KARMA

Peace Was Never an Option

Dennis Rae

The Karma Files™

Published by *The Karma Files™*

Distributed by *New Warrior Productions™*

Written By Dennis Rae © 2025 Dennis Rae. All rights reserved.

Kindle eBook (Amazon KDP) ISBN: 979-8-9988657-1-8

EPUB eBook *(Scheduled for wide release via Draft2Digital, IngramSpark, and global digital retailers after Kindle Select exclusivity ends.)* ISBN: 979 8 9988657 2 5

Paperback (Amazon KDP, IngramSpark) ISBN: 979-8-9988657-0-1

Hardcover (Amazon KDP, IngramSpark) ISBN: 979-8-9988657-3-2

Cover Design: Dennis **Interior Formatting:** Atticus **Developmental Editing:** Sofia, Terry, Jeff **Special Advisers:** John, Ezekiel **Copyediting/Proofreading:** Sofia

For privacy and protection, only first names are listed for contributors.

Printed in the United States of America **First Edition Book One in The Karma Files™ Series**

The Karma Files™ and all related titles, logos, and taglines are trademarks of New Warrior Productions™.

Author's Note

To those who have put their lives on the line for what matters most, we can never repay you. What we can do is honor you.

Our armed forces are the backbone of our freedom, and the fight ahead will demand their strength, resilience, and unwavering commitment to protecting our future. But protecting our warriors doesn't stop on the battlefield; We must stand for them when they return, just as they stood for us.

To those who made it home, and to those who never did, we honor you. We remember you. And we recognize the truth: There is real evil in this world, and it is only through the courage of those willing to fight that we remain free.

We stand together, or we fall apart.

Epigraph

"The only thing necessary for the triumph of evil is for good men to do nothing."
— Edmund Burke

Contents

PROLOGUE

Steel Lake, Northern California

Twisted branches of old-growth blue oaks strangled the last traces of daylight as wind howled through them, splintering the fading light into fractured streaks that danced across the dust-coated windows of an isolated cabin deep in the woods.

Inside the cabin, the air was thick.

The sour iron tang of blood, sharp pine, and rancid body odor suffocated the small space.

A dim lantern flickered against the stained wooden walls, throwing warped shadows that stretched and writhed with each pulse of light.

The silhouettes of the men standing guard loomed larger, distorted like specters waiting their turn. Jax Carson rolled his shoulders and let out a long, exaggerated sigh. Violence was routine now. He flexed his fingers, then shook out his hands like a fighter between rounds.

His lips pulled back in a grin that never reached his eyes, just teeth, tension, and the promise of pain. This was as close as he came to joy.

"I'm tired of hitting you, Dale." His voice was casual, like they were just two guys talking shop. "I just need the truth. I mean... cops are supposed to tell the truth once in a while, right?"

The men standing guard around the cabin broke into laughter, low and mean.

At the center of their grim circle sat Dale Harrison, a local deputy, bound to a chair, unrecognizable and broken. The shredded, bloodstained uniform hung from his frame. His face was swollen, gashed, and purple with bruises. His head lolled forward, breath rattling in his throat.

The five men surrounding him wore various Carhartt jackets stiff with dirt, faded flannels soaked in sweat, and mud-caked boots that dug into the wooden floor. They weren't just enforcers. They belonged to the land, shaped by its hardships. Large-framed, broad-shouldered, their faces bore the weight of a world that had never given them anything for free.

Different men. Different pasts. The same unspoken bond, a hunger for dominance in a world that had stripped them of everything but violence.

Jax studied Dale for a long moment, fingers tapping against his leg like Morse code before an ambush. His leather jacket creaked as he shifted, flannel hanging loose beneath it. Young as he was, his viciousness had moved him up the ranks fast.

He crouched before Dale, balanced on the balls of his feet, arms draped on his knees. The scar that ran from his left temple to his mouth twitched, his tell when he was about to hurt someone. It didn't always need to be physical.

"See, Dale, I liked you. You were mean. Mean enough to make yourself useful." He shrugged. "But you ain't smart."

Dale gulped, his Adam's apple jerking like a fishing bobber yanked beneath the surface, signaling a fish fighting for its life. He kept his gaze low, fingers twitching against the rope that held him to the chair.

Jax watched. Let the silence stretch, suffocating.

"And now you got me in a tough spot. I don't like tough spots."

Dale's voice was a hoarse whisper..

"I didn't talk to nobody."

Jax raised an eyebrow, nodding as if considering it.

"Yeah?"

He glanced at his men, their eyes gleaming with sick anticipation.

He crept closer.

Dale flinched, his breath hitching as Jax reached out.

For a brief second, Jax's fingers lingered on Dale's swollen face, almost gently. Dale tensed. Shoulders shaking. Waiting. Dreading.

And then.

CRACK.

Jax backhanded him hard, snapping his head to the side.

Dale groaned, spitting blood onto the dusty floorboards. The cabin settled into a thick silence. The only other sound was his ragged breathing, punctuated by the occasional whimper from his dog.

Freckles.

She cowered in the corner, shivering, left to die by the group. Her sleek coat of brown and white speckles, which inspired her name, was now matted with blood. Her soft brown eyes flicked toward her master in quick, sorrowful glances.

Her tail, once wagging energetically, was now tucked tight between her trembling legs. Blood dripped from her mouth, swollen lumps marking the spots where brutal kicks had landed. Punishment for trying to shield Dale from harm.

She struggled to even lift her head, whimpering softly. Heartbroken. Helpless. Her hind leg was twisted beneath her, her back broken. Yet, through the agony, she kept looking toward Dale, devastated she could no longer protect him.

She flinched when Jax leaned in close, his breath hot against Dale's ear.

"I don't like repeating myself, Dale." Jax's voice was lower now. Controlled. "You were skimming. Moving product on the side. We know it. You know it. So just tell me who else you told. We know who you sold to. That's why we're here."

Dale coughed, struggling to keep his head up. "I—I just took a cut, man. That's all. I needed extra cash."

Jax let out a short, humorless laugh, glancing at his men before looking back at Dale.

"You really think that's the problem? You think I care about a few missing bricks?" He shook his head. "'Cause I do. We can't have that. But right now, I need an answer."

Dale's breathing turned ragged, his ribs throbbing with every inhale. He didn't answer.

Jax leaned in closer. "We know where your family is, Dale." He let the words sink in.
"North Carolina, right?"

Dale's good eye widened, the pupil trembling.

"Our reach is everywhere, Dale. You know that. We know everything—except who you talked to at the FBI."

Jax pulled out his gun, aiming it at Freckles. He waited for Dale to look up and see the weapon.

"This is your last chance, Dale. Tell me who you talked to, or I kill your fucking dog. I'm tired of hitting you."

Dale's whole body went rigid. "No—I didn't talk to anyone."

Jax grinned, standing to his full height. His scar twisted with joy. "Yeah."

Dale opened his mouth, but no words came. His swollen lips trembled, breath shuddering.
"Please."

BANG.

Jax shot Freckles.

Silence blanketed the room.

The smell of gunpowder and death hung in the air.

Dale breathed in ragged sobs. He gulped for air like a fish out of water. Blood, sweat, and tears poured from his broken face.

"I didn't tell anyone, I swear."

Jax slipped his gun into his back waistband. Then, gently, he cradled Dale's head in his arms.

"I know."

With brutal force, he twisted Dale's neck.

It didn't break on the first try.

Dale's body convulsed. His breath escaped in ragged bursts. The failed attempt had severed part of his brain stem but left him alive. Barely.

Jax exhaled, disgusted by Dale's dying, fishlike sounds and movements. He stepped forward, planting his feet as he reset his grip.

Then, with a guttural grunt, he yanked Dale's head harder.

A sickening crunch.

Dale's body went limp, sagging forward in the chair. Jax stepped back, breath steady. His cold eyes flicked with annoyance as he scanned Dale. He looked down at his own hands.

Disgusted, he wiped them on Dale's bloodstained back, using the shirt like a dish towel. He sniffed, nose wrinkling in irritation.

"Oh, did he shit himself? Figures." Jax exhaled sharply and shook his hands. "Fuck this. Let's get out of here. Drinks are on me."

He strode toward the flickering lantern, his looming shadow stretching across the walls, growing, distorting, swallowing the room whole.

CLICK.

Darkness.

The men piled into a rusted red van, its engine coughing to life before peeling out. In its wake, dirt kicked into the air, swirling through long shadows as the day faded into night.

The wind had died with Dale, leaving the lake and the nearby town eerily still. Those who remained clung to what was left, lost in the shadow of a place once known for its lush forests and booming lumber industry.

Now hollowed. Rotting.

When the mills closed, so did the future.

With no industry, the town lost everything, even its shield.

Fewer police.

Fewer answers.

And fear filled the silence.

People stopped asking questions. Stopped speaking altogether.

Because in a place like this, silence wasn't weakness. It was survival.

And those who broke it rarely lasted long.

***

Northern California, Trinity Highway

The deep, throaty growl of an 18-wheeler's J-brake rumbled through the forest, shattering the stillness of the two-lane road. The driver adjusted speed on the winding downgrade, the weight of the massive rig pressing into the pavement as it cut through the dense woodland.

Bryce Rath leaned forward in his leather seat, his matte black 4x4 Jeep Wrangler roaring up the hill in the opposite direction. The V-8 engine devoured the road, each turn demanding his full attention. Sunlight filtered through gaps in the canopy, flickering between the branches until, flash, a sudden burst of burning light stabbed through the dirty windshield, blinding him.

His grip tightened on the wheel. Instinct took over. He fought the disorienting glare, forcing himself to stay steady, resisting the urge to drift into the path of the oncoming semi. The thunder of its diesel engine and the acrid scent of burning brakes clung to the air, thick, heavy, familiar.

The moment passed. But his mind didn't.

The sound. The smell. The blinding light. It yanked him backward, dragging him into a memory he'd spent years trying to forget.

***

Kunduz, Northern Afghanistan — Flashback

The wind ripped through the valley, thick with the acrid bite of dust and distant diesel fumes. The air carried the stench of burning garbage, a smell Bryce had come to associate with places like this.

From his perch atop a crumbling ridge, Staff Sergeant Bryce "Karma" Rath pressed his cheek to the stock of his M110 sniper rifle, tracking the convoy as it slithered toward the abandoned compound below.

The village clung precariously to existence, a husk of bullet-riddled buildings held together by anger and loss.

His heartbeat slowed. Breathing steady. He exhaled, careful not to stir the dust beneath him.

Below, the trucks, rusted Soviet and Russian war relics, leftovers from decades of conflict, scavenged and repurposed by warlords, ground to a stop at the gates, their frames groaning under the weight of cargo not meant to be found.

Bryce eased back and flipped open his weatherproof notepad tucked against his chest rig.

The range card stared back at him. Fan-shaped and worn, drawn by hand at first light five days ago. He'd arrived under a moonless sky, waited for dawn, then mapped every structure, marked every line of sight, and noted every blind spot. Distances, angles, firing lanes, all logged in tight block script. He had made detailed sketches and notes to ensure he knew every inch of the world in front of him.

Gate: 310 meters.

South wall breach: 420.

Ridge crest: 950. No-go unless the world turned sideways.

He glanced at the treetops. Wind had shifted—now a steady breeze from the west. He marked it down: 5 mph @ 1400 Hold: L1.2.

The rest was burned into memory, but he read it anyway. Calm. Deliberate.

He closed the pad, tucked it back in, and settled behind the glass.

Then he saw movement.

Men spilled out of the trucks like ants swarming a carcass.

Bryce's grip tightened on the rifle. His jaw clenched. Tactical. Organized. Too good.

This wasn't some ragtag militia guarding a local warlord.

"Karma, how we lookin'? Sitrep."

Captain Marcus "Hawk" Daniels' voice crackled through Bryce's earpiece, low and steady, laced with the unspoken edge of a man who trusted his gut.

Bryce shifted, his ghillie suit blending into the rock.

He had infiltrated the area alone, building his hide under the cover of darkness. Cold rations. No fires. No movement. No mistakes.

His job was simple: maintain overwatch, confirm the targets, and neutralize any threats if things went south.

But in Afghanistan, nothing was ever simple.

Bryce exhaled, adjusting the scope. His crosshairs swept the growing cluster of bodies.

"Falcon One, intel was bad."

His voice was steady, but his pulse thumped in his skull.

"Security's doubled, cartel-backed militia. Four trucks. Twenty-plus tangos. Possibly ex-military."

His scope settled on a man emerging from the armored vehicle, carrying the unmistakable posture of command.

"They're carrying something heavy. Could be the weapons cache we've been tracking."

A flicker of movement at the edge of his vision.

Bryce didn't move, just let his eyes scan outward.

A sniper? Lookouts? Spotters?

Too early to tell.

But this was wrong.

Too coordinated. Too clean.

"Good copy," Hawk's voice crackled back. "We'll wait for the handoff. Hold your position. Keep eyes on target."

"Copy."

His finger rested on the trigger guard. Not the trigger.

Not yet.

Inside the compound, Hawk's MARSOC team, six operators, some of the best in the Corps, remained in the shadows. Waiting.

The plan was simple.

Capture or kill.

They'd been smuggled in two days ago, hidden inside a gutted water truck—modern-day Trojan horses jammed into the heart of enemy territory.

Now?

They were pinned.

All exits compromised.

Bryce's crosshairs swept through the convoy.

Every movement, every angle, burned into memory before his rifle settled on the biggest threats.

"Falcon One, three DShKs—12.7mm. RPG-7s mounted on the lead vehicle. Movement is disciplined, trained. Possibly Afghan Special Forces. Two-man fire teams covering every angle."

A pause.

Hawk exhaled. "Not some warlord's security detail."

"Negative. This is professional."

The wind blew along the ridge. Light static came through the earpiece.

"Copy, Karma. Hold position. Tasked to capture in the act. Standby for confirmation."

Bryce's finger tapped against the trigger guard.

Not a nervous habit.

A calculation.

Below, the cartel leaders stepped forward. Hands shook.

Bryce's grip tightened.

"They just made contact. Waiting on confirmation."

"Copy, Karma. Standby for go or no-go."

His scope swept through the compound.

Something was wrong.

No crates were moving.

No keys were being exchanged.

His heartbeat slowed.

His breathing thinned.

This wasn't a deal.

It was an ambush.

Bryce shifted. Adjusted his angle.

He exhaled, talking into his mic.

"Two more trucks just arrived from secondary exfil. We're boxed in."

"Good copy," Hawk replied, voice tight.

Bryce's brain fired through contingencies.

Best shots.

Fallback points.

Ways out.

He scanned farther, past the primary group, past the vehicles, looking for what didn't belong.

A flicker of movement on the opposite hillside. Low. Fast. Synchronized.

"Falcon One, incoming hostiles, five o'clock. Fast movers, full tactical loadout. Not cartel, not militia. This is a cleanup team."

Inside the warehouse, Hawk's voice sharpened. "Say again, Karma?"

Bryce stayed locked in, tracking the vehicles as they closed in. No hesitation. No drifting. Clean military spacing.

"They're not here for the deal. They're here for us."

He felt it now.

The slow, tightening noose.

The way shadows shifted in the hills.

The unnatural calm before the storm.

No insects. No birds.

Not even the wind dared to move.

Hawk's voice came in low, edged with grim certainty.

"Shit. We're compromised. Karma, can you take them out?"

Bryce's jaw flexed.

His scope tracked the incoming fire teams, tight formation, staggered advance, zero wasted motion.

Suppressors. Thermal optics. Coordinated sectors of fire.

Not cartel.

Not militia.

Military.

No patches. No flags.

Just methodical, professional execution.

Kill team.

"Negative. They're layered. I fire, and the rest collapse on my position."

He adjusted his angle.

"The incoming force just doubled what's already on the ground."

Silence.

Heavy.

The kind that fills your lungs with lead.

"This isn't reinforcement," Bryce continued. "It's termination protocol. The teams on the ground locked us in. These guys are here to finish it."

Hawk's voice came back, clipped and cold.

"Falcon One to Base Command, mission is compromised. Primary exfil is no longer viable. Request immediate QRF support. What's their status?"

No reply.

Bryce shifted his position again. Watched one of the lead vehicles slow, rear doors opening.

Operators dropped out fast, weapons up, already moving to cover.

Silence.

The kind that stretches.

That presses down on your ribs.

"Falcon One, be advised, your QRF is under heavy contact. RPG fire at the LZ. They're twenty mikes out, no clear path to you."

A slow exhale.

They had no backup.

Inside the compound, Hawk recalculated.

His team was no longer the hunters.

They were prey.

Hawk spoke in a measured tone. "Shift to hard cover. We're in for it."

"Copy," Ramirez grunted, shifting behind a crate.

"Gibbs, your entryway is exposed. Fall back to the support beams. Cover our six."

"On it."

The warehouse was a graveyard of old battles.

Bullet-riddled walls.

Rotting crates stacked like tombstones.

Shafts of light filtering through holes in the ceiling.

It offered little protection.

But it was all they had.

Hawk's voice was calm. Controlled. Final.

"You know the ROE. Do not fire until fired upon."

Each team member replied in low, measured tones.

"Copy."

And then nothing.

Just silence.

The kind that filled every crack of the world like a slow-rising tide.

The wait had begun.

Nothing moved.

Not the wind.

Not the dust.

Not the men in the compound.

The world shrank to this moment.

The breath before impact.

Bryce's eyes flicked to the Predator feed.

A silent, unblinking Demi-god watching from above.

Infrared signatures shifted into formation.

He adjusted the crosshairs on the tablet.

Marked the warehouse.

The perimeter.

The exits.

His breathing slowed.

Every muscle tensed.

Through the scope, he watched the fire teams tighten.

They weren't guarding anything anymore.

They were preparing.

His earpiece crackled.

"Gibbs, weapons check."

Thumbs grazed safeties. No clicks. No movement wasted.

"Hot."

"Ramirez, confirm fallback positions."

"Two points. East wall, southwest breach. But neither are good."

Bryce clenched his jaw. They all knew it.

His own exit routes were worse. The terrain offered little cover.

One sniper couldn't shift the tide.

His finger hovered over the trigger guard.

"No wasted rounds," Hawk commanded, his unwavering voice grounding the team. "Make them count."

A slow exhale.

Crosshairs tracked the shadows creeping closer.

The drone feed flickered.

They were out of time.

Bryce tapped his throat mic. "Falcon One, Hellfire on standby. Copy ROE."

"Copy."

His thumb hovered over the radio switch.

Nothing left to say.

The world stopped.

That awful, empty hush.

Like the ocean drawing back before a tsunami.

They waited.

They waited.

Then a muzzle flash.

The world erupted.

The old Russian DShK—12.7mm of raw Soviet firepower, still deadly after all these years, roared to life, cutting through the walls like a hose to a sandcastle. Its screaming mechanical rattle barked, echoing up the canyon as it shook the truck holding it.

Bryce's crosshairs snapped to it.

Exhale. Squeeze.

One down.

Another DShKA continued.

Shift. Squeeze.

Another turret gunner down.

Hawk's voice tore through the gunfire.

"Do it, Karma! Copy Danger Close!"

No hesitation.

"Command, this is Karma, request immediate fire mission, danger close. Co-ordinates inbound!"

He hit send. Returned to his rifle, focusing on the largest threats to his team. Taking them out one by one.

A response came from his earpiece.

"Wilco, Karma. Hellfire inbound. ETA sixty seconds."

Bryce gave a slight nod, a quiet rhythm of recognition, and pushed forward, locked in on protecting his team. Aim. Squeeze. Aim. Squeeze. Each target fell, a pink mist marking one less threat.

He kept dropping bodies, adjusting for distance from memory alone. RPG at the gate, three-twenty. Exhale. Squeeze. Down.

No wasted motion, only lethal accuracy. Squeeze. Down.

The mag clicked dry. He slammed in a fresh one, racked, and kept firing.

The Predator drone glided silently at 25,000 feet.

A muffled whoosh, followed by a falling star.

Bryce stayed locked in.

Scope snapped to another RPG team.

Exhale. Squeeze.

Down.

Another raised a launcher.

Squeeze.

Another body crumpled.

Another target fell. He keyed the mic.

"Thirty seconds!"

Rounds slammed near his hide. Another whistled past his ear.

He didn't flinch.

He kept firing.

Then—

CRACK.

A sledgehammer to the ribs. His Kevlar holding back the bullet, but his side exploded in pain.

He steadied the rifle.

No time. No pain. Just the mission.

Another round—

CRACK.

His shoulder. White-hot agony.

He forced the scope up.

One. Two. Three.

More bodies dropped.

Reload.

Then—he saw it.

A second smoke trail.

His stomach dropped.

Not right.

He checked the tablet.

His breath caught.

Two Hellfires.

"How?"

One wasn't heading for the target.

Bryce kept firing as he shouted into the mic, forcing his lungs to work. "Ten seconds! Negative impact. Second missile is off course. Hawk! Hellfire is going internal. Move!"

Too late.

The first missile screamed in.

The shockwave flattened everything.

Trucks flipped. Bodies vanished.

Then, like a camera flash, the second missile struck.

Direct hit on the compound.

Fire swallowed the world.

The blast ripped Bryce from his hide, launching him backward.

His vision swam.

Nothing left.

Heartbeat pounded.

Hand fumbled for his radio.

"Falcon One, this is Karma," he called out into the silence, deaf to his own voice, lost in the ringing void.

Static.

"Do you copy? Hawk, do you copy?"

Nothing.

Just ringing silence and blinding white.

He was weightless, drifting through fire and static.

No sound but the scream in his skull, until something else broke through.

Laughter. Cracking firewood. A night beneath the stars with his team.

"Karma." Hawk grinned at Bryce. "That fits."

That voice, steady, familiar, cut through the haze like a flare in a dark night sky.

Then it was gone.

The weight of the earth slammed against him.

He felt the planet's rotation driving him deeper into the ground.

He couldn't move.

His body fought for shallow sips of air. Every breath burned.

Every heartbeat drove fire from the earth's core through his veins.

The roar of rotor blades surged in the distance. The QRF was closing in.

But the ATAK, the Android Tactical Assault Kit, told the only truth that mattered.

His was the only heartbeat left on the battlefield.

Then—

Darkness.

Chapter One

New Life

Steel Lake, Northern California

Country music spilled from the weather-beaten bar, its melody drifting into the cool night air. Bryce's Jeep rolled to a stop, tires crunching over loose gravel. The music lingered, as if trying to distract him from his thoughts.

The bar sat like a forgotten relic, lost in the woods, its walls held together by time and whiskey. The distant hum of the interstate whispered beneath the thick canopy of redwood, Douglas fir, and cedar. A single, dim light flickered above the doorway, struggling against the approaching dark. Smoke curled from the kitchen chimney, the only other sign of life. It was the kind of place people came to drink, fight, or forget.

Bryce stepped out, stretching his arms overhead to work out the tightness from hours behind the wheel. His six-foot-one frame was hard to hide, even beneath a loose shirt that masked the width of his back. Faded tattoos and old scars covered his arms, remnants of a life spent pushing past limits for survival... for those he swore to protect.

His eyes swept across the lot. A rusted red van hogged three spaces in the back. Bryce exhaled, already annoyed.

The bar's door creaked open, triggering a motion sensor that painted him in light, like a rockstar on stage. He scowled, shifting instinctively into the shadows. Too exposed. Smoke from the grill wrapped around him, thick with the scent of grease and charred meat, the only thing pulling him forward.

Inside, the air was thick with stale beer, cigarette smoke, and stories no one wanted to tell. Amber lights flickered against grime-coated walls, their glow struggling through the haze. The sacred redwood bar gleamed at the center, an island of alcohol-fueled refuge surrounded by battered tables and worn leather booths.

The crowd was sparse. Muted conversations and the occasional burst of laughter filled the room. A group of guys in dirty work boots and stained Carhartts slouched in the back, getting drunker as the night got darker.

Everyone here had clocked out, wrecking their bodies just to scrape above the poverty line, or being crushed beneath it.

Bryce pulled his cap low, shadowing his face as he moved through the bar, reading the room the way most people scroll through social media.

Threats. Cover. Escape routes.

It was ingrained; even retirement couldn't erase it. His movements were effortless, precise, designed to be unnoticed. No energy wasted. No attention drawn.

He found an open section at the bar and settled onto a stool. The bartender approached, sizing him up. Experienced eyes took in Bryce's frame, his posture, the way he scanned the room.

A napkin slid across the counter.
"You look hungry."

Bryce nodded.

"You want a beer?"

Another nod.

"Cheeseburger and fries? Best thing on the menu."

The menu landed in front of him.

Bryce didn't glance at it, just gave a thumbs-up.

"What kind of beer?"

Bryce shrugged. His low voice cut through the room.
"You choose."

The bartender studied him a moment longer, then took the menu back and moved toward the fridge.

Bryce watched the bar as he waited. Almost everyone was staring at their phone or watching one of the three outdated TVs hanging over the bar, likely the only upgrade this place had seen in two decades. No one talked. Not really. They scrolled, they drank, they scrolled again. People only talked when someone leaned over to show their screen.

The bartender's movement pulled Bryce's attention back as he set a bottle on the napkin in front of him.
"What brings you around here? Family?"

Bryce shook his head.
"Fishing. I'm a guide. Just scouting the area for some runs."

The bartender lifted an eyebrow, unimpressed.

"Cool," he muttered, already turning away, more interested in mixing a cocktail for someone else.

Bryce took a slow pull from his beer, letting the bitterness settle.

Disconnection. He'd felt it in every town, every stop. And it wasn't getting any better.

Bryce took another sip, letting the cold bite settle before glancing at the TV above the bar. An NFL game played, the teams decked out in pink accents that overshadowed the home colors he remembered from childhood. He tried to focus, but not out of any genuine interest, just something to pass the time.

Another sip. Another shake of the head.

On the screen, a player ripped off his helmet, screaming at the officials. The crowd at the bar grumbled, a mix of jeers and half-hearted cheers, but Bryce wasn't sure if they were more annoyed at the game or at each other. The bickering on the field felt wrong. Too much noise, too much ego.

Back in high school, the field was sacred ground, not a stage for tantrums. Coach Larson's voice echoed in his mind, clear as it had been all those years ago: *"Play with discipline, or don't play at all."* That lesson stuck, long after he left the gridiron behind.

A commercial break pulled him from his thoughts, loud, chaotic, flashing images of overpriced trucks and politicians faking sincerity. He exhaled, fingers absently tracing the condensation on his glass.

He shifted his gaze to another screen. A basketball game. Different sport, same story, overgrown kids whining to refs, arguing every call like entitled children.

Frustration gnawed at him. These days, kids didn't learn from coaches or fathers. They mimicked the worst behavior of their idols, absorbing every act of defiance against authority like scripture.

A country song hummed through the speakers, low and melancholic. Bryce never grew up on country, but now it felt like the only music that still seemed to hold onto respect and honor.

His thoughts drifted, steeped in a lifetime of war and conflict.

How does a society survive if respect for authority vanishes?

What's the point of protecting a culture that doesn't respect itself?

Another sip. Another glance at the third TV.

This one was worse. Pundits screaming over each other, spewing rhetoric instead of reason. The screen flickered with endless debates, a carousel of outrage.

When did civilized discourse become extinct?

These talking heads were supposed to be watchdogs for truth. Instead, they were mouthpieces for whatever sold.

Bryce chuckled bitterly into his drink, shaking his head.

The world had changed.

Or maybe he had.

He leaned back, rolled his neck, and cracked his knuckles. The discomfort lingered, tightening in his chest. He'd felt more at peace in a war zone than he did in a crowded room. It was hard to reintegrate when you felt like a shadow, present, but never whole. Just a reflection cast on the world, not a part of it.

He exhaled sharply, dragging his focus back to the present. The bar. The people. The two worlds he had lived in, separated by an ever-widening gap.

One world believed itself safe.

The other knew better.

His eyes drifted toward the door, but his stomach growled, reminding him why he was still here.

A sharp whisper drew his attention. Across the bar, a couple sat in the corner, locked in a hushed argument. Their faces were just silhouettes, but the tension was unmistakable, the clipped, hushed tones, the tight fists on the table.

It stirred something in him.

Old memories of voices raised in anger, of nights spent trying to stop something he never could.

Anger, he knew, burdened everyone it touched.

He realized he'd been watching for too long.

He took a sip of beer. A slow breath. The cold liquid steadied his nerves.

He scanned the room again, sensing how quickly realities could collide with devastating force. There was a fragile order to the world. Like a freeway accident, life seemed orderly until one distraction sent it spiraling into disaster.

Bryce knew that history repeated itself like those crashes, foreseen but inevitable when complacency set in.

One second of inattention could change everything.

Then a voice cut through the tension.

"Hey, we want more beer!"

A table erupted in laughter. One of them waved at the waitress, but she ignored him, busy with another table. Egged on by his crew, the man rose, posturing like the alpha of his pack. He sauntered toward the bar, his balance betraying the weight of his buzz.

He reached the bar, using his arm to steady himself. He burped. "Hey."

The bartender, still busy with other patrons, waved him off. "Jax, order from Gabby. It's quicker."

His eyes landed on Bryce. Sizing him up. Waiting for a reaction.

Jax's face tightened with annoyance. He'd spent more time in the gym than in any classroom, church, or therapist's office, places that might have given him insight into the anger and insecurity driving him now.

The waitress delivered Bryce's hamburger, ignoring Jax entirely.

Jax tapped her on the shoulder, his voice sharp. "Hey, can we get another round, or what?"

She didn't turn toward him, just glanced over her shoulder. "Yeah, Jax, I'll bring it over shortly."

Jax turned back to his table, throwing an arm over a chair.

"Drinks are coming," he announced, more for his own ego than anything else.

He took a slow sip of his beer, eyes flicking toward the bar.

The waitress was still talking to Bryce, still smiling. She leaned against the counter, the soft light catching the curves of her face. "So, are you from around here? I've never seen you before."

Bryce took a bite of his burger. The one he'd been waiting for the whole damn day. He chewed, savoring it, then washed it down with a sip of beer before answering. "Just passing through. Heard you get your meat from local farms and had to stop. Hard to find that anymore."

She smiled, tilting her head. "I'm locally grown."

Bryce glanced up, smirking.

Jax, still watching, clenched his jaw.

His beer was almost empty.

He shoved off the chair and stalked toward the bar, shouldering in between them.

His empty bottle thudded onto the counter. "Where are my fucking drinks, bitch?"

The waitress stiffened. A forced, polite smile flickered across her face, one she'd had to use far too many times. She didn't even look at Jax before turning and walking away, serving another table instead.

Jax's knuckles whitened around his bottle. He turned to Bryce. "Who the fuck are you looking at, old man?"

Bryce exhaled through his nose, amused.

Old man.

He was only thirty-three, but the years of war had carved deep lines into his face, hardened his eyes, and thickened his skin. He laughed to himself.

The deep rumble of Bryce's laugh only stoked his frustration. His lip curled.

Bryce didn't bother responding, just took another bite of his burger.

Jax flexed his fists, feeling the alcohol-fueled surge of invincibility. He'd spent years in the gym, turning himself into the kind of man people feared.

But something about this guy, this calm, unbothered man, was unraveling him.

Jax sneered, thinking he could force fear into Bryce.

He grabbed his empty beer bottle and smashed it against the bar.

But glass breaks in unexpected ways.

A jagged shard sliced into his hand.

Jax stared at the bloody mess, momentarily stunned. The rest of the bottle slipped from his grip and shattered on the floor.

Bryce moved.

A blur of efficiency, practiced control.

In one seamless motion, he snatched a nearby bar towel, wrapped it around Jax's bleeding hand, and used the same momentum to break his wrist.

Jax howled in pain, knees buckling as Bryce forced him onto a stool, twisting his arm into an unnatural angle.

Before Jax could react, Bryce relieved him of the gun tucked into his waistband.

He leaned in, voice a muted, menacing growl.

"You won't be needing that. I don't need you hurting innocent bystanders, something I'm sure you enjoy."

Jax gritted his teeth, sweat beading on his forehead.

Bryce examined his work.

"You've got a distal radius fracture. Any more trauma, and you could tear your extensor and flexor tendons. If that happens, no more use of your hand."

Bryce smirked.

"There goes your date night, judging by your personality."

Jax glared, but Bryce wasn't finished. His deep voice cut through the pain like a blade.

"Let me guess. You drive the red van out back?"

Jax's eyes widened. Fear flickered beneath the throbbing agony in his shattered wrist.

Bryce tightened his grip, just enough to keep him from moving.

At the table, Jax's crew watched in stunned silence. The bar was frozen; all eyes locked on the unfolding scene.

Bryce held Jax's wrist at a downward angle, letting gravity and blood pressure force the shard from his hand.
It dropped to the floor with a soft clink.

Jax let out a sharp breath, face paling further.

Bryce shifted his stance, instinctively wrapping the towel tighter, applying pressure to slow the bleeding. His hands moved with practiced ease, dressing the wound and stabilizing the fracture. Second nature.

Jax, now shaking, realized he was at Bryce's mercy.

All that bravado, all that arrogance, gone.

Bryce didn't let go.

His grip stayed firm, one hand bracing Jax's wrist, the other gripping the back of his neck.
Jax tried to twist free, but Bryce tightened just enough to remind him he was trapped.

A low, guttural groan escaped Jax's lips, equal parts pain and fear.
The fight had been torn from him like the shredded bar towel now holding his ruined wrist together.

Jax's eyes darted to his friends, searching for backup. But they were still frozen, still trying to process what had just happened.

Bryce leaned in, his voice a deep, menacing whisper, his smile not reaching his eyes.
"Don't even think about asking your friends for help. That'll just mean more of you needing stitches. Maybe a few casts for broken bones. And trust me, you don't want that."

He waved casually at the group like they were all in on some strange joke, shrugging his shoulders in mock amusement.
"Now listen, you fuck, keep pressure on that wound on your way to the hospital. You're lucky. This could've been a lot worse, but I don't feel like going to jail tonight."

Bryce tightened his grip slightly, feeling Jax stiffen in response.
"Now pay your fucking tab, and make sure you tip your waitress for putting up with your bullshit."

Jax's face twisted in pain and realization. This could have ended much worse.

He reached into his pocket with his good hand, pulled out a thick wad of cash, and tossed it onto the bar.

The bartender plucked the money, taking only what was owed before sliding the rest back. He suppressed a laugh, but his eyes gleamed with amusement.

Jax moved carefully, like a dog caught in a trap, knowing any sudden movement could bring more pain.

The usual cocky fire in his eyes was gone, replaced by something new and uncomfortable. Fear.

His hand trembled slightly as he retrieved the leftover cash, peeling off forty bucks and dropping it onto the counter.

Bryce watched him, amused.

"That's a good start."

Jax kept his gaze down, refusing to look Bryce in the eye.

But Bryce wasn't done.

With lightning speed, he seized Jax's hand again, shoving it against the wound.

Jax let out a strangled grunt of pain.

Bryce leaned in, his voice low and edged with something far darker than before.

"If I see you or your boys again, none of you will walk away."

He forced a smile, nodding toward the confused, hesitant group still watching from the table.

"Do you understand?"

Jax barely nodded, his lips pressed into a tight line.

Bryce clapped him hard on the back, not friendly, not gentle, sending Jax stumbling forward.

His legs trembled as he staggered back toward his crew, looking disoriented. Like a marked animal released into the wild, wounded and wary.

But the adrenaline still coursed too fast, his balance gone.

Jax tripped over his own feet, slamming face-first onto the floor.

Bryce chuckled, shaking his head.

He motioned toward the table.

"Hey, I think he had too much. Poor guy. Looks like he'll need stitches."

The group, seeing their alpha reduced to a mess, nodded, choosing pack mentality over loyalty.

They laughed at Jax, reveling in the sight of their leader brought down hard.

Jax gritted his teeth, humiliated, but didn't fight back. He knew better now.

They hauled him up, half-supporting, half-dragging him toward the exit.

Blood dripped down his arm.

He didn't even look back.

Bryce casually checked the gun he'd taken off Jax, confirming the make and model by feel. Safety was still on.

He tucked it under his shirt, his movements smooth, automatic.

The bartender leaned over, grinning.

"Food's on the house, man. Let me get you a fresh burger, without broken glass on it."

He nodded toward the door.

"That guy's been a prick his whole life. Seeing the look on his face? Worth every damn penny."

His tone shifted, just a little.

"But listen, man, if I were you, I'd get out of town after you eat. That guy runs with a dangerous crowd."

Bryce acknowledged the advice with a slow nod. He knew when someone was giving him a fair warning.

He scanned the bar.

Too much attention.

More than he wanted.

"I'll take the burger to go."

The bartender nodded, already moving.

Bryce looked at his beer but didn't drink. Could be glass in it.

Instead, he slid it aside, clearing the fractured shards from the bar with a slow, deliberate motion.

His body was still wired, the tension in his muscles refusing to fade.

Adrenaline lingered, like an old enemy.

He breathed slowly, controlled, forcing his pulse back to normal.

But his right hand still twitched.

It was instinct. Muscle memory.

His body searched for the comfort of a weapon, something he could trust.

Not to kill.

Just to be there when needed.

Restraint always came at a cost.

And Bryce preferred not to pay it.

He had nothing to prove.

And everything to lose.

The bartender returned with a fresh beer, setting it down in front of him.

"This is from the ladies in that booth."

Bryce exhaled, suppressing a smirk.

He glanced toward the booth.

Eyes were already watching him.

The bartender gestured toward a group of middle-aged women in the dimly lit corner, dressed up for a rare night out.

Their makeup was a little too perfect, their hair styled just a little too much, their eyes glinting with just enough mischief.

They smiled and waved at Bryce.

He lifted the beer in acknowledgment, offering a slight nod. A silent thanks.

Taking a sip, he set the glass down, conscious of the weight of every glance in the room.

The brief silence after Jax's departure had stretched a little too long.

Conversations had died down, replaced by whispered speculation.

The waitress reappeared, placing a fresh burger in a to-go box in front of him. "Here you go. And... thanks for taking care of that asshole."

She stayed, fingers tracing the bar's edge. Watching him. Willing him to notice her.

Her eyes searched his, wanting to know more.

"I'm off tomorrow if you want to go out."

Bryce picked up the box, his expression easy, unreadable.
"I'd love to, but I have to hit the road."

She smiled, pulling a napkin from her apron and scribbling her number on it.
"I'm Gabby."

Bryce tucked the napkin into his pocket, placing a crisp twenty on the bar in return.

He extended a hand, strong and callused, firm but measured. No bravado. Just quiet control.
"Bryce. Nice to meet you. See you around."

Gabby took it, biting her bottom lip as she sized him up, easing into his grip. There was nothing forced in his touch. Only calm strength, with something brutal buried beneath.
"I hope so."

As he turned to go, she leaned against the bar, watching.

Bryce stepped back into the shadows, moving toward the exit.

A quick scan of the room told him what he already expected. Two men glaring at him, their jaws tight, fists clenched under the table.

They thought they were owed something.

She gave him her number.

Not them.

The entitlement in their eyes was unmistakable, fueled by alcohol, bruised egos, and a lifetime of never being the biggest man in the room.

Bryce didn't stare them down, didn't need to.

He noted their positioning, their posture, the way their hands rested too close to their belts.

He'd seen this movie before.

And he knew how it ended.

At the door, he glanced toward the booth of women.

They waved wildly as if he were setting off to sea, about to disappear forever.

He was sure the alcohol had something to do with their enthusiasm.

The door creaked as he pushed it open.

He waited a beat, letting his eyes adjust to the dim light.

If Jax's crew was out there, he wouldn't be stepping into a blind spot.

He finally moved, his stride casual, but his right hand stayed close to his belt, ready.

The motion sensor flooded the doorway with light. Bryce kept one eye closed, preserving his night vision, then darted into the darkness, moving like a shadow beyond the reach of the bulb.

Outside, the air was cooler, heavier, the scent of pine mixing with the distant burn of diesel.

His eyes swept the lot, scanning for movement, silhouettes, anything out of place.

Nothing.

For now.

The moon hung low as Bryce strode toward his Jeep, anticipating the first warm bite of his burger. But first, he had unfinished business.

The gun.

He reached the vehicle, opened the door, and retrieved a pair of rubber gloves, slipping them on like a surgeon preparing for work.

He released the magazine, popping the rounds into a lockbox. Ammo was precious. No sense in wasting it.

With practiced ease, he wiped down the weapon, clearing any trace of himself.

Then he dismantled it, breaking it down into pieces too small to matter.

He scanned the lot.

A trash can bolted to a tree at the edge of the parking lot. Perfect.

He moved, but unhurried, placing the pieces into separate bags he found in the trash, ensuring no one would ever fire this weapon again.

The gloves went in last.

The lid closed with a quiet finality.

Gone.

He returned to the Jeep, slid in, and started the engine.

As the deep hum of the tires filled the cab, he finally opened the burger container and took a bite.

Still warm. Still good.

He shifted into gear, easing the Jeep onto the road.

One last glance in the mirror.

No headlights were trailing him. No suspicious movement.

But that didn't mean he was in the clear.

He knew how this worked.

Those two inside?

They wouldn't let it go.

Guys like that never did.

Maybe not tonight. Maybe not tomorrow.

But eventually, they'd convince themselves they needed to make a move.

Bryce had seen it before: weak men feeding off each other's worst instincts, convincing themselves they were strong.

It wouldn't end well for them.

Bryce took another bite of his burger, forcing himself to enjoy the moment before it disappeared.

He didn't know what was coming next.

But he knew one thing for sure.

The fish bite early.

And by sunrise, he'd be long gone.

Chapter Two

Diminished Returns

Pacific Coast of Mexico

Jagged cliffs and gentle beaches shaped the rugged west coast of Mexico, a hidden paradise where time moved at its own pace.

A small panga fishing harbor clung to the sleepy coastline, its wooden dock and last remaining weathered boat standing defiant against the relentless march of progress.

This was the last of its kind on this stretch of the Pacific, a relic of simpler times, when the sea provided for those willing to earn their keep. The larger fishing companies had choked out men like Miguel, their unchecked expansion leaving behind a wake of unintended consequences, much like the abandoned nets that strangled the sea.

Illegal overfishing had decimated marine life, throwing the delicate balance into chaos, a decline that would soon affect everyone, no matter how long they chose to ignore it. Still, Miguel clung to the old ways.

Not because he believed he could win, only because it was all he had left.

Miguel's body was weathered by years of hard labor beneath the coastal sun, his skin marked by salt and time. The wrinkles on his face and hands were as deep as the creases of the ocean on a windy day. His faded overalls, a gift from his late wife fifteen years ago, draped over his thinning frame.

The shirt beneath was old, its origins forgotten, but its scent was familiar. Fish. Sweat. And the emptiness of his loss. The day his wife died was the last day he cared about his appearance. She had been out buying groceries when an errant cartel bullet ended her life.

Miguel pushed the memory away as he stepped out of his fishing shack, its walls stacked high with nets waiting to be repaired. Some had been there longer than his overalls. The dock creaked underfoot as he walked to the edge, swallowed by the silence of a place that once thrived.

Nothing around him had changed, yet everything did. The sea still rolled in with the tide. The sun still set in the west. And the small panga harbor still clung to existence, just like he did.

It had once been alive, families working together, children's laughter echoing across the water. Now, waves softly lapped the deteriorating wood.

His son had left five years ago. Since then, the house had become too big, too expensive, too full of memories. Miguel sold it to keep the marina, the only thing left worth holding onto.

His wife's death eliminated funds for his son's education; mere survival dominated his finances. Miguel had to pull his son from his school and taught him the family trade, how to be a panga fisherman. But his son had learned something else. His education had given him bigger dreams. Friends who only liked him when he didn't smell like fish.

One day, he stopped helping at the marina. And started working for Javier Bravalez.

The cartel leader who owned everything in the town.

A screech of tires yanked Miguel from his thoughts. His son's shiny red Toyota Tundra tore into the empty lot, kicking up a tight spiral of dust that swirled like a small tornado, twisting the air with the emotions about to be unleashed. The truck skidded to a hard stop in front of the shack.

Luis stepped out. His gold-rimmed shades. His flashy Miami Vice clothes. A caricature of the man he thought he needed to be.

His sidekick, equally overdressed, sprayed cologne to ward off the scent of the marina.

Miguel took in the sight of his son, so different now, yet still carrying the face of the child he and his wife had loved.

The sweet boy who used to laugh at the docks, excited by everything.

He would wake up before dawn to help haul nets and bait lines, wanting nothing more than to be like his dad.

Miguel had once believed he would inherit this life.

So much had changed.

Luis's voice snapped him back. "Dad," he said, the disdain evident. "Javier wants the marina. You need to give it to him. He's doing me a favor, and you need to go with it."

His Spanish sounded different now. Harder. Like the gangsters he ran with.

Miguel stared at his son, his exhaustion deepening. He heard the words, but it took a moment for their meaning to sink in. Javier wanted the marina. But Miguel knew one thing.

He had no life without the sea. The pain of his son's words was almost unbearable, but Miguel knew he couldn't show it. There had to be another way. He needed to talk to Javier. Not through his fool of a son.

Miguel had known Javier long before he became a jefe. Before the gold-rimmed glasses, the yachts, and the trail of bodies. Maybe, just maybe, he could negotiate something better. But the idea of bargaining with the man who had taken everything from him made his stomach turn. He needed to clear his head.

Fishing always helped him think. The sea was the only place he found peace.

Ignoring his son's protests, Miguel turned and walked toward his last remaining panga boat. Luis, used to being ignored, shrugged and climbed back into the truck. As the engine roared, gravel and dirt sprayed across Miguel's old blue car, a childish insult from a son who no longer respected his father or his heritage.

Miguel's body protested as he climbed into the boat, the physical pain a welcome distraction from the war in his mind. The boat's gentle rocking calmed him, but as he reached for the starter cord, nothing. He pulled again. And again. Nothing.

He checked the gas tank, half full. The battery, fine. Still, the engine refused to turn over.

Frustrated, he slumped back, staring at the empty marina that once gave him purpose. Maybe this was the sign. Maybe the fight was already over.

Miguel shook his head. Refusing to give up, he pulled hard on the starting cord.

Then a low growl rolled across the water.

At first, he thought it was his engine sputtering to life. But no, the sound was coming from somewhere else. Growing louder by the second.

Miguel sat up, scanning the horizon.

And then he saw it. A sleek, dark wood Riva Ariston cutting through the water like a knife.

Miguel's heart sank.

He recognized the man at the helm.

They called him Javier Bravalez. El Rey de la Muerte. The King of Death.

Some believed he was not just a man, but death itself.

There were rumors of caves filled with shoes.

More than any warehouse could hold.

Each pair was left behind by someone who crossed him.

Some said there were ovens underground.

It was the rumors that kept control, but it was his rage that everyone feared most.

Death was just the result.

The boat glided into the marina, its presence an unspoken declaration of power. Javier's men moved with precision, leaping onto the dock, securing the ropes in one fluid motion. Every step reeked of control.

Javier was dressed for a yacht club, white boat shoes, blue slacks, a crisp linen shirt, a man who didn't belong here but owned everything. The gold-rimmed sunglasses and wide-brimmed hat made one thing clear: wherever he went, he was in control.

Three armed guards flanked him, their eyes sweeping the area with military discipline. Behind them, two businessmen in suits clutched their briefcases, knuckles white.

Miguel ducked lower in his boat, praying to go unnoticed. But it was too late.

A guard spotted him. He raised his rifle; the scope trained on Miguel's chest. Miguel was trapped, like a fish on a hook.

Javier stepped onto the dock, his gaze sweeping the marina with cold calculation. He spoke to his men in low tones, pointing out various spots on the pier. Miguel strained to hear the words.

A guard's voice crackled over the radio, confirming Miguel's location. Javier paused.

His head tilted.

With a small, almost imperceptible smile, he turned. And walked toward Miguel's boat. His entourage trailed behind him.

Miguel's heart pounded. This was it. The moment that would decide everything.

Javier's footsteps echoed on the dock's wooden planks, each one bringing him closer. Closer.

Closer.

"Señor Miguel," Javier called out, his voice smooth as glass. "I've heard so much about you."

Miguel rose. His body trembled with fear. And rage.

He had no choice now but to face the man who took everything from him. The man who now stood before him, ready to take even more.

Chapter Three

Freedom

The crisp early morning air breathed life into the mist rising from the river that wound through the mountainside, carving a path like a snake, searching for prey. The water nourished everything it touched.

Bryce stood in its rushing flow, using only the energy he needed to cast his hand-tied Royal Wulff fly. Made with peacock feathers and calf tail hair, it whipped through the air with precision, slicing through the nearby chirps and calls of the birds. The fly shimmered as it danced and twisted, settling in a still section of the tributary.

The birds, startled by the foreign sound, returned to their war cries as the sun climbed above the dark horizon, casting golden rays that cut shadows across vast mountains forged by ancient tectonic turmoil. Bryce found peace in the silent ritual of fly-fishing.

The fly bobbed in the water, a delicate dance on the surface, creating tiny ripples that spread outward. It sank, and with a flick of his wrist, Bryce snapped it free from its descent. The fly zipped back and forth, joining the harmony of the morning insects. He released it from its rhythm of flight, letting it settle where he wanted, dancing atop the flowing water before sinking again into a deep pool beside a fallen tree.

The sun rose higher, and just as the fly submerged once more, the line went taut.

ZZZZZZ.

The reel screamed as a fish struck, tearing through the peaceful calm of dawn. The fish fought for its life, but Bryce, a master of control and efficiency, maneuvered his fly rod with the precision of a seasoned predator. He methodically pulled his prey toward shore, every move calculated, every ounce of energy conserved.

Its body shimmered in the sunlight, a sleek blend of silver and chrome, with subtle hints of pink and green along its sides. The fish thrashed, its strong, torpedo-shaped body glistening as it fought for the last moments of its life. Its alert eyes and hooked jaw added to the sense of awe, a symbol of wild beauty.

A muscled grin broke Bryce's stoic expression as he lifted the large steelhead trout from the water, admiring its continued fight for life. Wishing it no extended pain or misery, he killed the fish with swift, expert knife movements, gutting it in one fluid motion. The entrails splashed into the river as he placed the fish on a rock, kneeling beside it. His deep timber voice whispered,

"Thank you for your life."

Bryce finished his prayer in silence and washed his hands in the river. He stood, stretching, as the harmony of the current and its controlled chaos fed life into his soul. The sun had climbed higher, casting a warm glow over the landscape. He grabbed the fish and his fly rod and walked back into the mountains.

Later, sitting on a rock, Bryce stared into the distance, lost in thought. The remnants of his fish breakfast sat on a plate nearby, the fire reduced to smoldering embers that sent playful wisps of smoke into the air. A sudden sound in the forest sent birds into flight.

Bryce's eyes narrowed, scanning the treeline, his senses sharp from years of battlefield survival. Satisfied of no immediate danger, he poured the rest of his coffee onto the dying fire, methodically cleaning up his camp.

At the river's edge, the monitor on his hip vibrated. He washed his plates, leaving the fish carcass for the forest's scavengers. Every move was deliberate, honed by experience. To ensure safety, he spread the campfire's ashes and embers with a stick. He poured water over the fire, starting from the outside and moving toward the center, drenching the embers until they were cold. He stirred them, ensuring no hot spots remained. When satisfied, he collected the cooled ashes, packed them for disposal, and returned the rocks to their original resting spots around the camp.

Bryce wiped the sweat from his brow and chuckled to himself. "I need to get more propane. This is absurd."

He walked the perimeter of his campsite, picking up small tripods with mounted sensors. Breaking each one down, he packed them away as routinely as tying his boots. With the last one in hand, he approached his extended-cab Jeep Rubicon Wrangler.

The matte black finish made it blend into the forest like a shadow, and its battle-worn exterior bore the scars of countless trails. Retrofitted for survival, the Wrangler was equipped with a snorkel, suspension upgrades, skid plates, all-terrain tires, and a robust front winch. The machine, like its owner, conquered any terrain.

Bryce opened the back of the Jeep, moved his binoculars aside, and set his backpack inside before closing the hatch—everything in its place. The Jeep's interior was a fortress of utility: cabinets and lockboxes welded into the bed, a rooftop tent that tucked into a storage rack, and a non-reflective solar panel powering his gear.

He sat on the welded bumper, taking a moment to enjoy the simple satisfaction of a job well done. His gaze swept over the campsite, pristine, as if he had never been there. Reaching into another locker, Bryce pulled out a map and compass. He oriented himself using the surrounding topography, his scarred, calloused finger tracing his planned route. The map showed a small town near his destination, where the river opened into a large lake. He folded the map and tucked it into his pocket.

After gulping down the last of his water from a canteen, he shook it dry and secured it back in its holder. With one last look around, Bryce leaned against the Jeep, taking in the scene.

A hawk cried out, riding a thermal updraft high above, a lone predator gliding effortlessly through the sky. Bryce admired its grace, knowing that beneath the hawk's beauty lay a relentless drive to survive, just like his own. He smiled at the bird's presence, feeling a kindred spirit in its solitary hunt.

With a deep breath, Bryce climbed into the Jeep and fired up the engine. The powerful 6.4-liter V8 roared to life, its growl reverberating through the muted forest. He put the Jeep into gear, and it crawled up the rugged path, the trail behind him soon to be erased by nature's relentless march.

The forest, once his sanctuary, faded into the distance as Bryce began the next leg of his journey. He moved like an apex predator, quiet and focused, shaped by war and driven by purpose.

As the Jeep crested the ridge, he cast one last look at the river, its silver thread winding through the valley like a lifeline in the vast wilderness. The call of the wild lingered, tempting him to stay.

But with a final shift of the gears, he left it behind.

The road ahead was uncertain. Bryce had never needed certainty. He only needed the will to keep moving forward.

Chapter Four

Old Sheriff In Town

At the center of town, the sheriff's office leaned into the wind, a squat, cinder block relic with flaking paint, bulletproof glass, and a porch light that flickered out of habit, not hope. It looked less like a place of authority and more like a forgotten corner waiting for graffiti and trash to claim as theirs.

A few blocks away, the sawmill sat cold and hollow. It was once the heartbeat of the valley. Now it stood rotted and picked clean, like the carcass of a beetle-ridden tree.

That's how it starts.

Not with fire.

Not with sirens.

A town like this doesn't have to fall to be lost.

It just has to be forgotten long enough for something worse to take root.

Inside the sheriff's office, the air was heavy, thick with stagnation and subdued resignation.

The phones barely rang. The staff moved slow. And no one pushed Sheriff Wilson harder than he pushed himself, which wasn't much at all.

Elected unopposed for fifteen years, Wilson didn't run a sheriff's department. He ran a personal fiefdom.

His office was a stark contrast to the crumbling department around him.

Where the station was outdated and under funded, Wilson's office was plush and excessive. A solid oak door replaced the standard government gray. Plush leather furnishings and a mahogany desk screamed of self-importance, giving the office the air of a prize won on a game show rather than the workspace of a public servant.

Wilson sat behind the desk, his bulk spilling over the armrests of his oversized chair. The phone in his hand looked almost ridiculous in his thick fingers as he dialed with deliberate impatience. His voice, deep and dripping with entitlement, carried through the office.

"Hello, this is Sheriff Wilson. I was told the woman you sent me would be submissive. Well, she wasn't, and now she's gone. I need a new one, and her found."

He glanced around, remembering how far his voice carried. He lowered it, but kept the venom.

"I've got a meeting with Agent Jack, and yes, this is a secure line, idiot. Just get it done."

His double chin quivered as he clenched his jaw. Frustration simmered. He huffed through his nose, trying to calm his temper, an old habit, and a failing one.

"Get it done. I give you protection; you give me what I fucking ask for. Now hurry up. What? No, stupid, I can't send my deputies to find my fucking sex slave, or whatever you want to call her. Just get her back. Or at least find her. I don't need my wife finding out. Hurry the hell up."

A knock on the door interrupted him.

His rage shifted gears without warning.

The phone slammed down.

"Yes, come in."

Cheryl hesitantly entered, her small frame tense, the weight of working under Wilson aging her beyond her years. Her uniform, though neat, did little to hide the unease in her movements. She cleared her throat.

"Um, sir, the new deputy, Pete, is here to replace..."

She faltered.

She didn't want to say the name.

Wilson glanced up. His fingers drummed against the polished wood.

"Who?"

Cheryl hesitated, her stomach twisting.

"Dale, sir. Deputy Dale Harrison."

Wilson's eyes flicked over her body, his face confused for a second. Then, a burst of fake recognition.

"I know who the hell Dale was, dammit. He'll turn up. I'm sure he's hungover or something. Who's this Deputy Pete?"

Cheryl moved carefully, choosing her words as cautiously as her steps. She'd learned how to survive Wilson's moods.

But something about this morning made her stomach twist tighter than usual.

"Sir, you said we had to fill the Deputy position as soon as possible, Sheriff," she said carefully. "Pete grew up here, but he just finished his probation in Carson County... And Agent Jack is here to see you."

Wilson leaned back, his chair groaning under his weight, his gaze lingering on Cheryl longer than necessary.

"Come in, Cheryl. No need to whisper."

She inched closer, gripping the edge of the folder in her hands.

"Come closer so I can hear you, dear. I won't bite," he said with a hungry smile. "Hard."

"Um, Sheriff, Pete's here. Do you want to talk to him before he goes out on patrol?" She gestured awkwardly toward the door, desperate for an exit.

Wilson waved her off, already losing interest. "No need. Tell him I'll call him later. And send Jack in."

Cheryl moved to the door, grateful for the chance to escape, careful not to draw attention or turn her back on him. Once outside, she winced as the heavy door slammed shut behind her.

Wilson didn't acknowledge Jack until the agent was already sitting across from him.

Jack sprawled out in the chair like he owned the room, tapping his fingers against the armrest. "What's up, Sheriff?"

Wilson flashed a toothy grin. "What can I get you to drink, Jack? Pour me one, too."

Jack sighed, pushing himself up. He knew Wilson wouldn't start talking until he got what he wanted.

He walked to the bar, poured two tumblers of whiskey, and handed one over.

"We still have a problem," Jack said. "I'm not sure how high it goes."
Wilson eyed him, taking a slow sip.

Jack leaned in. "I've been keeping Taylor-May and her family in check, promising full federal protection through WITSEC. New identities. Relocation. The works. But now Javier says they've been in contact with someone else at the FBI."
He locked eyes with Wilson. "You're sure it wasn't Dale?"

Wilson exhaled through his nose, swirling the whiskey in his glass. "Dale didn't tell anyone. We know that much."

Jack nodded, took a gulp, then grimaced at the burn. "We need to be sure before this blows back on us. I've spent too much time making Javier's rival syndicate the operational focus. Trust me, I don't like getting on Bratva Zmeya's radar. But they know better than to start a war with Javier or fuck with us while we've got him and the government as a shield."

He paused, voice lowering. "It's a tight line to walk. We have to be smart. Strategic. He made it very clear what happens if we lose control of the narrative." Jack swallowed hard. "And he scares me more than the Russians."

Jack's eyes hardened. "If there's another contact, another voice whispering in the right government ears, we're fucked. And if our own government doesn't get us, the Russians will, or if we fuck up, were are getting the next donkey ride from Javier and I sure as shit don't want any of that."

Wilson finally looked up from his drink.

Jack watched him closely. "And who the hell is Pete? Did you want to tell me you were going to replace Dale? Is this guy going to steal drugs or tip off someone that I just outlined would be really fucking bad for us?"

Wilson waved a hand dismissively. "Pete will fall in line quickly. His family lives in this town. Don't worry about it. I got it covered."

Jack exhaled through his nose, frustrated. "We need to be clean, or we're no good to Javier. The fucking King of Death. If we lose control of this, we're dead. Simple as that. We have to control how the family dies. The family is more dangerous alive. It needs to look like the Russians took them out. Got it? First, we have to know if they talked to anyone else?"

Silence settled between them, thick as the whiskey in their glasses.

Jack broke eye contact first, stepping back toward the bar. He poured another round, letting the quiet stretch until it got under Wilson's skin.

Wilson drummed his fingers impatiently.

Jack took a slow sip, eyes locked on the sheriff. "Dale, just disappearing doesn't look good. Loose ends make people nervous."

Wilson shrugged, feigning indifference. "It happens."

Jack slammed his glass down, rattling the ice. "Not to us."

Wilson's jaw tightened, but before he could respond, Jack gestured toward the sheriff's phone.

"Make the call. You know what needs to be done."

Wilson glared but obeyed, swiping through his contacts until he found the right number. He hit dial.

The voice on the other end answered on the second ring.

"Yeah, boss?"

Wilson's grip tightened around the phone. His voice dropped to a low growl.

"Jed, pick up John Mills. Find out who he's been talking to at the FBI."

A pause.

"Yeah, but…"

Wilson's patience snapped.

"I don't care how you do it. Just clean the house. No loose ends."

He ended the call, tossing the phone onto the desk like it disgusted him.

Jack watched him for a long moment, then nodded. "Good."

Wilson exhaled, tipping back the rest of his whiskey. "So, when do we start with the yachts? I want something high-end that fits my lifestyle."

Jack's expression darkened. He set his glass down with deliberate force.

"Don't get too comfortable. You're as expendable as anyone else."

Wilson narrowed his eyes. "Is that a threat?"

Jack's voice was calm. "It's a fucking promise."

A beat passed.

Then, finally, Wilson leaned back, waving him off. "Yeah, yeah. I got it."

Jack stood, straightening his jacket, then headed for the door.

Wilson watched him go, his fingers drumming on the desk.

Jack didn't look back.

But both men knew, this was only the beginning.

Chapter Five

Meet The Locals

Bryce's Jeep roared down a winding country road, its tires drumming across cracked pavement, soaking up every jolt through reinforced suspension. The road blurred into greens and browns, a narrow artery carved through towering trees and jagged rock.

Outside, the world was raw and untouched, a stark contrast to the rusted gas stations and boarded-up stores he had passed. Every town looked the same. Industry gone. Businesses empty. People scraping by, scavenging whatever was left.

The Jeep's speakers crackled to life, breaking the monotony of the engine noise. "What's up, Ant?"

A deep, familiar voice boomed through the speakers.

"Karma! Thought you'd be off the grid, running from civilization."

Bryce grinned. "You caught me in transition. What's going on?"

"I'm getting married in Sweden next year. And you're on my groomsmen list. Don't even think about saying no."

Bryce laughed, shaking his head. "Count me in."

"Good. Oh, and I just sent you that podcast I mentioned. Listen to it when you get a chance. We need to catch up before next year. Maybe I'll fly out."

Bryce nodded, even though Ant couldn't see him. "Sounds good. I'll check out the podcast now."

"Perfect. Talk soon, brother."

The call ended.

A notification pinged the email from Ant. Bryce tapped the link.

A voice filled the Jeep. Low. Measured. But with an edge beneath it, like someone used to saying hard things out loud.

What number tips a society into chaos?

A pause.

Bryce didn't know the number. But he'd felt it. Seen it. The quiet tipping point when people stopped sharing and started staking out sides.

Survival is simple in small numbers: tribes, families, tight-knit communities. Scale it up, and survival shifts. Cooperation becomes domination. We stop building bridges and start digging trenches.

His grip tightened on the wheel. He remembered rooms where silence meant trust and others where silence meant someone had a weapon under the table.

A second voice, calmer, more clinical, cut in.

People think laws and tech make us civilized. But we're the same creatures we've always been, fighting over food, power, and beliefs. We just have better tools now.

Bryce turned up the volume. They kept striking nerve after nerve, not because it was new, but because it was true. Brutally true.

His jaw tightened, instinctive. Like pressure on an old wound, painful, but earned.

It was the kind of hurt that came with healing, like a deep muscle finally stirred after being ignored too long.

Most people couldn't sit with this. They flinched, deflected, talked over it. But not him.

This hurt in the right way.

This was truth with teeth. And he welcomed it.

When scarcity hits, we retreat, clinging to sides, to identity. Demonizing the other is easier than asking: what if division itself is the tool of control?

It's always someone else. Bryce had seen entire villages torn apart because someone didn't belong. The flags changed. The language and accents changed. But the result never did.

A third voice joined in. Older. Worn.

It doesn't take much. The French Revolution started with food shortages. Rome fell when loyalty fractured. The Arab Spring began with one man. Sometimes, it only takes one.

One spark. Bryce had seen men with matches and others made of dry kindling. Most didn't know which one they were until it was too late.

Technology gives us a choice, the first voice said. Star Trek or Star Wars. Progress or dominance. Intelligence or power. And we're making that choice right now.

He exhaled. It hit closer than he wanted to admit. He never cared much for Star Trek, boldly going where no man had gone before, until he got older and realized the real fiction was different lifeforms working together.

Man always wants to conquer.

If only the world could be more like Star Trek, championing intelligence and common ground instead of constant war and picking sides.

Chimps violently fight for dominance within their hierarchy. Humans? We consume rage through media, politics, and feedback loops. Fear becomes fuel. And the more we feed it, the more it defines us.

We draw imaginary lines, pick sides, and dig in. Opinions harden into beliefs. Beliefs become filters, the lens through which we see the world. And once that lens is set, no one stops to clean it.

It becomes reality. Everything and everyone bends to fit it.
And that's a tough way to find common ground, hard to solve real problems when we're so busy creating imaginary ones.

Bryce had seen as much violence in so-called civilized countries as anywhere else.

The chimps had nothing on us.

So what do we build...help bots or war bots? Because war bots don't choose. We make that choice.

A silence followed. Then a colder voice, detached.

Right now, somewhere in the world, a drone is deciding if a man lives or dies. Not a soldier. An algorithm. And the people who built it? They sleep fine.

Bryce's jaw flexed.

He could still hear the whine. Then the flicker of the tablet. Screaming. Gunfire.

The second whine tore through the sky, through his brain.

The radio screamed. He screamed.

Then...White.

Endless. Blinding. White.

He'd seen what the drone feed didn't show. What it never showed. The blood. The fire. The broken pieces of his memories scattered through the wreckage.

He'd called it in. He gave the coordinates. And they trusted him.

His thumb tapped send, same rhythm, same reflex as the trigger.

Aim. Breathe. Squeeze. Shift. New target.

Only this time, there was no next.

This was the last.

The last target.

The last of everything he knew.

They called it mission success. Labeled it friendly fire. Wrote it off as an acceptable loss.

He was the only one left to argue.

His hand tightened on the wheel.

He didn't remember the blast. Only the ringing silence afterward. And the way the weight never left his chest.

He'd never blamed the drone operator. Or even the mechanic.

It was a freak misfire. It was doing what it was built to do.

The problem was, so was he.

A new voice now, sharper. More urgent cut through his thoughts.

We can discuss the technical aspects: firewalls, networks, systems, and safeguards.

But people live in parallel worlds.
Some live above the fallout. Shielded. Disconnected. Their theories never touch the ground. Their rhetoric echoes in safe rooms, ideas that only breathe in a vacuum.

While others can die for every choice made.
Because in the real world, decisions have weight. And theory doesn't bleed.

That one landed. Hard.

Take the AI trolley test. A train's about to kill twenty people. You can flip the switch, kill one instead. Still murder. And what if the one is your child?

He didn't flinch. He'd pulled the lever more than once. But the math never added up afterward.

A softer voice now. Reflective. Tired.

We're losing sight of why we fight. If intelligence, kindness, and wisdom were valued like fame and fortune, don't you think men would evolve?

Bryce didn't answer. He wasn't sure men wanted to evolve.

Men kill for power. But what if real power came through peace?

Think about it. We don't lock our doors because we're afraid of women.

Bryce shifted in his seat. His mind flashed to villages where girls had no doors to lock. Where a woman could be dragged out, blamed, punished, and erased.

He muttered, barely audible, "That's not culture. That's just control."

The final voice entered now. Quiet. Unshakable.

And here's the trick: some in power, hidden in the shadows, don't want peace. Not really.

They sell sex, not safety. Keep the world hungry. Desperate.
They pull strings, manipulate systems, all for their gain.
Because a world full of strong, wise men and women?
That's a world they can't rule. Can't control.

A breath.

Look at it. Even religion unites as much as it divides.
Unless we find common ground, or a common enemy that wounds all of us, we stay trapped in the loop.

Us versus them. Fighting over labels and translations.
Never realizing how much we share... and how little there is to fight about.
Until people start questioning what they're reacting to, start thinking critically, challenging what they're fed, we'll never get out of the trenches.

Bryce exhaled, slow, sharp. He remembered what his guide had told him at the sweat lodge:

The right wing and the left wing are part of the same bird.
The world felt exactly like that. Two sides, both convinced they were right.
No middle. No balance. Just war.

The most dangerous war is the one we don't even notice.
It spreads like an endless fire, thoughts that flicker and burn long after dark, stealing sleep, stealing peace.

A war of the mind. Fed through screens. Waged in homes. Rooted in fear.
Fueled by unchecked rhetoric until even our hearts forget how to heal.

His fingers flexed on the wheel. He gave a small, automatic shake of his head, like trying to erase the thought before it carved too deep. He'd seen what happens when people believe too much. When the cause matters more than the people. When the mission becomes the god.

They'll kill for an idea and justify it with a flag, a label, an opinion.
Then...A roar.

A filthy off-road truck burst from a dirt trail ahead, oversized tires slinging mud through the air. Confederate flags bolted to its rusted bed.

Bryce jerked the wheel. Narrow miss. Mud splattered his windshield, streaking his view.

Instincts flared. His grip tightened. Adrenaline spiked.

Same locals everywhere. Always looking for a fight.

The world tilted.

For a split second, the road faded, replaced by another. Hotter. Louder. Deadlier.

The Humvee's windshield glowed with dust. The air was thick with heat.

A sun-scorched road stretched ahead, the convoy grinding through it, engines howling.

A beat-up Toyota Hilux cut in front, AKs bristling from the truck bed, a faded black flag snapping in the wind.

Ansar al-Sunna militia.

The men in back taunted them, laughing, waving like they owned the road.

Bryce, riding shotgun, steadied his rifle, sighting through the window. His finger hovered on the trigger guard.

The radio clicked.

"Stand down. Stay on task."

His grip tightened. Something was off.

Then...

BOOM.

A deafening explosion. The lead vehicle vanished in a fireball of twisted metal.

Dust. Chaos. Screams.

Gunfire tore from the treeline. AKs screamed on full auto. RPGs streaked smoke, chaos raining down. A coordinated ambush.

The radio crackled, voices drowning in panic.

Bryce moved instinctively, shielding his head, shouting, returning fire.

"FUCK!"

The road snapped back as the wipers cleared away the past, revealing what was ahead.

The dust and fire faded. The heat of Mali was gone.

The podcast droned on, but Bryce hardly heard it.

His right hand hovered near the quick-release lock box close, but not touching. His fingers flexed, squeezing the tension away.

He just needed to feel the weight of a weapon.

Not to use it. Just to know it was there.

Something familiar. Something that had always had his back when nothing else did.

He focused on his breathing, letting the tension settle. Training took over, the same discipline that had kept him out of bad situations before.

Step back. Assess.

Were they drunk? Looking for a fight? Or just dumb?

Either way, it didn't involve him.

The Jeep's tires gripped the road, waiting for his decision.

His heart hammered.

This wasn't a war zone.

No IEDs. No snipers. No ambush waiting in the treeline.

Just some idiots playing games.

Bryce exhaled and eased off the gas. His heart pounded against his ribs, breath steady but tight. The truck shrank in the distance. His fingers twitched near the quick-release lockbox.

He knew he wasn't in a war zone.

But his body hadn't figured that out yet.

The podcast kept playing, but it was just noise now.

Annoyed with himself, he shook his head. Reacted too fast. Letting them pull him into something pointless.

The fight that doesn't happen is always the best one.

He eased down again, eyes flicking to a weathered sign: GAS UP AHEAD.

Gauge was low. He could use the stop.

He needed to ground himself. Gas, stretch, get out of his own head.

As he rounded the bend, an old gas station came into view, a relic of another time.

The sign was rusted, barely legible. Two faded pumps stood alone under a flickering light, struggling against the morning gloom.

A hand-painted WE HAVE ICE sign clung to the window, the letters faded and peeling.

Bryce rolled to a stop, scanning the lot. His fingers twitched.

Always check. Always be ready.

The truck that almost hit him sat in front of the gas station, taking up every space like it owned the place.

His jaw clenched.

Figures.

Bryce pulled his Jeep to the furthest pump, eyeing the faded sign taped to the machine.

CASH ONLY.

No need to go inside. Nothing good would come of it.

With nothing else to do, he grabbed a rag from the passenger seat and stepped out, rolling his shoulders as he stretched.

A thick slime of wet mud streaked across the windshield—a fresh reminder of his introduction to the locals. The wipers had only smeared it into a dirty haze, leaving slow, murky trails down the glass. He tossed the rag back into the Jeep and grabbed the windshield squeegee from the pump.

Cold water mixed with the mud, swirling into brown rivulets that dripped onto the pavement as he worked.

Satisfied, he stepped back, giving the windshield one last pass before tossing the squeegee back into its slot.

Moving to the rear of the Jeep, Bryce pulled out the ashcan he'd stored from his campsite. Along the fence, the gas station had a disposal can for campers—one of the few conveniences left in a place like this.

Yelling erupted from inside the store.

"I don't give a shit, old man! I don't care who your daughter's fucking. I'm not paying for shit!"

Bryce's movements slowed, his focus shifting toward the commotion.

Jake and Marty came barreling out, all noise and attitude.

Jake, the truck's owner, carried his fat like muscle. He strutted to the driver's seat with a 12-pack under one arm and a bag of jerky in the other.

Marty followed, part grizzly bear, all muscle, no brains.

One massive hand hoisted a case of beer against his hip; The other clutched chips and more jerky.

He yanked on the truck door. Something had to give.

The beer hit the pavement with a dull thud.

Two cans burst, spraying foam across the gravel.

"Shit," Jake muttered, not even looking down.

"Hurry up, stupid."

Marty grabbed the dripping case, slipped, and lunged for the door as Jake fired up the engine.

He barely got his foot in before the truck shot into reverse, tires shrieking. He stumbled but recovered, athletic reflexes saving him.

"Do that again," he snarled, "and I swear to God, I'll knock your damn jaw off."

Jake just grinned. Marty's threats were as empty as the beer cans they'd left behind, the same as they always had been since first grade.

As they sped off, Jake's grin widened when he spotted Bryce.

He spat a stream of tobacco onto the pavement and flipped him off. More habit than hatred.

Bryce didn't react.

He just watched them disappear down the road.

Then, with a shake of his head, Bryce tossed the rag into the Jeep, grabbed his wallet, and walked inside.

The bell above the door chimed as he stepped in. The scent of old wood, motor oil, and fresh produce settled around him.

His instincts kicked in, the quiet habit of scanning a room without looking like he was scanning a room.

The layout was familiar.

Camping gear and hunting supplies in one corner. Fresh produce and meats in the coolers. Frozen goods humming behind fogged-up glass doors. Car batteries and tools lining the back wall.

But what caught Bryce's attention was the wall behind the counter.

A folded American flag rested in a glass case.

Below it, another banner, a white field with the Army's blue insignia.

A scarlet scroll beneath it read: *United States Army–1775.*

Beside it, a ribbon, green, yellow, and red.

Vietnam.

A black-and-white photo sat framed beneath the banners. Edges worn, but carefully preserved.

Young men in fatigues stared into the camera.

Faces hardened by youth lost to war.

A patch with a red taro leaf and a yellow lightning bolt rested beside the frame—the insignia of the 25th Infantry Division.

Bryce stood there a moment longer, taking it all in.

This wasn't just decor.

It was a lifetime of sacrifice.

A story told without words.

Movement caught his eye.

Near the beer cases, an old man knelt, cleaning up a shattered bottle of wine.

Gray beard. Late sixties, maybe.

His denim overalls were frayed at the seams, stained with grease and dust. His white shirt was smudged from work.

A Vietnam service hat sat low on his brow.

The old man looked up, weariness in his eyes.

Not fear.

Not anger.

Just the weight of tired acceptance.

Bryce nodded, his voice calm.

"I got his license plate, if that helps."

The man shook his head, dismissing the offer as he returned to his task.

"Thanks, but I don't think it'll help much."

Bryce understood.

He wandered down an aisle, picked up a fishing pole, then glanced back at the old man.
"You've got just about everything you could need in here."

The man struggled to his feet, his rusty tin pail sloshing with water, wine, and glass.

He limped to the counter and set it down with a sigh.
"We try."

A flicker of pride returned to his voice.

Bryce grabbed two bottles of water, then scanned the meat section. A fresh ribeye caught his eye.

"This local?"

The man nodded, pride flickering behind tired eyes.
"From the next town over. Got it in yesterday."

Bryce grinned, picked the biggest steak, and added it to his basket.

He grabbed potatoes, fresh vegetables, garlic, and onions, then headed to the counter.
"I'll take eighty on pump one, and whatever all this comes to. Oh, and some ice and that cooler."

The man rang everything up, then hesitated, adjusting his glasses.
"That'll be two-fifty. Cash only."

His voice carried a quiet apology.
"The gas and the wine... they're not cheap."

Bryce handed over three crisp, hundred-dollar bills.
"Keep the rest, for the broken bottle. And for the beer and jerky they took."

The man's face lit up, surprised, grateful.

Bryce held out his hand.
"I'm Bryce."

The man gripped it firmly, eyes steady.
"John. Pleasure to meet you."

Bryce nodded toward the flag.
"Thank you for your service."

John's eyes welled up.
He steadied himself against the counter.
"There was a time when... I wouldn't have let something like that happen."

Bryce met his gaze.
"Means you're wise. Don't worry, they'll get what's coming to them."

John opened his mouth, then stopped himself with a light nod. Instead, he let a small smile crack his face.

"Yeah. Thank you."

As Bryce turned to leave, his hands were full, but everything felt light compared to the weight in his heart. He paused at the door.

A flicker of instinct.

He glanced back.

John, limping back with the pail, struggling to get back on his knees again to scrub the last remnants of glass and wine. His movements were slow. Tired.

The bell above the door jingled as Bryce stepped outside. His mind was already far away.

Lost in memory.

The dusty air of the store faded.

Thick, suffocating smoke took its place.

A war-torn village, crumbling in the haze.

Bryce squinted through the heat distortion, scanning the wreckage.

Through the dust and fire, he saw him...

An old Iraqi man, kneeling in the ruins, sifting through what was left of his home.

Dust clung to his wrinkled skin. His hands trembled as they pushed aside broken bricks and shattered glass.

He looked up, eyes hollow, searching for something, someone, who wasn't there.

And Bryce recognized the expression immediately.

The same sorrowful smile.

The same resignation.

Blood trickled down Bryce's cheek, warm and sticky from a cut above his brow.

He tried to speak, his voice caught in dust and smoke.

"Are you hurt? Where's your grandson?"

The old man crumbled at the words.

His trembling hands lifted, pointing to a collapsed pile of rubble.

Tears carved tracks through the dirt on his face.

He was saying something, a whisper, a prayer, a plea, but Bryce didn't hear it.

The moment faded through static and ash.

"Can I help you?"

Bryce blinked, pulled back into reality.

The store reappeared. The haze was gone. The war was gone.

John looked up from the floor, his expression eerily familiar.

Bryce's throat tightened.

"No... sorry." His voice was hoarse. Distant, like it belonged to someone else.

He swallowed hard, shaking off the last traces of the memory. Instinctively, his shoulder moved to his brow, wiping at blood that wasn't there.

"Thank you again, John. Have a great day."

His voice was barely above a whisper.

John didn't respond.

Bryce stepped outside, the bell ringing softly behind him.

The feeling lingered.

The image of John scrubbing the floor wouldn't leave his head.

Bryce rolled his shoulders and cracked his neck, working to let it go.

But war never really lets go.

It just waits.

He lingered a second longer, watching John through the glass.

Then, with a slow exhale, he headed for his Jeep to fuel up, now that he was stocked.

Janice emerged from the back like a rock fighting the current, steady, unyielding.

She was powerful, worn, and moved with the grace of piss and vinegar. She was sharp, unbothered, and ready for whatever came next.

She carried a fresh case of beer, balanced on her hip.

She glanced at her husband, still on the floor, scrubbing. "He was nice," she muttered, setting the case beside the wine bottles.

Her voice was gravelly from years of smoking.

Then she added half to herself.

"I hope he doesn't stay long."

John rose, wincing as he straightened.

He met his wife's gaze, his voice low and tired.

"We should leave too."

Janice paused, a crooked smile creeping across her lips.

"Yeah. Never thought I'd hear you say that."

She hesitated. Then, after a moment.

"Jed called. He wants to talk to you."

John's face darkened, like a storm rolling in.

His voice didn't rise. Didn't shake. Just flat. Final.

"Fuck Jed."

No hesitation. No need to explain.

The kind of answer you only give when you've lived the reasons behind it.

Janice sighed.

She stepped forward, leaned in, and kissed him soft, fleeting, final.

"Go see him, John. I've got things to do in the back. Let me know when you leave."

Then, without another word, she turned and disappeared into the storage room.

John watched her go.

Then he turned toward the window, looking out, lost in thought.

Just in time to see Bryce's jeep disappear down the road.

***

Bryce leaned back into his seat, hands steady on the wheel. The engine hummed beneath him as the road unfolded ahead.

The steady thrum of electronic music filled the cabin, pulsing in rhythm with the road.

The landscape unfolded before him, rolling hills, towering mountains, a sky stretched wide open.

The podcast's last words echoed in his mind:

We are on the brink. Every choice we make, every reaction, decides what comes next. Do we build bridges? Or dig trenches? Star Trek or Star Wars?

Bryce exhaled a long and slow breath.

The question lingered. Heavy.

But there was no answer.

His grip tightened on the wheel.

And with the road wide open ahead, he kept driving toward whatever came next.

Chapter Six

New Partnerships

The G650 Gulfstream sliced through the hazy blue sky, its sleek black fuselage gleaming as it banked over the jagged Mexican coastline. Built for international routes and high-stakes landings, it now descended onto a private runway, rare, discreet, and deliberately unseen.

Below, rugged cliffs jutted into the sea, where waves crashed with a violence that matched the tension in the air. Coastal forests stretched inland, thick and impenetrable, hiding more than just wildlife. The golden beaches, untouched by tourists, told their own story, a place of wild beauty and darker truths.

Inside the jet, the chaos outside felt a world away.

Polished mahogany paneling gleamed under the soft morning light that filtered through tinted windows. The faint creak of leather seats, the low hum of the engines, and the rich aroma of fresh coffee had given the cabin an air of understated opulence.

He didn't just sit. He occupied space. Effortlessly. Absolutely. Authority didn't follow him, it orbited him like gravity.

The kind of power that required no introduction.

His tall, lean frame was draped in a tailored suit, cut with precision, every stitch a quiet declaration of wealth. His face was a study in balance, with angular features and a beard trimmed to add to the air of control he carried in every breath.

His dark, fathomless eyes didn't just observe. They deconstructed, analyzed, anticipated. He read people like open ledgers, scanning for strengths, debts, and vulnerabilities. He didn't see moments. He saw moves.

The sleek smartphone rested against his ear, his voice smooth, deliberate. Every word carefully chosen. Every sentence carrying purpose, not conversation.

His English was flawless, honed through years at elite Western universities, but a melodic undercurrent of Arabic lingered in his cadence.

"The next phase is secure." A pause. Measured. Certain. "We expand distribution through the farms. Javier and I will finalize today."

His words were precise, casual only on the surface. In this business, every word carried lives.

On the other end of the line, a voice just as composed, just as dangerous: "Good. Ensure everything stays contained. We cannot afford exposure. Our interests must remain... invisible."

Zayed's fingers tightened slightly around the phone, a rare flicker of thought crossing his sharp features.

This wasn't just business. It was a chess match played across continents. One misstep, and the entire board collapsed.

Outside, the coastline stretched wider, revealing the true nature of the land.

Between the dense patches of wilderness, hidden enclaves emerged, reminders that the untouched beauty of this place existed alongside brutal, unspoken violence.

A landscape shaped by power and blood.

The plane didn't just land. It arrived.

A ghost on the tarmac, sleek, silent. A whisper of power, landing without being detected.

The ground took the weight, but the balance of control shifted.

Silence.

Only the distant rumble of waves and the soft hum of the jet's engines winding down.

A rush of fresh, salty air cut through the sterile luxury for just a moment before the world of wealth and control snapped back into place.

Zayed stepped out, his movements unhurried, precise.

Every step measured. Every breath controlled.

His shoes, polished to a gleam, clicked against the asphalt as he approached the waiting black SUV, its tinted windows reflecting the jet like a dark mirage.

Around him, his entourage didn't move. They flowed. A silent current of control, watching everything, missing nothing. The perimeter was secured and accounted for. The terminal was discreet, tucked into the landscape like an afterthought, and the security was formidable, unseen, unwavering, and absolute. Every exit was covered. Every line of sight accounted for.

This was not a place for mistakes.

Chapter Seven

Let's Eat

Miguel's pulse thudded in his ears as he stepped off the edge of his panga boat, his boots striking the cold, uneven planks of the dock.

The salty air tugged at his worn clothes, but it did nothing to calm the rising dread as he faced Javier Bravalez and his entourage.

His gut twisted. Not just fear, but that bone-deep certainty a man feels when he knows it's already over.

His whole life, built on hard work, family, and a legacy of survival, now felt fragile, dissolving under the shadow of Javier's ruthless world.

The thought of losing everything he had spent years building gnawed at his gut.

His son, lost to addiction and empty ambition, might not even realize his father was gone.

Miguel swallowed hard, trying to steady his voice as he approached Javier.

"Hola, Javier. ¿Qué puedo hacer por ti?"

He tried to inject some normalcy into the words, but they fell flat against the thick tension between them.

Javier met his gaze, an expression cold and unflinching.

This wasn't about business, it was about power.

Miguel knew that.

Asking why was like asking a predator why it hunts.

Javier didn't need to explain himself. The reason was simple: control.

His face was unreadable, but a glint lingered in his eyes, a mix of amusement and disdain.

This was a man who had mastered the art of fear, who used violence like an artist used a brush, controlling people and cities with every calculated move.

He didn't need to lift a finger to instill terror.

But for now, he needed the marina intact. Its purpose unchanged.

It still had value, as a front, a veil of normalcy amid the chaos Javier orchestrated behind the scenes.

"You'll stay, Miguel," Javier said, his voice like a blade wrapped in silk. "You'll sell your fish to my restaurant. Be part of the town. A good man. A family man."

"And you'll act normal."

Miguel's hands trembled, but he nodded, trying to mask his unease.

The flicker of relief inside him was fleeting, like his breath under water. Only when he came up for air everything would be gone.

He wasn't naïve enough to think this offer was a kindness.

It was a leash, Javier's way of wrapping his hand around Miguel's throat without applying pressure. Not yet. Like a cat toying with its prey. A game only he gets to play.

A man who once hung bodies from bridges was now offering him a lifeline, but it came with chains attached.

Javier turned and gestured toward the boat.

"Go change. We're heading into town for a meal. There's much to discuss."

Miguel nodded again, his throat tight, as he made his way back to his small fishing shack.

Every step felt heavier than the last, like he was walking to his own execution.

The shack, once a symbol of everything he had built, now felt like a cage.

Inside, he rifled through his modest belongings, fingers brushing the rough fabric of his Sunday best, clothes reserved for church and family, the only formality he owned.

As he dressed, the weight of it all hit harder.

His life was no longer his own.

Two of Javier's men entered, their eyes darting about the small space, seeking hidden weapons or tricks.

Miguel didn't flinch. He just stood, silent, resigned, while they swept his life for threats that didn't exist.

When they finished, they nodded and stepped back outside, their silent presence a constant reminder that his fate was no longer his to command.

Dressed in his best clothes, Miguel stepped out of the shack and walked toward the dock.

Javier stood waiting, his eyes sweeping over the marina with a look of concealed contempt.

To him, everything here was a tool. Something to be bent or broken as needed.

"Vamos," Javier ordered, already turning toward the boat.

Miguel's heart sank as he followed.

He could feel the weight of his home, the dock, the marina pressing down on him.

The old wooden planks groaned underfoot as he walked, each creak echoing the uncertainty of his future.

The rhythm of the ocean slapping against the posts now felt like a countdown.

The boat's engine roared to life, cutting through the stillness with jarring intensity.

The guards untied the ropes.

Miguel boarded, gaze low, like a man already condemned.

He felt like the lobsters in his traps.

The boat surged forward, its powerful engine carving through the water, forcing him back into the leather seat. He didn't fight it.

He stared ahead, unmoving, as the marina, his home, his past, shrunk into the distance.

This boat was nothing like the humble panga he'd spent his life on.

Sleek. Polished. Its powerful engine cut through the water.

To Miguel, it wasn't a boat. It was a coffin, slick and gleaming, waiting to seal itself shut.

He glanced over the side, watching the endless expanse of ocean roll beneath them.

It should have comforted him. He had spent his life on this water.

But now, it mocked him, a reflection of how quickly everything had spiraled out of his control.

High above, a private jet sliced through the sky, descending toward the hidden runway.

A predator overhead, silent, watching.

A reminder: nothing here belonged to Miguel anymore.

Not even the sky.

A world of wealth, violence, and ambition, where power reigned, and the powerless served as pawns.

Miguel clenched his jaw, trying to shake the growing dread as the boat cut toward its destination.

This wasn't the life he had imagined.

But it now held him captive.

His only hope was to find a way through without losing everything.

The sun sank, bleeding red into the water as Javier's boat sliced through the waves.

Every mile felt like another step away from the world Miguel had known, deeper into the depths of Javier's control.

He could only hope that, somehow, he would survive whatever awaited him at the end of this journey.

Chapter Eight

New Honey Hole

Bryce's scarred black Jeep climbed an overgrown logging trail, its suspension flexing through deep ruts as the tires gripped the rocky terrain.

As the Jeep reached the ridge, the valley unfolded before him, an untouched expanse of wilderness. A large lake mirrored the sky, its surface broken only by a river cutting through the mountain valley before cascading into a foaming waterfall. Mist clung to the peaks, the last wisps of morning clouds dissolving under the rising sun.

The Jeep came to a stop. Bryce rolled down the window and shut off the engine. The light ticking of the motor cooling was the only sound that wasn't nature.

Birds chirped in the trees, locked in their daily skirmishes, while the river below nursed the valley with its gentle rush.

It reminded Bryce of a sweat lodge he attended when he first got back. He'd sat cross-legged on the cool, dark earth, deep inside a traditional lodge. The stones, pulled glowing from the fire, radiated in the shadows, brought back to their original form. Steam had settled over him like a heavy blanket on his soul. The deep, steady breathing of those around him grounded him, proof he wasn't alone. Wasn't dreaming.

He'd wanted to leave. To flee the pain in his body and mind. But then, the elder, whom he'd only met a week before, dipped a wooden ladle into a bucket and poured water gently back into it.

The trickle whispered through the underground chamber. Then the elder's voice, low, centered, cut through Bryce's spiraling thoughts.

"This is the first music of the land."

He poured water over the hot rocks. Steam surged up, thick and cleansing.

"And this is the second song."

Bryce smiled at the memory.

Finding comfort in discomfort.

He'd never agreed with anything more than that first song, the song of water. The music of life.

He chuckled to himself. Maybe that's why he became a guide. An excuse to always stay near the water.

He breathed it in its beauty, its purity.

He'd lived on both sides of the coin.

Despite its beauty, he'd seen and walked through the opposite.

He tore open a bag of jerky with his teeth and took a bite, savoring its rich, smoky flavor. A moment of peace.

He washed it down with a sip of water, then set the bottle aside.

He stepped out, stretched, and studied the trail ahead. Assess. Plan. Execute. His boots crunched on loose rocks as he walked the rutted path, calculating the safest descent. The embankment was steep, unstable in places, but manageable instinct first, calculation second.

He slid down in one smooth motion, logging every loose rock, hidden root, and silent threat. Task complete. Data logged. He bounced back up the hill with surprising agility for his six-foot-one, two-forty frame, honed for power, conditioned for speed.

Back at the Jeep, Bryce fired up the engine. He engaged the sway bar disconnect, improving articulation, then tapped Hill Descent Control and let the Rock-Trac system take over.

The Jeep descended like a predator, its weight flowing over the terrain. Tires gripped loose soil, adjusting with each jolt. Loose bark and leaves slid under the wheels, but he stayed in control.

At the bottom, the forest closed in. Bryce parked facing the exit, the Jeep settling onto level ground.

Time to set camp.

The rooftop tent unfolded above the Jeep, rising like a fortress. Bryce paused, breathing in the pine-scented air, damp earth mixing with a faint ocean breeze.

Home.

He opened the cab, retrieved his 9mm Beretta, checked the mag, and secured it in a holster inside the tent. Habit. Instinct. Preparedness.

Bryce had a concealed carry permit. Multiple, but after years on the road, slipping between states and jurisdictions, he'd learned not to rely on paperwork. Some places offered better protection for carrying it. Others, safer not to. He adapted. Stayed legal when he could, invisible when he had to. Sometimes, the smartest move was leaving the weapon locked up and blending in.

The lockbox clicked open. Bryce pulled out his Glock 17, Gen 5, RMR on top, SureFire light underneath. Grip tape wrapped the frame, simple, quiet, effective. He'd carried older models for years, but this one stayed closest. Worn in. Scarred. Reliable. A bond born in the fire. One of the few things he still trusted.

He gripped it, feeling the weight. Not just steel, but history. Purpose.

He clipped the holster to his belt. There was peace in its weight. In its truth. He slid the Glock in, and it embraced the rig like an old friend.

Now he felt whole. Grounded. Ready to enjoy his new home, if only for a moment.

Next, he pulled his SAT phone, scanned the screen. No calls. Relief flickered through him, but he didn't show it. He locked it away.

Pack on, he moved methodically, setting the first sensor, a tripwire without the wire. Then another. A layered net. Unseen but unbreakable.

Three more went down. Tight square pattern. Perimeter armed.

Back at the Jeep, he pulled a tablet and linked it to the sensors. A soft beep confirmed the connection. Another device, no bigger than a pager, vibrated in his hand. He clipped it to his belt.

If anything crossed the line, he'd know before they did.

He ran a hand along a cylindrical case mounted to the Jeep. The combo lock clicked open.

Inside, three fly rods rested in perfect order.

The Sage X Series, sleek, adaptable.

The Winston Boron III Plus, raw power for unforgiving waters.

The Hardy Zephrus, refined and precise.

He scanned the river's current and knew today's choice.

Sage X.

The others slid back into place. Lock sealed.

He selected a Hatch Finatic reel from a side locker and secured it with practiced ease. The soft click grounded him, a familiar sound in an unpredictable world.

He threaded the tippet, knotted a barbless fly with clean, practiced motions. A ritual. A return to something real.

He grabbed a protein bar from the cooler and refilled his canteen. The meat went into a scent-proof bag, locked away.

Scanning the pristine camp, he exhaled.

Everything in its place. Order in the wilderness.

He locked the Jeep, slung the canteen strap over his shoulder, and gripped the rod in his right hand.

The monitor on his hip vibrated as he crossed the perimeter.

A silent acknowledgment.

A small smile tugged at his lips.

The shift was complete.

No longer a visitor.

Now he was the hunter.

Chapter Nine

Arrival

Zayed's SUV cut through the jungle like a blade through flesh, clean, unrelenting, inevitable.

The convoy moved with purpose, blacked-out and bulletproof. But the jungle pushed back. Dense foliage pressed in from all sides, branches clawing at the paint, vines hanging low like nooses from the canopy. The road narrowed, swallowed by green. Out here, everything wild fought to reclaim its space.

Then, the treeline broke, and the sky blazed crimson and gold. Midday light knifed through the mist, casting jagged shadows across the dirt road. A warning, not a welcome.

They passed through villages unmarked on maps, hunched homes, satellite dishes rusted and cockeyed, children frozen at the sight of the convoy. Men stepped aside without meeting their eyes. Doors closed. Dogs fell silent.

It wasn't the vehicles that frightened them.

It was who rode inside.

Each tinted window rang with a Pavlovian bell of violence, conditioned by fear at every glance.

Javier's reach stretched long out here. No uniforms. No announcements. Just the knowledge that power had arrived, and it was best not to look too long at its face.

As the SUV rolled toward the villa, the light faded. Walls rose. The jungle receded. And the silence thickened.

Inside, Zayed is silent.

He knows what lies ahead.

Javier Bravalez.

A man whose name is spoken in reverence and fear.

A man who built his throne from blood and an empire whose loyalty is a currency traded, not given.

This meeting isn't just about money.

It's about survival.

A palace of opulence in the middle of the wild.

Wrought-iron gates, tall and unyielding, yawn open at their approach. The convoy rolls into a sprawling courtyard surrounded by high walls, guarded by men who know better than to trust anyone.

The estate is a contradiction: a palace wearing a cage's bones.

Wealth built on bones. Beauty carved from obedience.

Zayed steps out of the vehicle, his shoes crunching against the gravel. The sun casts long shadows behind him, but he moves with precision, unaffected.

A large man emerges from the entrance, a human blockade, built more for intimidation than diplomacy.

His voice is polite but hollow. "Your men must wait outside. No one enters but you."

A ripple of danger passes through Zayed's spine, but his face remains impassive.

"Of course."

He turns, gives his men a single nod. The leader of his security detail doesn't argue, they all knew this risk the moment they arrived.

The convoy pulls away.

Zayed is alone.

The doors of the villa swing open, and the cool air inside swallows him whole.

The hallway stretches, a gallery of wealth. Marble statues. Priceless paintings. Each one, a silent taunt.

You don't belong here. You will never belong here.

Zayed moves through the hush of decadence, his mind already three steps into the meeting.

Every word, every gesture, will dictate the power balance.

Every move has been rehearsed.

But in places like this, where loyalty is measured in survival, nothing is ever truly controlled.

The scent of aged leather and faint cigar smoke lingers in the air as they approach a dark wooden door, its polished surface reflecting the dim, golden glow of the chandelier.

The guard pushes it open.

Inside, power takes form in silence.

The room is a statement, wealth and intimidation woven together.

A bar stretches along the wall, an arsenal of rare liquors standing like trophies from a world too expensive for most to exist in.

Two deep, black leather couches sit across from each other like adversaries locked in a standoff.

Between them, a low coffee table of pure obsidian, cool and unyielding.

Above, a chaotic painting of blood-red strokes. More violence than art. Chosen for effect, not beauty.

The air is heavy.

Somewhere out of sight, a clock ticks.

Time feels slower here. Pulled under the weight of anticipation.

Zayed doesn't sit. He won't.

The couch is a trap wrapped in leather. An illusion of ease. A silent demand to lower his guard.

Not today.

The guard steps aside. "Javier is on his way. Can I get you anything while you wait?"

Zayed doesn't look at him.

"No."

One word. Sharp. Final.

The guard nods and disappears through a side door.

Zayed is alone.

But not unobserved.

The room breathes around him, its silence not an absence of sound, but a presence of control.

The air itself coils, waiting for the first move.

This isn't a meeting. It's a battlefield where bullets are the last resort.

A test of patience. Of nerve. Of absolute control.

Beyond the window, waves slam into jagged rock as if even nature senses the danger.

Farther out, a yacht sways within the protection of a man-made seawall. Even the ocean cannot touch Javier here.

Zayed's pulse slows.

There is no room for weakness.

No room for error.

The walls press in. The weight of the unspoken war grows heavier.

This isn't just business.

This is survival at its most ruthless.

Chapter Ten

Fresh Air

Bryce walks in peace, the valley stretching wide before him, untouched and alive.

A small smile tugs at his lips as he breathes in the crisp mountain air, letting it fill his lungs, grounding him in the present.

A break in the clouds reveals a pristine bend in the river, a hidden world seen only by the patient and the silent intruders.

He settles onto a flat rock, watching the water move. Listening to the wind dance through the trees. The river hums with energy, a slow-moving rhythm that soothes his restless mind.

The outside world falls away.

He sips from his canteen, chewing a protein bar as his eyes scan for the telltale ripples where fish wait to strike.

He picks up his Sage X Series fly rod, running a calloused hand along its grip, feeling its familiar weight. Standing, he moves carefully along the riverbank, searching for the perfect approach.

Shadows give you away. Footsteps send them scattering. Move like the river. Let it carry you.

Bryce moved like a cloud over water, silent, precise, undisturbed.

His boots touched the wet, rocky bottom with delicate precision light, exact. He never applied more weight than needed.

Nothing was stable, but everything was predictable. His breath moved with the wind, steady and unseen.

He doesn't move against the river. He moves with it. Never disturbing more than necessary.

He unhooks his barbless fly, letting it dangle in the morning air, its shimmering thread catching the light.

The reel clicks as he pulls more line, the comforting sound settling him deeper into the moment.

A roll-cast is the best option here, tight quarters, limited space to work with.

His wrist flicks forward.

The fly cuts an elegant arc beneath a low-hanging branch, landing with the whisper of falling leaves.

He draws it back, letting it hover for a heartbeat before it disappears into the sky again.

Bryce falls into the rhythm of the cast, the world around him fading into the sound of moving water and the measured beat of the reel.

Then...ZZZZZZZ

The reel screamed, tension surging as the fish fought the line.

The hunter is now the hunted.

A grin spreads across Bryce's face.

The fight is on.

The rainbow trout explodes against the pull, a silver-green missile surging through the current.

It fights like hard not used to being the prey. It will do anything to survive.

Bryce lets it.

Strength against patience. Instinct against control.

Bryce holds steady. It's a barbless hook. He has to be patient.

The fish twists, trying to shake free, diving for deeper water.

Bryce moves with it, careful not to let the line snag on the river's hidden obstacles, fallen branches, slick rocks, the tricks of a desperate escape.

He steps down the shore, matching the trout's movements, keeping its head up.

One last pull.

He lifts it from the water, iridescent scales flashing. Its gills pump, fighting for air.

Bryce grips it gently, freeing the fly with practiced ease.

For a moment, he admires its beauty: the sleek body, the primal determination in its black eyes.

He kneels by the river, pushing the fish back and forth, forcing oxygen-rich water through its gills.

"You're lucky, big guy. I'm eating steak today."

With a final push, the trout flicks its tail and disappears into the current.

Bryce stands, stretching, watching the river settle again as the sky shifts to deep amber.

Time to head back.

As the sun dips below the treeline, Bryce moves around camp with silent efficiency, the lanterns casting a soft glow from their halos.

The warm light sets the tone for the night.

His friend Anthony once shared a Swedish word with him, *mysigt*. Pronounced *mee-sikt*. It meant cozy comfort, the kind of ease that creeps in when the light is just right.

Bryce never knew he needed it until he felt it.

The Jetboil stove hums as he preps dinner on the Jeep's tailgate, his makeshift chef's table.

He cuts potatoes, onions, and vegetables, tossing them into a pan with butter, letting them sizzle and pop over the heat.

Nearby, his ribeye rests, waiting for the chill of the forest air to fade so the meat can cook evenly.

Bryce inhales deeply, savoring the smell of pines, damp rock, and the faint salt of ocean air finding its way through the trees.

The cast-iron skillet, the only thing he ever inherited from his family, waits patiently.

It will never need replacing. Like him, it was built to last.

Smoke curls from the pan. It's time.

Bryce drops a thick pat of butter, watching it melt and gild the skillet in gold.

The ribeye hits with a satisfying sizzle, drowning the insect hum beneath pure heat and fat.

He tilts the pan, basting the steak in a mix of garlic, butter, and heat, cooking it to perfection.

Beside him, his coffee cup held a deep red pour of wine, an earned, silent toast to the day. After beating his addiction to pills, alcohol never became his enemy. He knew many who weren't so lucky.

Funny how everyone fights for balance in their own way.

For some, it's a glass of wine.

For others, it's poison in a bottle, a glass, or a can, kryptonite disguised as comfort, leaving wreckage in its wake for everyone who cares.

He never thought of himself as a wine drinker, but tonight it's perfect. He shrugged his head, thinking how the older he got, the more he realized how little he knew about the battles people fought inside their own minds.

He took a smooth drink.

The Merlot hit like a memory, dry, dark, with just enough bite to remind him he was still alive. Notes of smoke and black fruit cut through the scent of steak sizzling on the cast iron, grounding him in the moment.

No burn. No rush.

Just control, poured into a coffee cup.

Bryce plates the steak, golden-browned potatoes, and tender vegetables, pouring the remaining butter over the top before taking his seat.

He bows his head.

"Thank you for your life."

He lifts his cup, takes a sip, then cuts into the ribeye, medium rare, the juices pooling like liquid gold.

The first bite melts.

For a long moment, Bryce just eats, breathes, and exists.

No war. No past. No future.

Just the fire, the river, and the delicate promise of another dawn.

Bryce leaned back in his chair, savoring the bite of steak, letting the rich flavors linger. He glanced up at the night sky, the vast openness above mirroring the solitude that surrounded him.

It's been months since he's had a meal like this. Not for lack of means, but because people cost more than they're worth. Big grocery stores draw attention, and he prefers to stay off the radar. But it's more than that. Aisles stacked floor to ceiling feel obscene. He's seen children fight over crusts of bread in war-torn towns. Watched men kill for a sip of clean water. Here, people complain about the wrong brand of coffee. Some doors are easier left closed, especially after you've lived in a world that had none.

A breath of a chuckle escapes as a memory surfaces. One of the many absurd moments from deployment.

On one tour, his team leader had a ridiculous curse: every time the guy opened an MRE, the enemy attacked.

It became a running joke. Eat before he does, or don't eat at all.

Bryce takes a sip of wine, swirling the deep red in his cup.

He's seen alcohol destroy lives, just ask his family.

But tonight, it's perfect. Just a humble toast to a meal and a day well spent. Then...

The monitor on his hip vibrates.

Bryce stands in one motion, his gun already drawn, his body moving before his mind fully catches up.

The forest has gone silent.

No branches rustle. No insects chirp. Nothing.

He grips the remote in his free hand, thumbing it like a flashlight beneath the gun, waiting.

He's not listening for sound, he's listening for weight.

Click.

Twenty thousand lumens detonate the dark.

A massive black bear freezes in the light, its haunches level with the Jeep's bumper.

Bryce exhales. Not a threat. Just hungry.

"Sorry, buddy, I can't share this meal with you."

The bear sniffs the air, unblinking.

Bryce's thumb moves over the remote.

The Jeep's floodlights flash, the horn honking twice.

The bear vanishes into the trees, as silent as it had appeared.

A second vibration on his hip confirms its retreat.

Bryce lowers his gun, his body still coiled from the surge of adrenaline.

He walks to the back of his Jeep, popping open the tailgate. The LED work light clicks on, shifting the makeshift kitchen into a perfect workbench.

From a secured drawer, he pulls out a Heckler & Koch MR762, loading a 7.62x51mm NATO magazine with calm, practiced movements.

Better to have it. Never want to need it.

Satisfied, he locks up the Jeep, reclaims his seat by the fire, and clicks the remote.

The lanterns bloom again, casting warmth across the camp.

Bryce raises his cup to the rising moon, the forest's cadence returning in slow, steady waves.

He finishes the last of his wine, but sitting still has never suited him.

He gathers his plate, utensils, and the H&K, slinging it over his shoulder. Then walks toward the river, boots silent against damp earth, the fire fading behind him. The monitor buzzes again as he crosses his perimeter. At the water's edge, he switches on his headlamp, scanning for movement before kneeling to wash his dishes with biodegradable soap.

Rinsing his hands, he scrubs away the remnants of the day, a ritual as much as a necessity. Once everything is cleaned and packed away, he brushes his teeth, gives himself a quick sponge bath, and returns to camp. He turns on the burners one last time, burning off any residue on the cast iron. His movements are automatic. Practiced. Each step, part of the unspoken discipline that keeps a man alive. Satisfied, he packs everything down, locks the Jeep, and climbs into the tent, zipping it closed behind him.

Click. The outside lights fade, leaving only the glow of his Kevlar-lined tent. Above his bed, the gun rack sits empty. Bryce checks the H&K, clears the chamber, pops the mag, reloads the round, and locks it back in place. His Glock joins the Beretta on the side panel. Shoes and pants go in the corner, ready to grab in seconds.

He lays back against the pillows, pulling up the electronic tablet to check his perimeter feed. The LED screen reflects in his eyes, a 3D map of his surroundings pulsing in blue light. Everything is around him has settled in for the night. Secure. He turns off the tent's light, shifting to his side, staring up at the stars through the bug netting beneath the sliding solar panel. The moon rises, painting the landscape in silver. For a moment, everything is perfect.

Then... his breath comes too fast, his pulse a war drum beating back the memories.

Bryce isn't awake, but he's already moving.

The gun isn't something he grabs. It's already in his hands.

The darkness isn't empty. It's waiting.

But there's nothing there.

He already knows why he's awake. His mind replays it like a reel that won't stop spinning. The dreams never change.

He wipes a hand down his face, sweat slicking his brow, and checks the monitor again. Clear.

"Shit, Karma." His voice is a broken whisper. Bryce lowers the gun, hands clenching, unclenching.

The only movement in the stillness. A single tear rolls down his cheek. He wipes it away. Holsters the weapon. Focusing on his breathing, he slows his heart, staring at the ceiling of the tent as his body forces itself to relax. The monitor's glow dims. The forest breathes. Sleep comes.

Chapter Eleven

Breakwater

Miguel sits frozen in the back of the boat as Javier steers around a jagged rock outcropping, revealing a hidden cove tucked between sheer cliffs.

This isn't just a natural harbor. It's man-made, sculpted to protect the massive 27-meter Kereon yacht anchored at its heart, a floating fortress of wealth and power.

As the tender slows, its engine purrs like a contented beast, and the men aboard fall silent. On the dock, uniformed guards stand at attention, ready to secure the vessel.

Miguel can't look away.

The yacht isn't just big. It's suffocating. A palace adrift, floating above men like him, untouchable and unreachable.

The weight of it isn't only in its size. It's in what it represents. It presses down on him, a physical reminder of how little control he has left.

Javier steps off first, his polished shoes clicking against the wooden planks with casual authority. He takes in the scene, pride swelling in his chest, not looking back as he surveys the marina.
With a flick of his thumb, he motions to Miguel behind him.

"You can fish here anytime you want, Miguel," he says, his voice rich with satisfaction. "No one dares come within three miles of my marina. It's my own private paradise."

Miguel nods absently, though his attention drifts, not to the mansion or the wealth surrounding him, but to the water below.
A school of fish swirls beneath the surface, their silvery bodies shimmering in the fading sunlight.

They move with instinct and purpose, unbothered by the world above.

For a moment, Miguel is drawn into their rhythm, their existence. Simple, quiet, free. But the group moves forward, climbing the winding path up the hill, and that moment of calm unravels.

Each step away from the water chokes the air from his lungs. The climb isn't steep, but it might as well be. Each step feels heavier than the last, every breath harder to catch. The weight in his chest isn't just pressure. It feels like chains.

The mansion looms larger with every step, its pristine white walls glowing in the last light of day, a kingdom built on blood and loyalty.

From a side path, a woman appears with two small children clutching her hands.

Her eyes scan the group, pausing when they land on Miguel.
She studies him, not like the others do. Not as an asset, and not as a liability.

She sees him as a man.

Miguel meets her gaze. For the first time in years, he feels exposed. Not in danger. But seen. Not as a pawn. Not as a piece in someone else's game. But as a man breaking under the weight of his choices.

Her expression softens. Then, without a word, she gathers the children and disappears into the mansion.

Miguel watches her go, a strange sense of loss settling in his chest.

Javier, oblivious, scrolls through his e-tablet, flicking through pages of data.

To him, this is routine. Another meeting. Another deal. Another piece of his empire falling into place.

But Miguel knows better. This meeting isn't about business. It's about survival.

At the top of the hill, a guard steps forward from the security station, posture rigid.
"Your guest has arrived," he announces, voice clipped and professional.

Javier finally looks up, a slow, sharp smile spreading across his face.
"Excellent. Bring him to my office."

Without waiting for a response, he strides toward the mansion.
His entourage falls in behind him like shadows, obedient and silent.

Miguel lingers. He should follow. But his feet refuse to move.

The weight in his chest becomes unbearable, his pulse hammering against his ribs. His eyes drift back down the path, back to the dock, the water, the fish still circling in the shallows.

And then he sees it.

A fishing pole rests against the guard shack, the line coiled and prepped, waiting for its owner's next break.

Miguel doesn't think. His hand closes around the fishing pole.
Something real. Something he knows.

He steps toward the shack and knocks. A guard answers, expression unreadable.

Miguel's voice is low but steady as he works to find the words.
"Can I use your pole? I'd like to fish at the dock. Is that okay?"

The guard eyes him for a long moment.
Then nods.
"Sure."

Miguel takes the rod, feeling its familiar weight in his hands.
Without a word, he turns back down the hill, each step easier than the last. By the time he reaches the dock, the sun is slipping beneath the horizon, painting the sky in deep blues and purples.

The water shimmers. The school of fish returns, unbothered, unchanged.

Miguel sits at the edge, legs dangling over the side. The fishing pole rests beside him, untouched. He doesn't cast a line. Not yet.

Instead, he leans back, eyes fixed on the endless expanse of water before him. The tension in his shoulders ebbs with the rhythm of the waves. The weight in his chest begins to ease.

The worries.
The fear.
The choices.
They fade.

On the water, there are no deals.
No power struggles.
No expectations.

Here, he can just be.

But he knows this peace is only temporary. Because at the top of the hill, his fate awaits. And soon, he'll have no choice but to face it.

But not yet.

Miguel picks up the rod, casts his line into the water, and waits.
The ocean welcomes him back. The tide doesn't care who owns the land. The fish don't answer to Javier.

Here, for a breath, for a heartbeat, he is free.
And for now, that's enough.

Chapter Twelve

New Day

Bryce wakes early, his breath visible in the cold morning air as he breaks down camp. The marine layer has rolled in and out, leaving a thin veil of dew clinging to the ground, a quiet warning. The scent of pine and damp earth fills his lungs, mixing with the rhythmic chirps of a black-capped chickadee that sound like it's calling out, "Cheeseburger. Cheeseburger."

Bryce smirks despite himself. But even in this tranquility, tension curls at the edge of his thoughts, a shadow never far behind.

He shoves the last perimeter tripod into the back of the Jeep and pulls his Glock from his hip, running his thumb over the grip. A mutter escapes him. "Come on, Karma. You don't need to be so damn paranoid. You're going fishing." With a click, he locks the Glock in the lockbox, shutting the Jeep with a finality that matches the coolness in the air.

Slinging his pack over his shoulders and securing his fly rod in a carrying cylinder, Bryce heads toward the river, the trees casting long shadows across the trail. The river's constant white noise should be calming, but something prickles at the back of his mind. He pauses near the rapids, pulling out his map, eyes narrowing as he scans the hillside's changing terrain. Checking his watch, he tucks the map away and starts hiking over the mountain ridge, his pace quick, efficient, instinctual.

As the incline steepens, Bryce scales a rocky cliff, each movement precise, each step calculated.

Then he stops. Kneeling behind a boulder, his senses flared. Slowly, he raises his binoculars, scanning the horizon. A bear lumbers across a distant mountainside, unaware of him.

Bryce exhales, smirking. "At least you're going in the right direction. Good luck, big guy." His muscles loosen for a moment.

The air shifts. A different scent, a thick, earthy scent, drifted through the trees, part sweet, part sharp.

Not natural to these woods.

It hit Bryce like a ghost from the past.

The soft powdery sweetness of poppy fields under Afghan sun, floral, dry, laced with something bitter underneath.

Mixed with the pungent, resinous weight of marijuana, skunky, green, and unmistakably alive.

Together, it smelled like desperation. Like lives already broken, just waiting for the body to catch up.

He'd smelled it before, in valleys full of silence, guarded by boys with rifles and hollow eyes.

Crossing the ridge, Bryce moves through the trees, emerging into a clearing, and his pulse spiked. Fields of crimson poppies stretch for miles. To the left, rows of marijuana plants choke the riverbanks. His stomach tightens.

This isn't a casual fishing spot. This is a high-level drug operation, hidden deep in the wilderness.

Bryce's eyes sweep the valley, tracking movement. Vehicles with oversized tires and motorcycles litter the area, not campers, not hikers, but enforcers. And then his gaze locks onto something worse. A rusted red van parked near an old shack.

Jax's van from the bar.

Bryce exhales sharply. "Shit. This is the last party I want to join." His hand instinctively reaches for his gun, but his fingers close around nothing. It's locked in the Jeep. Damn it.

His mind runs through exit routes, scanning for the cleanest way out. Then a sound. A slap of flesh against flesh. A scream follows. Bryce's blood runs cold.

Dropping to his stomach, Bryce pulls out his binoculars again, sighting in on the shack below.

John.

The old man from the gas station, tied up, bleeding.

Head slumped forward, mouth swollen, blood dripping from his temple.

Jed looks down at John.

"We know you're talking to Jack at the FBI. We just need to know who else you're talking to. You tell us now and I can let the rest of your family live."

Bryce's jaw clenches.

Nearby, Jake and Marty from the gas station stand smirking, surrounded by skinheads, bikers, and backwoods enforcers.

Jax, arm in a cast, watches from the sidelines, face twisted in amusement.

John spits blood on the ground.

Defiant.

He just looks Jed dead in the eye as Jed steps forward.

A giant of a man, fists still slick with blood, grins as he wipes his knuckles on his jeans. Then he backhands John again, sending him toppling over on the ground.

"Stupid old man. Just fucking tell us. I ant got time for this."

Bryce lowers the binoculars, exhaling slowly and controlled. "Shit. Fuck this." His brain runs through options, but none are good. He is alone. Unarmed. Deep in enemy territory.

This was supposed to be a fishing trip. Now? It's a goddamn war zone.

The sound of another slap echoes up the mountain. Bryce shifts into the cover of a nearby bush, pulling out his SAT phone, dialing the volume down as he makes the call.

"911, what's your emergency?" Bryce keeps his voice low and urgent. "Yes, I'd like to report a gang murder in progress."

"A gang murder?" The dispatcher sounds confused. "Where are you, sir?" Bryce grits his teeth, forcing patience. "I'm in the middle of the forest. Go to these coordinates, and you'll find a crime." He rattles off the latitude and longitude, keeping his voice steady.

A pause. "Do you have an address, sir?" Bryce shakes his head, biting back frustration.

"There is no address. It's the middle of the woods." He hangs up, muttering under his breath. "I'd like to report a gang murdering, what the fuck, Karma."

A phone rings below. Bryce freezes.

Jed pulls his phone from his pocket, voice carrying up the mountainside. "Hello? Yeah. Shit." His head snaps toward John. "Put this piece of shit in the cage. Someone called the cops."

Two men grab John, dragging him toward a rusted dog kennel near the shack. Bryce watches through his binoculars as the rest of the gang grabs their weapons, eyes scanning the hills through scopes and binoculars.

"We're gonna find you, fucker!" Jed's voice booms through the valley.

The gang spreads out, moving through the trees in a loose, sloppy search pattern. Bryce moves low, deliberate, shifting to better cover.

The buzzing of a rattlesnake stops him cold. His eyes flick down.

"Shit. Tattle tail."

In one swift motion, Bryce drives his knife into it, then buries the head before moving on.

A dust cloud appears on the horizon. Bryce raises his binoculars.

A sheriff's cruiser speeds down the dirt road toward the camp, kicking up dust. Bryce whispers through gritted teeth, "Now you're fucked."

But something's wrong. No one in the camp reacts.

The sheriff steps out, adjusts his belt, and waves Jed over. They exchange a few quiet words. Then the sheriff nods toward the cage. "Get it done, or I'll find someone who will."

The cruiser peels off, leaving a trail of dust in its wake. Jed turns back to his crew. "Let's go hunting, boys."

Engines roar to life as dirt bikes and trucks tear up the mountainside.

Bryce exhales slowly. The balance shifts.

He's hunted before, felt the thrill of being unseen, waiting for the perfect moment to strike.

Now the game has changed. They're no longer watching John. Their eyes are on the woods. That's their first mistake. They don't see it yet. And by the time they do, it'll be too late.

Bryce shifts the knife along his forearm, the hilt pressing against his pinky. He darts down the ridge, keeping to the shadows as he closes the distance to the cage. The gang isn't organized, a mix of city thugs who don't belong in the woods and hunters who move with experience. Some stumble through the brush like drunken tourists, scanning the hills clueless as to their quarry.

Bryce watches everything, controlling his breathing, preparing himself for something he never thought he'd do again. They aren't worried about John. Not yet.

He kneels behind a thick oak tree, barely fifty feet from the cage, tracking movements. One wrong step, and it's over.

His mind sharpens. Tactical thinking takes over. Calculate the angles. Count the threats. Plan the exits.

He shifts into the state of mind he knows best. He is the predator. And they are his prey.

Bryce slips through the brush, each step controlled, every movement a whisper against the earth. He reaches the cage, eyes locking onto John.

John slumps against the bars, blood dripping from his temple. His face is unrecognizable, swollen, battered, and beaten. A ragged breath escapes him, a bloodied spit hitting the dirt.

Bryce whispers, "John, can you move?"

A beat. John squints through swollen eyes.

"Who's there?" His voice is raw.

"Shh, it's Bryce. We met at the store." John tries to move, but his body can barely respond. He manages to grunt. "Run. Get away."

Bryce's eyes flick back to the gang. They're wandering, frustrated, confused. One of them, Gary, gives up first.

He slips on leaves on a steep incline, crashing down. "Fuck this."

Bryce watches him trudge back toward the camp, peeling off his biker jacket. Marty steps toward the cage, spitting in disgust. "All this for some old piece of shit?" He kicks the cage hard, making it rattle.

John flinches. Bryce doesn't move.

Gary stomps toward his bike, shaking his head. Marty is alone. Isolated. The weak link.

Bryce counts the steps. Four paces to close the distance. One strike. Knock him out. No need to kill, not yet. Just no noise, no struggle.

He exhales. Silent. Swift. Deadly.

Bryce springs from cover, closing the distance in a blur of motion.

Before Marty can react—Bryce slams him down.

His hand clamps over Marty's mouth, muffling the guttural scream as they hit the dirt. Bryce moves to control him, knock him out if he has to, but the struggle is brief.

A sickening snap. Marty's neck twists at an unnatural angle, caught against a protruding tree root. Bryce stills, breath measured. Marty's body goes limp. His eyes stare blankly at the sky.

Bryce exhales. "Damn it."

No time to second-guess. He rifles through Marty's pockets keys, a phone, and a wallet.

Belt. He'll need it. John looked bad.

Bryce unlocks the phone with Marty's face, disables security, and pockets it. Then, grabbing him by the armpits, he drags the body into the brush, hiding it from sight.

Back at the cage, Bryce pulls a crowbar from a nearby shed and snaps the lock. He climbs inside, crouching next to John.

John struggles to lift his head, eyes puffy and half-swollen shut. He doesn't flinch. Doesn't pull away. He just looks at Bryce like he's been holding out for him.

Bryce speaks low. "John, talk to me. Where's the worst of it?"

John shifts, jaw tightening. "Side. Feels... deep."

Bryce nods. Triage mode. Prioritize. Assess. Stabilize.

He peels back the torn shirt, exposing the stab wound, deep, oozing, sluggish but steady. Could be a nicked organ, maybe liver. Pressure now. Belt to hold compression.

Pulse weak. Breathing shallow.

He presses down hard. "Does this hurt? Give me a number one to ten."

John groans, biting down. "Eight."

Still coherent. Still fighting. Not in shock yet.

Bryce rips a strip from his shirt. "This is gonna hurt. Don't scream." He presses it into the wound, cinching it tight with Marty's belt.

John shudders under the pressure. A tear rolls down his cheek, but he doesn't scream. Doesn't beg.

Not now. Not ever.

Bryce registers it. Respects it.

The honor in the moment is hard to release.

Something ignites inside him, something buried.

He has an enemy. And someone worth protecting. He feels alive again.

His purpose, his skills, they matter now. They can be used.

Bryce shakes it off, and shifts lower, checking the legs.

Bruises. Swelling. No jagged breaks. Not critical. Move on.

He lifts an eyelid. Slow pupil response. Minor concussion. Not his biggest problem.

He checks the belt again, pulling it tighter around John's torso. "This is not my best work, but it'll hold for now."

Bad. But not fatal if they get to a hospital soon.

Bryce's hands keep working, already thinking five steps ahead. It isn't perfect. But it'll have to hold.

"Okay, we're moving."

He glances up. The gang is still spread out in the woods. He looks back at John. "This is gonna hurt."

With a grunt, Bryce hoists him onto his shoulders, careful not to jostle the wound. John stifles a cry, arms trembling as he clings to Bryce's neck.

"You're doing good," Bryce whispers. "Stay with me."

They reach the row of trucks parked near the camp.

A brand-new Toyota TRD catches Bryce's eye, but a quick tug on the door handle confirms it's locked.

Shit.

The last thing he needs is to set off an alarm.

Bryce scans for another option.

That's when he hears it—

A twig snaps nearby.

Bryce drops into a crouch, his hand instinctively finding his knife.

A figure stumbles out from behind a tree, fumbling with his belt buckle.

Jax.

His broken wrist slows him down, and for a second, he doesn't see Bryce.

Then his gaze lands on John, slumped by the truck.

Jax sneers.

"How the hell did you get out?" His eyes dart around. "Where the fuck's Marty?"

His hand fumbles for his gun.

But Bryce is already moving.

One step. One strike.

The knife slides in before Jax even registers the attack.

His eyes go wide, confusion mixing with fear.

A crimson torrent sprays in violent pulses.

Bryce twists the knife, ripping through the artery.

Jax tries to scream, but his vocal cords are already shredded, his body jerking violently as he staggers backward.

Bryce watches the life drain from his eyes.

Then—silence.

He wipes the blade on Jax's shirt and sheaths the knife.

This wasn't bravery. It was a necessity.

Bryce drags Jax's body into the nearby underbrush, patting him down.

A gun. A pocket knife. A spare magazine.

Bryce takes what's useful, wipes the blood from his hands, and returns to John, crouching beside him.

John blinks through swollen eyes, his breathing uneven. He doesn't ask who Bryce is. He already knows. His voice is a rough whisper.

"Special Forces?"

Bryce doesn't hesitate.

"A friend."

John exhales, a dry chuckle caught somewhere in his throat.

Bryce tightens the bandage on his wound, his voice softer now.

"You deserved more."

John doesn't move, but Bryce can feel the weight of the words land.

"You all did."

John's face hardened, not with anger, but with something deeper.

Something buried too long.

"Yeah," he muttered. "You get used to it."

Bryce looked at him. Eyes steady. Unwavering. Locked on his soul.

"Not today."

John says nothing more. He just nods in appreciation. His eyes glisten, but he doesn't let the tears fall.

Bryce continues scanning the area.

The old Ford truck catches his eye.

A rusted pile of shit.

But Bryce looks at Marty's Ford key in his hand.

"Perfect."

He lifted John and carried him to the truck.

Yanked open the door.

The smell hit him thick with rotting fast food, old beer, vomit, and rust.

But he didn't flinch.

Just breathed through it and got to work.

As long as it runs.

That's all that matters.

Bryce eases John into the passenger seat, fastening his seatbelt.

Then, moving fast, Bryce pulls his knife again.

He slashes every bike tire and every truck tire in the camp that isn't out looking for him.

If they try to follow, it'll be on foot.

Satisfied, Bryce climbs into the driver's seat.

His fingers tighten around the key, hand shaking slightly.

He looks at John.

"If this truck starts how I think it will, we'll have to drive fast and know where we're going."

He pulls out his map, unfolding it, his scarred fingers tracing over the terrain.

"We're here." His voice is calm but urgent. "Do you know where the hospital is?"

John's eyes are unfocused, his breathing uneven.

Bryce checks his pupils wider than they should be.

Shock is setting in.

John blinks, struggling to focus, then nods.

With effort, he lifts a shaking finger, pointing ten miles past the gas station.

Bryce exhales sharply.

"Shit. That far."

His eyes search the treeline.

Still no movement.

But that won't last.

Bryce grabs John's seatbelt, cinching it.

"Let's hope this guy kept gas in his truck."

He slides the key into the ignition.

Takes a breath.

Pauses.

He squeezes his hand, steadying his nerves.

Then he turns the key.

The truck sputters, coughs, and belches smoke.

It sounds like the engine might just die right there.

Bryce holds his breath as the engine roars to life.

Bryce slams it into reverse; The old gears clanking like they might fall apart.

He glances at John, who manages a weak shrug, the best he can muster.

Bryce shifts into gear, paying it won't die on him.

The truck complains less this time, its old engine groaning but hungry to eat up the ground.

Bryce shakes his head and stomps on the gas.

The tires spit dirt, the truck fishtailing before gripping the road.

They're gone.

Every mile is a fight. The old Ford rattles, its engine coughing like it might die any second.

Bryce grips the wheel, eyes scanning the road. Ten miles. Too far. Too slow.

John shudders beside him, breath coming in weak, shallow gasps.

"Stay with me, John."

No response.

Bryce slams the gas pedal harder. "This piece of shit better not die on us."

He steals a glance at John. His breathing is shallow. His skin, pale and slick with sweat. Shock is setting in.

Bryce tightens his grip on the wheel.

"Stay with me, John."

Still nothing.

Up ahead, the road veers hard to the right. Bryce stomps on the brakes, the truck fishtailing through loose gravel as he yanks the wheel. The tires scream, the frame groans, but it holds.

Then he straightens out, slams the pedal down, and drives harder.

Faster.

The logging road blurs past. The old truck lurches as it spits mud and gravel across the forest.

He calculates the route to the hospital, already running through the questions they'll ask when he gets there.

A long way to go.

A lot to explain.

But if it saves John's life—

It'll be worth it.

Chapter Thirteen

Bad Boys

Bryce grips the wheel, guiding the battered truck down the winding dirt road, its tires skidding on loose gravel. The forest looms on either side, dense and unforgiving.

Every rut and dip threatens to rattle the truck apart, but Bryce handles it with precision, his muscles working instinctively as he navigates the uneven terrain.
Next to him, John is silent, his breathing shallow but steady.

The road twisted and turned, then spit them out onto the highway.

The same spot where Bryce had first run into Jake and Marty the day before.

Without hesitation, he yanks the wheel, jerking the truck onto the asphalt, gunning it in the opposite direction of the gas station.
Beside him, John stares out the window, his face lined with pain and something deeper, regret.

Bryce glances over at him, taking inventory.

"You doing okay?"

John turns, eyes reflecting a lifetime of hardship.
"Yeah. Thank you. It wasn't always like this."

Bryce nods, keeping his eyes on the road.
"I'm sure."

They drive in silence for a moment, the weight of the past hanging between them.

John breaks it first. He nods toward the dense forest lining the road, his voice rough.
"The new growth, at least twenty years old now."

Bryce flicks a glance over, keeping the conversation alive.
"What was this place like when the mills were still running?"

John offers a sad smile.
"You would've liked it then. This town... it accepted me when I got back from the

when I got back from the war. It was the only place that made me feel like it was worth it. I met my wife here. It was a beautiful little town. Hard work got you a good life."

Bryce absorbs the words, nodding.
"Yeah, I would like that."

Then his gaze sharpens.

A sheriff's cruiser barrels past them in the opposite direction. Its lights are on but no siren.

Instinct tightens in Bryce's chest. He watches it through the rearview mirror.

John exhales sharply.
"Yeah. The whole town's a fucking shell now. You notice how everything's cash only?"

Bryce didn't take his eyes off the mirror.

He watched as the cruiser disappeared around the bend, its engine fading into the trees.

A flicker of relief passed through him, brief, but real.

"Yeah," he muttered. "Cash-only means you can wash money anywhere. The whole town's just one big laundromat."

John stares down at his bloodstained hands, his voice barely above a whisper. "Once they killed the mills, we lost all our work. That's how the cartel crept in, money laundering, drugs... They own everyone now."

His voice falters. Then panic spikes in his eyes.
"My daughter. My wife. Oh, Lord."

John turns, grabbing Bryce's arm with surprising strength for a man who should be unconscious.
"Please, Bryce. You have to save them. You can leave me on the side of the road, just save them. They're my everything. Please."

Bryce keeps one hand on the wheel, the other gently prying John's grip away. "Relax. It's okay. I'll get you to the hospital. Then we'll get the feds involved, find some police that aren't on the payroll. Whatever works to change this. This isn't my fight, John. I already killed two people today. You understand, right?"

John droops his head, desperation in his eyes.
"Please..."

A second sheriff's cruiser roars past them.

But this time, it doesn't keep going.

The lights flash. The siren screams to life.

The cruiser makes a hard U-turn.

It's coming straight for them.

Bryce curses, fingers tightening around the wheel. His jaw clenches.
"Everyone in town, huh?"

John's head lolled toward Bryce. His voice was thin, frayed at the edges.
"Not everyone... only the ones they need."

Bryce mutters under his breath, glancing at the mirror.
"Well, they have a good response time. I'll give 'em that."

John's grip tightens on the armrest.
"Floor it."

Bryce raises an eyebrow.
"I don't think that's gonna work."

John's expression is resolute.
"What other options are there?"

Bryce sighs.
Then slams his foot on the gas.

The truck lurches forward, the old engine groaning in protest as they tear down the highway.
For a moment, it feels like they might actually outrun the cruiser.

Then—
CLUNK. BAM.
The truck chokes.
Steam pours from under the hood.

The old Ford sputters and dies, steam hissing like a final curse.

Bryce guides it to the side of the road, muttering under his breath.
"Way to go, Karma. Shit."

John shifts beside him, groaning, his hands trembling as he wipes blood from his chin.

Bryce glances at the rearview mirror.

Red and blue lights exploded in the mirror, flooding the cab in violent flashes.

The siren wailed. It's shrill, closing in fast.

Whatever came next, it was already here.

The sheriff's cruiser slows to a stop behind them, dust curling in the beams.

Bryce exhales, rubbing his face.
"Well, this is gonna suck."

John swallows, his voice raw with pain.
"Let me do the talking."

Bryce nods.

John gently reaches over, taking the gun next to Bryce and tucking it between the seat and the door.

He looks over at Bryce.

"I've known Pete since he was a little boy coming into my shop to buy worms to go fishing. He's a good boy. He will listen."

Bryce's eyes flick to the meth pipe on the floorboard.

"Mind kicking that under your seat?"

John tries, but his leg barely moves.

Bryce sighs, toe-tapping it out of sight just as the deputy steps out.

He focuses on his breathing, watching through the side mirror.

The young deputy emerges from his cruiser, adjusting his belt with deliberate slowness.

Then he hesitates.

He reaches down, pulls out his wide-brimmed hat, tries to put it on, then takes it off, wipes his forehead, tries again.

The wind catches it. He gives up, sheepishly looks around, and sets it on the driver's seat.

Nerves.

Bryce mutters, "Shit." He looks over at John.

"This is probably his first real stop, and now he has to handle a stolen truck and two unknowns. Not good."

The radio crackles on the deputy's shoulder.

"Unit 4, what's your location?"

Pete presses the button.

"Uh, just pulled over a 1970 green Ford pickup."

He puts the hat back in the cruiser, closes the door, and walks toward the truck.

"License number?"

The deputy squints at the plate.

"F—Foxtrot, U—Uniform, C—Charlie, K—Kilo, Zero, F—Foxtrot, F—Foxtrot."

Static comes from the radio. Worse than silence.

Dispatch replies.

"So, the plate says 'FUCK OFF'?"

Pete exhales sharply, rubbing his temple.

"Correct."

"It's been reported stolen."

Pete frowned.

"Yeah. That's why I pulled it over."

His radio crackled. Static, then a voice:

"Sheriff Rick says to call him on his cell."

Pete glanced around, eyes narrowing.

"That was fast," he muttered.

He patted himself down, one pocket, then another.

Third try, he found the phone. He pulled it out, thumb hovering.

Didn't dial.

Just stared at the truck.

Something wasn't right.

Instead of calling, he walks forward.

Gun resting on his hip, Pete knocks on the window with his phone.

Bryce rolls it down, trying to be as smooth as possible not to alert the deputy.

Pete freezes when he sees John.

The older man is slumped, his shirt soaked in blood, his face pale.

Pete's stomach twists.

"Shit."

"Pete," John rasps.

The deputy steps closer.

"John... John Mills?"

John nods weakly.

"Yeah, Pete. This man saved my life."

Pete's eyes narrow.

"What happened?"

John shifts, wincing.

"Jed and Marty did this to me." His voice was a shell of its usual strength.

"They were gonna kill me."

Pete's jaw clenched.

"Who else was there?"

John coughed, spitting dark blood onto the floorboard.

"Whole damn crew. Same ones who burned down Old Man Davis' place last year."

Pete flinched.

Bryce's eyes stayed locked on him, tracking every twitch, every breath. Watching for the shift.

The reach.

But all he saw was a good kid, stuck in the wrong moment.

The deputy's hand lingered near his gun, but his eyes showed doubt.

Bryce recognized that look.

He's conflicted. Not stupid.

Bryce moved slowly, reaching into his jacket.

Pete tensed, hand snapping to his weapon.

"Easy, kid," Bryce said, voice calm. He pulled out his wallet, flipped it open to his driver's license.

"You want my ID, right? Here.

Pete hesitated, then took the license, glancing down.

"Bryce... Rath. License Number B..."

John coughed again, blood streaking his lip.

Pete exhaled hard and keyed his radio.

"Dispatch, I've got John Mills, he's in bad shape. Requesting an ambulance. ASAP."

Static hissed. Then:

"You talk to Fred?"

Pete frowned.

"No. I'm talking to you. I need medical assistance, now."

Another pause. More static.

"Call the Sheriff."

Pete's jaw clenched.

"Is an ambulance coming or not?"

"Call the Sheriff."

Pete's pulse kicked up.

What the hell was going on?

He keyed the radio again.

"Dispatch, confirm. Is an ambulance en route?"

The wind stirred, stretching the silence like a held breath.

Then his phone rang.

Pete stiffened.

He stepped away from the truck, answering quietly.

"Sheriff?"

Fred's voice was cold. Steady.

"Pete, listen to me. That man in the truck? He killed Marty and Jax."

Pete's stomach dropped.

"Sir, how do you know? The truck was just reported stolen."

"Check your phone."

Pete pulled it up.

A grainy game camera image appeared, a man dragging a body through the woods.

Bryce. His face was too clear to mistake.

Timestamp: twenty-five minutes ago.

Pete's pulse spiked.

Fred's voice returned, hard as iron.

"Listen real close, Pete. You let him go, you're not just fired, you're under arrest. Obstruction, aiding a suspect, take your pick. Don't test me. You got it?"

Pete's eyes flicked to John's bloody shirt.

"Yes, sir."

He hung up, eyes scanning the road, trying to make sense of it all. He should've already called for the ambulance, not waited for permission.

But something about this didn't sit right.

John Mills was a good man. Marty wasn't.

His gut tightened.

His training said one thing.

His instincts said another.

Gun drawn, eyes locked, he marched toward the truck, his voice steady but tight.

"Hands up where I can see 'em. Now."

Bryce stilled, raising his hands slowly.

Beside him, John stirred.

"Pete... what are you doin'?"

Pete's grip tightened on the gun.

"John, the Sheriff says this guy killed Marty and Jax. It's his picture on the game camera, dragging Marty's body."

John's face twisted, caught between pain and disbelief.

"Pete... be honest. You know how long it takes for anything to move around here. So how the hell they already got his photo?"

He coughed hard, blood flecking his shirt.

"Where's Dale? You replaced him, right? He just disappears and you show up? That's not strange to you?"

Bryce's jaw clenched, but his tone stayed calm. He held Pete's gaze.

"It's a good question, Pete. Think about it. Where exactly was that camera? Near the grow farm, or the cage they kept John in?"

Pete's hand trembled.

Nothing made sense.

Bryce stayed focused.

"Kid, let me take him to the hospital. Then you can arrest me. Call for backup, do whatever you need. But if he dies here, you're the one that has to live with it."

Pete hesitated.

His stance was firm, but the doubt in his eyes betrayed the weight he was carrying.

This was his first big stop. His first real moment of control.

"Step out of the vehicle. Slowly."

Bryce glanced at John. He struggled to lift his head.

His voice was weak.

"Do as he says, Bryce. Please."

Bryce met John's eyes.

He read the weight behind them.

This kid isn't the enemy.

With slow, deliberate movements, Bryce reached outside the window, opened the door handle so Pete could see both hands, and stepped out smoothly.

The moment Pete saw him, his posture shifted, an instinctive step back.

It wasn't fear.

It was recognition.

Bryce didn't move like some guy who hit the gym to look good for the ladies.

He didn't strut. He didn't need to.

He moved like a man trying to blend in, but couldn't.

Too smooth. Too exact.

Strength coiled beneath every step.

There was a density to him, a weight only trained eyes could see.

This wasn't a man looking for a fight.

This was a man tired of killing.

Fighting was a child's sport in his world.

Pete adjusted his grip on the gun, suddenly unsure.

Bryce kept his hands visible.

"You're doing fine, kid."

Pete didn't lower the gun.

His grip was firm, stance textbook, but inside, something twisted.

At the academy, they brought in pros.

SWAT instructors. Retired Special Forces.

Even UFC guys to demonstrate aggression, control, pressure.

None of them felt like this.

Bryce didn't puff his chest. Didn't flex.

Didn't need to.

He just stood there, still, calm...

But every inch of him radiated a coiled weight. Pete couldn't explain.

It wasn't size.

It was a density.

Like the air shifted around him.

Like violence lived just beneath his skin, waiting, not eager, not afraid, just *ready*.

Pete's brain screamed threat, even as his eyes told him the man hadn't moved.

It felt wrong. Instinctively wrong.

Not in a way he could name, but in the way animals sense earthquakes before they hit.

Like something ancient had walked into the clearing.

Like this wasn't a man, but the thing you send men to stop.

And worst of all, Bryce wasn't tense.

Pete was.

Heart pounding.

Palms sweating.

Breath shallow.

The training didn't cover this.

Nothing did.

Pete stepped back again, scanning his face.

"You military?"

Bryce held his gaze.

"I was."

Before Pete could respond, John groaned in pain.

Pete's attention snapped to him. He finally registered how bad John looked, pale, soaked in sweat, blood staining his clothes.

"Jesus, John..."

Pete leaned in, concern finally overtaking protocol.

"You need a hospital. Now."

Bryce seized the moment.

"Then let me take him. "

His voice rumbled at a different frequency, low, steady, impossible to ignore.

He didn't just control his body; he controlled the tempo. The space shifted, pulling Pete into his rhythm, calming him with nothing but tone and presence.

Pete turned back to him, torn.

"Look, I get it, you've got orders. But if you cuff me, John dies. Let me drive him to the hospital, and you can arrest me there. Hell, I'll give you my word I won't run, and that means everything to me."

Pete hesitated.

The weight of the decision pressed down, crushing.

Bryce gave him time to think and process the moment.

The radio crackled.

Dispatch cut through the silence:

"Pete, Sheriff Rick wants to know when you've got Bryce Rath in cuffs."

Pete gritted his teeth, frustrated. He looked at John. Then Bryce.

He keyed the radio.

"Do I have an ambulance en route or not?"

Silence hung in the wind.

Then the dispatcher's voice returned—flat and irritated.

"Is he in cuffs?"

Pete froze.

His hand trembled. The weight of his badge suddenly felt heavier.

Nothing like this was ever taught at the academy.

Bryce's voice remained steady. Calm. Controlled.

"We need to go. Now."

Pete's hand tightened around the gun.

"Shut up."

His voice cracked.

He was trying to convince himself more than anyone else.

"John, why are you in Marty's truck?"

John's voice came strained, thin.

"I told you, Pete. They were trying to kill me. We're on our way to the hospital. Jax fucking stabbed me."

John pulls back the makeshift tourniquet, revealing the deep, oozing wound.

Pete stares at it. His breath catches.

Bryce looks over his shoulder at John.

"What are you doing? You need pressure on that."

John gasps in pain but nods weakly.

Bryce turns back to Pete, his intensity burning into the young deputy's eyes.
"Let me take him. Arrest me after."

Pete visibly struggles.
"I can't."

He keys his radio.
"Dispatch, I need an ETA on the ambulance, north on Old Valley Road, about three miles from John's Gas Station. Over."

A static-filled pause.

Then, the dispatcher's voice, dripping with sarcasm:
"You talk to Fred?"

Pete's frustration boils over.
"YES, I talked to Fred! Did you relay my request?"

More static.

Then a mocking response:
"Yes, an ambulance is on its way."

Pete exhales sharply. He refocuses on Bryce, gun still raised.
"John, help is coming. But I have to cuff him before that happens."

John groans, pleading with Pete.
"Pete, we need to get out of here now. They're going to kill us. Look at me—come on, son. They'll kill you just for getting in the way."

Pete looks torn.

"I'm sorry, John. I need to arrest him. But I'll make sure you and your family are protected."
Pete straightens. His voice hardens, trying to regain control.

"Mr. Rath, on your knees. Hands in the air."

Bryce glances at John.

John nods weakly.
"Just do it, Bryce. We can work this out."

Bryce lets out a slow breath.
"Shit."

He kneels. Hands raised.

Pete steps forward.

He reaches for the cuffs on his belt.

The snap is stiff. He has to focus to get it open.

The silence is deafening. SNAP.

Pete pulls out the cuffs.

They jingle as he fumbles to open them.

Then a rumble of powerful engines approaches from the distance.

Bryce hears it first.

Then Pete.

They both turn toward the road.

Two massive 4x4 trucks roar down, skidding to a stop, blocking both lanes.

Dust kicks up in thick clouds as four men spill out.

Tim and another rough-looking thug, both armed with machine guns, leap from the first truck.

From the second, Eric emerges, cold-eyed and composed, his weapon held like an afterthought. Too confident. Another man steps out from the passenger side, almost a foot taller than Eric.

Pete's face drains of color.

The handcuffs slip from his grip, falling to the ground.

Instinct takes over. He steps back, raising his gun on the larger threat. His voice shakes, but he holds firm.
"Stop right there! Drop the weapons now!"

Eric tilts his head, amused. His lips curl into a smile that never reaches his eyes.
"Sorry, can't do that, Pete."

He steps closer, rifle aimed at Pete, but his eyes are locked on Bryce.
"This guy killed Marty."

Pete tightens his grip on the gun.
"That's why I'm taking him to jail, so the law can process him."

Eric chuckles, shaking his head.
"Our law, not the state's."

He gestures toward the woods, his tone dropping, quieter, more insidious.

Eric smiles.

But there's no warmth in it, just calculation.

"Look, Pete. I know you're new. I know you wanna do the right thing."

His voice softens, mocking.
"So let me help you."

He steps closer, lowering his voice.
"You're about to make a choice you can't take back."

A pause, just enough time for Pete to feel the weight of it.
"Think about your family, kid. Think about your future."

Pete stiffens but doesn't move.

Eric steps closer, his voice almost fatherly now.
"Just give him to us, and we'll be gone. You can say you found the truck empty."

Pete swallows hard.

He's young. In over his head.

Bryce watches him grapple with the weight of his decision.

Pete shakes his head, stepping back.

"No. Just leave, Eric. Now."

His fingers reach for his radio.

"Dispatch—"

The crack of gunfire tears through the air.

Pete jerks violently, once, twice, three times.

His body crumples like a rag doll, collapsing beside Bryce.

"Shit, Tim!"

Eric spins on him, furious.

"I told you..."

Bryce doesn't waste the opportunity.

He rolls forward, grabs Pete's gun, and yanks his body behind the truck for cover.

A hail of automatic gunfire erupts, ripping through metal and shattering glass.

Bryce presses two fingers to Pete's neck—nothing.

The kid is gone.

Bryce mutters a quick prayer, then rips the extra magazines from Pete's belt and yanks his radio free.

Eric's voice cuts through the chaos, frustrated and condescending.

"It's Marty's fucking truck! I was gonna give it to his kid. God knows he didn't leave him shit. Think before you start shooting, dumbasses!"

He turns to his men, barking orders.

"Spread out! Shoot the fucker, not the goddamn truck!"

Bryce moves.

Fast.

He slides to the passenger side, peeking just enough to spot movement—Tim creeping along the police cruiser.

BAM—Bryce fires.

Tim drops, screaming, clutching his leg.

Bryce shoots him in the head.

Automatic fire erupts again, bullets chewing through the truck's metal frame.

"STOP! FUCKING STOP!"

Eric screams, but Bryce is already moving.

He rolls under the truck as rounds tear through the air above him.

A pair of boots step into view.

Bryce fires. Blows out the man's kneecap, then delivers a second shot to the head.

The body collapses.

Another silhouette. Big boots. Bigger target.

Bryce fires. Takes out the knee. Then ends it.

Six shots. Three lives gone.

A choked curse from Eric.

"What the fuck, man!"

His voice cracks, realizing Bryce has taken them apart one by one.

Bryce hears it, the click-clack of cowboy boots.

Eric is retreating.

Then, the deep roar of an engine.

Bryce knows what's happening before he sees it.

Eric's running.

The truck peels away, tires screaming against pavement.

Bryce stays low, behind cover.

More sirens. Heavy engines. Dirt bikes scream in the distance.

Reinforcements are closing in.

Bryce moves fast, gathers weapons, extra magazines, and phones from the dead.

Then he looks at the truck.

John's body is slumped in the passenger seat.

He's choking on blood. The bullets have ripped through him.

John's hand trembles as he grabs Bryce's sleeve.

Blood bubbles at his lips, but he fights to speak.

"My wife's at my gas station. Promise me. Please. Save my family."

His fingers tighten.

Bryce's eyes are locked on John's.

"I promise John."

Then, like a crashing wave on the shore, his grip fades.

He'd stayed alive just long enough to give his last message to Bryce.

The life drains from his eyes.

Bryce exhales through his nose.

"Fuck."

He places a hand on John's shoulder, just for a second. He closes John's eyes and says a silent prayer.

Then he moves.

The sirens are closing in from both directions.

Bryce turns and sprints into the dense forest, the thick underbrush clawing at his clothes.

He pushes harder, feet pounding the earth, heart hammering.

At the top of a ridgeline, he drops behind a rock outcropping, chest heaving.

For the first time since this started, the weight of it crashes over him.

The rage. The grief. The exhaustion.

Bryce's fury detonates. Raw. Uncontrollable.

He slams his fist into the dirt, the pain grounding him but doing nothing to stop the storm inside.

"AHHH! FUCK!"

The sound shatters the silence, echoing through the valley

Then—nothing.

The forest watches.

Unmoved.

Unforgiving.

Bryce wipes his eyes.

He has a mission.

He lets himself have that moment. Just that moment.

Then he moves.

He digs into his pack, pulling out a compass and map.

Studies the terrain. Tucks them away.

The sirens grow louder. Vehicles screech to a halt.

Bryce vanishes into the shadows of the forest.

Chapter Fourteen

Hide and Seek

The sun shrinks lower over the horizon. It's been three hours since the shootout. Police tape cordons off the entire area.

A chaotic mix of police cruisers, big 4x4 trucks, motorcycles, dirt bikes, and an ambulance clogs the roadside.

Medics stand around, unsure of what to do with the bodies.

It's a full-blown clusterfuck. No one is in charge, and no one is qualified to be.

Everyone yells over each other, posturing for control, arguing about who outranks whom, who saw what, and who's to blame.

They're confused, pissed, and hungry for revenge.

The hounds snarled like demons, chains pulled tight as they lunged forward, muscle, spit, and instinct. Their handlers stood unmoved. Sun-leathered arms. Grease-black fingernails. Cowboy hats rotted with sweat and time, crowning faces carved by heat and hate. They didn't speak. They didn't need to. The dogs did it for them.

The search party is an odd collection of stereotypes of bikers, rednecks, and skinheads, standing in a loose semi-circle, watching Sheriff Fred.

The sheriff lifts his bullhorn, its crackling feedback silencing the yelling crowd.

Behind him, Marty's old Ford sits riddled with bullets, looking more hole than metal.

Fred stares at it, his fist tightening at his side.

His jaw clenches so hard his cheek muscle twitches.

CRACK.

He slams the bullhorn onto the truck's hood.

"How the HELL did they miss him shooting that much? Jesus FUCK!"

He spits, chewing on the rage like its tobacco in his cheek.

Then, he lifts the bullhorn again.

"Alright, listen up! Bubba's dogs will sniff this bastard out. This is a shoot-to-kill situation. I've deputized all of you."

The assembled men glance at each other, some nodding in approval, others gripping their rifles tighter.

Fred lets his eyes sweep over the group, his voice dropping lower.

"We're hunting smart. Keep your space and don't shoot each other. Move together. If you see something, call it out. Follow Bubba."

He lowers the bullhorn and leans toward Bubba.

"Let 'em go."

Bubba grins widely, eyes gleaming with anticipation.

He looks down at the dogs straining at their leashes.

"Get 'em."

Foam sprays from their jowls as they lunge, claws raking the ground like they're digging graves.

The hounds SNAP forward, their leashes jerking so hard Bubba stumbles, but he recovers fast, more agile than you'd expect.

The barking turns feral, less sound, more war cry.

Bubba laughs, barely keeping control as they drag him toward the trees.

The group follows, excitement mixing with nerves as they take in the damage to Marty's truck, a brutal testament to the firepower Bryce brought to the fight.

At the roadblock, impatient drivers honk their horns, stuck behind the blockade.

The sheriff keys his radio.

"Let's reroute everyone at Junction 6."

Dispatch crackles back.

"Sir, that'll take them an extra hour just to get gas or go home. Can we open a lane instead and control the flow?"

Fred grinds his teeth and spits again.

"You have my orders. Now follow them. This is a crime scene, and I'm on a manhunt. Get it done. And get those damn bodies off the road before they start to stink."

Dispatch pauses, then responds, resigned.

"Copy."

The dogs stop at the rock Bryce hid behind, sniffing wildly, circling.

The group of hastily deputized men slows.

Guns come up.

The bravado from before starts leaking away with each step they fight their way into the deepening woods.

Gary edges up to Tank, voice low, glancing around to make sure no one's paying attention.

"So we're about to walk into this thick-ass forest to hunt the guy who, just to be clear, killed Marty with his bare hands, shoved that half-a-bear-man into a bush, slit Jax's crazy-ass throat, and shot three dudes in the forehead while they played OK Corral with Marty's truck?"

Tank squints at him.

"Yeah?"

Gary lowers his voice.

"We're gonna get Lyme disease as a best-case scenario here. This shit is dumb."

Tank rolls his eyes, but Gary isn't done.

"Bro, I feel them already." Gary slaps the back of his neck, whipping around like something's crawling on him.

"A tick's gonna crawl up my ass, inject its alien spit, and next thing you know…" He swats his arm, shuddering.

"I'm in the hospital getting my brain drilled for Lyme disease while y'all are getting fucking dismembered by Rambo."

Another hard slap and scratch over his arm.

"Yup. Fuck this."

Tank grimaces, shifting his boots over the forest floor.

Gary leans closer. "I saw *Rambo* when I was a kid. Fuck this."

Tank opens his mouth to respond.

BEEP.

The sheriff's bullhorn cuts through the air. "Let's move! The dogs are on the scent. He couldn't have gone far. Let's go, boys!"

The hounds bark louder, dragging Bubba deeper into the trees.

Tank gives Gary one last look, sighs, then keeps walking.

Gary lingers, muttering as he slips on pine needles.

"Fuck. This. Shit."

Chapter Fifteen

Keep Moving Forward

The forest thickens.

Towering trees swallow the last rays of sunlight as Bryce moves like a shadow through the underbrush. Adrenaline pulses through his veins.

It has been years since he engaged an enemy, since he was in a real fight. But now, with a target on his back, he feels more alive than he has in years.

Not even the private sector gave him this kind of clarity. Being a hired gun was hollow.

This is different.

This is about his word. About honor. About setting something right that should never have gone wrong.

Some things do not fade. Some things haunt you until you do something about them. At least they do for Bryce.

That's what makes him different. That's what makes him Karma.

He glides through the terrain, every movement precise, every breath controlled.

Ahead, the treeline opens into a meadow. The gas station sits beyond it, exposed and vulnerable, surrounded by empty road and fading light. A bad place to cross.

Bryce kneels behind a massive oak and scans the area.

From here, he sees everything: the gas station, the road, and the lone police cruiser idling out front.

He pulls his binoculars. Watches. Waits.

Inside, a deputy stands at the counter, talking to Janice. Bryce tunes into the police radio clipped to his vest.

"Sir, can we open the road back up?"

A gruff voice responds—Sheriff Fred.

"Go ahead, but keep this channel open. Any signs of him, you let me know right away."

Bryce switches off the radio and slips it back on his chest.

Then he sees it.

The moment Janice learns her husband is dead.

The deputy steps back, his body language softer now.

Janice stiffens. Her lips part.

She snaps.

Her grief explodes into rage. Her hands slam the counter, her voice cracking through the glass.

Bryce does not need to hear the words.

The deputy stumbles back, retreating toward his cruiser as Janice shouts, waving him off.

A few seconds later, the cruiser pulls away, kicking up dust.

She is alone now.

Bryce checks his watch.

Time is running out.

In the distance, the baying of bloodhounds echoes through the trees. They have picked up something, but he knows it's not his scent. That will take them longer.

There will be pain before they arrive. He knows that much.

Bryce moves. Staying low, he follows the treeline and circles to the back of the station.

A single four-by-four pickup is parked near the rear entrance.

A possible escape.

The dogs grow louder. Closer.

"Fuck it, Karma. Move."

He breaks into a sprint, boots silent over the damp earth.

The back door looms ahead.

He reaches for the handle.

It swings open.

Bryce reacts instantly, dropping back with his rifle raised and finger on the trigger. Janice screams, startled, her cigarette slipping from her fingers.

Bryce catches it mid-air, safeties his weapon, and lets it drop to his side. One hand clamps over her mouth as he pulls her inside, the rifle swinging from his shoulder strap.

He glances outside. Nothing.

Then he shuts the door behind them, sealing them in.

The small backroom is tense. Silent.

Bryce holds her firm, steadying her breathing.

"Ma'am, I tried to save your husband."

Her body trembles against his grip.

"They tortured him. They were asking who he talked to in the FBI."

Janice's eyes widen. Recognition. Horror.

Bryce lowers his voice.

"Do you know anything about that?"

A tiny nod.

"I'm letting you go now. Please don't scream."

Another nod.

Bryce lets go, eyes locked on her face.

He is not looking for fear. Fear is normal.

He is looking for the break, the tremble in the hands, the scream that will not stop, the thousand-yard stare.

The kind of panic that gets people killed.

He needs focus. Clarity. Even just a spark of it.

Because if she shatters now, they are both done.

She snatches the cigarette from his hand, fingers trembling as she takes a ragged drag.

"He hated when I smoked inside," she mutters, her voice cracking.

Bryce waits, letting her process.

She is holding it together, better than most would.

John married a strong woman. He would be proud.

But the hounds are closing in.

Bryce opens the door a crack and scans for movement, danger, anything that could get them killed.

"We do not have much time," he says finally. "I threw them off, but we have maybe thirty minutes before they are here."

Janice nods, but her mind is elsewhere.

"Did John tell you about our daughter?"

Bryce meets her eyes.

"Yes. But first, we get out of here. Then we figure out how to help her."

Her hand shoots out, gripping his arm, strong despite the tremble.

"You have to help her."

Bryce nods, his voice steady.
"I will."

She searches his face.
He gently pries her hand away.

"Do you have a place we can go? A trailer or a cabin? Somewhere no one would think to look?"
Janice hesitates, then nods.
"Yeah. Up north. No one knows about it."

Bryce nods.
"Then that is where we are going."

He moves swiftly, grabbing non-perishables, propane tanks, fishing weights, ropes, anything useful.
Behind him, Janice snaps out of her shock. Her movements sharpen. Her jaw tightens.

"Good. Pack what you need. We are locking this place up and not coming back," Bryce says as he stuffs canned goods, lanterns, bug spray, burner phones, walkie-talkies, first aid kits, and tools into a duffel.

Janice stops, glancing around the store—her store.
Then she spits on the floor.

"Fuck 'em. This is their place now."

Bryce flicks a look toward the four-by-four truck parked out back.
"Yours?"
"Yeah." She is already moving toward the door.
"Fill up the tank. And the gas cans."

She shoots him a look but does not argue, grabbing red jerry cans from a side shelf before heading out.

Bryce works fast, methodical. He loads boxes of shells, spare knives, and camping gear.
At the ammo section, he sweeps anything that fits their weapons into a bag.

His radio crackles.
"We got a call about a home invasion out on Chapel Hill."

Bryce freezes, listening.
Sheriff Fred's voice follows.
"Send a unit, but keep everyone else on the manhunt. We get him today."

The dogs are getting closer.
No more time.

Janice reappears with a shotgun in hand and a box of shells tucked under her arm.

"They are used to seeing me with guns," she says, slinging it over her shoulder. "Fuck 'em."

Bryce does not argue.

He hauls their gear to the front of the store and stacks it near the door.

Janice is already outside, pumping gasoline into the truck and tossing full jerry cans into the bed.

Bryce climbs into the truck bed and rearranges the supplies.

A rolled-up carpet, shoved against the side, makes for a quick blind.

He ties down the propane tanks and gas cans to ensure nothing shifts.

The store bell jingles. Janice steps back inside and grabs a few last items.

The radio crackles again.

"I think we found the damn trail again."

Bryce's heart pounds. He glances around, realizing he is exposed.

The distant barks of the dogs grow louder.

They are closing in.

Bryce moves fast, climbing into the blind and staying low.

He adjusts the makeshift cover to ensure he is hidden.

Through narrow slits in the fabric, he raises his binoculars and scans the area.

The store bell jingles again. Janice steps out, clocking the carpet blind in the truck bed. One eyebrow rises.

"Nice fort."

"Thanks. You hear the sirens and dogs? They will be here any minute."

She does not need telling twice.

The big-block V8 roars to life, tires screaming as the truck tears away from the gas station.

Bryce sinks deeper into his hide, rifle tight in his grip.

It is an action that always brings him balance.

The rifle gives him control. Everything else is a variable.

When the world spins sideways, this steel and glass stays true.

In a life built on chaos, it is the one thing that never lies to him.

The weapon has always been there. Steady. Reliable.

It does not judge. It does not fail unless he fails it.

Sometimes, he has cared for it more than himself.

That is something he has learned to change.

But not today.

He scans the terrain, breath steady.

Then he sees it.

Through the gap in the tailgate, a column of thick smoke twists into the sky.

Bryce raps on the cab window.

Janice slides it open.

"What?" she snaps.

Bryce jerks a thumb toward the rising smoke.

"Did you set fire to the gas station?"

She meets his gaze in the rearview mirror.

Defiant. Unapologetic.

"Yep."

She slams the window shut.

Bryce exhales sharply and shakes his head.

Sirens wail in the distance. More of them.

Janice did not just burn her business.

She torched the bridge behind her.

Bryce tightens his grip on the rifle.

The road stretches ahead, endless and uncertain.

The fight is not over.

It's just the beginning.

Bryce whispers to himself, barely moving his lips.

"No sound. No light. No movement."

The words are not a prayer. They are protocol.

Chapter Sixteen

The Hunt

Six dogs tore through the thick, relentless brush ahead, each bred for a different kind of problem.

They moved like a unit, every leash tailored to purpose, short leads for control, long ones for range.

Bubba knew exactly how much slack to give.

The Malinois surged forward on tight leads, jaws clenched, eyes scanning like heat-seeking missiles.

A Dutch Shepherd flanked wide on a longer line, tongue lolling, gaze sharp as a blade.

The two bloodhounds stayed low, leash slack, dragging the scent trail like scripture.

Behind them, the pit-mastiff mix pulled hard against a reinforced tether, all torque and rage.

And last, the Blue Heeler Mix bounded ahead on a loose runner, built for speed and flush work.

The dogs lunged forward, muscles coiled and rippling beneath sleek fur, jaws snapping at the scent trail.

Leashes strained, Bubba trudged behind, sweat pouring, but unfazed.

Three-fifty and built like a tractor, but he moved like he'd been born in the mud.

People saw fat.

They missed the force beneath it.

Most only made that mistake once.

Bubba wasn't just big; he was mean. And he carried his weight like a man who had spent his life knocking down anyone foolish enough to doubt him.

The dogs weaved through the underbrush, noses twitching, locked onto Bryce's scent with unrelenting focus.

The group followed in loose formation, struggling to match the pace as the forest closed in around them.

Branches scraped their faces, roots snagged their boots, and the air grew thick with the acrid mix of sweat and frustration.

Each man fought his own battle of fatigue and pride.

The man they were hunting, Bryce Rath, had made fools of them twice already. He'd killed their friends and he will pay for that.

They wouldn't let him get away a third time.

Not with the crew they had.

No one escaped this kind of lineup.

No one expected much from city boys, but at this point, they'd take all the help they could get.

Gary and Tank ran distribution back in the city, where Harleys and leathers made sense.

Mid-tier movers. Route managers. Not manhunters.

They'd come up to finalize the next round of shipments.

Then Bryce tore through the region, and everything froze.

No product moved until he was handled.

And when Javier said jump, nobody asked why.

Now they were out here, motorcycle boots in the dirt, lungs on fire, wondering what the hell they'd signed up for.

They'd started the chase with a bet: How long before Bubba keeled over from a heart attack?

Six brutal miles later, it was Gary and Tank wheezing like old hounds, while Bubba moved on without a word, steady as ever.

Even their usual smart-ass remarks had dried up, especially after the sheriff chewed them out for slowing the group down.

Gary had managed a middle finger in response, but even that had felt like a chore.

Tank wiped his brow.

"How much longer we chasin' this guy?"

Bubba stopped dead in his tracks.

Gary sucked in a breath, watching the group up ahead stop.

"I dunno, but I ain't feelin' good about this."

Gary and Tank approached from a behind as anger and confusion crawled over Bubba's face. He yanked the leashes hard, working to control his dogs to get back on the scent.

The dogs, trained killers, bred to hunt, whimpered.

Not barked. Not growled.

Whimpered.

Tails tucked. Ears flat. Pulling back.

That had never happened before.

The group froze.

Scanning the woods.

Listening.

Waiting.

Something had shifted.

The sheriff narrowed his eyes.

"The hell you doing?" he snapped at Bubba.

Bubba didn't answer right away. He was staring at the ground, frowning.

Then he took a slow step forward, looking at the trees ahead.

The rest of the group stiffened.

They could feel it now.

Something off.

No one spoke. Even the radio kept buzzing in the background.

"Unit 3, we've checked the roads. No sign of him on the west side."

"Unit 5, perimeter's still clear. Nothing moving toward town."

"Sheriff, you copy?"

The sheriff, still sucking in painful breaths, strained to see what Bubba was doing.

The radio crackled from his belt. A constant chatter, pulling focus.

He talked into the radio. "Copy. Keep looking."

He reached down and shut it off. *Click.*

Silence.

Something wasn't right.

Something was dangerously wrong. The sheriff looked around at his men.

They were silent. Each looking off in different directions, frozen in the moment.

He had seen Bubba hunt down five men in a single day.

Men who knew the woods. Men who had a day's head start.

But this?

This made no damn sense.

Bubba shook his head, frustrated, eyes dark.

"No. That ain't right."

He spat in the dirt and crouched low, scanning the ground for a sign.

A fresh boot print. A snapped twig still green at the break.

Crushed grass. Turned soil. Nothing.

Then he looked up.

Eyes tracing the lower branches, searching for scuffed bark, a fresh break or a smear of dirt where a boot might've caught hold.

A man didn't vanish.

Sometimes he just went up.

And the dogs never thought to look in the trees.

Bubba searched for anything to reveal where Bryce had been or where he was going.

The sheriff wiped sweat from his brow.

His voice was tight.

"Bubba, what the hell's going on?"

Bubba lifted a meaty finger and pointed at the dirt.

"Trail's gone."

The sheriff squinted.

"So what? Maybe it just..."

"No." Bubba's voice was low. Sharp. Final.

He knelt, dragging thick, scarred fingers over the ground.

His voice was quieter now. Controlled. Calculated.

"The scent. His tracks. They ain't covered. Ain't faded."

Bubba rose slowly.

His massive frame coiled, tense, like a man waiting for the crack of a gunshot.

His eyes scanned the forest, but not like a hunter anymore.

Like prey.

Then, finally, he said it.

"It's just... gone."

Tank frowned as they caught up to the group. Something felt... off.

Like they had just been here.

Like the trees had shifted when they weren't looking.

Gary and Tank came to a halt as they rejoined the group.

Their movement was too loud, too clumsy, drawing eyes and irritation.

They looked around, oblivious to the danger coiling tighter with every step.

Tank shot Gary a glance, uneasy.

"...Didn't we already come this way?"

Gary, still catching his breath, looked around.

His brow furrowed.

"...I... I think so."

He exhaled.

"Shit. I think I took a piss over there last time."

Gary stepped forward, squinting at a large tree.

"Well, shit. I did. Hell, I might have to go again."

Bubba exhaled.

Slow.

Unsteady.

That got everyone's attention.

Gary stopped mid-step. He could see it in the locals' eyes. Something was off.

He knew

Bubba never got rattled.

Yet here he was, staring into the trees like they held something unnatural.

Bubba's voice dropped to a near whisper.

"...I've heard stories."

The sheriff cut a glance over.

"What the hell are you mumbling about now?"

Bubba finally turned to face him.

No grin. No swagger. Just that slow, steady stare.

"My uncle fought in Vietnam. Used to talk about the jungle like it was alive. Said the trees had eyes.

Not ghosts. Not spirits. Shadows. The kind that moved quiet through the trees, fast, smart, and mean."

He glanced up at the treeline now, scanning. Not paranoid. Calculating.

"I know you've heard of jungle warfare... but this, this is different. This is more like canopy warfare. In the jungle, you'd find tunnels, camps, something. A trail. A boot print. Some sign of life. But canopy warfare...That was a whole other beast. Nothing left behind. No sound. No bodies. Just men gone, like the trees swallowed 'em whole."

Bubba looks around at the trees, lost in thought. "Said platoons went dark without a single shot.

No screams. No firefight. Just... gone."

He wiped sweat from his brow, still watching the brush like it might move.

"One time they brought in local trackers, guys who grew up in that terrain, knew how to follow trails a snake couldn't see.

Didn't matter.

They vanished too.

Sometimes all they'd find was a snapped strap or blood up on the leaves.

Sometimes not even that."

He spat in the dirt, slow and deliberate.

"This feels like what my uncle used to talk about... when he got real drunk. Nothing scared him. Not much, anyway.

But when he started in on this... It was the only time I ever saw fear in his eyes."

Bubba paused, eyes scanning the trees.

"He talked about the same quiet. Same weight in the air. Like something's out there, watching. But no sign. No movement.

No tracks. No trail. Nothing. And if that son of a bitch climbed up into these trees..."

He turned to the sheriff, voice low.

"Well, Sheriff... We're not tracking him. He's tracking us."

The way he said it, low, certain, made the air feel heavier.

Bubba took another slow look around.

Deliberate. Calculating.

Then, voice lower still:

"This ain't normal, Sheriff. Not even close."

He turned back.

"This is a man leading us where he wants."

Bubba exhaled.

He mumbled to himself.

"...And we just walked right into it."

Then—

A snap.

A whip.

A scream.

One of the men, one of their best hunters, was yanked off his feet.

A tensioned stick snapped loose, its sharpened point stabbed into his leg like a hook. A split second later, the rope went taut and his body launched upward, slamming into the tree.

SLAM!

He hit the tree trunk hard, spine-first, rifle tumbling from his hands.

CRACK.

A bone-snapping, stomach-churning sound.

But he didn't die.

He screamed.

A long, ragged, gut-wrenching scream.

It kept going. And going.

His leg twisted at a sickening angle.

His arms jerked, spasming, caught in the rope's merciless grip.

A wet gurgle, somewhere between a sob and a scream.

Bubba moved first.

He stepped forward, kneeling beside the trap. It was set four feet up the tree.

He stared at it.

His breath slowed, realization darkening his face.

"Shit..." he muttered.

He glanced up at the sheriff.

"This was made for people."

The sheriff frowned. "What?"

Bubba pointed at the way it was set.

"This wasn't meant to hurt the dogs."

He turned, locking eyes with the sheriff.

"He set it just high enough to catch us, not them."

The tracker kept screaming, a broken, shuddering wail.

A man in pain.

A man meant to feel every second of it.

The wind shifted.

And that's when they heard it.

Sirens.

Distant.

Growing.

The sheriff snapped his head up.

His gut twisted.

He turned up the radio.

It crackled to life.

"Sheriff. Fire Chief Lyle again. This thing's burning fast. If we don't move in now, we're losing the whole damn structure."

Another voice, Deputy Raines, urgent:

"Sir, Lyle's asking if it's safe to start suppression. Do we move in or not?"

Bubba's voice.

Low.

Steady.

Unshaken.

"Sheriff."

He nodded toward the smoke.

"How the hell did he get over there?"

The sheriff hesitated for just a second.

Then he clicked the radio.

"All units, hold perimeter. We're on our way."

The sheriff looked over at the man, still screaming.

"Shit. Someone cut him down. Let's go."

The pack shifted.

The screaming didn't stop.

The fire loomed ahead, swallowing the sky.

The sirens grew louder.

The group moved out, pushing through the last stretch of trees.

It was a hard march now.

Legs burned.

Boots felt heavy.

Nobody spoke.

Nobody dared.

They carried the injured tracker, still screaming in agony.

That sound clung to them, trailing even as it faded into the distance.

Nobody wanted to be next.

The forest thinned.

They hit the tree line and stopped cold.

They saw it.

A pillar of black smoke twisted into the sky.

The building was half-consumed in flames.

A handful of firefighters stood outside their trucks, helmets on, arms crossed.

Waiting.

Watching.

Pissed.

Red and blue police lights spun in the haze, strobing against the thick smoke.

The heat hit them even from here.

Then the dogs caught it.

Heads snapped up.

Noses twitched.

Muscles tensed.

They lunged. Hard. Barking and sniffing.

Nearly ripping the leashes from Bubba's grip.

Bubba gritted his teeth, holding them back.

The sheriff stepped closer.

"Talk to me."

Bubba didn't answer right away.

His arms strained against the leashes, sweat dripping from his temples.

The dogs were locked in now.

Focused.

Determined.

A frenzy of barking.

No confusion.

No hesitation.

They had him.

Finally, Bubba grunted.

"They got 'im."

The sheriff's eyes narrowed.

"He's here? You're sure?"

Bubba nodded.

"Yeah."

His voice was flat.

No excitement.

No triumph.

Just fact.

The sheriff took a deep breath, then clicked his radio.

"All units, hold perimeter. Confirmed. He's here, or he was here. The man is armed and dangerous."

They all turned toward the gas station.

At the fire.

At the wreckage.

At the place where Bryce Rath had been...Or where he was still waiting.

For the second time, the hunt slowed.

This time, it wasn't fatigue.

It was something worse.

Hesitation.

Nobody wanted to be the first to step forward.

Nobody wanted to be the next one screaming.

Bubba yanked the leashes hard.

The dogs resisted, muscles still taut, still eager.

But they listened.

Bubba exhaled.

Shook his head.

Then turned.

The sheriff frowned.

"Problem?"

Bubba kept his eyes forward, like the sheriff wasn't even there.

"I'm done."

The sheriff squinted.

Bubba jerked his chin toward the flames.

"My dogs ain't tracking through fire, Sheriff."

The sheriff folded his arms.

"You quitting?"

Bubba eye's locked onto the sheriff.

His face didn't show anger or frustration. Just cold certainty.

"I came to track, Sheriff. Not to die in a goddamn explosion."

The sheriff's jaw tightened.

"I need every shooter I got."

Bubba wiped sweat from his brow, then spat into the dirt.

"I'll be back with my guns. But not my dogs."

A sharp whistle.

The dogs whined, but obeyed.

Bubba turned, leashes in one hand, pulling them away.

The sheriff watched him go.

The fire burned hot.

The sheriff clenched his jaw and ripped the bullhorn from his belt.

"Bryce! We know you're in there!"

His voice boomed over the roaring fire.

"Come out with your hands up!"

Nothing.

The sheriff clicked his radio.

"Talk to me. What's the situation?"

A voice crackled through.

"Sheriff, it's the Fire Chief. We need to move in and put this out. Now!"

The sheriff's jaw tightened.

"Negative."

"Sir, this thing's about to go—"

"I'M IN CHARGE HERE!"

The sheriff's voice ripped through the radio.

Then—The first explosion.

The force tore through the clearing, slamming men to the ground.

The radio crackled.

"Sheriff, do you hear that?! If that fire reaches the underground tanks…"

The second explosion hit.

A shockwave blasted through the air.

The sheriff was blown off his feet.

His back slammed into the dirt.

His ears rang. His head spun.

Flames roared into the sky.

The sheriff pushed himself up, coughing.

His uniform was covered in soot and dust.

Men scrambled, wounded and disoriented.

Firefighters rushed in, battling to keep the flames from spreading.

Gary and Tank arrived, breathing hard.

Gary slumped against a tree. Tank bent over, hands on his knees.

They had just caught up.

Now they wished they hadn't.

They stood frozen at the treeline.

"Holy shit," Gary muttered.

"You think he's in there?"

Tank shook his head.

His voice was barely a whisper. "I don't care. I just want a beer and to get the hell out of here."

They stood in silence, disgusted by the scene, watching as two deputies carried out a broken tracker.

He groaned. A jagged branch had speared clean through his thigh.

Blood splattered onto the dirt.

Gary looked over.

"Fuck this shit."

Another man had his leg mangled, his screams stifled by clenched teeth.

A third tracker's voice cut through the smoke as he spoke to a paramedic.

His tone was hollow. His eyes stayed locked on the injuries in disbelief.

"Do you know how hard it is to make a trap that only injures people?"

His voice dropped lower.

"Do you know how hard it is to make that and not hurt animals? While you're being chased?"

Nobody answered.

The man exhaled.

Pointed at the one impaled through the leg.

"He built that to only hurt. Not to kill."

A beat.

His voice dropped again.

"That takes planning. Precision. I thought this guy was on the run."

A deputy stared at the trap, pale.

"That ain't luck."

The man nodded.

"Damn right it ain't."

The sheriff turned away.

Pulled out his personal phone.

A few rings.

A low, controlled voice answered.

"Yeah?"

Fred rubbed his forehead, his free hand still shaking from the blast.

"It's Fred. We got a problem."

A pause.

"Go on."

Fred watched the fire rage as the firefighters rushed to contain it, hosing down the structure before it spread.

"There's some special forces freak out here. He killed four of my guys, one with his bare hands, one with a knife, and three with a handgun. Center of the damn forehead. And they had fucking machine guns. They got off more than a hundred rounds. He shot 6 times. He bested my tracker and his dogs while building some kind of trap designed to only maim my men. I mean, who the fuck can do that? I don't know where he is, but I'll find him. I just need some extra help when I do. I'll send over what we have. An ID my deputy pulled before he died."

His voice was low.

"I'm sure we can handle this. But listen, we can't let this go national. We need to handle this as fast and quiet as possible. I need more help. Your kind of help."

Silence was dragged out as he waited for a response.

"You sure about that, Sheriff?"

Fred didn't answer right away.

He just watched his men groaning in pain, carried past him.

This wasn't a manhunt anymore.

Bryce Rath had turned it into war.

"Yeah..."

Fred exhaled, slipping the phone into his pocket like it weighed a hundred pounds of regret.

The tracker's voice lingered in his head:

"That ain't luck."

"Damn right it ain't."

The sheriff clenched his jaw, watching the wreckage smolder.

Hunters wouldn't be enough.

He needed trained killers.

He wasn't going to catch Bryce alive.

That much he knew.

Chapter Seventeen

Escape

Janice drove the old truck, taking out her anger on the turns.

It rumbled deeper into the mountain road, tires grinding over loose rock pried from crumbling walls, once grated and reinforced for logging trucks that ran this route year-round.

No one maintained it now.

The forest was taking it back.

Bryce watched through the hide as the smoke grew higher into the sky.

Suddenly, a fireball bloomed, wide and violent, lighting up the treeline like a second sun.

Seconds later, the boom rolled in, low and distant, like thunder rumbling off the hills.

Bryce shook his head in disbelief. He checked his watch, calm as ever.

"Four years since you've been in jail…" he muttered. "It's been good, Karma."

He glanced in the rearview mirror at Janice, deadpan. Pointing at the fireball. "You see that? We're one gust away from lighting up half this mountain."

Janice barely reacted. Her eyes locked on the fireball in the rearview mirror. "Fuck 'em."

She slammed the back window shut and stepped on the gas.

They drove in silence, passing forests, abandoned farms, and collapsed houses swallowed by overgrowth.

The truck turned off the main road, disappearing into the trees, its tires kicking up dirt and gravel as it veered onto an overgrown path.

Janice slowed, guiding the truck onto a washed-out dirt road.

She killed the engine and cracked open the back window.

"This is gonna be bumpy as shit. We haven't used this road in a while. Parts of it washed out in the last few storms."

Bryce nodded, stepping out and stretching.

He studied the road ahead.

"This looks steep. You sure your truck can handle it?"

Janice shot him a look.

Unimpressed.

"Shit yeah. But your little fort back there needs some adjusting."

Bryce grinned, glancing at his makeshift concealment and nodding in agreement.

He handed Janice a semi-auto rifle.

"Here. Keep watch and erase as much of your tire tracks as possible. Let me know if you see anyone coming."

Janice checked the rifle, keeping the muzzle down and away from herself and Bryce. Smooth. No hesitation.

She popped out the magazine, ejected the chambered round, reloaded, and locked it back in place.

Safety on.

She shouldered the weapon, adjusted the scope, then walked down the road.

On the way, she snapped off a branch, dragging it like a rake over their tire marks.

Bryce watched, impressed.

Smart. Efficient. Careful.

He turned back to the truck.

Bryce lifted the gas and propane cans, checking for leaks.

Satisfied, he cinched them down, tight and secure, no room to shift or spark.

He laid the carpet flat, climbed in, and strapped down the remaining supplies.

Once everything was locked down, he grabbed his rifle and hiked down the road to check Janice's progress.

She had erased most of the tracks, using the branch like a makeshift rake.

Bryce nodded, smoothing out a few extra spots.

"I'm impressed."

Janice grimaced, meeting his gaze.

"I watched a lot of movies as a kid."

Bryce chuckled, waving her back to the truck.

She turned, walking up the hill in a crisp stride.

Then a siren wailed in the distance.

Both instinctively dropped behind a bush, weapons ready.

Four massive fire trucks roared past on the main road, followed by two police cars.

Bryce watched them pass.

A slow, nagging guilt crept into his gut.

He was partly responsible for putting them to work.

"Hope they put it out fast... before they bring in spotter planes or helicopters."

Janice didn't answer. Her red-rimmed eyes said everything. She'd already lost too much.

Without a word, she turned, climbed back up the hill, got in the truck, strapped in her rifle with the seatbelt, and started the engine.

Bryce lingered, watching her.

Her entire world had changed in hours.

He moved to the back of the truck, scanning the area through his scope.

No movement.

He climbed in, knelt on the carpeted truck bed, checked his weapon, and knocked twice on the side. "Let's go."

The truck clunked into four-wheel drive as the hubs locked in.

Bryce breathed out, gripping the rifle.

He was ready to fire out the back if anyone spotted them.

His eyes flicked to the strapped-down gas and propane cans.

He muttered under his breath,

"I hope no one sees us."

The truck lurched forward.

Bryce's head snapped back against the carpet.

He braced himself, planting his feet against the wheel wells for stability.

The truck bucked and jerked up the eroded path.

Branches scraped the sides, their echoes amplifying inside the metal bed.

Bryce watched the walls shake, half-expecting them to buckle under the strain.

The climb was brutal.

The truck lurched through switchbacks, tearing through loose rocks.

It crawled reluctantly up the final ridge.

Then a clearing opened up.

Nestled in the middle of the forest sat an old hunting shack.

Janice opened the back window.

"The cabin's up ahead."

Bryce jumped out, landing softly.

He pointed to her rifle strapped in beside her.

"Keep the truck running. Turn it around so we can leave fast. Tuck it under the trees. Be ready for anything."

It wasn't just a hunting cabin anymore.

Now it was cover, because they were the ones being hunted.

Chapter Eighteen

House Call

J avier stood at the window of his private office, high above his empire, where luxury masked an ever-present current of danger.

His white linen shirt was crisp, sleeves rolled to his forearms, revealing glimpses of tattoos that snaked up his arms, a silent testament to his violent rise to power.

His tailored jeans balanced casual comfort with calculated opulence, a reflection of his command.

Outside, the vast estate stretched before him, a kingdom by the sea.

The Pacific shimmered on the horizon.

Below, nestled in the cliffside marina, his 27-meter Kereon yacht rested, an emblem of wealth and fierce dominion.

Javier turned from the view, letting it slip away as he faced the room.

His office was a fortress.

The heavy wooden door, intricately designed, was secured by fingerprint and retinal scan locks.
Inside, old-world sophistication blended with quiet menace.

Dark wood paneling lined the walls, exuding power.

A towering crystal chandelier cast long, shifting shadows.

At the room's heart, an immaculate desk stood like a throne's platform, stacks of documents, encrypted communication devices, and ledgers meticulously arranged, each a cog in the machine of his cartel's operations.

Behind it, an ornate high-backed chair.

Where Javier commanded his world.

Bookshelves lined the walls, filled with volumes on law, power, and strategy, a façade of legitimacy masking the brutal reality beneath.

But behind those books:

Concealed compartments.

Hidden safes.

Each filled with sensitive information, valuables, and weapons.

On one wall, a massive, detailed map dominated the space, tracking his territory, trade routes, and shifting cartel alliances.

A war map, charting past victories and battles yet to come.

Atop the desk, a leather-bound ledger lay open, financial records, transactions, cartel dealings.

A testament to Javier's meticulous nature.

And a weapon, ready to be turned against anyone who dared cross him.

This wasn't just an office.

It was a command center.

Where whispers shaped the underworld.

Zayed sat across from him, silent. His expression was unreadable.

The tension between them was thick, a blend of mutual respect and wary calculation.

Javier scrutinized him, his sharp gaze betraying nothing.
"The marina will be built in three months." His voice was steady, each word weighted with certainty. "Once that's in place, you can begin construction on the resort."

Zayed nodded, considering the words.

Before he could speak, the heavy wooden door creaked open.

Javier's eyes flared with irritation.

His men knew better than to disturb him here.

But he suppressed it, keeping his tone controlled.

"Yes?"

The man crept inside, a folder clutched in his hands.
"Señor, hubo un problema—"

Javier cut him off, voice sharp.
"English. In front of our guest."

The man swallowed.
"Sorry, sir. There was a problem at one of our Northern California distribution centers."

He cleared his throat.
"The operation is on hold due to complications."

He kept his eyes low, avoiding contact.
"They're requesting reinforcements. Heavy casualties after a confrontation with a local family."

Javier leaned back in his chair, muttering with disdain.
"A contractor..."

His eyes narrowed as he flipped open the folder.
Irritation deepened, but beneath it, calculation.

"What does this have to do with me?"
His voice was flat. Cold.

He skimmed through the details.
"It's their problem. They need to fix it."

The assistant shifted.
"They're requesting someone with military skills, sir. They don't want to involve additional law enforcement."

Javier sighed, tossing the folder onto the desk.

The annoyance was clear, but so was the unspoken understanding of the situation's gravity.

"Fine."

The assistant bowed and exited, closing the door behind him.

Zayed, silent through the exchange, leaned forward, eyes locking onto Javier's.

A smooth, confident smirk.

"I may be able to help."

Javier's interest piqued.

He leaned back, studying him.

"Go on."

Zayed chose his words carefully.
"I know individuals who would appreciate the opportunity to utilize their skills, and move into more prosperous positions."

He let the words land.
"If I can assist you and accelerate our project, all the better."

Javier's eyes narrowed.
"Interesting. Go on."

Zayed's tone was calm.
"They're well-trained. Loyal. Operate under your command, answerable only to you. All they require is clean documentation and a chance to prove their worth. If they succeed, they could take on leadership roles within your security operations if you could use them. If not, they can go back into the shadows."

A pause.
"All I ask is that no pictures ever be taken of these men. Officially, they no longer exist."

Javier's smile crept in, slow and deliberate. It was the kind of smile that made your skin crawl.

Calculated. Cold. Full of promises best left unspoken.

He leaned back.

"Ah... what the Americans call a sleeper cell?"

Zayed held up his hands, a slight grin tugging at his lips.

"They live to kill, no hesitation, no conscience, no questions."

He met Javier's gaze.

"And I do mean anything."

Javier turned back to the window, his eyes on the Pacific's endless horizon.

The sun was setting, casting a blood-red hue across the water, a fitting backdrop for the decision he was about to make.

"And what do you get out of this?"

His voice was soft, laced with suspicion.

Zayed's eyes darkened.

A flicker of restrained anger beneath his composure.

Still, his tone stayed measured.

"We want to create new streams of income that can't be tracked digitally, new avenues that will benefit us both."

Javier turned back, his smile slow and knowing.

"They will need to clean up everything. And everyone."

He let the words linger, then added, low and cold,

"Wipe the slate clean. Then we talk about your team taking over the area."

His gaze sharpened.

"If they prove themselves. And if they obey orders, we can make something work."

Javier doesn't blink. "Remind them a bullet cuts through many skills if they try anything else. Deal?"

Zayed held Javier's gaze, then glanced at the folder.

"May I?"

Javier nodded.

Zayed reached for the folder with smooth precision, flipping it open.

Then, with the ease of someone who operated in shadows, he pulled out his phone.

A sleek, encrypted satellite model.

It looked like a standard iPhone, but it wasn't.

Designed for secure, untraceable communication, it was a device even government agencies struggled to intercept.

He dialed a number, meeting Javier's gaze.

"Deal."

Then, into the phone. "I have a mission. Three will do. I'll send the details through our links. Thank you."

His fingers moved fast, sending encrypted data through channels only a select few in the world could access.

He looked back at Javier, a satisfied smile forming.

"It's done. Have your men send the details to the link I just provided."

Javier leaned back, fingers steepled, a predatory grin spreading across his face. "This will be a good trial to see if we can do business."

Zayed nodded, his smile tinged with the same cold satisfaction.

"Indeed."

As Zayed rose to leave, Javier's gaze drifted back to the ocean.

The sun had vanished.

The sky deepened into an endless, blood-dark blue.

Night had come and with it, the promise of violence, power, and control.

Javier's empire was on the brink of expansion.

And nothing would stand in his way.

This wasn't just business.

It was a board being set, pieces already moving.

And by the time anyone realized the game had begun, it would already be over.

Chapter Nineteen

Cabin in the Woods

Janice's exhaustion pressed down as she backed up the truck where Bryce told her to park, every turn of the wheel demanding more than she had left.

After hours of adrenaline, fear, and survival, her eyes nearly closed the moment the truck stopped beneath the canopy. She kept the truck running. The idea of trying to escape now was almost impossible. She looked over at her weapon and back at Bryce.

Bryce scanned the brush, weapon steady, never taking his eyes off the trees. "Cabin door unlocked?"

He looked back at her, speaking in a clipped whisper.

She shook her head no, her movements sluggish but certain.

Bryce caught everything, her slumped shoulders, the tight flick of her fingers on the wheel. But this wasn't the time to coddle. Too close to safety to make a mistake now. Even a small one.

"Okay." His voice was a steady whisper. "Give it to me. Wait here. Don't go in until I clear it first."

Janice fished the key out of her pocket.

A rusted metal spike dangled from it, repurposed into a makeshift keychain.

Her hands shook slightly as she handed it to Bryce.

"Here," she managed, her voice raw from the day's strain.

He took the key with a nod, then turned to the task at hand.

Bryce moved with the silent precision of a predator, scanning every inch of the cabin's weathered frame.

The place had seen better days.

The logs, once rich brown, had faded to a silvery gray, scarred by time and weather. Yet the cabin stood firm, like an old soldier, battered but unbroken.

He reached the front door, hand brushing against the thick wood.

It was locked, just as Janice had said. A small relief, but still worth noting.

He continued his sweep around the perimeter, his senses sharpened as the last of the daylight slipped away.

Sixty feet behind the cabin, the land plunged into a valley.

A large lake glistened at the mountain's base, its surface disturbed only by the occasional ripple from a fish or the wind.

The setting sun cast a golden glow over the water, but Bryce had no time to appreciate it.

His focus was on ensuring they weren't walking into a trap.

His eyes swept the ground, scanning for footprints, broken branches, anything that hinted at recent movement. Nothing. Area appeared cold. Time to lock it down.

Evaluate. Fortify. Hold.

They'd come through the low brush.

Chokepoints were limited. Coverage was thin near the treeline.

Stack and breach made no sense here. They'd blitz the front. Keep momentum. Break them fast.

Muscle memory engaged. Time to prep the kill zone.

He continued his patrol, pulling out his notepad, sketching a rough sector diagram and jotting down quick observations.

The terrain was rough, but it offered real defensive advantages.

The cabin sat on elevated ground. Good line of sight. But the surrounding trees and brush gave plenty of concealed approach options.

He scanned the terrain in quadrants, falling into old habits.

Then he flipped perspective. If he were coming in heavy, how would he do it?

They wouldn't use the trees. Too open. Too exposed.

A staggered line, moving fast, bounding in overwatch pairs.

The steep drop behind the cabin limited retreat options. Any good team would recognize that as a trap, no escape, no fallback.

They'd favor a full frontal push. Overwhelm and dominate.

Sniper would take the ridge. Suppression fire from above while the assault team pushed center mass.

Ran the scenario start to finish. Checked every sector, every approach, every soft point.

This is combat chess. Live board. No resets. Stay ten steps ahead or die. Shape the battlespace before contact.

Enemy had fire superiority and the terrain advantage.

They were already in check.

Only move now was first strike.

No rules. No second chances. Just violence, precision, and survival.

Bryce continued his approach.

Each step deliberate.

Fast. Quiet. Precise.

Near the clearing's edge, he found an old fishing boat under a tarp.

He checked for tampering. Clean.

A sonar fish finder was still mounted inside. Might be useful.

Later.

By the time he circled back to the front, Janice was already waiting. Rifle in hand. Eyes sharp.

Bryce motioned for her to stay put.

"So much for keeping the truck running," he muttered under his breath.

His eyes narrowed as he turned to the door, every muscle ready.

Raising a finger to his lips, he signaled for silence.

Then, with calculated precision, he unlocked the door.

The hinges creaked as it swung open.

A dim interior greeted him.

Bryce moved inside, staying close to the wall, avoiding open spaces where he could be an easy target.

He swept the room, clearing each corner with practiced ease.

The cabin's interior was a time capsule of a simpler era.

Wooden walls were adorned with old tools, animal pelts, and faded photographs.

An enormous stone fireplace dominated one corner, its presence both comforting and a potential liability.

Furniture was sparse but sturdy, a testament to old-world craftsmanship.

A rough-hewn table, carved from a centuries-old tree, bore the marks of countless meals and stories shared.

Bryce moved down a short hallway, clearing a small bathroom.

The air reeked of the outdoors.

A composting toilet fed into a pit beneath the cabin.

Off-grid.

No water.

No bills.

No paper trail.

For now, that was a good thing.

The bedroom was small, only large enough for a queen-sized bed and a closet that smelled of old tools and oil.

Bryce rifled through it; blankets, hunting jackets, rusted tools.

All useful in their own way.

He grabbed a saw, tested its weight, and nodded.

It would do.

Back at the front door, he found Janice leaning against the frame.

Tears traced silently down her dirt-streaked face.

She fought to hold them back, to stay composed, but the strain was too much.

Bryce's heart clenched at the sight, but he knew better than to show it.

"It's clear," he said softly.

Janice nodded, wiping her eyes with the back of her hand.

She pulled out a cigarette, hesitated, then lit it with a shaky hand.

Bryce reached out, placing a hand on her arm.

"We shouldn't smoke. Not outside. Please, do it inside."

Janice gave him a sad smile, the kind that spoke of loss and too many broken promises.

"John never wanted me to smoke inside," she murmured, voice trembling.

She exhaled slowly, smoke curling between them.

"Well, now I can."

She turned, stepping inside, the cigarette dangling from her lips, smoke trailing behind her like a ghost of the past.

Bryce watched her go.

Then turned back to the work.

He headed down the hill, saw in hand, toward a thicket of trees.

He worked fast, cutting thick branches to camouflage the truck.

As he dragged them back up the hill, the forest grew darker, shadows stretching long with the fading light.

Layer by layer, he covered the vehicle, making it nearly invisible from above or at a distance.

For the final touch, he rigged a rope to the branches, tying it to a nearby tree.

If they needed to leave in a hurry, a single tug would clear the canopy away.

Satisfied, Bryce grabbed the shotgun and a carton of cigarettes Janice had left behind, then headed back to the cabin.

Inside, Janice was unpacking supplies, her movements mechanical, her mind tormented, fighting back tidal waves of emotion, each one threatening to pull her into an abyss soaked in pain and memory.

Bryce set the shotgun on the table and handed her the cigarettes.

"I'm making this our staging table," he said, voice gentle but firm.

Janice, eyes swollen and red, nodded, clutching the carton like a lifeline.

"I need to cover the windows before we turn on any lights," Bryce said. "We'll only use red light."

Janice's voice was barely a whisper. "Why?"

"Red light preserves our night vision. Harder to see from a distance."

He cut a tarp and secured it over the windows.

"The lanterns have a red setting. Can you load the batteries while I finish this?"

Janice nodded, too tired to argue.

She moved like a shadow, fading in the growing dark.

Bryce handed her a headlamp set to red mode, casting the room into an eerie crimson glow.

"The fish finder in the boat. Can I use it?"

Janice shrugged.

"Help yourself."

Bryce paused, almost placing a hand on her shoulder, but thought better of it.

Her eyes flashed, anger flaring, and fading as she turned toward the door.

"Wait," Bryce called after her.

She turned, eyes narrowing.

"I was just getting firewood."

Bryce shook his head.

"We can't light a fire. Too risky."

Janice muttered a curse and kicked a log near the fireplace, her voice rising. "Then how are we supposed to stay warm? How in the hell do we even know if they're coming?"

She held back tears, her voice cracking into a whisper.

"How are we supposed to survive?"

She slumped into the nearest chair, drained, emotionally and physically spent.

Bryce knelt down beside her, meeting her eyes. His voice was steady, but not cold.

"I'll take care of it. You're not alone in this."

He stood and shifted into briefing mode. Calm. Clear. Certain.

"We've got thermal layers, jackets, and enough blankets to stay warm through the night. I'll rig the fish finder into a perimeter alert system. I'll connect the transponder to the walkie-talkies and run fishing line across key approach points. If anyone trips the line, the signal will transmit back to the fish finder monitor. We'll know they're coming before they know we're here."

He nodded toward the windows.

"We'll close the shutters. During the day, I'll uncover one line of sight per wall. Just enough to spot movement or take a shot if needed. But we never cross in front of a window. Ever. That's how people get killed. Understand?"

She didn't answer right away. Just lit another cigarette.

The smoke curled upward, soft and slow.
She exhaled a long stream, eyes fixed on the ceiling.

Then, shaking her head, she looked down and placed her hands on her knees, like she was about to break.

Then she stood and walked to the kitchen.

Bryce watched her go, then turned back to his work.

He checked the window coverage, ensuring no light would leak out.

He walked through the rest of the cabin, exploring its strength.

Bryce ran a hand along the inside wall, solid pine, aged and dense. Not perfect, but thick enough to stop most small arms.

He knocked twice near a seam. Dead sound. No hollow echo. Good.

High-velocity rounds would punch through eventually, but not fast. Not clean.

He eyed the table in the center of the room, solid, heavy.

It wouldn't tip over easily, but it would stop a .308.

Maybe even stall a belt-fed long enough to set up his next move.

Not ideal. But workable.

He didn't need to win the fight here.

He just had to control it.

Bryce slipped outside to check for light spill.

The forest was pitch black now, alive only with the faint stirrings of nocturnal life.

He moved along the cabin's perimeter, slow, deliberate, eyes scanning for light leaks, reflective surfaces, anything that might silhouette them.

No shine. No flash. No bleed.

Satisfied, he slipped back inside without a sound.

Janice was in the kitchen, her movements slow, deliberate.

She worked over a hot plate wired to a car battery under the sink.

The faint sizzle of food breaking the silence.

The smell of something cooking soon filled the air.

He checked in on her, watching her work. He knew the night was silent. The weight of what was coming would press down on her.

He could feel it in the way Janice moved, in the slight tremble of her hands as she prepared the meal.

The quiet moments were always the hardest.

Especially when there was nothing left to do but wait.

After a while, Janice called him over to the small table, where she had set out two plates of canned beef stew mixed with stale bread from the pantry.

A simple meal.

But the aroma was familiar, a small comfort in a world that had stopped making sense.

They sat down, the red glow of the lantern casting long shadows across the room.

For a few minutes, they ate in silence. The only sounds were spoons scraping against plates.

Bryce finally broke the silence.

"We should plan shifts for the night. One of us stays awake at all times. Keep watch. We'll do three on three off. Does that work for you?"

Janice nodded, gaze fixed on her plate.

"I'll take first shift," she said, though there was no conviction in her voice. "I'm not sure I can sleep, anyway."

Bryce studied her, then nodded.

"Alright. Wake me in a few hours."

Janice looked up then, her eyes searching his face for something, reassurance, maybe. A reason to believe they'd make it out of this.

"Do you think we'll make it?"

Her voice was barely above a whisper.

Bryce didn't answer right away.

He knew better than to offer false hope.

But he also knew they needed to hold on to something. Anything."We've made it this far," he finally said, his tone even, measured. "We've got a chance. But we have to stay sharp. No mistakes."

Janice nodded, but doubt lingered in her eyes.

She didn't push.

Just turned back to her dinner.

After they finished eating, Bryce helped Janice clean up, then made sure everything was set for the night.

He laid out supplies within reach.

Checked the blackout curtains one last time.

Secured the front and back doors with makeshift barricades.

Janice dropped into the chair, rifle across her lap, her weariness undeniable. Her grip on the weapon told a different story.

She looked weary, but determined. Bryce appreciated that. He knew he could trust her and that's saying a lot in this world.

Her eyes scanned the dark, as if willing the world to stay quiet just a little longer.

Bryce lingered for a moment, watching her, before heading to the bedroom.

He stretched out on the bed, clothed, rifle within reach.

The mattress was lumpy. But it brought relief.

Darkness closed in.

Despite the tension knotting in his stomach, exhaustion eventually claimed him.

Bryce fell asleep fast.

He did not get his normal fitful, fragmented dreams that made no sense. Faces. Places. Ghosts of the past all woven into the dread that had followed him since the nightmares began.

He woke with a start.

The stillness of the cabin pressed in around him.

He focused his breathing and listened to the house.

Straining to hear anything out of the ordinary.

But there was only the faint sound of Janice's steady breathing in the other room.
Bryce forced himself to relax.

Reminded himself Janice was on watch. He looked at his watch. It had been three hours.

Eventually, he heard the soft creak of the bedroom door.

Janice's silhouette appeared in the doorway, outlined by the dim red light from the other room. She stood there, as if gathering the strength to speak.

"Your turn," she finally said, her voice hoarse with exhaustion.

Bryce nodded, swinging his legs over the side of the bed, reaching for his rifle.

He was on his feet before he was fully awake, his training kicking in automatically.

She looked like she could barely stand.

Dark circles hung under her eyes, puffy from crying. Bryce figured that's what had kept her awake.

Her shoulders sagged under the weight of everything they'd been through.

Bryce felt a pang of sympathy.

But there was no time for that.

"You did good," he said quietly as they passed in the narrow hallway.

Janice didn't respond.

Just gave a weary nod before disappearing into the bedroom.

Bryce heard the soft thump as she collapsed onto the bed.

Moments later, the cabin was quiet again.

He killed the red lights, letting the dark take the cabin.

Then he took up position by the window, eyes scanning the treeline beyond.

The night was calm.

Too calm.

The kind of stillness that pressed with unspoken tension.

Bryce kept his rifle close, every sense on high alert as he settled in for his shift.

The hours crawled.

Bryce was used to the wait.

Danger came when you least expected it. He knew that.

He moved from window to window, peeling back his makeshift curtains to monitor the night. Bryce's mind drifted to the days ahead, locking in the steps like a checklist burned into muscle memory.

First, secure the cabin. Reinforce the perimeter. Control the high ground. Set the traps. Then get the girl.

Once she was safe, the Jeep became the lifeline.

Mobility meant survival. The tools he had on the jeep would secure their next steps.

After that, reach out to the old team. Tap whatever intel they could offer.

The hard call would be to Troy.

But he trusted him.

Troy was the JAG who tried to prosecute him and the one who saved him.

Now he was deep in the CIA. Deep enough to disappear someone without leaving a paper trail.

He had the contacts. WITSEC. Off-book liaisons. Assets buried inside the Bureau. Troy could move through the cracks between the Feds, the locals, and anyone else who had been bought.

Funny how the only person he trusted was the man who once came after him. But that was how he knew what Troy stood for.

And that was rare in a world full of political pawns.

If there was a way out, Troy would find it.

Somewhere off-grid.

Untouchable.

And anyone standing in the way, they wouldn't be standing for long. But if he could avoid civilian casualties, he would.

It wasn't just the right thing to do; it made getting out clean that much easier.

As the first light of dawn filtered through the trees, he felt a flicker of relief.

They'd survived.

They'd made it through the first night, but Bryce knew better than to think they were safe.

For now, that was enough.

But with daylight came new dangers.

Quietly, Bryce rose, rifle in hand.

The brief refuge of night was over.

It was time to move again.

To stay one step ahead of whatever, or whoever, was coming next.

Chapter Twenty

Welcome to America

Dawn broke, casting long shadows over the sprawl of steel and concrete.

The bare carcass of the construction site was taking shape. Another soulless subdivision rising from the dirt, built to trap families in debt and routine.

It was the largest project in the area, an ideal place for someone to disappear.

Engines grumbled to life at the entrance, slicing the cool air with misty exhaust.

Headlights cut through the lingering dark as workers emerged, faces set with the day's grind.

The vehicles included dust-covered pickups, rugged bulldozers, and towering cranes, all ready for another day of relentless labor.

Among them was Ahmed.

To everyone here, he was José, just another undocumented worker, toiling for pennies on the job site.

At five-nine, his frame was unassuming by design.

He wore strength like camouflage, meant to be missed until it was too late.

A man of few words, he kept to himself.

Never stood out.

Never drew attention.

Invisible.

Yet beneath the ordinary exterior, Ahmed was the linchpin of a sleeper cell.

Chosen for his unwavering loyalty.

His sharp intellect.

His unparalleled leadership.

He moved through the site with purpose, lifting, carrying, blending in.

The skilled laborers shouted and postured, jostling for rank, the same scene on every job site in America.

Ahmed hefted a stack of two-by-fours, relishing the burn in his muscles.

"Hey! Get someone to help or carry less. I don't need you showing up at the ER saying you work here. That's a headache I can't afford," the foreman barked.

Fire flashed in Ahmed's eyes.

But he set the wood down.

Picked up a smaller stack.

"Lo siento," he muttered without looking up.

"Yeah, well, save it. Don't let me catch you doing it again," the foreman snapped, stalking away.

As he carried the wood deeper into the site, his phone buzzed in his pocket.

He set the stack down.

Slipped into an empty room.

Glanced around.

Pulled out the phone.

Answered in Spanish.

"Hola."

A flat, robotic voice.

"In action. Use links."

The line went dead.

Ahmed felt something close to happiness, a rare emotion.

One last look.

Then he left the lumber and this world behind.

His body moved with deliberate lethargy, blending into the site's rhythm.

But his mind raced ahead to the mission.

Jet-black hair, now streaked with gray, told the story of countless missions.

His eyes, piercing and brown, had seen the world's darkest corners.

Held the weight of the secrets he carried.

He had shaved his beard last year when the old president opened the border.

That was the moment he and his fellow warriors slipped through.

Unnoticed. Unchallenged. Welcomed.

His past was a labyrinth of deadly skirmishes and victories. Victories that had earned him the right to be here now.

The mission was his penance.

His redemption.

A burden he carried alone.

Until now.

***

On the bus to Northern California, Ahmed sat in silence.

Surrounded by oblivious enemies.

The steady hum of the engine filled the space, masking the storm inside his mind.

He needed sleep.

Uncertain when he'd get another chance.

As he closed his eyes, a rare peace settled over him.

For the first time in years, he felt alive.

The weight of his mission granted him a moment's rest.

Chapter Twenty-One

Ready Room

The morning light pressed against the curtains, but none of it made it through.

The cabin was dimly lit, his red headlamp swept across the old wood in a slow arc, while the other red lanterns placed throughout the room cast fixed shadows that stretched and curled like warning signs.

Bryce sat at the thick redwood table as he unpacked his bag, lining up the confiscated phones like evidence on a war table.

Smoke from Janice's cigarettes drifted through those shadows like passengers on a subway, silent, aimless, headed to unknown destinations.

His headlamp steadied as he connected the inverter to the fishing batteries he'd scavenged earlier, then plugged the phones into a surge protector.

A faint hum filled the quiet as each device powered up.

Bryce watched the screens, confirming he still had access through the unlocked app.

With quick, precise movements, he jotted down the phone numbers for each device.

Then he pulled out a burner phone, dialing each number to confirm the lines were still live.

The soft, rhythmic beeps of ringing echoed back at him, each one confirming a successful connection.

Satisfied, he hung up and moved to the next phase of his plan.

In the kitchen, he rummaged through drawers until he found a box of Ziploc bags and a roll of aluminum foil.

He sat back at the table and got to work.

Mind focused.

Hands steady.

Each confiscated phone was sealed in plastic, then carefully wrapped in layers of foil. His own makeshift Faraday bags.

He called one of the wrapped devices.

No signal.

Perfect.

He repeated the process for each phone, the light crackle of foil filling the room.

Bryce glanced at his watch, calculating how long to leave them charging.

He set a countdown for an hour, enough time to power them up before cutting them off.

Every second counted now. Bryce crossed the room and grabbed his SAT phone. The cracked keyboard mocked him.

He pressed the power button.

Nothing.

Frowning, he pried open the back.

The motherboard crumbled apart in his hands.

Broken. Useless.

"That's five grand down the drain," he muttered, tossing it aside in a bin for extra parts.
"At least I didn't pay for it."

He let out a breath and refocused. He laid out the confiscated weapons beside ammo bags and tools he'd picked up earlier.

One by one, he removed the magazines, checking each firearm, matching them with the appropriate ammo.

His mind switched to inventory mode, his training taking over. At the bottom of a bag, he found two gun-cleaning kits and set them aside.

Janice entered from the kitchen, carrying a steaming cup of soup.
"Got this warmed up for you," her voice was weak but steady.

He hadn't realized how hungry he was until the smell hit.

He took the cup, nodding his thanks.
"Appreciate it," he said, his voice rougher than intended.

Janice lingered.

Her eyes were red, brimming with unshed tears.

Then, finally, she said it.

"How are you going to get my daughter back?"

Heavy words, ones she'd clearly been holding in.

Bryce sighed, setting the cup down.

He'd been expecting it. But he still wasn't ready.

"I'll find a way," he said finally. "Once I know we're safe here, I'll get her."
His voice was steady, absolute.

"We have to play this smart. Stealth and strategy. That's all we've got."

Janice shot him a dry look, equal parts exhaustion and sarcasm.
"Sure. It's good to know we got something."

She walked over to the table.

Then froze.

Her eyes locked on something.

She pointed.

A framed picture hung on the wall. A recent photo, only five years old.
John, Janice, and Taylor-May stared back at them.

Taylor-May had warm brown hair, a happy smile, and bright, lively eyes.
They all wore that same smile. A memory from a different time. The three of
them looked happy.

A real, genuine happiness, the kind that couldn't be faked.

Janice's voice was barely above a whisper.
"That's my daughter."

Bryce didn't respond immediately.

Instead, he stood. Stepped closer. Studied the photo. Memorized her face.

But memory wouldn't be enough.

Without a word, he pulled out his phone, snapped a picture, and slipped
it back into his pocket.
"I'll need that," he said simply.

Janice watched him, her expression unreadable.

She didn't question it. Didn't protest. She just took another slow drag
from her cigarette, her thoughts somewhere far away.

Bryce returned to his seat, his mind already working ahead.

Now, if he found her, he'd know for sure.

Janice exhaled, staring into the empty fireplace.
"Well... God bless you," she muttered. "I don't know where we'd be without
you."

Bryce didn't say anything. Didn't need to.

The moment lingered between them.

Unspoken.

Understood.

Bryce got back to work, picking up his wire cutters. He glanced at his
worktable.

She took a slow drag from her cigarette, exhaling through her nose as she watched him.

His hands were steady as he spliced the walkie's wires into the fish finder's system.

Bryce hadn't pulled this trick since the sandbox, when a kid with a goat nearly blew their whole convoy to hell.

He'd learned fast. And remembered everything.

His movements were precise, practiced, each motion a step toward reinforcing their defenses.

Janice watched him for a moment, then spoke.
"So... what exactly are you trying to do?"

Bryce didn't look up.
"I'm modifying the transducer. If I can rig this up right, it'll act as a motion detector. It won't pick up every little thing, but if something big moves out there, we'll know."

Janice raised an eyebrow.
"So we're trusting some fishing gear to keep us alive?"

Bryce chuckled, shaking his head.
"You got any better ideas?"

Janice huffed out a breath, but there was no real fight behind it.
"Fair enough."

He finished tweaking the wiring and turned his attention back to the range card open on the table.

Grabbing a pencil, he refined a few lines, marking potential choke points, cover positions, and the fastest routes down the ridge.
He had sketched out everything.
He flipped the page.
One side detailed a 180-degree field from the road to the cabin.
The other showed the back side, the valley below and the ridge rising up the far side.

Janice leaned over his shoulder, eyes scanning the rough map.
"So what's the plan? We sell art down by the river?"

Bryce tapped the page, ignoring the joke but appreciating it all the same.
"You could try selling lemonade down the road."

"Depends how they come. Full team, we slow them down. Small numbers, we pick them off as they try to hide."

Janice's face hardened.
"You're talking about killing them."

Bryce met her gaze, unflinching.

"I'm talking about surviving."

She held his stare for a long moment.

Then exhaled and nodded.

Janice sat across from him, eyes locked on the photo of her daughter. Her jaw tightened.

"I know they're coming for me, too."

Bryce didn't deny it.

He set his pencil down, reached for his sidearm, and slid a spare magazine across the table.

"Then you'd better be ready."

Janice picked it up, turning it in her hands.

She wasn't a fighter.

But she wasn't going down easy, either.

Bryce checked his watch.

The phones were charged enough.

He stood, unwrapped the first from its foil casing, and moved to the table.

Janice watched him, curiosity creeping in.

"You gonna call them?"

Bryce smirked.

"Something like that."

With steady hands, he powered up the first phone and scrolled through the messages.

Names. Numbers. Locations.

Breadcrumbs left behind by men who thought they were the hunters.

Bryce intended to flip the script.

He cracked his neck and exhaled slowly.

The game had already begun.

They just didn't know it yet.

Bryce kept his eyes on his work, the soft scratch of his pencil the only sound filling the cabin.

She took another drag from her cigarette, smoke curling in the dim light.

"John never did nothing like this," she muttered. "Didn't plan ahead. Didn't think about ambushes or escape routes. Just took life as it came."

Bryce looked at her.

"John was part of a special team."

Janice blinked. "How do you know?"

Bryce nodded. "It was on the wall at the gas station. The 25th was tasked with clearing villages, destroying infrastructure, and disrupting supply lines."

Janice exhaled smoke and dropped the butt into a can.
"Well... I know he didn't have any of the training you had."

His voice was even, but there was weight behind the words.
"I wish they all had more training."

He paused, tapping his pencil against the edge of the table.
"What we learned from them made me who I am today."

His gaze flicked to Janice.
"I just hope it's enough, because there won't be a second chance."

Chapter Twenty-Two

Bad Delivery

An ordinary delivery van rolled up to a quiet, well-manicured house in the suburbs.

One of those neighborhoods where everything looked just a little too perfect.

The kind of place where nothing bad ever happened.

Not yet.

The man who stepped out was the definition of ordinary. Average height, average build, the kind of face you'd forget a minute after seeing it. His tan uniform, simple button-up and matching pants, was as unremarkable as the van.

Even the logo belonged to a small-time courier service. The kind subcontracted by the big players. The kind that didn't ask questions. A perfect cover for someone who, legally speaking, didn't exist.

He moved methodically, weaving around a couple of plastic toys scattered across the lawn. His face stayed neutral, but inside, resentment churned.

These kids, so carefree, so sheltered, had no idea what it meant to grow up in a world of fire and steel.

No idea what was coming.

He reached the freshly painted front door, set the package down, and rang the bell with cold efficiency, already turning to leave before the door even opened.

A woman in a bathrobe answered.

Her eyes crinkled with warmth, her smile light and pleasant, no clue about the kind of predator standing in front of her.

"Thank you," she said, blissfully ignorant.

"You're welcome." His voice was polite. Measured. It took effort to keep the disgust off his face.

She waved and shut the door, already moving on with her perfect little life.

Oblivious.

The door clicked shut.

His smile dropped. His face twisted, dark, bitter. A sneer pulsing with rage.

She was just like the others, entitled, blind, content in their comfort.

Oblivious to the wolves already at their door. If he had his way, her world would burn. He'd take everything from her, tear it from her hands like justice owed.

Just like he had with the others.

"Praise Allah," he whispered. "I will have my way."

Thinking about his boss made his blood boil. A woman like that giving him orders? It was a daily insult. He hated her. Everything she represented. The framed photos on her desk. Her perfect little family. Bright-eyed kids grinning back like they had any idea what the world really was.

All part of the same sickness.

Weak. Soft. Spoiled.

He clenched his fists. Imagined the fear in her eyes the moment she realized what he was. He'd wipe that smug smile off her face.

One day.

But not yet.

He had to stay patient. Blend in. Play the part of the obedient, grateful worker.

For now.

His phone buzzed.

He scanned the street, no eyes on him. Then pulled it out. The message blinked across the screen:

IN ACTION. USE LINKS.

A genuine smile spread across his face. Sharp. Cold. Real. He didn't hesitate. He answered.

The flat, robotic voice on the other end snapped him back into focus.

This was it. What he'd been waiting for. A rush of adrenaline hit. His heart pounded.

Finally.

He hung up without a word. Sat there for a moment. Eyes closed. Breathing it in.

The wait was over.

The engine rumbled to life as he merged back into traffic.

The world around him blurred into a haze of ordinary life, cars, houses, playgrounds full of laughing children.

All of them were oblivious.

Clueless of the storm brewing in his mind.

His hands gripped the wheel, steady, controlled.

He rehearsed the plan again. Every detail. Every step. He had been patient. Watching. Waiting. Biding his time.

But now?

Now it had begun.

His smile widened, slower, darker this time.

Soon, they would all know what it felt like to have their world torn apart.

They wouldn't see it coming.

Until it was already too late.

Chapter Twenty-Three

Keep Going

The cabin was dim and heavy with the stale residue of Janice's cigarettes, smoke and exhaustion woven into the very fabric of the space.

At the cluttered workbench, Bryce pushed aside a soldering gun and a tangle of wires.

His focus locked on the fish finder, now transformed into something far more dangerous.

Each walkie-talkie, meticulously paired and labeled, was connected to the fish finder's motherboard by thin strands of fishing line.

Bryce checked the setup against his hand-drawn map, making sure each label matched the numbered quadrants.

He gave one line a careful tug. The fish finder chirped. The screen lit up, highlighting the correct quadrant.

Bullseye.

It worked.

Bryce exhaled. A small wave of relief washed through him.

He stood, stretched his aching shoulders, and chewed a strip of beef jerky as he planned his next steps.

A sudden rasp of coughing snapped him out of focus. He looked over.

Janice lay asleep on the couch, curled beneath a blanket, breathing rough and uneven.

Bryce shook his head. Said nothing.

She needed rest.

He turned back to the table.

The burner phones were lined up, charging off the boat batteries, each labeled with numbered tape strips.

At the far end of the table sat his most dangerous work. Five camping propane tanks, rigged with fishing weights and thick black duct tape.

Wires snaked from each valve, ending in wingnut fuses.

Improvised explosives.

Bryce picked up a modified burner phone, its back rigged with a protruding wire.

He used a multimeter, then dialed the number taped to another phone, tied to a marked quadrant on the map.

A soft beep.

A charge spike.

He hung up.

One by one, he repeated the test, each trigger system confirmed and logged.

By the time he finished, the table had become a battlefield map, phone numbers taped to their strike zones.

Bryce packed fast.

Burner phones. Spare wingnuts. Wire cutters. Extra line.

His stomach clenched.

One wrong number.

One midnight call, everything would change.

Shaking off the paranoia, he zipped the bag shut.

Poured the last of the soup into a coffee mug and carried it back to the workbench.

He sipped slowly.

His eyes flicked to Janice.

Still asleep.

Snoring rough, rasping, occasional choking coughs rattling in her throat.

Bryce set the mug down and made one last sweep of the cabin.

The red lanterns glowed low, no light leaking outside.

From the back closet, he pulled the thickest jacket he could find, warm enough for the cold, loose enough to hide gear and his headlamp.

In the kitchen, he grabbed a cardboard box and a Sharpie.

Scrawled NO TRESPASSING in jagged black letters.

Aged it with coffee and water until it looked like it had been ignored for years.

Once prepped, he loaded the walkies, fishing line, and tools into a duffel bag, tossed in a can of WD-40 for good measure.

The propane tanks were last, handled with care, strapped tight in their own bag to prevent movement.

Bryce checked his weapons.

Handgun secured in his waistband.

Rifle slung over his shoulder.

He took one last inventory of the room, then killed the lamps and his headlamp.

The cabin plunged into darkness.

Bryce eased the door open, stepping into the chilly night without a sound.

It closed behind him with a soft click, sealing in the cabin's warmth.

He crouched low, letting his eyes adjust to the dark.

For a long moment, he listened.

Stillness.

No movement.

No voices.

But he knew better than to trust silence.

He drew a slow, steady breath.

Then moved forward, vanishing into the trees.

Chapter Twenty-Four

Clogged Drains

The dim glow of his flashlight cut through the crawl space as Hassan slid forward on his belly, tracing a pipe beneath an old house.

He was a large man, broad frame, poor fit for tight spaces, yet every movement was precise. Practiced.

Despite his deep-seated disdain for America, instilled since childhood by his father and religious leaders, he couldn't help but admire the craftsmanship of the homes he serviced.

Hassan's background was as brutal as it was unforgiving.

In his homeland, disobedience meant violence.

He was raised to hate the freedom he now witnessed daily.

And yet, in two and a half years of plumbing, he had found something he never expected: passion.

Not just duty. Not just cover.

He enjoyed it.

The order. The problem-solving. The simple victories.

Fixing something broken gave him a kind of satisfaction he never thought possible.

In a life trained for destruction, plumbing had become his rebellion.

His peace.

A part of him even looked forward to the work. Even knowing it couldn't last. He had only been allowed to read and write after proving himself in battle.

But once he could, he devoured knowledge. Languages. Machines. Strategy. Plumbing, in its own way, was mental combat.

Precision. Patience. Pressure. A discipline he secretly embraced and enjoyed.

His flashlight swept the PEX piping.

A clean tear. A rat chewed through it. An easy fix. The simplicity of the solution filled him with pride.

Back at his white Sprinter van, Hassan stowed his tools with care. He whispered a quiet prayer of thanks for another day's work done well.

Lawn mowers buzzed in the distance. Children's laughter carried on the breeze.

The moment broke when his phone vibrated.

Shattering the peace.

He expected another service call. Answered smoothly. The name Omar, his alias, rolled off his tongue.

"Hello, this is Omar."

A flat, robotic voice cut through the line.

His pulse dropped. Cold.

"In action. Use links."

The words were simple, yet they carried the weight of inevitability.

Hassan's stomach tightened.

It had begun.

Driving back to his base, a nondescript house in a lower-income suburb, his mind raced.

The mission he had been dreading was now reality.

Backing the van into the garage, he moved with calculated precision, unlocking a hidden closet and loading large, heavy Pelican cases filled with specialized equipment into the vehicle.

The house was sterile. No personality. No warmth. A shell. Nothing more.

He wiped every surface.

Cleared every trace.

Clothes. Tools. Documents.

Packed.

His watch beeped.

Maghrib.

He paused.

Knelt.

A moment of faith before war.

***

The van was packed. His existence here, erased.

The garage door clattered shut behind him, sealing away what was.

He pulled onto the highway, merging into the stream of ordinary, unsuspecting Americans.

His orders were clear:

Rendezvous at a Sacramento train station.

With a general he'd never met, Ahmed. A fierce warrior. Respected. Feared.

Their target:

Bryce Rath.

With militia support, they would eliminate him.

Success meant new identities.

New operations.

And if they pulled it off, long-term placement with greater purpose. A focused mission. A future.

He knew the rules.

Succeed. Or die. No getting caught. No failing.

Then vanish.

Until the next call.

As the van hummed toward its destination, Hassan tightened his grip on the wheel, his mind already calculating the days ahead.

This was just the beginning.

Bigger than this city. Bigger than this country.

A storm was coming.

And Hassan was ready.

Chapter Twenty-Five

Make it Happen

Bryce dropped low, freezing mid-step. The air was sharp, damp earth, pine, tension. He began a silent environmental sweep. Listened. Sensed. Every cell alert.

Clutching his rifle, he swept through the darkness, eyes absorbing every shadow, every shift of wind.

The obscured moon cast a ghostly silver glow over the landscape. He glanced back at the cabin, its sturdy logs a silent testament to security.

The wilderness swallowed him whole, broken only by the rhythm of his breath as he prepped for the night's tasks.

Under cover of darkness, Bryce moved with practiced silence, each step measured.

The forest was his ally. Its shadows, his cloak. He paused often, listening, tuned to the smallest shift in the forest's nocturnal rhythm.

First task: get the propane tanks in place.

The tanks sat cold inside his duffel, metallic, unforgiving.

One wrong wire. One misfire. One lucky bullet.

That's all it would take.

He exhaled.

No room for hesitation.

At a rocky, pre-scouted site, Bryce set the bags down, red headlamp dimmed to a soft glow, just enough to work without casting shadows.

One by one, he planted the tanks in shallow, concealed positions behind natural cover, fallen logs, rock shelves, tight choke points.

He knew once the trip lines snapped, the fish finder would chirp; short, sharp bursts of sound. Enough to wake him.

Enough to warn Janice.

When they attacked, he'd let the sensors guide him. Every trip line a breadcrumb.

He'd fire in short bursts from shifting angles, making it seem like they were all in the cabin.

Naturally, they'd dive for cover, thinking they were closing in.

But Bryce would be herding them.

Not toward victory. Toward the traps. Toward the kill zones.

The Cabin's thick log walls would shield his position as he moved, never staying in one spot, always one step ahead.

They'd think they had him surrounded. But they were already surrounded. Trapped and receiving exactly what they'd come to deliver.

The hunters, now the hunted. Just like fish chasing bait. Bryce took no joy in it. But he felt no remorse, either.

This was their choice.

His was to survive and honor a dying wish.

If they stayed away, good.

But if they came... He wouldn't lose sleep.

This was the part of the job that made sense. Kill or be killed.

No emotions. No second chances.

Just gravity, velocity, and the law of the universe.

Working quadrant by quadrant from memory, he wired a modified phone to each tank.

Black duct tape sealed moisture out. Connections were tight.

Each phone was bagged, buried, and covered with forest debris. Camouflaged. Undisturbed.

When the last tank was set, he rubbed dirt on a weathered NO TRESPASSING sign and drove it into the ground, covering his tracks with its placement, just as he had with the others.

He sat back, listening.

Still nothing.

Good.

Hearing nothing, he gathered his equipment and moved to the next phase.

Motion sensors.

Walkies buried and rigged to chirp if jostled.

Fishing line strung across narrow approach paths like a spider's web.

To keep animals from setting them off, he coated each trip line with WD-40.

The scent was sharp, unnatural, enough to keep the wildlife at bay.

Only a human would miss the warning. Only a human would trigger the line, deaf to nature's signals.

By first light, his work was done.

The cabin wasn't just a shelter now.

It was a trap. A limited fortress.

Designed to buy them seconds, when seconds meant survival.

Exhausted but sharp, he eased the cabin door open, every step placed to avoid a creak.

Inside, Janice was still out.

Adrenaline had worked its way through her system.

Bryce untied his boots, needing to be out of them for as long as possible.

He turned up the fish monitor.

Grabbed a bottle of water.

Padded to the back bedroom, avoiding every squeaky floorboard from memory.

Sleep came fast.

No dreams, just pure rest.

The kind he hadn't had in years.

****

Bacon pierced the air.

He moved before thinking, wide awake, auxiliary mode engaged.

Then came the coffee. The scent hit harder than any alarm. His mind snapped alert before his body did, muscles still wired from years of waking up ready to fight.

The cabin stirred as the sun climbed over the mountain. That smell had pulled him from sleep like a rope.

Janice greeted him with a skillet of eggs and a hardened smile.

A rare comfort in a world that no longer offered them. Bryce didn't say it, but this was against every protocol.

The smells would carry farther than sound. But they were still alive. He'd give her this little win.

They ate.

Talk turned tactical.

Bryce laid it all out. Security protocols, hard rules, and contingency plans.

No more cooking. Only cold rations from here on.

No guesswork. No surprises. Stay alert. Do not get curious. Do not make noise.

Janice took comfort in the structure. In return, she opened up. She talked about the cabin, her daughter, and the weight she carried.

She admitted she had become an informant for the FBI.

She was not turned. She went to them.

She had planned to give them all up.

Not out of anger, but because she wanted to save them.

Bryce listened. He said nothing.

Then he promised he would handle it.

After breakfast, he cleaned every weapon, checked every mag, and reloaded every round.

One missed detail could cost everything.

He prepped his bag.

Went over the route to the house.

Confirmed every variable he could.

Then he gave Janice the plan.

Instructions.

Timing.

Fallback points.

Escape route.

He left quickly, slipping into the trees.

The cabin stood behind him, fortified, waiting.

Bryce disappeared into the forest.

One man against the coming storm.

Chapter Twenty-Six

Who's coming here?

Supervisory Special Agent Jack sank into the oversized couch, eyes scanning the room. The extravagance was excessive. Floor-to-ceiling windows framed a panoramic view of the river winding through the mountains, the golden glow of dusk reflecting off the water.

"We're fucked, Fred."

Sheriff Fred sauntered over, handed Jack a tumbler of whiskey, and sank into the leather chair behind his grand mahogany coffee table, waving off Jack's words like a drunk waving away the check. Dodging the conversation completely, pretending like he still had control.

"Look, we just need to get rid of this guy and that family, and we're back in business. Now, going after him didn't work out. Sure, he's got some training, but we've got more men, more guns, and the fucking cartel. How bad can this guy be?"

Deadpan Jack flipped open a folder and slid it toward Fred.

Bryce Rath stared back, clean-shaven, crisp military uniform, chest full of ribbons and medals.

Most of the documents were heavily redacted, more black lines than text.

Fred sipped his whiskey, squinting at the file.

"MARSOC? Sounds like some Star Wars shit. What the hell's that?"

Jack's expression darkened. He snatched the folder, his fingers tightening.

"You see how much of this is blacked out?" Jack tapped the pages, holding it up for Fred. "The stuff we can read is bad enough. What's hidden is worse."

Fred waved his glass dismissively.

"So what? That was in the past. He got hooked on painkillers and ended up in jail. He slipped out on a technicality. We've got former SWAT, military guys, and other hard hitters on our team. Hell, I was in the service."

Jack shot out of his seat, slamming the folder onto the table.

"What kind of fucking service were you in that you don't know what MARSOC is? Fred. Look closer. His last mission? Three broken ribs, two bullet wounds, and a fractured skull. He didn't just survive, he finished the job."

He flipped to another declassified section.
"Then this, he walked away from an ambush that took out his lead truck in Mali. Most of his convoy got wiped out. Thirty confirmed kills of Al-Qaeda-affiliated JNIM fighters."

"Read it. The lead vehicle hit an IED. Then came the RPGs. The AKs." Jake looked at the sheriff, hoping some of the information he gave would sink in.
"And he took them out while saving lives in the process."

Jack's jaw clenched.
"Fuck this guy. He's bad news."

Fred chewed the inside of his cheek like he'd seen this show before. And didn't like the ending.
"He's one guy. Sure, he evaded Bubba and the dogs, but he's still just one guy."

Jack's fist slammed down on the table. Pain shot up his arm. He didn't care.

"You're missing the point, Fred! He's a ticking time bomb. Exactly the kind of problem we don't want coming for us."

Fred snorted.
"Jesus, Jack, you act like this guy is Jason fucking Bourne."

Jack's face didn't move.
"He's worse."

"Oh, come on," Fred groaned. "One guy. That's it." He jabbed at the folder. "He's now the most-wanted man in three states. We'll flush him out, blame PTSD, and kill him in a shootout. Page twelve news. Nobody cares."

Jack exhaled through his nose.
"You still don't get it."

Fred chuckled, swirling his drink.
"He's an addict with PTSD, Jack. How much of a threat can a broken man be?"

Jack downed his whiskey, gaze hardening.
"PTSD doesn't erase training. If anything, it amplifies it."

He looked at Fred with disgust.
"Addict? Are you fucking kidding me? It's not like he was shooting heroin. He got hooked on painkillers after getting shot three times. His team was wiped out in a friendly fire mishap he blames himself for. You try going through any of that and not taking something."

He pointed at the file.

"Every man I know would've done the same. He's fought battles we can't imagine. And now? He's here. Evading capture. Dropping bodies."

Jack pointed at the file.

"That doesn't sound like a man who's lost his edge."

Fred shrugged.

"He's one guy. A fugitive. Blood on his hands. He won't get far. We've alerts across three states."

Jack pushed away from the table, pacing.

"Fred, he's got a Silver Star. A Navy Cross. A Purple Heart. Eleven tours. Africa. Afghanistan. South America. And that's just the stuff that isn't blacked out."

He paused, flipping to a redacted page.

"He's tied to CIA black ops."

Fred grinned like a man who just sold the family cow for magic beans. Only this giant was real, and it killed everything it touched.

"Relax, Jack. Javier called in a specialized team. The heavy hitters. They'll clean this up, and we can move on."

Jack froze.

"Javier? Are you out of your goddamn mind?"

The name hit like a sucker punch. His mouth went dry. He knew what Javier's people did. He'd seen it firsthand. No favors.

No survivors. Just scorched earth.

Fred chuckled again, still proud of his 'solution.'

"What? They're just muscle. They'll handle our problem. Simple."

Jack's stomach dropped. His pulse kicked up. Cold crawled across his skin.

"Fred. Do you even realize what you've done?"

He rubbed his face, pacing now, the weight of the situation pressing like a boot to his chest.

"Javier doesn't clean up messes. He erases them."

He turned, eyes locking onto Fred's clueless smile.

"You didn't bring in help. You opened the gates."

Jack looked around, taking it all in. Then softly, "You opened Javier's box, Fred. And now it only closes with all our blood."

Fred barked a laugh, his gut heaving as he reached for his drink. His fingers fumbled, the reach awkward, clumsy. After a graceless moment, he finally wrapped his hand around the tumbler, leaning forward like a beached walrus.

"All I know," he said, grinning, "is they're coming with enough firepower and skill to handle our problem."

Jack massaged his temples, his voice dropping slow and dangerous.

"You're not handling it, Fred. You just subcontracted our entire authority to mercs."

"This is how operations spiral."

Fred scoffed, waving him off.

"As long as they can't pin a badge on their chest or sit behind a desk, they still need us."

Jack's pulse thundered in his ears. His glare could've shattered the window.

"Fuck you, Fred!"

He snatched his glass and hurled it against the wall.

It exploded on impact.

Shards rained down as Jack stormed out and slammed the door behind him.

The echo lingered.

And just like that. Fred was alone.

And the grin faded.

He stared at the glass on the floor, at the wet splash of whiskey bleeding into the carpet.

The smell of liquor and bad decisions clung to the air.

For the first time, doubt crept in.

His fingers trembled as he reached for his phone.

He dialed. A familiar number.

Two rings.

"Don't speak," Fred rasped. "I'll explain when I see you. Stay longer on your trip. No credit cards. Just cash. Don't come home. Not yet. Things are about to go sideways."

She hesitated.

"Fred..."

Click.

He hung up.

The mountains still stood.

The river still flowed.

But Fred's world?

It was about to burn.

Chapter Twenty-Seven

Downward Facing Goodbye

Bryce crouched at the forest's edge, scanning the quaint suburban development through his binoculars. The two-story townhouses, with their manicured lawns, stood in stark contrast to the rugged wilderness behind him.

Despite the peaceful appearance, Bryce remained vigilant, searching for any signs of danger or inquisitive neighbors.

He saw movement through a second-story window. A woman. Her movements were sharp and precise as she transitioned into a warrior's yoga pose.

Bryce narrowed his eyes.

Her form was tense. Not the kind of tension that came from stretching. This was readiness. Like she was preparing for a fight, not relaxation.

Could this be Taylor-May?

Bryce pulled out his phone, checking the picture he took back at the cabin. It was her.

He exhaled sharply.

"Great. Like mother, like daughter."

A garage door rumbled open in the neighboring house. A car backed out slowly.

Bryce knew this was his only window.

Stashing his binoculars and phone, he darted from the treeline. His closest approach had been pre-planned minimal exposure.

At the back door, he tested the handle locked. His eyes scanned the frame for contact sensors. Nothing.

Good. No security system.

His gaze dropped to the ground, searching.

There. A misplaced rock.

He picked it up casually, like he belonged.

Underneath: a key.

With quick precision, he unlocked the door and slipped inside as casually as if he lived there.

Inside, silence.

Bryce moved carefully, scanning and memorizing the layout.

Then a woman screamed.

"Come on, you bitch! Stop your fucking smiling and finish this fucking hell!"

Bryce froze.

Gun up. Muscles taut.

He ascended the stairs in controlled movements.

At the top, he found the source: a screen flickering with a yoga instructor guiding a calm session.

Okay, and breathe into this position, letting all your stress float away with the good pain you are feeling.

Taylor-May barked at the screen, "Fuck you, bitch. If you were here, I'd fish-hook you and make you eat my shit."

Bryce blinked.

Jesus Christ. She's got a mouth on her.

Taylor-May stood in warrior pose, with her back to him, focused.

Bryce set his gun behind the kitchen island, planning how to start the conversation.

He saw nothing easy. Searching the room one last time, he made his approach.

One clean motion.

He locked her arms, gripping her far wrist and pinning it across her body. His other arm wrapped tight around her mouth and neck, immobilizing her.

She tensed, solid as steel.

Then...

She relaxed.

She knew.

She recognized the control.

Bryce released her mouth, keeping her wrist locked as he pulled out his phone. He tapped the screen. Held it in front of her face.

Janice's face filled the screen, red, tear-swollen eyes locked on the camera. A translucent triangle hovered at the center.

The video waited.

Bryce released her wrist and stepped back, feet staggered, hands loose but ready.

Just in time.

She spun.

Muay Thai elbow.

Bryce rolled with it, dodging most of the hit. Still, her fingernail raked his nose, drawing a thin, immediate line of blood.

"Shit. Really?"

He stepped back, fists clenched, every nerve screaming to strike. But he didn't.

Taylor-May squared up.

Stance perfect.

The yoga instructor droned in the background, oblivious to the standoff.

Okay, now breathe and feel your heartbeat with the rhythm of the life you want. You should be in complete peace now.

Bryce wiped the blood from his nose, staring her down.

Something in her eyes was sharp, wild. He expected resistance, but not like this.

"You think rolling up on me like some back-alley mugger is the move?" she snapped, breathing hard.

Bryce wiped his nose again, nostrils flaring as he leveled an icy stare.

His voice dropped low, edged with steel.

"Turn the yoga shit off. Listen to what your mom has to say."

Taylor-May's chest heaved, adrenaline still coursing through her. She didn't move, her fists still half-clenched, her entire body coiled with fight-or-flight tension.

Bryce held up the phone.

"I don't want to be here," he muttered. "I have to be here. So please listen. You've burned through the last of my patience."

Then, to his own surprise, he huffed a dry chuckle and wiped his bleeding nose with his sleeve.

"Shit. That hurt."

Her lips pressed into a hard line. Jaw twitching.

Then finally her eyes flicked to the phone.

With a sharp inhale, she grabbed the remote and switched off the TV.

Silence.

Bryce didn't look away. Didn't soften his stance.

Still breathing hard, she dropped onto the couch, shaking her head.

Like none of it was real.

Then, hesitantly, she hit play.

Janice's face filled the screen.

Baby.

Her voice cracked immediately, her face streaked with dried tears.

Bryce is here to help. He saved my life, honey.

Taylor-May's fingers dug into the couch cushion, but she didn't speak.

He tried to save your dad's, too.

A sharp, shaky breath escaped Taylor-May. Her whole body went rigid.

I'm sorry you have to hear about it this way, Janice whispered. *I'm sorry, baby. But you need to leave with him now.*

Janice's expression hardened, her grief twisting into fury.

Jed and the cartel killed your dad. We can't trust a single goddamn soul in this town, not the sheriff, not the deputies. No one. Come home now, baby. We're done here. Fuck this town and fuck them all.

Her voice wavered, just for a second.

You're all I have now, she whispered. *I need you home.*

A long silence. Janice looks off the screen.

That's all I got. Bring my baby home, Bryce.

The video ended.

Taylor-May sat frozen.

A single tear slipped down her cheek. No sob. No collapse.

Just a stare, locked on Bryce.

He was still wiping his nose with his sleeve, dabbing at the thin line of blood trailing down his lip from his nose. Like none of this rattled him.

Taylor-May launched from the couch, pacing the living room like a restless predator. Her hands clenched, then unclenched.

"I have to wait for that piece of shit to come home!"

Bryce's expression didn't change, but his shoulders squared slightly.

"I don't care what my mom says. I need to hear it from him," she snapped. "I was gonna marry that fucker. Eventually turn him over to the Feds. But shit. I was locked in this damn town. Fucking cartel."

Bryce nodded slowly, thinking. Processing.

Then he said it.

"Does he know you're an informant for the FBI?"

Taylor-May froze mid-step.

She turned her head toward him. Her face unreadable.

"How do you know that?"

Bryce exhaled through his nose, shaking his head.

"What's his name?"

She blinked.

"What?"

Bryce's gaze didn't waver. "What's your boyfriend's name?"

Taylor-May swallowed hard. Her breathing slowed. Her voice dropped to almost a whisper.

"Jed."

Bryce's world tilted. The name hit like a hammer to the ribs.

"No. No fucking way. That guy?"

He forced himself to breathe. To keep his face blank.

"He was the one interrogating your dad at the grow shack," Bryce said, voice low. "He's the one who beat him while he was tied up with a stab wound from Jax bleeding him out." He shook his head as the pieces clicked together. "He threw your dad in a dog cage. That's your boyfriend, your fiance?"

Another tear traced down Taylor-May's cheek, but still she didn't break. Her nostrils flared. She inhaled slow and deep through her nose, locking herself back into control.

"He was my boyfriend," she corrected sharply. "It was survival. Not love."

She turned away, gathering herself. When she faced him again, her eyes were clear. Focused.

"I have to hear him say it," she said, voice steel. "Then we leave. Non-negotiable."

Bryce stared.

She squared her shoulders, standing tall in the center of the room.

Then the garage door rumbled open downstairs.

Bryce's fists curled. He already knew how this would go.

"No time for negotiation. You win," he said, already moving. He snatched his gun from the floor and took his phone back from her hand. "Ask him. Quickly. Pack while you're talking."

Taylor-May nodded, but instead of packing, she started tidying. Straightening a throw pillow. Rearranging mail.

Bryce clocked the hesitation, jaw tightening. He tapped his watch, motioning for her to stay sharp.

She waved him off, wiping her face with the back of her hand.

Bryce slipped into the next room, leaving the door cracked just enough.

Thud. Thud. Thud.

Jed's boots slammed against the stairs like a giant in *Jack and the Beanstalk*. Each step groaned under his weight, his broad shoulders thumping the walls as he climbed.

A lazy drawl echoed up the stairwell.

"Hey baby! I'm home! You cook me somethin' good? I'm starvin'!"

Bryce peeked through the door, shooting Taylor-May a look.

This guy? Seriously?

She gave the smallest shrug, brushing him off like nothing was wrong.

Bryce closed the door again, leaving a sliver open.

Jed stomped into the kitchen and dropped a six-pack on the counter like he barely cared to hold it. Then he looked up.

Taylor-May stood in the living room. Frozen. Ready.

Oblivious, he yanked open the oven and slammed it shut when he found nothing inside. A pan clattered to the floor as he checked the stove, muttering curses. At the fridge, he grabbed a beer and popped the tab off with his teeth.

The whole routine felt rehearsed, like a mantra he repeated every time he came home.

Bryce crouched lower in the shadows, watching it all unfold like a twisted live-action *A Streetcar Named Desire*. He suppressed a laugh. He'd hated that movie in high school. The lead reminded him too much of his father.

Now, staring at Jed as he barked orders and gulped his beer, the resemblance was eerie.

Jed belched, scratched his ass, and ripped a fart.

Bryce winced. Full stereotype bingo.

If this were a sitcom, the tri-state audience would be applauding.

Jed's voice boomed through the house.

"Hey, Taylor, where's dinner? I'm starving!"

Two gulps later, the beer was gone. He crushed the can, then tossed it into the fridge and grabbed another.

Two more gulps. Gone. He crushed the can and, rather than throwing it in the trash, he tossed it back into the fridge before reaching for another.

Then he noticed Taylor-May staring.

His brows furrowed. "What's your problem? I don't get a kiss?"

He scanned her body, leering. "I like it when you wear tight things."

Taylor-May's face twisted with disgust.

Then she exploded.

"Hey, Jed, you fuck! I just heard my dad's dead!"

Jed blinked, slightly sobered. "Who told you?"

Taylor-May reeled. "What?"

Jed's expression shifted, his drunken haze evaporating.

"How the hell did you find out? Your mom? Where the fuck is she?"

He took a step closer, his voice rougher now. "Damn it, baby, I'm tryin' to protect you, but you need to tell me, right fucking now, where she is."

Taylor-May folded her arms, standing her ground.

"You knew? Does the whole town fucking know? I'm the last one to find out? Jed Jenkins, did you do it? Did you kill my dad?"

Jed's face paled. He stepped back slightly, trying to calculate his next move.

"Now, look," he said, suddenly calm. "I didn't kill him, but he was talking to the feds, Taylor. I'm sorry, baby, but we're in this shit deep."

He took another step toward her, gentler this time, like a man trying to corral a spooked horse.

"I had to fight to keep them from getting you."

Taylor-May looked at him like she was about to kill him.

"What about my mom?"

Jed turned away, already searching for another beer.

"We couldn't find her. We think the guy who killed your dad got her, too."

Taylor-May's fists clenched.

Jed cracked another beer, sipping like nothing mattered.

That was it.

She snatched the can, chugged it, locked eyes and whipped it at his head, following with a right cross that landed clean.

The half-drunk beer exploded across the floor.

Jed looked more pissed about the beer than the punch.

"Jed, you fucking killed my dad..."

Tears welled in her eyes.

"I hate you."

Jed wiped his lip, checking for blood. Nothing. He sneered.

Then, without hesitation, he backhanded her across the face, sending her sprawling to the floor.

Taylor-May lay stunned, blood trickling from her split lip.

Jed loomed over her, his anger sobering him up.

"I didn't want to do it, dammit," he muttered.

Then he reached behind his back and pulled a handgun, leveling it at her face.

Bryce moved.

Before Jed could react, the butt of Bryce's gun came down hard on the back of his head.

Jed crumpled with a heavy thud.

Bryce disarmed him, rolled him onto his stomach, and zip-tied his wrists and ankles in one smooth, practiced motion.

Taylor-May stared, still in shock. It had all happened too fast.

Bryce barely looked at her, expression cold, unreadable. He was already thinking ahead.

"We need to leave. Now. Does he have any weapons worth bringing?"

She didn't move. Just flicked her eyes between Bryce and the unconscious body on the floor.

Bryce clocked the hesitation. That was bad.

He sighed and dropped his voice into a terrible Schwarzenegger growl.

"Come with me if you want to live."

Taylor-May blinked, frowning. "What?"

Bryce rubbed the back of his neck. "Shit. That was the moment, and you're telling me you've never seen *Terminator*?"

"No, I mean yeah, I have. It was just... a bad impression."

"Wow." He pulled her to her feet. "Tough crowd."

He bent to check Jed's pistol, ejected the mag, and cleared the chamber. "Does he have more weapons?"

Taylor-May nodded, finally snapping back to reality.

Bryce studied her for a beat, then nudged her toward the hall. "Then pack. We need to go."

She didn't argue. Just turned and walked.

"Follow me, Terminator."

As she passed Jed, she kicked him in the face. Hard.

"Fucker."

Blood sprayed from his nose. Bryce smirked.

Damn. Solid kick.

He followed her into the bedroom, door open, line of sight locked on the unconscious giant still snoring on the floor.

Taylor-May yanked open the closet.

A full arsenal stared back at them: guns, ammo, tactical gear stacked like a militia startup kit.

Bryce raised an eyebrow. "I love rednecks."

Taylor-May scowled at the weapons.

"I wanted a closet for my clothes. He wanted this. Guess who won."

Bryce nodded at the armory. "Healthy compromise."

She wiped her lip, muttering, "That fucker," then squared her shoulders.

"We're taking his truck. It has a camper shell. Easier to stash this shit. Also? I need a shower."

Bryce shook his head. "We don't have time."

Taylor-May sniffed her armpit, grimaced, and shot him a look. "I smell like swamp ass and rage. Deal with this, I'm showering."

Before he could argue, she grabbed a duffel, tossed in some clothes, and disappeared into the bathroom. The door slammed.

Bryce exhaled and turned to the weapons. "Fine. I'll play personal shopper."

He stacked cases on the bed and flipped one open. "Oh, hello, M24. What do we have here?"

He lifted the sniper rifle, running a hand along the Leupold Mark 4 scope and the AN/PVS-27 NV clip-on.

"Thank you, night vision."

Then he found it, tucked in a hard-shell case near the back.

Bryce unlatched it, opened the lid. "Oh... shit."

Inside: a pristine set of PVS-31A dual-tube NVGs. White phosphor. Auto-gated. Custom-cut foam. Not cheap. Not civilian. Government-grade.

Bryce turned them over in his hands, admiring the craftsmanship. "Now we're talking."

This wasn't just expensive. It was next-level.

His mind ran through a dozen questions.

Where the hell did Jed get these? Military theft? Cartel channels? Or was he just a dumbass who didn't know what he had?

He clicked them on, flawless clarity.

Shit. These would help a lot.

Bryce smirked. "Alright, Jed. You're officially the most helpful person I've ever robbed."

He strapped the NVGs onto his head, flipped them up for later use, and moved on.

Popped open another Pelican case. "TRG-42, same scope, same night vision. Now this," he whistled, "is why walk-in closets shouldn't store clothes."

A SIG Sauer P226 Extreme sat in a thigh holster, perfectly oiled and loaded with an extended mag. It would do in a pinch, but he couldn't wait to get back to his Glock 17.

Bryce opened another drawer, five extra magazines. All 9x19mm Hydra-Shoks.

He glanced toward Jed, still face-down on the carpet, bleeding and snoring into the rug.

"Looks like we're getting a refund on your dowry, Jed."

Bryce walked over and nudged him with his boot. No response. "Do you even have savings, or was this your retirement plan?"

Still snoring.

"Thanks for leaving the safe open. Very considerate."

Back in the closet, he strapped on a Kevlar vest, grabbed two more, and tossed them onto the bed. He adjusted his own, slipped in extra SIG mags, then stepped out again, this time holding a fully loaded HK416 with three extra mags.

"Well, this is exactly what I needed," he muttered, slinging it over his shoulder. "But you really shouldn't have these, young man."

No time to sort through the rest.

Guess we'll take everything."

He hauled three cases and two ammo boxes downstairs, loading the truck with weapons, gear, and supplies.

Sweat beading down his temple, he wiped it and surveyed the haul. His eyes landed on some camo gear hanging near the back wall.

He grinned. "I really do love rednecks."

Ghillie suit. Camo jacket. Three extra-large tarps into the truck.

Then he spotted it a full propane tank.

Gave it a shake.

Still full.

He loaded it next, followed by a truck battery and a space heater.

By the time he finished, everything was squared away. Neat. Efficient.

Then the clomp, clomp, clomp of Taylor-May came down the stairs.

Wearing a pink camo jacket.

Bryce blinked. "What are you wearing? We're not going to the mall."

She shot him a look. "You really trying to police my outfit?"

He grabbed her duffel bag, eyeing the bright pink stripe. "You got anything less... pink?"

Taylor-May glanced down like she was just noticing. "Yeah."

She peeled off the jacket, revealing a base-layer camo shirt.

With another pink stripe across the chest.

Bryce's expression flattened.

"What?" she snapped.

"Not saying take it off," he muttered. "Just... do you have black?"

"In my bag."

Bryce waited. She didn't move.

He sighed, rubbing his temples. "Put it on. Please. If we're getting shot at, I'd rather you not be a walking target."

Taylor-May crossed her arms. "You calling me fat?"

Bryce blinked. "I've known you thirty minutes, and we're already here?"

She rolled her eyes and grabbed a plain hunting jacket from the rack.

"Sorry I pick fights so I don't have to talk about my emotions."

She glanced up at a high shelf. "Can you get that for me? I'll change."

Bryce grabbed the box filled with beakers, cylinders, and tubes.

Taylor-May smiled. Not joy. Satisfaction.

"Thanks," she said, already walking toward the kitchen.

"Be ready in ten minutes," she called over her shoulder.

"I'm ready now," Bryce muttered.

He yelled after her, "Leave your phone!"

Taylor-May turned, annoyed. "Seriously? I just paid it off."

She vanished into the kitchen.

Bryce shook his head. "Strange priorities."

Back in the garage, he resumed his sweep.

Found a compound bow, a bullet press, a full bucket of gunpowder.

That'd be useful.

He loaded it into the truck, shut the tailgate, then pulled out his map.

In the driver's seat, he flipped open his compass, double-checked the route.

Ten minutes.

He checked his watch. Again.

Then—thud-thud-thud.

Taylor-May came sprinting down the stairs, hair still damp, slamming the garage door button as she hopped into the passenger seat.

"Hurry up, Bryce Rath!"

Bryce froze halfway through, locking the tailgate.

She used his full name.

He exhaled, shook his head, climbed into the driver's seat, and turned the key.

The diesel engine roared to life.

A female country ballad poured through the speakers.

Where did all the real men go? I always chose the one who punched first. I liked it... until I was on the receiving end.

What are we doing—raising boys to think they can hit women?

Bryce grimaced and snapped the radio off.

Too close.

Beside him, Taylor-May wrestled with her seatbelt, yanking too fast and locking it up.

Again.

Her legs bounced. Nervous energy rolled off her in waves.

She was dressed right, black base layer under a camo jacket, but she wasn't settled. Not even close. Her fingers trembled as she fumbled with the garage door opener.

She kept glancing at the rearview mirror. Couldn't stop.

Bryce sighed, reached over, and pulled her seatbelt into place.

Click.

The garage door creaked open.

"Hurry the fuck up," she muttered, breath catching. "But don't speed away."

Bryce arched a brow but obeyed, easing the truck out onto the street.

Calm. Controlled.

Her hands still trembled.

"That fucker. Fuck him." Her voice cracked, but the rage beneath it was nuclear.

Bryce checked the mirrors. Kept scanning.

He looked back when he saw smoke curling from the house.

The garage door rolled shut behind them.

His grip tightened on the wheel. "Did you just light the house on fire?"

Taylor-May shrugged. Flat. Blank. "Kinda."

He stared at her, waiting.

She licked the blood from her lip, eyes forward.

Cold. Detached.

"He used to cook meth," she said, voice deadpan. "So I made it look like he was doing it again. Passed out. That piece of shit was waking up when I got there, so I knocked him out again. Staged it to look like an accident."

She turned her head, studying his reaction.

Bryce said nothing. He sped up, putting as much distance between them and the house as he could without drawing attention.

She kept going.

"I picked him up and dropped him, let his head hit the kitchen island. Left enough evidence to sell it. Then I cut his restraints."

Finally, she smirked.

The kind of smirk that came after justice. And maybe a little gasoline. "Thanks, CSI: Las Vegas."

Bryce shook his head and turned onto the main road, speeding up. The house shrank in the rearview mirror, but the smoke kept rising.

Then came the blast. The explosion lit up the mirror. A fireball swallowed the house.

Bryce exhaled. "You're your mom's daughter."

Taylor-May didn't flinch.

Just watched the flames grow in the side mirror.

Another explosion rocked the street.

She jumped.

Voice flat now. Almost numb. "I loved that house."

Bryce kept driving. Eyes forward.

Sirens.

Distant, but growing louder.

A car passed in the opposite lane. Civilian. Not a cop.

Bryce's face stayed neutral. Hands steady on the wheel.

"I hope no one else gets hurt," he muttered.

Taylor-May shook her head, eyes fixed outside.
"Every house near us is empty." Her voice dipped to a whisper. "I watched all my friends leave years ago."

Her fingers clenched.
"This town's a zombie. The cartel runs everything. It's just a shell. Corruption and destruction."

Her shoulders shook.

Her hands curled tighter.

"Fuck this town."

She touched her lip. Wiped away the blood.

Then she finally let herself cry.

Chapter Twenty-Eight

Family Reunion

A car passed in the opposite direction as Bryce pulled the truck over and killed the engine. He watched the vehicle disappear into the distance, checking the mirrors as he reached for a roll of duct tape. With a flick of his wrist, he shut off the headlights and disabled the dome lights inside the cab.

Taylor-May blinked. "What are you doing?"

Bryce didn't answer right away, just tore another strip of duct tape.

"Covering the taillights," he said flatly. "No reason to make it easy for anyone to follow."

Relief softened her features, and she gave a small nod. Without another word, Bryce stepped out, closing the door behind him.

Taylor-May sat rigid, her fingers gripping her seatbelt. Her heart pounded, the weight of everything pressing in. The cab felt suffocating. She forced herself to take slow breaths, trying to steady her racing mind.

Outside, Bryce worked fast, every move calculated, taping over the brake lights. His face flushed in flashes of red, then vanished back into shadow. Taylor-May watched him work, the flickering light making him look almost otherworldly. When he finally climbed back inside, he turned down the dashboard dials, dimming all the interior lights.

"Don't open the glove box or anything that lights up unless I say so," Bryce instructed.

A single tear rolled down Taylor-May's cheek as she nodded. "Yeah. Okay."

Bryce exhaled, watching her for a moment. "We'll get through this together. You hear me?"

Taylor-May swallowed hard, forcing a sad smile. "Okay."

With a final twist of the dial, complete darkness engulfed them. Bryce slipped on his night-vision goggles, a ghostly green hue illuminating his face as he adjusted the googles. He shifted the truck into four-wheel drive, and they crawled forward, swallowed by the dense, blackened forest.

Taylor-May gripped the stabilizing bar as the truck jostled over rocks and branches, the terrain unforgiving. The eerie quiet was punctuated only by the occasional snap of a tree limb against the frame. Her reflection in the darkened window stared back, hollow-eyed, unrecognizable.

Her voice wavered. "Why are you doing this?"

Bryce, his gaze fixed ahead, maneuvered the truck over a steep incline. "I don't want anyone to see us driving to the cabin."

Taylor-May shook her head. "No, I mean... why help us? Why are you doing all of this?"

A heavy silence settled between them, stretching over the sound of crunching rocks and dirt beneath the tires.

Bryce's voice was quiet. Almost distant. "I couldn't let them do that to your dad."

She stared, waiting, but he didn't elaborate.

A low branch scraped the window. She flinched. Clenched her jaw, forcing herself to hold it together.

Bryce adjusted the wheel, navigating a steep drop-off. "Look," he said, "I have a contact in the CIA who can get you into witness protection. I don't trust your FBI handler."

Taylor-May exhaled sharply. "Yeah. Me neither."

Tears welled, trailing down her cheeks. "Why does it always come to this?" she whispered. "I mean... I just did it, but why does it always have to end in fucking blood?" Her voice cracked. "He's gone. I killed him."

Bryce tightened his grip on the wheel as a rock clanked against the undercarriage.

"You didn't have a choice," he said. "He was never going to let either of you go. You survived. That's all that matters now."

Taylor-May buried her face in her hands, her body shaking.

Bryce didn't look at her, eyes locked on the path ahead. "We're almost there."

Lifting his night-vision goggles, Bryce pulled out a burner phone. His fingers moved swiftly before he hit send.

"I told your mom I'd text when we were ten minutes out."

Taylor-May sniffled, wiping at her face. She let out a hollow laugh. "I did like your joke, you know." She did a terrible Arnold impression. "Get to the chopper! AHHH!"

Bryce smirked.

Taylor-May looked over, a flicker of a smile tugging at her lips. "Sorry I hit you."

Bryce chuckled. "That was a great move. I was proud of you when you did that. And how you handled everything."

She blinked, startled by the words. She wasn't used to compliments.

Bryce put the truck in low gear, the engine growling as they crested a final hill.

"Thank you," Taylor-May said quietly. "My dad taught me to fight. To never be helpless."

She turned toward the window, her sobs now silent. The truck lurched, bouncing over a hidden boulder and slamming her into the doorframe. A sharp yelp escaped before she could stop it.

Bryce slowed the truck, maneuvering the final stretch. "Okay. We're almost there."

He eased the truck into a concealed spot near the cabin, tucking it beneath thick tree cover. The forest swallowed them in silence. Only the rumble of the engine gave away their position.

Lifting his night-vision goggles, he turned to Taylor-May. The faint green glow cast eerie shadows over her tear-streaked face.

"Get in the driver's seat," he said. "Keep the truck running. I'll check the house and make sure your mom's safe."

She nodded, but hesitation flickered across her face. Bryce could see it, the exhaustion, the weight of everything crashing down now that the adrenaline had burned off.

He leaned in. "Listen to me. If I don't flash my light three times in sixty seconds, you drive. Go to the next state. Find help. Got it?"

Taylor-May swallowed hard. "Why don't we just leave now?"

Bryce shook his head. He leveled his voice.

"They'll be on us before we know it. This is our shot to end it now, before they regroup. We flip their comfort zone into a kill box. That's how we seize control."

She exhaled sharply, but didn't argue.

Bryce reached for his rifle and opened the door.

Taylor-May grabbed his arm. "Thank you."

He met her gaze, nodded once, then slipped out into the night.

The forest was still. Too still.

He moved like a shadow, rifle low, scanning the tree line as he approached the cabin. At the doorstep, he knocked three times, controlled, deliberate.

A gruff voice came from the other side. "That you?"

Bryce kept his eyes on the trees. "Yeah. Don't fucking shoot me."

A smoker's cough rasped through the door. A second later, the scent of stale cigarette smoke leaked through the cracks.

"Clear," Janice muttered.

Bryce lifted his goggles as the door creaked open.

The dim red glow from the lanterns inside mixed with curling cigarette smoke, casting flickering shadows across the walls. It felt like stepping into a bad Halloween attraction.

And Bryce had a feeling the nightmare was just beginning.

Janice stood in the center of the room, barefoot, her stained hoodie hanging loosely over her frame. A half-burnt cigarette dangled between two fingers, the ash seconds from falling. Her eyes were sharp despite the lines of exhaustion.

Bryce grinned. "Jesus, do you have any cigarettes left?"

Janice barked out a rough laugh. "Shut up and get her." She slipped on her boots.

Bryce turned back toward the truck and clicked his red flashlight three times.

A moment later, Taylor-May flung the door open and sprinted past him, straight into her mother's arms.

Bryce watched them embrace, the red lantern glow painting their silhouettes against the trees. Smoke curled from Janice's cigarette, drifting into the cold air like an extension of her breath.

He muttered, "At least she listened to me."

After turning off the truck, he opened the tailgate, and began unloading gear, rifle slung over his shoulder. When he glanced back, they were still locked in their embrace, their whispered words lost in the quiet.

He sighed. "Ladies."

Both turned, wiping their eyes.

"Oh, shit, sorry, Bryce." Janice sniffed, clearing her throat. "Come on, honey, let's help."

Still holding hands, they walked toward the truck.

As Bryce hauled another bag inside, Janice suddenly stopped, then turned back.

Before he could react, she hugged him, hard.

Bryce stiffened. His arms hovered for a moment, unsure of what to do. Then, after a beat, he gave in and returned the hug, firm, but brief.

"Thank you, Bryce."

Her voice cracked. She pulled away, shaking her head. "Shit, I haven't cried this much, ever."

She turned back to Taylor-May, grabbing her hand again like she couldn't bear to let go.

Bryce watched for a long moment, caught off guard by the raw mother-daughter bond unfolding in front of him.

And for a brief second, something stirred in his chest, something he hadn't felt in a long, long time.

He shut it down.

Not now, Karma. Stay focused.

Janice and Taylor-May struggled to lift one of the Pelican cases. Bryce had already arranged everything inside, the weapons, tactical gear, and supplies lined up in perfect order.

Pulling out a camo net, tarp, and rope, Bryce turned toward the front door.

Taylor-May wiped sweat from her brow. "What can we do now?"

"If you two want to make dinner and spend some time together, I'll take care of the truck," Bryce said, not looking up.

Janice reappeared from the kitchen, tossing him a bottle of water. He caught it midair and nodded.

Taylor-May hesitated. "Wait... dinner?"

Bryce took a swig. "Yeah. You still gotta eat."

Taylor-May snorted. "Right. Because this is so normal."

Bryce clenched the empty bottle, knuckles whitening. He said nothing, just set it on the counter, turned, and walked outside, closing the door behind him.

The air shifted the moment he stepped onto the porch.

The forest was still.

No wind. No rustling leaves. Not even the distant hoot of an owl.

Just dead air, and his own pulse pounding in his ears.

The cabin stood strong among the trees, an island of warmth in a sea of cold isolation.

Inside, soft laughter echoed. A mother and daughter finding a sliver of normal in a life that had never been.

It was inviting.

Safe.

But it wasn't. Not when you were in the war zone. Think. Plan. Move. Keep them safe.

It never was.

Bryce exhaled slow, steady. Forced focus. Secure basecamp. Get to the Jeep. Contact Troy. Get them safe. Simple. Tactical. He could focus on that.

Bryce turned, eyes scanning the cabin's thick timber walls. Inside, the soft clinking of whiskey bottles whispered into the night, a reminder of what they'd almost lost.

It should've felt good. But he didn't allow himself to feel.

His jaw tightened. Not now. Not here.

With a breath, he started moving, boots crunching over gravel. His eyes swept the treeline, the ridgeline, the sky. He mapped angles, read shadows, registered threats. Hands steady. Mind locked in.

Work the problem, Karma.

He secured the truck beneath the tarp and tightened the rope in a trucker's hitch, easy to release in seconds. Climbing into the driver's seat, Bryce gripped the wheel. His fingers flexed over the leather. Then let go.

He shook out his hands, forcing the tension loose. Breathe.

Rubbing his temples, he shut his eyes for just a second. His grip had shaken when he opened the truck door. He hated that.

Refocusing, he ran the mental checklist: Truck covered. Propane tanks staged. Motion sensors in place. The work was done.

Now he had to go back inside the cabin.

He looked around one last time, then exhaled and stepped out of the truck. Every step toward the cabin felt heavier than it should.

At the porch, he hesitated. His hand hovered over the knob. Trembling. Again.

Jaw clenched tight. Not now. Not in front of them.

He took a slow breath, firmed his grip, and turned the handle. The door creaked open.

Heat struck him. Chili simmered on the hot plate, smoke clung to the air, the low cadence of laughter and gentle sobs wrapped in a red glow that now felt softer, tinged with celebration and quiet appreciation, all beneath a veil of reflection.

Too much contrast from the cold silence outside.

He stepped in and locked the door behind him.

He needed an anchor.

Something solid.

So he walked to the table and placed both hands on the maps and gear, his version of prayer.

Out of the corner of his eye, Bryce saw them watching him.

Taylor-May stood by the kitchen counter, whiskey glass in hand. Her lip was still swollen, eyes red from crying.

Janice sat slouched in the worn armchair beside the lantern, exhaling a slow drag of smoke.

They weren't looking for answers. They were waiting for him to make sense of their world and how to survive it.

Taylor-May raised her glass slightly. "Want some Jack?"

Bryce didn't look up. "No alcohol. Not until we're clear."

She let out a slow breath, drained the glass, and set it down.

"Fair."

She grabbed a fresh bottle of water and pressed it into his hand. "You should eat. We made chili."

Bryce took it but didn't move toward the food.

Taylor-May watched him, brow raised. "You don't eat?"

"I eat," he muttered. "When I need to."

Janice scoffed. "Bullshit. You're running on fumes, son."

Bryce finally met her eyes. "I've gone longer on less."

Janice shook her head, exhaling smoke. "Damn military boys. You'd rather starve to death than admit you need something."

Taylor-May nudged the bowl closer. "Just eat the fucking chili, Rambo."

Bryce hesitated.

Then sat.

Grabbed the spoon.

It was hot. Spicy. Simple.

But it was good.

It tasted like something he hadn't let himself have in years.

It tasted like home.

Taylor-May plopped into the chair across from him, watching him eat like some feral animal she'd just rescued.

"See? Not poisoned."

Bryce smirked, taking another bite.

A long moment stretched between them.

Janice leaned back, cigarette resting between her fingers.

"So what's next, soldier boy?"

Bryce swallowed and set the spoon down. "We finish securing this place. Then I head out before sunrise. Gotta reach my Jeep. That's our real way out."

"You're leaving?" Taylor-May's voice tightened.

"Not for long."

"You just got us safe. Now you're bailing?"

"Safe's temporary. We need more than a hideout. We need a plan."

Janice nodded. "And you got backup?"

"I've got people. People I trust more than your FBI handler."

Taylor-May frowned. "Why not trust the FBI?"

Bryce's voice dipped. "Because I've seen what happens when someone inside's dirty."

Janice's gaze sharpened. "And you think they are?"

Bryce nodded. "I think the cartel has people in every branch of law enforcement. Your FBI handler? He was watching, but he wasn't protecting. Your sheriff? Hell, I don't know how many people across the counties, or even states, are compromised. This doesn't feel local anymore."

Taylor-May exhaled sharply, running a hand through her hair. "So what the hell do we do?"

Bryce leaned forward, tapping the map. "We move smart. We set traps. We keep them on the defensive, even when they come to us."

Janice studied him. "You talk like you've done this before."

Bryce met her gaze, expression unreadable. "I have."

The air in the room shifted.

Janice flicked her cigarette into an empty beer can. The sizzle filled the silence.

Then she looked back up at him.

"Well, I like you, Bryce. But I like you better if you keep my daughter breathing."

Bryce locked eyes with her. "That's the plan."

Taylor-May leaned back in her chair, staring at the ceiling. "Fuck, I hope this works."

Bryce exhaled, standing. "It will. Because we don't have another choice."

He checked the window for light leaks, already thinking three moves ahead.

Behind him, Taylor-May watched, her expression unreadable.

He wasn't just a soldier.

He wasn't just running on instinct.

He was something else entirely.

And for the first time in a long time, Taylor-May felt something strange. She felt safe.

Bryce moved to the workbench, grabbing a propane tank.

"There are a few large lakes on the map. We stage the boat on one side, a truck on the other. If it comes to it, it buys us time."

He nodded toward the warped floorboards near the kitchen.

"The hole. We need to finish it."

Taylor-May raised an eyebrow, swirling the whiskey in her glass.

"Well, let me know after you think it over," she teased.

Janice laughed.

Bryce shot them both a flat look.

"Guns. Hole. Boat. Truck."

He turned to Taylor-May. "Before I covered Jed's truck, I checked for a LoJack. Didn't find one, but we move it anyway. No chances."

Taylor-May half-followed, distracted. "Yeah, okay," she mumbled, handing the map to her mom.

Bryce returned to the workbench. He lined up fishing weights, black duct tape, and a camping propane tank.

Carefully, he began attaching weights at measured intervals.

Taylor-May watched him.

"You're not gonna blow up some dumb animal if it wanders through, right?"

Bryce didn't look up. "No. I'll spray enough WD-40. Keeps wildlife away. They hate the smell."

Taylor-May smiled, impressed.

"Thought of everything, huh?"

Bryce shrugged.

"I hope so."

He took a long drink from his water bottle.

His hand trembled slightly.

Taylor-May noticed. She didn't say anything.

He looked at them both.

"No more alcohol. That needs to be your last drink until we're safe."

Janice nodded, no hesitation. Taylor-May looked reluctant. But she didn't argue.

Bryce paused.

Then, finally, he said it.

"I watched your dad die. I couldn't save him."

Silence.

Janice bowed her head, rubbing her temples.

Taylor-May's grip on her glass tightened.

Bryce checked his watch.

The soft beep cut through the room as he silenced it.

He stretched his back, slow and stiff.

"I need sleep before I leave. Don't go near this table. If anything beeps on the fish finder, get me. Quietly."

Taylor-May nodded, her whiskey suddenly forgotten.

"We will."

Janice added, "Yes. Thank you, Bryce."

Bryce nodded once and stepped into the bedroom.

Chapter Twenty-Nine

Sleep

Bryce stepped into the bedroom and sank onto the edge of the bed, rubbing his forehead.

His body ached. Exhaustion pressed against the edges of his mind like a rising tide.

He pulled his handgun from his vest, slid it under the pillow, then lay back and stared at the ceiling.

It had been one thing with Janice—survival under fire, driven by adrenaline and instinct.

But now both of John's girls were under his care.

No backup.

No intel on the enemy.

Too many unknowns.

His mind wouldn't shut down.

Every laugh from the other room twisted the knife.

Because they trusted him.

Because failure wasn't an option.

The mission was clear.

But the weight hit differently now.

He didn't have time to unravel it.

And he couldn't afford to.

A single tear slid down his cheek.

He wiped it away—steady, calm—and shut his eyes.

He thought through his training.

In through the nose for four counts.

Hold. Let it burn through the noise.

Out for six. Slow. Controlled.

Again.

It wasn't just a breath. It was a reset.

Heart rate dropped.

Edges sharpened.

Focus returned.

This was how you stayed alive.

Not by pretending it didn't matter.

But by carrying the weight, then releasing it.

Like a current you step into, then let pass.

He almost laughed.

Maybe that's why he'd been doing so much river fishing.

"Come on, Karma," he whispered. "Breathe. You need sleep. Focus."

A soft knock at the door cut through the quiet.

He sat up, instincts spiking, hand already drifting toward the gun beneath his pillow.

"Yeah. Everything okay?"

The door creaked open. Taylor-May peeked inside.

"Can I come in?"

Bryce blinked, rubbing his temple.

"Um, yeah."

She slipped inside, hugging her arms.

"I need to grab some blankets before you pass out. Don't want you shooting me just because I got cold. That'd kind of defeat the purpose of you saving my life."

Bryce exhaled a tired chuckle, rubbing his forehead.

"Yeah, it does." He gestured vaguely. "Help yourself to whatever you need."

Red lantern light spilled into the room, casting long shadows that danced across the walls.

Taylor-May moved to the closet, yanking open a door, her movements unhurried, yet deliberate.

Bryce watched her for a moment before sinking back onto the pillow, eyes on the ceiling.

Taylor-May turned, blankets piled in her arms, then hesitated. She looked down at him, wanting to say something, but couldn't find the words. She walked to the door, then turned and pulled it almost closed, just enough for the red light to slip through.

She padded across the room and knelt beside his pillow.

"Who's Karma?"

Her voice was soft. Teasing at first.

But when Bryce turned toward her, the crimson light caught his face. Raw. Haunted.

The joke died in her throat.

The answer landed heavier than she expected.

"It was my callsign. Now it's a nickname."

Something in the way he said it pulled her closer.

"Oh... okay."

She shifted, sitting on the edge of the bed.

The weight of the blankets in her lap gave her something to hold on to, something to fidget with as she searched for the right words.

"Look..." She cleared her throat.

"I want you to know we appreciate everything you're doing. And I can see it."

She met his gaze.

"I can see how much you're holding onto, what you've done to get us here. We're not helpless. We're capable. And as much as you're here for us, we're here for you, too."

She reached for his hand, hesitating for just a second before squeezing it.

"Sorry, that was my from-the-heart speech, using the only words I know and, okay, maybe a little bit of Jack. A lot of Jack, actually."

She let out a breathy laugh, shaking her head.

"But what I mean is... don't keep it all bottled up. The weight's always heavier in your head than it is out in the world."

She hesitated, her thumb brushing absently over the back of his hand.

"That's what Dad always told me. Took me a while to appreciate it, but he was always right."

She held back tears, shaking her head.

"That man went through so damn much."

Bryce turned his head, his gaze locking onto hers in the dim glow.

Taylor-May exhaled, her voice quieter now.

"He carried so much on his own. I thought he was invincible. But no one is. Not even him. Not even you."

Bryce swallowed, looking away, but his grip on her hand tightened.

A tear slipped down his cheek.

"It creeps up on you," he murmured. "You take a hundred knockout punches to the chin and keep going. But then, one soft hit lays you out flat. It stacks up... until it all just collapses."

He exhaled sharply.

Taylor-May studied him in the dim glow, then leaned in and pressed a soft kiss to his cheek.

She didn't pull away right away, and Bryce didn't stop her.

Then, without a word, she dropped the blankets in her arms but held onto one. As she went to drape it over him, she hesitated, then slid in beside him as the blanket came down. She eased in close, guided his arm around her waist, and settled quietly against his chest.

For the first time in days, maybe even years, Bryce let himself exhale.

He relaxed into her, melting into the moment.

It felt good. Real. Honest.

"You're not alone, Bryce Rath," she breathed. "Thank you."

They lay there in silence, letting the weight of the night settle between them.

Taylor-May sniffled, her voice a whisper.

"It'll never go away, will it?"

A soft sob escaped as Bryce pulled her in tighter.

Bryce tightened his hold as she gripped his arms like an anchor.

"Taking a life stays with you," he murmured.

Taylor-May shivered.

"I don't feel bad about killing Jed," she said, voice distant. "He was like a deer for survival. Or a bug that shits in your food. But what happened to Dad…"

She turned, staring up at the ceiling, then over at Bryce. "I feel hollow about all of it. I don't feel better after killing him… but I do feel better knowing he can't hurt us, or anyone else, ever again."

Her hand rested on Bryce's chest, fingertips rising and falling with each breath.

She looked into his eyes and felt it, not just a bond. Something more.

He had saved her life.

She had taken one.

And now, in the quiet aftermath, she had more in common with this stranger than with anyone she'd ever known.

It terrified her.

And yet, it settled something inside her, too.

"I'm sorry," she whispered. "Do you want company? I just barged in."

Taylor-May began to shift away, unsure.

But Bryce's grip tightened.

"Stay."

She exhaled and turned back, pressing into his warmth like it was the only thing keeping her together.

Bryce's voice came low and steady, a soft vibration against her back. "Jed was a life. Every life has to matter... or nothing does. And if nothing matters, the world turns to chaos."

Taylor-May opened her eyes.
"You really believe that?"

Bryce hesitated.

"I try to. I have to. But the mind's a bottomless pit. Just when you think you've hit the floor... something passes you on the way down, or you pass it. It's hard to know sometimes."

Taylor-May tilted her head, looking into Bryce's eyes, caught between a smirk and astonishment. "That's some deep shit, Karma."

Bryce let out a tired laugh, shaking his head.

Taylor-May turned to face him. Her expression softened until she saw his smile fade.

His jaw clenched.

"I thought I left this behind," he whispered. "But now I see... everything I've been trained to do—it's the only thing that'll keep you both alive."

His voice dropped heavier.
"The system's broken. Maybe it always was. And everyone thinks they're fighting for the right cause."

He turned, meeting her eyes.
"But fighting for something real? For someone worth it? That feels good. A good I haven't felt in years. A purpose for who I am. What I can do."

He looked away, jaw tight, eyes fixed on some distant memory he didn't want to name. Then he turned back, his gaze steady, unflinching.

There was no judgement in his eyes. Only strength. And honesty. Now they searched hers. Quietly. Carefully.
"How did you even get mixed up with the cartel?"

Taylor-May exhaled slowly, the breath catching in her throat.

She shifted slightly, pressing closer to his warmth like it was the only thing keeping her from floating away.
"Same way you end up in a nightmare." She looked down at his chest, fingers brushing gently over a faint scar beneath his shirt. "You don't walk into it. You slip."

She hadn't thought about it in years. She'd been surviving, not reflecting. Not asking how she got here, only how to keep moving forward.

But now... a distant memory surfaced. Her dad laughing. Her mom smiling. A time before.

It hurt. Maybe that's why she buried it so deep.

She choked a little, trying to get her voice back. "When the logging industry dried up, people needed something to hold on to. Drugs became the new economy. Then the cartel showed up, like flies on rot. Ready to profit off desperation."

Her voice thickened. "We adapted. Survived the only way we knew how. Take what's available and make it work."

She turned back to him, eyes searching. "Do you judge me for getting caught up in this shit?"

Bryce didn't flinch. Didn't look away. And for the first time in a long time, he saw someone he truly understood.

"I understand completely." His voice was low. Steady. "That's how I met Troy."

Taylor-May turned over, inching closer. "Troy?"

"He's my contact in the CIA," Bryce said, his tone shaded with reluctance. "The last person I ever thought I'd call."

Taylor-May bit her lip, watching him closely. "What happened?"

Bryce didn't answer. She saw it, the storm brewing behind his eyes.

"You don't have to tell me," she said softly. "It's okay."

But her presence grounded him. Her warmth. He knew she wouldn't judge him.

So he let it out.

He exhaled, gaze fixed on the ceiling. "I went AWOL after my last tour in Afghanistan."

Taylor-May's brow creased. "What?"

Bryce hesitated. The words tasted like rust. "They called it PTSD. Survivor's guilt. I tried to self-medicate after they cut back my pain meds from surgery and rehab. I started selling pills to get them cheaper... that was just the next step in the spiral."

Taylor-May didn't say a word. She just stayed with him. Still. Listening. Waiting.

"Why?"

Bryce looked at her for a long moment. The weight of it all, the years, the loss, the guilt, pressed down like a slow wave, drowning him.

For the first time in years, he let himself talk.

"I didn't show up for training after they cleared me. I wasn't ready. I was a mess.

Self-medicating, self-destruction, selfish."

He stared at his hands, fingers tracing invisible scars, ones deeper than skin.

"After my team... after everything collapsed around me, and I couldn't stop it, knowing I played a part in it, I was... lost."

His voice was quiet. "They called it friendly fire, but my team was killed."

Taylor-May didn't move. Didn't speak. Her eyes caught the faint red glow from the other room, glassy, unblinking, just her quiet strength beside him, saying more than anything else could.

Janice's snore cut through the silence like a chainsaw.

They both laugh.

Janice's continued muffled snores were the only reminder the world still turned.

She didn't look away.

She moved closer, holding Bryce now. The contact pulled him back from the edge.

Bryce swallowed, his throat tight.

"After I got back, I was never fully back. Part of my soul, my heart, my mind... it died with them. I took a few rounds. Suffered some head trauma..." he let out a bitter chuckle, "Head trauma. That's an understatement."

His voice dropped lower, almost a whisper.

"They gave me painkillers at first, but then the headaches wouldn't stop. It became a cycle—too many, not enough. Body hurts. Mind hurts. Everything hurts."

He exhaled, long and slow.

"I lost my wife. My friends. My family. Thank God we didn't have kids..."

His fingers curled around hers, anchoring himself.

"Ironically, they saved my life when they threw me in the brig."

Taylor-May wiped at her cheek. "How?"

Bryce smiled, shaking his head. A ghost of something that once was.

"Troy."

She blinked.

"Troy?"

"He was part of the JAG team that came after me. The MPs kicked in my door without a warrant. Dumbest thing I ever did, but in the end? Best thing that could've happened."

Taylor-May arched a brow, a small smile tugging at her lips. "Talk about karma."

Bryce smirked, the first real flicker of light in his eyes.

"Something like that."

She held his gaze, her expression warm, understanding, and strong.
"So, Troy?"

Bryce shifted on the cot, exhaustion settling deep into his bones.

"He was in charge. He was honest, but he didn't let me slack. He was good at his job. I respected him, even when he was coming after me. He wasn't wrong."

"I was."

The words felt heavy. Honest. Final.

Bryce exhaled.
"But I got sober. Then I got out. Did a few private sector jobs. Made good money. But I was over it."

His voice softened.
"When I saw Troy had joined the CIA, I wasn't surprised. He was damn good at his job. It was good to see him using his skills to go after people trying to destroy our country."

Taylor-May didn't speak right away.

She studied him through the shadows.
"I'm glad they busted you."

Bryce turned his head toward her.

For a long moment, they just stared at each other.
"Me too," he whispered.

Taylor-May saw how tired he was.

She wanted to stay, but knew it would be selfish.

He needed sleep. And they needed him rested.

Her hand touched his face.
"Good night, Karma. Thank you for talking to me."

Taylor-May slowly pulled herself up.
She leaned down, kissed his forehead, picked up the blankets, and slipped out of the room, closing the door behind her.

Bryce exhaled and laid his head back down. He ran a hand over his tired face, let out a quiet laugh, and then rolled over.

And let sleep take him.

Chapter Thirty

The Teacher

The colossal silhouette of Javier's yacht loomed overhead, its towering frame casting a long shadow across the dock where Miguel sat, his legs dangling over the edge. The water beneath him lapped gently against the wooden planks, a stark contrast to the firestorm waiting for him beyond this fleeting moment of peace.

Miguel cast his line without thinking, away from the hull, into the murk. This was the only thing that ever brought him peace. And right now, he needed it more than ever.

Soft footsteps on the dock pulled Miguel's attention. A young boy approached, wide-eyed, flickering with a mix of curiosity and hesitation as he watched Miguel reel in the lure with practiced ease.

Miguel offered a kind smile. After a gentle pause, he extended the fishing rod. The boy hesitated, then reached out with both hands, his face lighting up as he took the handle. His excitement was infectious, stirring something deep within Miguel, a joy he hadn't felt in years.

Miguel guided the boy's small hands over his own, teaching him how to flick his wrist just right. The first cast barely cleared the dock, landing with an unimpressive splash, but the boy beamed with pride all the same.

A woman approached, cradling a sleeping baby in her arms. Miguel recognized her from earlier. He'd seen her walking near Javier's estate. Her graceful movements and composed expression now softened with warmth as she watched her son.

She settled beside him, her shoulder brushing his as she adjusted the baby.

"Thank you for this," she said softly, her voice riding the gentle breeze. "It's been a long time since he's had a chance to just be a kid."

Miguel waved off her gratitude, though his throat tightened at the sincerity in her voice. "Thank you," he said. "I'd forgotten how children's laughter can lighten everything. Thank you for reminding me and for letting me share a moment in your lives."

The boy let out a triumphant cheer, pulling up his catch. Nothing but a tangled mess of seaweed. He groaned in exaggerated disappointment before dissolving into laughter. The woman joined in, shaking her head affectionately.

For a moment, Miguel allowed himself to forget.

The high sun chased away the shadows of Javier's ship, casting a golden shimmer across the water. The boy's laughter echoed off the dock, mingling with the rhythm of the tide. It was so achingly familiar, so much like the days he'd spent with his own son, teaching him the art of patience and precision in fishing.

But then heavy boots thudded against the dock.

Miguel knew before he turned.

A squad of Javier's guards approached, their movements sharp, their eyes cold. The air shifted. The warmth evaporated as quickly as it had come.

Miguel exhaled and rose to his feet.

"Miguel." One of the guards motioned for him to follow. No explanation. None was needed.

He turned back to the woman and her children, his gaze lingering, trying to hold on to the moment just a little longer. The boy now held the fishing rod, his earlier joy dimmed by the presence of the men. The woman, though silent, radiated understanding and something else.

Pity.

Miguel forced a smile for the boy's sake. "Keep practicing. Next time, you'll catch something real."

The boy nodded, confused but listening.

Miguel turned and walked away.

Each step up the hill felt heavier, as if the weight of his past and the inevitability of what came next conspired to drag him back down. He resisted the urge to glance over his shoulder.

But he could feel their eyes following, burning into his back.

And he knew, with muted certainty, that he was leaving behind something precious.

A fleeting moment of peace that already felt like a distant dream.

But one he would work hard to remember.

Chapter Thirty-One

Put Some Pants On!

The morning sun pierced through the tiny gaps in the boarded-up windows, fractured beams scattering across the dim room like broken glass. Bryce sat motionless at the rustic table, a ghost in a ghillie suit, his face streaked in mottled green and brown. Before him lay the disassembled pieces of a TRG-42 sniper rifle and an HK MP7—silent declarations of the day's grim intentions.

The house was still wrapped in sleep, but Bryce moved with precision. His hands, steady and deliberate, worked through the rifle's components, cleaning, oiling, reassembling. One magazine of .338 Lapua clicked into place. Three more slipped into the Kevlar vest beneath his ghillie suit.

Then came the MP7. Same ritual. Clean, check, load. His SIG Sauer sidearm followed, drawn, inspected, holstered. He looked forward to getting his Glock back, but this will do.

Each motion was mechanical. Muscle memory. Discipline forged in fire.

With weapons prepped, he packed only what mattered: water, binoculars, protein bars, an extra box of ammo. All placed with the precision of a surgeon into his rugged pack. He stretched his stiff muscles, rolled his shoulders, then moved into the kitchen, pouring himself another cup of coffee as his eyes swept across the table of maps and gear.

The map was marked Xs and Os in a coded language only he understood. A blueprint of escape and war.

He took a bite of a power bar just as movement stirred in the rest of the house. Janice and Taylor-May, groggy and slow, shuffled from their makeshift beds. The last remnants of sleep faded, replaced by the cold weight of reality.

The sound of water trickling echoed from the bathroom from Janice.

Taylor-May stumbled into the kitchen, still half-asleep, dressed in a loose T-shirt, no pants. She grabbed a mug and poured coffee like it was life support.

"Mornings suck without running water," she muttered, voice thick with sleep, eyes flicking toward the other room, knowing damn well it wasn't water.

Bryce didn't look up. He was focused on the mission. He points at the map. "I've marked the locations, Xs are explosives. Os are surveillance beacons. Stick to the Os and you're safe."

She took a sip, processing.

Then, with a smirk, she tilted her head. "Kisses and hugs, huh?"

Bryce exhaled through his nose, fighting the smirk threatening to rise. She leaned over the table, her shirt riding just high enough to test his discipline.

"Not what I intended," he said, dry. "But sure. Kisses kill."

Their moment cracked under the sharp sound of Janice's voice from the hallway.

"Jesus, Taylor-May. Put some pants on."

Taylor-May scowled, tugging her shirt down with a glare. "It's a hundred degrees in here."

Bryce, grateful for the distraction, turned back to the table.

He gestured to the burner phones neatly lined in a row.

"Each phone corresponds to an IED location. If you see movement, confirm with the scope or binoculars before triggering, could be wildlife, could be them."

His tone dropped, calm but final.

"Either way, be ready to move. If something blows, grab what matters and go."

Taylor-May's smirk faded. The weight returned.

Janice studied the map, sharp and focused.

Bryce strapped on his pack and stepped toward the door.

"You make a terrible damsel in distress," Janice muttered, eyes still on the map.

Taylor-May blinked. "What the hell's that supposed to mean?"

"It means focus," Janice said evenly. "This isn't a game."

Taylor-May looked at Bryce, maybe expecting a quip.

But Bryce only pulled his hood up, adjusted his gear, and stepped out into the light.

The door closed behind him.

Taylor-May stood there, gripping the table. And just like that, she already missed the sound of his voice.

Chapter Thirty-Two

Dude, That's My Jeep

A cool ocean breeze swept over the jagged cliffs, carrying the distant cries of a circling buzzards. Bryce knelt at the edge, silent and deliberate, blending seamlessly with the terrain. Through his binoculars, he scanned the valley below, a rugged stretch of wilderness that marked the beginning of his five-mile trek back to the Jeep. He'd have to cross another mountain range and a second valley, a brutal gauntlet that demanded precision and patience.

He moved carefully, choosing his descent down the cliffside with practiced ease. Slipping into the treeline, he used the dense foliage as cover, his gaze sweeping constantly for signs of an ambush. The serenity of the landscape was deceptive, masking the very real threat lurking within its shadows.

Adjusting his pack, Bryce shifted the weight of his weapons, redistributing the load for better balance as he navigated the slope. Loose rocks threatened to send him tumbling, but his footing held firm. When he reached the summit of the next ridge, he stayed below the crest, avoiding the silhouette effect against the sky. Finding cover behind a rock outcropping, he dropped to a knee, unfastened his TRG-42 sniper rifle, and extended the bipod.

With slow, deliberate movements, he set the rifle into position, keeping the muzzle hidden behind the rocks. Peering through the scope, he dialed in his focus toward the distant ridge where his jeep was parked.

Still there.

Untouched.

But something wasn't right.

Bryce adjusted the scope, tracking fresh tire marks that led to a cluster of camouflaged hunting blinds tucked into the treeline. A flicker of movement caught his eye. A rifle barrel twitched.

"Weekend warriors," he muttered. "Shit."

He lowered the rifle and pulled his burner phone. No new messages. He tucked it away and pressed flat against the rock, crawling two meters left for a better angle.

Binoculars up. Slow scan.

He marked distances, cross-referencing his mental range card with the terrain.

Jeep — 350 meters.

First blind — 200.

Ridge gully — 150.

Wind — light from the west, steady.

Cover — thin. High exposure between the blinds and the ridge.

Everything was noted. Everything tracked.

The crunch of footsteps on gravel snapped his attention below.

Incoming.

Bryce stayed motionless, letting the sound of approaching voices drift up the rocky incline.

A voice irritated, and out of place, cut through the quiet.

"I'm just saying, man, we ride fucking bikes and handle shit where bikes go. Why the hell are we out here, where rednecks live for this outdoor shit? Look at us. We're both wearing white T-shirts, leather vests, and blue jeans. We can't hide from shit unless there's a goddamn Fonzie convention."

Bryce suppressed a smirk.

"Look," the second man, Tank, grumbled, "We kill this fucker, and we're back on the road."

Gary snorted. "Yeah, sure. The cartel has the FBI, DEA, ATF, and the sheriff on their payroll, and they can't find this guy? That doesn't ring any alarm bells for you?"

Tank threw up his hands. "Whatever, man. Just do your fucking job."

"What am I gonna do, wait behind a rock like some lawn ornament and blast him when he's already on top of me? This thing's only good up close."

A burst of static crackled over their radio.

"Hey, dipshits, what the fuck are you doing? Stop walking around and get back to the shack. Either change into camo or wait on the other side of the hill. Get the fuck out of there, man."

Gary started laughing. "Told you, fucker."

Tank flipped him off. "Fuck you, man." He pressed the radio to his mouth. "Yeah, it's all clear over here. Over and out." He shook his head. "That guy is a dick."

Gary scoffed. "They're all fuckwads. I hate working with these assholes. Everyone is on Javier's nuts. I'm gonna take a piss. Meet you back at the shack of horrors."

Tank grumbled and turned back toward the treeline.

Gary, muttering under his breath, wandered off toward the cliff's edge, fumbling as he unbuckled his belt.

Bryce moved like a shadow.

By the time Gary fumbled with his zipper, Bryce was already there, silent, invisible.

He didn't strike immediately.

He waited.

Waited until Gary shifted his weight, feet planted awkwardly. Waited until he was at his most vulnerable.

Then, in one swift motion, Bryce clamped a gloved hand over Gary's mouth, yanking him back against his chest. The cool press of a knife blade slid against Gary's throat.

Gary stiffened, his breath hitching.

Bryce's voice was calm. "I don't want to kill anyone, but I know they want to kill me. Do you want to live?"

Gary's eyes darted like a trapped animal. His bladder gave out.

A stuttering trickle hit the leaves, uneven, awkward, humiliating.

"Yeah," he choked. "I do."

Bryce wrinkled his nose. "Jesus. At least something's working. What the fuck, man, drink some water."

Gary glared back, but the knife at his throat and the hand clamped over his mouth silenced whatever comeback he had. The pathetic drip of his piss kept going, splattering leaves like a bad experimental jazz solo.

Bryce rolled his eyes. "You should get your prostate checked with that stutter-stream. Sounds like a leaky faucet trying to freestyle."

He sighed between the irregular patters. "How many out there?"

Gary hesitated.

The blade pressed harder.

"Ten. Dr. Ghillie."

Bryce smirked. "Who do you work for?"

Gary zipped up, weirdly unbothered. "The fucking cartel."

Bryce raised an eyebrow. "No shit. Which one?"

"Javier Bravalez," Gary muttered. "The last guy you wanna piss off."

Bryce let out a dry laugh. "Javier Bravalez, is that his real name?"

"Don't know. Don't care." Gary's tone darkened. "They call him *Rey de la Muerte*. King of Death. And trust me, he is."

Bryce snorted. "Here's the deal. I'm gonna knock you out and tie you up. Should take you about twenty minutes to get out of the zip ties. If I see you again, I'll kill you. Understood?"

Gary rolled his eyes. "Uh, yeah, buddy. That works for me. I need a nap anyway. This week's been fucked."

Bryce didn't waste another second. He struck fast, one clean blow, and eased Gary to the ground. He stripped the walkie and headset from Gary's vest, then used Gary's thumb to unlock his phone and opened an app to keep the phone unlocked. Silencing it, he shoved it in his backpack.

"Sorry, buddy," Bryce muttered as he tightened the zip ties and gagged him. "Might take longer than twenty minutes."

With practiced efficiency, Bryce moved back up the cliff, securing the walkie and slinging his pack into position. No wasted motion.

He pulled out his map and crouched low behind cover, scanning it with the precision of a man trained to calculate survival in seconds.

His finger traced the main road, likely the primary ingress for any reinforcements once the shooting started. Too exposed. Too obvious.

He followed the river downstream with his eyes, finding an overgrown logging trail nearly lost to time. That was his route. Quiet. Concealed. Off-axis from the main engagement.

He marked two alternate exfil routes, one along the ridgeline, the other through the gulch, both previously scouted, both viable depending on contact.

Terrain. Elevation. Line of sight. Every decision cross-referenced against his mental range card.

Primary route. Contingency. Contingency for the contingency.

This was standard doctrine. Always have a way out before you go in.

And Bryce never stepped into the unknown without a map of how to disappear.

A burst of static crackled through the radio.

"Anyone seen Gary?"

Tank's voice cut through the comms.

"You check his bike? He's usually not far from it," Bubba replied.

"Funny, shithead. If you see him, let me know. He went to take a piss and never came back."

Another voice cut in, sharper, on edge. "Orders are shoot to kill. Don't fuck around. This asshole killed Marty and Jed, and Jax. Shit, he killed all our damn friends! They said he cooked himself, but that's bullshit. He's out there and we need to be fucking ready."

Then came the gravelly drawl of Sheriff Fred, silencing the chatter.

"Stop talking and keep a lookout, idiots. We're hunting, so fucking act like it."

Bryce exhaled, steadying his pulse.

He checked his watch, still on schedule.

Below, the valley stretched out like a live-fire range. His battlefield. His terms.

The map beside him was marked. Enemy blinds, firing arcs, likely fallback routes, all sketched with surgical precision. No detail missed. No margin for error.

He folded it, tucked it away, and shifted into position.

Settling behind cover, he adjusted his scope, slow and deliberate, glassing one target at a time.

Range. Wind. Movement. Priority.

Each target filed away in order of engagement. Each shot was already played out in his mind.

All that was left was their choice. He had to give them a choice.

Slowly, he lifted the walkie to his lips.

"You have two choices," he said, voice low and cold. "Leave and live, or stay in your blinds and die. I'll give you five seconds to decide."

"Five... four... three... two... one—"

"Fuck you."

Bryce muttered under his breath. Wrong answer.

Through the scope, he saw Eric barking into his walkie, oblivious that he was already in the crosshairs.

A single squeeze of the trigger.

The bullet punched through Eric's forehead, misting the air with blood. His body crumpled like a dropped marionette.

Bryce didn't wait. He shifted positions, rolling to the next firing angle.

A man beside Eric reeled back, staring at the fresh spray of blood across his vest. His hands fumbled for his rifle.

"Don't do it," Bryce warned over the radio. "Just walk away."

The man hesitated, then lifted his rifle toward the cliffs.

His head exploded before he could pull the trigger.

Bryce scanned the valley.

Two hunters scrambled out of their blind, abandoning their rifles as they sprinted for the ridge, arms flailing, feet pounding the dirt.

Smart.

He let them go.

Rolling into a new firing position, he found the next blind just as a muzzle flash flared too close. A bullet chipped the rocks near his shoulder.

Bryce fired twice.

The first man crumpled, his body slumping over the ledge.

The second staggered, gripping his throat as blood pulsed between his fingers. He stumbled sideways, legs kicking, before collapsing in the dirt.

The walkie went dead. They'd changed frequencies.
Bryce spun the dial until static hissed, then a panicked voice bled through.

"Shit! We're losing people! Draw his fire, Gabe, just haul ass! We'll take him when he shoots at you! We got an idea where he's at."

A dirt bike roared to life.

Bryce tracked the rider. Waiting.

The dirt bike shot across the valley, a blur of wheels, dust, and desperation. The rider zigzagged hard, twisting the throttle wide open, trying to bait a shot.

He banked sharply behind a line of rock outcroppings, vanishing from the group's line of sight—just as planned.

But the idiot didn't see the ditch.

The front wheel hit hard.

The bike catapulted forward, launching the rider through the air.

Bryce watched, almost in awe.

"Ohhh..."

Weightless, the rider flailed midair, limbs twisting unnaturally before slamming into the ground with a grotesque crack.

His helmeted head wrenched sideways at an impossible angle.

Dead.

The bike sputtered to a stop, its front tire still spinning. A massive marijuana leaf decal on the side panel stared up at Bryce.

"Don't do drugs, kids," he muttered.

The walkie buzzed.

"Gabe? You okay? Say something, man."

Silence.

"Gabe, what the fuck, dude?!"

Bryce considered his options. Then, an idea struck.

He smirked as the plan formed, simple, cruel, and fast.

Bryce descended the cliffside with controlled steps, eyes scanning the treeline for movement, no surprises, no gaps.

He reached the body and knelt beside it.

With a grunt, he pried off the helmet, the broken neck resisting with a sickening twist.

He wiped the inside clean, quick but thorough, then slid it onto his own head, tightening the straps with practiced efficiency.

The walkie squawked again.

"Gabe, where are you, man?!"

Bryce hit the transmit button, disguising his voice in a lazy, stoner drawl. Using the facemask to muffle his voice.

"Uh... yeah... I'm good. Just, uh, I don't see him. I'm coming back. Where you guys at?"

"Dude, get your ass back here. We're setting up in the trucks. Gonna mow this motherfucker over with the fifty cal when he goes for his Jeep. Fuck this guy."

Bryce's eyes widened.

"Oh, wow... yeah, that sounds... cool."

Crouching next to the corpse, he stripped out of his ghillie suit, swapping it for the dead man's black jacket and camo pants. The fit was tight, but it would work.

He gave the MP7 a final check, ensuring the extra magazine was within reach.

Then, with a last glance toward the valley, Bryce mounted the dirt bike, revved the engine, and took off, heading straight into enemy territory.

Bryce retraced Gabe's path, avoiding another hidden trench. Gradually, he picked up speed, matching Gabe's approach vector, slipping into their routine like he belonged.

Up ahead, the last of the group had set up around a raised off-road truck. Two sat in the cab, while two more stood in the bed, one manning a mounted .50 caliber aimed at Bryce's Jeep.

All four were locked onto the cliffs, sweeping their sights between the Jeep and the valley, searching for movement.

Bryce rode up casually, waving.

The moment they all waved back, he struck.

His hand snapped to the MP7, flicking the selector to full-auto as he fired a sweeping burst. The truck became a slaughterhouse before they could react, bodies jerking violently from the impacts. Bryce dumped the bike mid-slide, transitioning into a low crouch, his weapon snapping toward potential threats.

Clear. Breathing steady.

Bryce swapped in a fresh mag from a practiced position, movement fluid ingrained.

He flipped the selector to semi-auto, one round per squeeze.

He pushed the visor up, locking it fully open. Not off, not yet, but enough to see clearly.

No distractions. No tunnel vision.

The MP7 came up, red dot steady.

Target. Breath. Control.

His eyes never stopped scanning. He moved cover to cover, staying low, keeping his profile tight, just another shadow in motion, a hard target to track, even harder to hit.

An outhouse door creaked open in the distance.

Through the red dot, the glowing bead rested center mass on Tank's chest, his rifle raised in surrender.

He spoke into his walkie, his voice too casual.

"Ah, this is Tank. Did you kill Gary?"

He waved, set the rifle down, then raised his hands again, pressing them against the outhouse doorframe with the walkie still in his hand.

Sirens howled in the distance, closing fast from the main road.

"Too convenient."

"Look, man," Tank continued, still waving. "Take your Jeep. I don't care. Just let me know. Did you kill him or not?"

Bryce moved low, staying unpredictable as he darted between trees, keeping his angles covered.

Finally, he clicked the walkie, his voice cold.

"How many more of you are waiting for me?"

"Just me now," Tank replied smoothly. "And I ain't waiting for you."

Bryce kept his MP7 locked on Tank, but his eyes swept the treeline, scanning for the inevitable double-cross.

Then, switching the walkie to his left hand, he pulled his Jeep key from his vest and pressed the alarm button.

Nothing happened.

Good sign.

He remotely started the engine.

Tank's voice crackled through the radio. "Hey, man. You're clear."

Bryce ignored him, moving fast, MP7 still at the ready as he sprinted for the Jeep.

He reached it in three strides, keeping low, weapon up, checking every direction.

No shots. No movement. Bryce yanked off the helmet and let it drop to the dirt.

In one fluid motion, he swung the door open, climbed in, tossed the MP7 onto the passenger seat, and slammed the gas, kicking up a storm of dust and dirt as he tore toward the shallow river crossing.

As the Jeep bounced hard over the uneven terrain, Bryce pressed the walkie back to his lips.

"He's 200 yards to your right, down by the cliff. I'm driving straight toward him."

The sirens screamed closer, red and blue flickering in his mirrors.

The river loomed ahead.

Bryce clenched his jaw and tightened his grip on the wheel.

Time to hit the water. His snorkel was ready, air routed high and dry above the engine.

Chapter Thirty-Three

No Time to Eat

A cold wind slipped through the hollow streets of the abandoned development. Three black SUVs glided over flawless pavement, their dark windows catching the gleam of lifeless storefronts. The town had all the earmarks of coastal luxury seen around the world, but there was no one left to admire it, not here, buried deep in Javier's domain in Mexico.

No open shops.

No pedestrians.

No life.

The convoy rolled to a stop before an upscale restaurant, its modern glass façade radiating calculated elegance.

Two security guards emerged before the SUVs stopped. They moved, eyes scanning every angle with the quiet confidence of men who had done this a thousand times. Satisfied, one gave a curt nod. The doors unlocked.

Javier stepped out first. He never rushed.

Miguel followed, his chest tightening. Something was wrong. He could feel it, not in the obvious way, not in the security presence or the eerie silence, but in the unshakable certainty that this was a meeting he had already lost.

Inside, the restaurant was a sanctuary of controlled luxury, rich wooden panels, fabric-lined booths, soft lighting that cast everything in a golden glow. Designed to soothe.

But Miguel wasn't soothed.

The staff moved with choreographed precision, silent nods, no direct eye contact. Their smiles were polite but mechanical, as if trained rather than genuine.

Javier led the way, guiding Miguel through the empty dining area into a private room. The chef was waiting at the entrance, his posture rigid, a strained smile on his face.

As Miguel stepped inside, the door clicked shut.

Not loud. Not aggressive. Just final, enough to send a ripple of unease through him.

The windows weren't just bulletproof: they were the kind installed in high-security government safe houses. Thick, polished, and flawless to the eye, but built to withstand blasts. Discreet protection, hidden beneath silent luxury.

Miguel didn't need to ask why.

Javier poured himself a glass of wine, swirling it as if this were nothing more than a casual dinner between old friends.

"It's about control," Javier mused, watching the deep red liquid spin. "A place to conduct business without interference. A haven where family outings feel normal... despite the extraordinary precautions."

Miguel said nothing.

A plate was set in front of him. Polenta. Crisped just right, topped with seafood. A dish meant to impress. But this wasn't a meal.

This was a performance.

Then the contract appeared.

It was placed beside his plate as effortlessly as the food slid forward like an afterthought.

Javier kept talking about investments, expansion, opportunities. But the numbers meant nothing. The figures were generous, but Miguel understood.

This wasn't a negotiation. Not a deal. It was a sentence.

The pen felt heavier than it should. His fingers trembled as he lifted it.

For a fleeting moment, his father's voice echoed in his mind, the way his hands had guided Miguel's the first time he signed a fishing license as a boy.

"Your name means something. Never sign it away."

A single tear slipped down Miguel's cheek.

No one acknowledged it.

His signature inked the paper. The contract vanished. The moment passed, erased as if it had never existed.

Javier took a slow sip of wine, smiling as if they had just closed a routine business deal.

Then he looked up. His voice was light.

"There will be more paperwork before the build begins, so... don't get hurt fishing."

Miguel's stomach dropped.

It wasn't a warning.

It was mockery.

The chef, still until now, sprang into action. He gripped Miguel's arm and guided him toward the exit.

His voice was steady. Practiced.

As if nothing had happened.

He spoke about sustainable fishing practices, like it was just another day.

Miguel barely heard him as they moved into the waiting SUV.

The door slammed, and Miguel flinched.

Outside, the world blurred past the window. It felt distant, dreamlike, wrong.

The SUVs pulled away in silence, tires kicking up dust along the empty streets.

***

They arrived at the old marina.

Everything looked the same, only it wasn't.

None of it was his.

Not his family's.

It was Javier's now.

He had taken everything.

Miguel stood alone.

At the water's edge, he sat on a weathered piling. It was the same one he and his father had replaced fifty years ago.

And he wept.

The creak of the docks.

The cry of the seagulls.

The distant bark of a dog.

The soundtrack of his life. His family's legacy.

Now it all belonged to someone else.

The contract in his hands might as well have been an obituary.

His family's name was buried beneath Javier's signature.

Everything he had fought to protect was gone.

And with it, a piece of his soul.

Because Javier didn't just own the marina now.

He owned Miguel's future.

And there was no escaping that truth.

Chapter Thirty-Four

Dukes & Hazards

The Jeep slammed into the river, water exploding in all directions with a bone-jarring splash. The icy spray hammered the windshield, momentarily blinding Bryce as the vehicle lurched forward, tires grinding over the riverbed's slick stones. He gritted his teeth as the Jeep clawed up the far bank, engine roaring in defiance, following the faint dirt bike trail like a wolf on the hunt.

He didn't slow down. The trail ahead dropped sharply, and Bryce angled the Jeep just right, the suspension groaning as it bounced over the ridge, landing hard but keeping momentum.

At the last moment, he skidded to a stop beside the ditch where Gabe's broken body lay, eyes sweeping the shadowed treeline for movement.

Without hesitation, Bryce vaulted from the Jeep. MP7 raised, knees bent as he moved low, sweeping the ridgeline for threats. His heartbeat thundered, but his breath remained steady. Controlled. This was his element.

At the rear of the Jeep, he swung open the tailgate, tossing his rifle and backpack inside with a solid thud.

Then, movement in the trees.

Bryce whirled, weapon locked and ready, only to find a man hobbling toward him.

Gary.

His legs were zip-tied at the ankles, forcing him to hop awkwardly across the uneven ground. His wrists were bound behind his back, his mouth gagged with his own sock, tied so tight it pulled at the corners of his mouth.

Despite his predicament, his eyes crinkled with unmistakable humor and frustration.

The moment their eyes met, he flipped Bryce off.

Bryce smirked, lowering his gun, lifting the walkie to his mouth.

"Tank. Gary's alive. He'll need cutters."

Still scanning the area, Bryce moved to where he'd stashed his backpack, sniper rifle, and ghillie suit.

He ripped the police radio from Gabe's motorcycle vest, then slammed the tailgate shut.

As he rounded toward the driver's side, Tank's voice crackled through the walkie. Irritated, but relieved.

"Ah, thanks."

Bryce cut the walkie short with a grin. "Fuck you too, Tank."

Climbing into the Jeep, he cranked the engine, easing it through the deep ditch before slamming the accelerator, tires kicking up dirt and rock as he sped across the valley floor.

He glanced at the map wedged between the seats, tracing his route with one finger. The logging road wasn't far. It was his best shot at vanishing before the next wave of pursuit.

Bryce drove fast, his foot heavy on the pedal, mindful of every bump, every shift in the terrain. One wrong move at this speed and he'd be flipped, dead, and gone before the cartel even caught up.

The Jeep skidded into a sharp curve, drifting through the turn. Rocks sprayed out behind him in a storm of debris. He punched the gas, racing toward the steep incline ahead.

Then a flash in the rearview mirror.

A sheriff's SUV bounced across the uneven ground, sirens blaring, closing in fast.

Bryce cursed. The logging road was a double-edged sword. It got him away from the immediate threat, but it funneled him toward predictable routes. If the cartel and law enforcement were working together, they'd know exactly where he was headed.

He hit the base of the hill, the Jeep growling as it tackled the incline. The wheels slipped, gravity took hold. For a sickening second, the front right tire lifted off the ground.

Bryce wrenched the wheel hard, muscles straining as he fought for control.

The Jeep lurched forward, tires biting into the rock at the last second.

Below him, the sheriff's SUV fishtailed out of control, spinning before it slammed into the ditch.

Bryce didn't wait to see the outcome. He hammered the gas, the Jeep surging over the final ridge onto the dusty, uneven stretch of the logging road.

He risked a glance in the mirror. The SUV was stuck, its sirens dead, half-submerged in the trench.

Bryce exhaled. "Hell of a day for a joyride," he muttered, eyes snapping back to the road ahead.

But something gnawed at him, a gut feeling he couldn't shake.

This wasn't over. Not even close.

The adrenaline began to wear off as Bryce glanced at his watch. 4:12 p.m. He pulled out his phone, scrolling through unread messages.

TAM: *You good?* (2:15 p.m.)

TAM: *Still alive?* WTF! (3:15 p.m.)

He quickly typed out a response.

BRYCE: *Clear. Back in four to five hours.*

A reply came almost immediately.

TAM: *Damn. That was close. Glad I didn't put my pants on. I almost sht 'em ;)*

Bryce smirked, shaking his head as he tossed the phone onto the passenger seat. He checked the battery level on the police walkie half charge. With a flick of his thumb, he switched it off, conserving power for later.

Reaching into the armrest, he pulled out his SAT phone, flipping it open as he steered around a rock hidden beneath the high weeds. His fingers scrolled through numbers, eyes flicking between the screen and the road.

He hit dial, tapped the speaker icon on the phone, and set it in the cradle on the dash.

The line connected.

A gruff voice answered, suspicious. "Who is this? How did you get this number?"

Bryce gritted his teeth, knuckles tightening on the wheel. "Staff Sergeant Bryce Rath. I got your number through private sector contacts."

A beat of silence followed by a slow inhale.

"Karma?" Troy's voice dropped, laced with wariness. "You better have a damn good reason to be calling me."

Bryce rolled his shoulders, trying to loosen the tension. "Troy, I've got a family that needs help. The cartel's after them. Some cartel guy Javier... Bravalez."

A slow, steady exhale from the other end.

Bryce checked the rearview mirror, gut tightening.

"Look, I know you're probably still pissed, but you're the only one I trust. I know how much of an asshole you are for the law, even after you moved into the CIA, which is... fucking lawless."

A pause.

Then typing.

Troy's voice came back flat. "Not gonna ask how you got my number or how you know I changed careers. We'll save that for later. But if you're messing with Javier Bravalez, you're in deep shit. His reach is global."

Bryce nodded. "Yeah, no shit. I think they've infiltrated the FBI, probably half the alphabet soup gang. That's why I'm calling you."

The Jeep hit a steep incline. Bryce focused on the terrain, eyeing the mountain ahead, mentally mapping the best route up. He locked the Jeep into four-wheel drive and began the climb.

A glint of metal flashed in the mirror, another sheriff's SUV creeping over the ditch, tracking his route. Sirens echoed below, converging on the valley.

Troy's voice crackled through. "You seriously can't stay out of trouble, Karma."

Bryce gritted his teeth, wrestling the wheel as the Jeep slid on a soft patch. The rear tires lost grip. For a heartbeat, the front right tire lifted.

He yanked the wheel hard, shifting the weight. The Jeep lurched forward, catching traction just as the SUV behind him slammed into the ditch at full speed, the siren ceasing.

Bryce barely smirked. "Right now, I feel like I'm in a bad episode of *Dukes of Hazzard*. But hey, at least you took my call."

He threw it into four wheel-high, accelerating onto the dusty logging road. Gravel and debris sprayed behind him, creating a curtain of dust that swallowed the road and obscured any snipers hiding in the hills.

Troy was still typing. "You know there's a warrant out for your arrest?"

Bryce leaned into a sharp turn. "I figured. It's bad. Local cops and every back-woods militia wannabe in town are on the payroll."

Troy cursed. More typing.

Bryce took a breath and went for it. "Feels good to help someone again. You wanna help me? Make me a contractor to keep this legal. That way I can finish this without Uncle Sam putting a bullet in my back."

More typing. Faster now.

A long pause.

Then: "Shit, Karma."

Bryce powered through a blind curve, eyes locked on the road.

Troy was considering it.

"Send me what you've got," Troy finally said. "Let me look into it. I'll get back to you."

The line went dead.

Bryce stared at the SAT phone, then muttered, "Thanks."

He slid the phone back into the armrest and shifted gears, navigating the rough terrain ahead. As the main road appeared in the distance, he eased off the gas and rolled the Jeep behind a cluster of bushes for cover. Switching into two-wheel drive, he kept the engine running.

Time for a reset. He turned on the police radio, taking it with him.

Climbing out, he popped the tailgate and rifled through his gear. A lightweight button-down shirt, clean enough. He yanked it on over his Kevlar vest.

The police radio crackled to life.

"Dispatch, this is Car 7, in pursuit, mile marker four. Over."

Bryce grabbed a towel, dumped the rest of a water bottle over his head, and scrubbed the dried blood and grit from inside the motorcycle helmet.

Water trickled down his face as he tugged on a beat-up fly-fishing hat, flipping the brim low to reshape his profile.

His hands moved on instinct.

He swapped the borrowed SIG for his Glock 17 and holstered it with care. Extra weapons stripped.

Glock secure.

Phones pulled.

Faraday bag sealed.

He shoved the devices inside, blocking any signal, and exhaled. His eyes narrowed toward the distant road.

Time to disappear.

The police radio hissed.

"Car 5 to Dispatch. Requesting assistance at mile marker sixteen. We have a 187, multiple victims. Need backup. Copy?"

"Copy. Units en route."

One-eight-seven. They were finding the bodies.

This is getting bigger fast.

Bryce's grip tightened on the wheel. It wouldn't be long now before every uniform and every fed in a hundred miles locked onto him like heat-seeking missiles.

He turned down a cracked suburban road. The skeleton of a once-thriving community. Ghost town vibes, but worse. The bones were still fresh.

Basketball hoops leaned at odd angles, backboards shattered, nets long gone. Faded *For Sale* signs slumped in weed-choked lawns.

A plastic tricycle lay overturned on the sidewalk, its wheels warped by heat and time.

This place had history. A future, once.

But that future had been stolen.

When the mills shut down, so did the town's heartbeat.

The lucky ones left. The rest? They adapted or got swallowed whole.

At the edge of the road, a malnourished dog let out a hollow bark. It wasn't angry. Just instinct.

Bryce barely looked.

But in the mirror, he saw it.

The dog sniffed the air, padded to the end of its chain, and sat.

Not in fear. Not in defiance.

In surrender.

It didn't fight.

It didn't resist.

It just accepted.

Bryce swallowed hard.

This shouldn't be happening here.

This wasn't war. This was America.

The radio crackled, pulling him back.

"Car 7 to Dispatch. Requesting additional units and body bags. Multiple bodies at the scene. Confirmed 187."

"Unit 3-Alpha to Dispatch: Possible visual on suspect vehicle, Jeep Wrangler, heading east through Covington neighborhood. Requesting confirmation. Over."

They're closing in.

He yanked the map from between the seats. Twenty miles ahead, a truck stop. His best shot at refueling and regrouping.

But the highways were death traps now.

Then, off to the right, an old frontage road veered away from the main route.

A shortcut. Less predictable.

He turned hard; the Jeep fishtailing as it peeled away from the highway.

"Unit 2-Bravo, I'm at mile marker four. No sign of the suspect. Requesting update."

"Hang tight, Bravo. Last sighting was closer to Covington."

Good. Let them chase a ghost.

The truck stop came into view.

Semi-trucks lined the pumps. Travelers milled about. Cash was king. No one asked questions.

But something was off.

Bryce felt it in his spine.

They had to have planted a tracker. There is no way they could have tracked him so fast.

He shut off the engine and climbed out, sweeping the lot casually.

No cops. No cartel.

Yet.

He moved to the rear wheel well and pulled out a tracking detector from a hidden compartment. He swept it along the Jeep's undercarriage.

Beep.

There it was.

Bryce knelt, pretending to inspect the tire. Underneath a small black box, magnetized to the frame.

He peeled it off and palmed it, eyes scanning the parking lot.

Then he saw it.

A red G-Wagon Mercedes rolled up, bass shaking the pavement. Flashy. Reckless. The kind of driver who thought the world bent for him.

Perfect.

The guy stepped out, baggy jeans, gold chain, flipping off a trucker before swaggering into the store like he owned the place.

Bryce smiled. That'll do.

He moved casually toward the G-Wagon, stretching like a man shaking off a long drive, his head low beneath the brim of the hat.

The nearby semi-truck revved impatiently, but he ignored it.

At the rear wheel, he crouched, pretending to adjust his boot.

In one fluid motion, he reached under the G-Wagon's chassis and attached the tracker to the vehicle's rear axle. The magnetic box snapped into place, undetectable to an untrained eye.

Bryce stood, dusted off his hands, and walked back to the Jeep without so much as a glance toward the G-Wagon.

To anyone watching, he was just another guy stretching his legs. Nothing suspicious, nothing worth remembering.

He could already picture the cartel's enforcers and corrupt cops tailing that flashy vehicle for miles, chasing a ghost while their real target vanished into the night.

As he finished fueling, Bryce scanned the busy station truckers, travelers, local roughnecks... all oblivious to the underground war unfolding around them.

Inside the convenience store, he kept his head down, avoiding the security cameras as he grabbed a burner phone, bottled water, beef jerky, and a few extra essentials. He paid in cash, offered a polite nod, and kept his eyes low. Just another forgettable face. Then he slipped back outside without a sound.

The G-Wagon's owner strutted out of the store and fired up the engine. It roared to life. Loud, cocky, oblivious. He had no idea what waited for him. Music blasted, rattling the glass as he threw it in gear.

Bryce smirked as the SUV peeled away. His little gift was already in place.

With a final glance around the truck stop, he climbed into the Jeep, started the engine, and pulled out slowly. He merged onto the highway, heading in the opposite direction. He followed the map to a exit to a frontage road. Pulling off, he drove a little above the speed limit.

His hands were steady on the wheel, his mind clear. The tracker was gone. The police and cartel were chasing the wrong lead.

For now, he was in control.

As the sun dipped lower, its glare cast long shadows across the road, making it difficult to see far ahead. He needed to get off the main roads.

Turning down another old road, Bryce eased the Jeep into the overgrown driveway of an abandoned Victorian house. The mailbox at the end had been smashed to splinters long ago, the work of bored kids. The house itself stood like a forgotten monument, vines creeping up the siding, paint peeling away in strips, its grandeur reduced to a ghost of the past.

He maneuvered the Jeep around back, parking it inside what had once been a garage. The doors had rotted away, leaving only a skeletal frame.

It was perfect. Hidden from the road but easy to escape if necessary.

Bryce grabbed his MP7 and swept the area. In the corner, he spotted a rat-chewed tarp, stained and rotting, but usable. He cut small slits into it with his knife, ensuring he'd have sightlines outside before draping it over the Jeep.

Settling inside, he peeled open a bag of jerky. His hands trembled slightly as he reached for a moment of stillness, working to control his breathing.

The police radio squawked, snapping the silence in half.

"Unit 5-Alpha, this is dispatch. We have a possible location on I-5. Proceed with caution and await backup."

"10-4. Proceeding with caution."

Bryce sighed and turned the volume down. He took a bite of jerky, savoring the familiar taste that grounded him. His muscles, tight with tension, began to relax. He washed it down with a swig of water, then studied the map.

All routes back to the cabin required major roads. The logging trails would be a safer bet if they didn't take him back toward the crime scene.

Checking his watch, he made his decision.

He'd wait until nightfall to move. Less traffic. Fewer eyes.

Stretching out, he scanned his surroundings once more. His next step was securing the area.

Slipping out of the Jeep, he moved through the property with silent, measured steps, his MP7 at the ready.

The house stood like a monument to forgotten time. Once proud, now swallowed by moss and memory. Vines snaked up the walls. Grass devoured the cracked driveway. Time had stripped away its former glory.

Bryce circled the perimeter, scanning every shadow, every blind spot. His fingers rested on the steel of his weapon. Ready, but not anxious.

Each room inside was swept with the same precision. His eyes adjusting to the dark, his ears tuned to the slightest movement.

Cobwebs clung to forgotten corners. Sunlight leaked through cracks in the walls, painting eerie patterns across the dust-covered floors. He moved carefully, checking old furniture, doorways, anything that could conceal danger.

As he cleared the last room, he stepped outside, inhaling the crisp evening air.

The house was secure.

Back in the Jeep, Bryce finished the last of his jerky, washing it down with a slow sip of water.

The world outside was silent.

Waiting.

He unfolded the map, tracing a familiar route with his fingertip.

An old service road lay a few miles east. If he hit it under cover of darkness, he could reach the cabin without drawing attention.

For now, he allowed himself a rare moment of stillness.

He locked the doors. Turned the radio down to a faint hum. Reclined the seat just enough to ease the strain in his shoulders.

Outside, the last streaks of sunlight filtered through the slits in the tarp, casting shifting bands of gold across the Jeep's interior. Fleeting warmth. Fading light.

He set his alarm for thirty minutes past sundown.

His fingers brushed the grip of his MP7. An instinct, a habit, a precaution.

Then, with his weapon within reach and his mind still calculating the next move,

Bryce closed his eyes.

And for the first time that day,

he let exhaustion take him.

Chapter Thirty-Five

Old Friends

The Sacramento train station, usually a bustling hub of travelers, stood deserted in the late hours of the night. Moonlight filtered through the arched windows, casting long, ghostlike shadows across the marbled floors. The silence broke only with the distant echo of footsteps.

An ornate chandelier hung like a forgotten jewel in the grand hall, its crystals catching the faint light. The high, vaulted ceiling stretched into infinity, an architectural monument to a bygone era. Rows of wooden benches, once filled with weary passengers, now sat vacant, their worn surfaces whispering stories of travelers long gone. They lay in hushed anticipation.

Dimly lit corridors led to the platforms, where train tracks extended like fingers into the dark. The occasional flicker of a forgotten overhead light revealed graffiti-scrawled walls, a testament to the transient lives that passed through.

The rendezvous was set in the heart of the station, where shadows concealed intentions and echoes masked conversations.

A white Sprinter van pulled into the half-empty parking lot. Hassan stepped out and approached a vending machine, his baseball cap pulled low to hide his face from security cameras. He bought eight bags of chips, four candy bars, six bottles of water, and one Coke. Items chosen to mislead anyone who might later analyze the footage. Nothing that hinted at how many were actually inside.

He returned to the van, set the bag down, and grabbed a bottle of water and a bag of chips for himself. Without a word, he slid the rest toward the back, where Ahmed and Nadir sat in silence.

The van merged onto I-80, the dark ribbon of highway stretching before them. After thirty minutes, Ahmed shifted into the passenger seat.

"As-salaam alaykum."

Hassan and Nadir smiled. Hearing their native tongue again was a muted relief. Ahmed felt it, too. It was the first time he had spoken his language since leaving home two years ago.

"Wa alaykum as-salaam," they answered in unison.

Ahmed let the words hang for a moment. A small peace in a war none of them could name.

Then, in perfect English: "As much as I'd like to keep speaking freely, we don't use our language here. Not until we return home. No prayers. No signs. Nothing that can expose us. Allah will understand."

They nodded without hesitation.

Ahmed continued. "First order of business. We have forty-five civilians. Most can shoot and hunt. A few are trained officers. They've given us a house to use, but we need to stay low. Be ready to leave the moment Bryce Rath and the family he's protecting are dead."

Again, they nodded.

Ahmed sipped from his water bottle.

"Have you read up on him?"

Both men nodded again.

"We've got the advantage. For now. He's expecting civilians and dirty cops, not trained soldiers. That window closes fast. Nadir, secure dirt bikes and stash extra fuel. We'll need them for exfil or pursuit. Use the old logging trails to gain distance before we regroup."

He opened the chips and ate a few; the crunch filled the silence as the van barreled forward.

In the distance, the vast mountains loomed.

"We'll stop in about an hour for gas and food," Ahmed said, checking his watch. "Stick to rural stations. They have fewer cameras. And remember, we're all immigrants from South America. Broken English and Spanish only if we need to communicate."

He turned toward them.

"We speak English around them. If we need to 'speak privately,' we use Spanish. But only say what you'd say in English. Some of them will understand. If you have questions, ask in the van before we arrive. After that, we are cartel hitmen. Nothing else."

His voice was calm, unwavering.

"Many brothers here are ready to join us. We must not jeopardize the future."

Hassan and Nadir nodded.

The van vanished into the dark, its silence louder than thunder. A storm was coming. And all they brought was devastation.

Chapter Thirty-Six

Lost City

A bottle toppled in the garage, snapping Bryce awake, weapon already in hand. He strained to hear the sounds outside the Jeep. Night had fallen around him, making it impossible to see beyond the confines of his temporary shelter. Checking his watch, he turned off the alarm, then reached for the police radio, switching it off as quietly as possible.

He ensured the dome light was disabled before opening the door, preventing any unwanted glow from giving away his position. A rattle of a can farther away confirmed something was moving outside. Carefully, he reached into the back of the Jeep, retrieving his night-vision goggles. He tried to look through slits in the fabric draped over the vehicle. No vehicles obstructed his exit. That was a good sign.

He unlocked the door and peered out through the driver's side window, searching for any threats. For a tense minute, silence pressed in around him. He exhaled slowly. He had to move. Had to neutralize whatever made that noise before it became a threat.

Opening the door without a sound, he slipped beneath the tarp and swept his weapon across each quadrant, checking for movement. A rustle in the bushes beside the garage put him on high alert. He shifted his grip, finger brushing the trigger, when a large raccoon lumbered out, sniffing the air. Bryce exhaled and pulled his finger away from the trigger.

"Thanks for the wake-up call, buddy," he muttered, voice barely above a whisper. The raccoon sniffed again, its glowing eyes reflecting back at him in the night vision. "You smell my food? Sorry to disappoint, but I don't share."

The animal scurried closer to the Jeep before pausing to stare at Bryce. He sighed, relaxing.

"You hungry?" he muttered. "I could share some jerky with ya."

But the raccoon darted away before he moved.

Bryce smirked. "Figures. Another picky eater."

He removed the tarp from the Jeep, folding it and storing it back in the garage. Then he pulled out his map, confirming his route, before climbing into the driver's seat. He started the engine, leaving his night vision goggles on as he inched down the gravel driveway. The path, once well-traveled by a family that had likely left for better opportunities, was now overgrown and forgotten.

At the end of the road, Bryce removed his goggles and checked both directions for movement. Seeing no headlights, he turned right, flicking on his lights and setting a steady pace to avoid drawing attention. He switched on the police radio.

"Unit 16, we are thirty minutes to southbound Five, marker thirty. Awaiting backup."

"10-4. Units en route. ETA forty minutes. Copy."

Bryce grabbed a piece of beef jerky while cracking open an energy drink. He took a long swig, letting the chemical concoction jolt his system awake. Then—bright headlights pierced the windshield, temporarily blinding him. He squinted.

"Turn down your brights, asshole."

As the truck roared past, recognition struck. The deep growl of the engine, the oversized tires—Jake's truck. Bryce glanced over just in time to see Jake's dumbfounded expression, wide eyes locking onto Bryce. Jake pointed frantically.

"Of course it's you," Bryce muttered, swinging the Jeep around. He veered into a muddy meadow, wheels kicking up dirt as he gunned the engine for momentum. Jake's truck peeled away in retreat.

"Idiots," Bryce muttered, shifting gears.

He rolled down the window and switched to automatic, leveling the MP7 with his left hand.

A short burst, controlled and precise, tore through the truck's tires.

The lift kit and oversized wheels betrayed it.

The truck jolted left, then flipped end over end, a blur of steel and sparks.

Beer cans and loose gear exploded out of the cab as it rolled down the road, finally skidding to a stop on its roof.

Wheels still spinning.

Smoke rising.

Slowing the Jeep, Bryce parked in a defensive position. He reloaded before stepping out, creeping toward the wreckage. The stench of gasoline filled the air. Inside the cab, Jake slumped against the steering wheel, blood trailing from his forehead. Another man lay unconscious beside him, a gun still clutched in his limp hand.

Bryce swept the area, collecting their rifles and sidearms. He picked up a phone from the floorboard, its screen lit up. A call in progress. He pressed speaker.

"Jake? You there? Jake, what in the hell do you want? Jake?"

Bryce sighed, hanging up. He looked down at Jake, disgusted.

"You know, it's not safe to talk on the phone while driving." His thoughts flickered to John. Anger burned through him. "You just won't stop. You're like a damn virus."

His eyes locked on a gas can in the bed.

He yanked it free, gave it a shake.

Sloshing. Half full for him.

Half empty for them.

"You've had this coming for a long time."

Using Jake's own hand, he opened the glove box and found a road flare. Perfect. He grabbed a dirty rag near the wheel well and soaked it in gasoline.

Bryce doused the truck's interior and tossed the can inside.

"What a mess."

He struck the flare. The red-blue flame hissed to life, casting flickers across the wreck. One last look and he tossed it in.

The gasoline caught with a violent whoosh, flames licking up the seats.

The men began to scream.

Bryce took no pleasure in it. Raising Jake's handgun, he ended it. Two shots center mass each head.. Then he emptied the rounds from it and wiped his prints and tossed the weapon into the growing fire. He doesn't need to get anyone else hurt.

One last sweep of the area through his rifle's scope confirmed he was alone.

Then he sprinted back to the Jeep and floored the accelerator.

In the rearview mirror, the truck exploded, causing a fireball to erupt into the sky.

Shaking his head, Bryce muttered, "Those women are a bad influence."

He turned onto a side road, checking his watch. He grabbed his burner phone and typed: *30 min ETA.*

Seconds later, a reply lit up: *About time, Karma!*

Bryce chuckled, pocketing the phone. He sped toward the cabin, the glow of the fire fading in the distance, leaving only darkness behind.

Turning right onto a smaller, unlit street, he accelerated. The ghost community no longer cared about his speeding. The only neighborhood watch came from rats and owls, each locked in its own fight for survival.

He turned down a side road, then back onto the main one leading to the cabin's turnoff. His eyes scanned every direction, ensuring no one would see him pull off the road. Once there, he shut off the Jeep and stepped out, tapping the taillights, watching for movement.

Slipping back into the seat, he pulled on his night vision goggles, shifted into four-low, and let the Jeep crawl up the old road. The green glow filled the cab, casting eerie reflections on the tinted windows. The Jeep growled, a predator slipping through the dark.

Bryce's head bobbed slightly from the weight of the goggles as he climbed the incline. At the base of the last hill, he pulled out his phone and sent a message:

I'm pulling up now. Please don't shoot or blow me up.

He waited, scanning the hillside.

Slowly, he crested the ridge and spotted the cabin, dark, appearing empty. The two trucks were camouflaged so well that they looked like thick brush swallowed by shadow.

His phone vibrated. The glow half-blinded him through the night vision. Wincing, he turned the SAT phone to dark mode and alternated eyes to balance the vision strain.

"Hey, Ant. Thanks for calling me back," Bryce said quietly.

A deep voice answered, relaxed but alert. "Yeah, buddy. What do you need?"

Bryce reached into the armrest, grabbed a Bluetooth headset, and slipped it on.

"Look, I'll pay whatever. Or Troy will. If I do this right. I need to know where the money's going, and anything else you can get."

He fought the wheel as the Jeep climbed a steep curve.

"Well, let's see what we can find. This is not getting you out of coming to Sweden, but I know if you're reaching out to the guy who arrested you, then it's serious. You really know how to pick your vacations, Karma."

Bryce laughed. "There's no way I'm missing Sweden. I liked your podcast, too. I'm digging trenches here for sure. I'll send you everything within the hour."

"Copy. I will be ready. You sure about Troy? I have other contacts."

"Look, his team failed him, but he's solid. I trust him. He was never in the wrong. I was."

"Yeah, okay. If you say so."

A pause.

"Thank you, Ant. I'll connect the SAT to the laptop and text you when it's up."

"Go get 'em, Karma. I got you."

"Thanks, Ant."

He parked in front of the cabin, removed his goggles, and flicked on his headlamp. Grabbing two car batteries from the back, he approached the porch just as the cabin door creaked open.

Cigarette smoke drifted out, curling into the cold air. Janice and Taylor-May stepped into the glow—automatic weapons slung, exhaustion on their faces.

Janice barked, "Who were you talking to?"

Bryce hoisted the batteries. "A friend. He'll help with SATCOM and intel."

As he passed, he added with a smirk, "If you wanna be on the cover of *Guns & Ammo*, you gotta smile."

Janice spat off the porch. "Are we getting out of here, or what?"

The smirk faded. His cold stare shut down the conversation. They stepped aside.

"I need to upgrade our security," he said as he carried the batteries inside.

Back at the Jeep, he rummaged for more gear. Janice and Taylor-May followed, rifles now slung casually.

Taylor-May kicked one of the Jeep's massive tires. "Hell of a rig, Karma."

Bryce turned, backpack over one shoulder. "It's done the job. Could be better."

"You got high standards?" she teased.

He looked back over his shoulder. "Once you've driven an armored Hummer, everything else feels like a tin can."

Janice and Taylor-May laughed.

"That's a relief," Taylor-May said, nudging her mom. "He likes Hummers. Big surprise there."

Bryce kept walking. "Gets me where I want and lets me live how I want. I'm good with that."

Taylor-May called after him. "You rich, Karma?"

From inside: "Nah. Sold my house. Bought this instead."

Janice and Taylor-May examined the Jeep. Admiring the welded lockers, camouflaged storage, and clean utility. Everything served a purpose. Nothing wasted.

"You think he built it himself?" Taylor-May asked.

Janice nodded. "Wouldn't surprise me. He's one scary, sweet badass."

They each grabbed a side of a heavy Pelican case.

"That's the only compliment I've ever heard you say," Taylor-May smirked.

Janice huffed, shifting her grip. "Not many people are worth it. Shit, this thing's heavy."

"What about me?"

Janice groaned. "Nice job blowing up that asshole boyfriend of yours."

Taylor-May grimaced, a flicker of guilt and annoyance crossing her face. She responded flatly, "Thanks."

Chapter Thirty-Seven

Close Encounters Of A New Kind

The Sprinter van rounded a bend, headlights washing over the ruins of John and Janice's old gas station.

Where the pumps and tanks once stood, a crater yawned like the eye of a dead volcano.

Moonlight silvered the jagged edges.

Ash clung to the concrete.

Char streaked the earth beneath the broken treeline.

Hassan slept in the back.

Nadir, riding shotgun, studied the map in his lap, then looked up at the burned-out ruin.

He glanced at Ahmed, who drove without a word, eyes locked on the road ahead.

"That's where they lost them," Ahmed muttered.

Nadir shook his head, still staring at the destruction. "Shame the forest didn't burn like that other town. Probably too wet from the marine layer. Would've made tracking them easier."

He exhaled sharply, rubbing a hand over his face as he surveyed the tangled underbrush and overgrown forest. "Strange values. They'd rather protect an idea than prosper by managing the land."

Ahmed's lips curled into a faint smile as another car's headlights swept over them. He nodded. "This is how they fall, by their own hands. They fight over foolishness, argue about their weakest, even the air they breathe, while their nation crumbles. And we? We grow stronger. Allah has willed it." His voice dropped, firm with conviction. "Let's make sure they never recover."

Nadir nodded, gripping the map tighter, thinking about his family and everything he'd given up. The realization hit him like a release. "Praise Allah."

Ahmed heard the fire in his voice. He was proud to fight alongside him. Their eyes met for a brief moment before Nadir returned to scanning the map.

"In two miles, make a left."

They drove in silence. Hassan's snores competed with the van's suspension, which squeaked rhythmically under the load.

"Turn here, that big house on the left." Nadir pointed to the sheriff's residence. Ahmed guided the van into the long driveway, slowing as they approached.

They each pulled their hats low, obscuring their faces in shadow. Ahmed shifted the van into park behind the sheriff's cruiser and looked at Nadir.

"Remember, my name is Jose."

Nadir nodded. "Gus. Short for Gustavo."

Hassan stretched, waking quickly, refreshed and ready. He adjusted his hat low over his eyes. "And I am Omar."

The van doors opened, and the three men stepped out. Hassan slung a heavy duffel over his shoulder, the seams straining under its weight.

The front door creaked open. Sheriff Fred stepped onto the porch, eyeing the three strangers with unease. He walked down the steps slowly, hands on his hips. Ahmed approached first, extending a hand.

"Hello, Sheriff. My name is Jose. This is Omar and Gus."

The sheriff hesitated, then finally shook Ahmed's hand. "Well... bring your stuff in. I'll set you up with a room."

Ahmed studied his face as his tone cooled. "Thank you. We'll need to change and use the restroom. Then we'll be ready to meet your men. There's much to do."

The sheriff paused, then nodded, turning back toward the house. "Yeah, sure. I'll have my deputy round up the guys at his place. You can head there now if you want."

Ahmed stopped him, placing a firm hand on the sheriff's shoulder before he could move. His grip was iron, relaxed, almost casual, but decisive. He gave a slight nod to his men, signaling them to look away.

Lowering his voice, Ahmed tightened his hold. "Open the app. Give me your phone. Now. And turn off every camera in this house."

The sheriff stiffened. His mouth opened, then closed. When he met Ahmed's gaze, the fight left him. That wasn't a look of negotiation. It was a promise.

"Uh... yeah. Sure. No problem." The sheriff fumbled for his phone. Ahmed took it, his fingers moving fast. He disabled the security system, scrolled through the footage, and deleted every frame of their faces and vehicle.

Ahmed didn't loosen his grip. "Fred, if you ever take a picture of us again, I will kill you and everyone you've ever made contact with. Do you understand?"

Sweat rolled down the sheriff's forehead. "Yeah. I can do that."

"Perfect." Ahmed nodded to his men, who followed him toward the porch. Over his shoulder, he asked, "Do you have a lock on their location?"

They stepped into the house, checking the room for threats. Ahmed gestured for his men to clear the rest of the interior, then turned his focus back to Fred, eyes locked on the sheriff's phone.

Fred swallowed hard, watching his house and now his phone slip out of his control. "Yeah. We found a deed to a hunting cabin Janice inherited after her father died. Took some digging, but I'm sure that's where she's holed up. We sent a hunter. He didn't see movement, but he saw Jed's truck covered really well. He almost missed it, but the sun reflected his side mirror. From there we flew a drone, but couldn't see much."

Ahmed nodded, still working through the phone. "Excellent. We'll change, then meet your men. I'm installing a wipe app. If you take another photo, it deletes your phone and everything tied to it. This is your one and only warning."

Fred's hands trembled. "Yeah. My deputy. No cameras. I'll tell them."

Ahmed handed the phone back, but didn't move further inside. "No. We'll go alone. Call them now. Warn them however you need to. If anyone has a photo of us. We kill them."

He watched Fred carefully. His eyes drilled through him, reading every twitch of discomfort.

"When the time comes, I'll provide comms. I'll tell you what to do and what to say. We'll be in the shadows. You'll be the puppet."

Fred's face darkened. "That's not what I was tol—"

He never finished.

One moment he was upright, the next, flat on his back. A knife pressed against his throat. Ahmed moved like fog, mounting him in one fluid motion. Fred's arms were pinned. His gun was already gone.

Fred gasped, Ahmed's weight pressing into his ribs. The blade barely touched his skin, but the message was carved deep.

Ahmed's whisper was ice. "You were told to obey."

Fred's face turned gray. "Yes, sir. I got it."

Ahmed stood. Hassan and Nadir moved to unload the van after securing the house

The sheriff staggered to the sink and turned on the faucet with shaking fingers. In the window's reflection, he saw a stranger, a man who had just stared death in the face.

Ahmed reappeared in the doorway, tossing the sheriff's gun onto the counter.

"This is how it works now. You do your job. Keep your people calm. And when the time comes, follow orders."

The sheriff clenched his jaw and nodded, sick to his stomach.

Ahmed's eyes glittered with amusement. "Good. Let's get to work."

Chapter Thirty-Eight

Upgrade

Taylor-May and Janice kicked the door open, struggling through the narrow frame as Bryce sat cross-legged on the floor, swapping out the car batteries he'd rigged into a makeshift charging station.

"Where you want this?" Taylor-May huffed, both women straining under the weight of the heavy case. "Why are these so damn heavy?"

Bryce got up and walked over, resting a hand on one of the cases.

"They're all lined with Kevlar," he said. "Lids are reinforced with AR500 steel. It stops a .308 no problem. Heavy, sure, but they double as mobile cover when shit gets loud."

He gave the case a firm knock with his knuckles.

"Built 'em to haul gear and stop bullets. Multi-use matters when you're always moving and not a fan of getting shot."

Bryce grabbed the handle, effortlessly taking it from them. "Thanks."

He carried it over to the table, setting it down before reconnecting the three large car batteries already wired together with an inverter. He knelt, checked the voltage with a multimeter, and adjusted the output until it was right. Only then did he glance up. Both women were watching him.

"There are a few more in the back of the Jeep," he added, turning his attention back to the surge protector, ensuring it was properly distributing power.

Taylor-May and Janice exchanged a look before heading back outside.

"I sure hope the next one's heavier," Janice muttered. "I was hoping for a hemorrhoid."

Taylor-May snorted at her mom's joke. "Yep, here it comes. Shit."

They grabbed another case, each gripping a handle as they trudged slowly toward the cabin.

Meanwhile, Bryce stepped onto the porch, NVGs perched on his head, backpack slung, HK in hand, Glock 17 secure in its holster.

"I'm heading out to tighten the perimeter," he said, his voice low, calm, deliberate, already thinking three steps ahead.

Taylor-May rolled her eyes, fake-whining, "I was just getting used to the fish finder, but sure, let's remodel everything."

Bryce smirked, stepping closer and lowering his voice. "We have maybe a day at most before they find us. We should be as silent as possible. Keep the door closed as much as we can." His expression softened. "After this is over, I want you two to make me laugh for days. Sound good?"

Taylor-May leaned in, whispering back, "Deal. But you can't wear the goggles in the bedroom. Candles only."

Bryce chuckled, whispering in return, "Deal."

With that, he vanished into the forest, silent as a shadow.

Janice frowned, scanning the darkness. "Where the hell did he go?"

Bryce moved carefully, sweeping the perimeter.

He studied the treeline, scanning for sightlines that offered a clean shot toward the cabin.

Every angle mattered. Every shadow had potential.

He stepped lightly, avoiding the fishing line tripwires he'd rigged earlier.

Now, he placed his own motion sensors, higher up, buried in the branches.

Silent. Precise. Off-book.

A small hum blinked to life on his receiver.

Now he could see the world in three dimensions.

Little wins. Stack enough of them, you stay alive.

Satisfied, he made his way back inside.

As soon as he stepped through the door, cigarette smoke hit him, thick and clinging. The smell of chili simmering on the stove tried to compete, but was fighting a losing battle.

Taylor-May and Janice were chuckling in the kitchen, sharing a drink.

Bryce set his gear down and pulled out his iPad, exhaling as a full 3D scan of the area appeared on the monitor.

Taylor-May and Janice wandered over, peering at the screen.

"So, what's this do?" Taylor-May asked, pointing.

Bryce turned the monitor toward them. "This is our perimeter. It's set fifty yards out in a full 360-degree view."

Janice squinted at the display. "What are all the red dots?"

Bryce glimpsed at her. "The IEDs I made."

Janice turned to look at him, then at Taylor-May. "Shit."

The low murmur of the police scanner played in the background, a constant reminder of the outside world.

Taylor-May dropped onto the bench beside Bryce, eyeing the gear around him. "So, you just… camp with all this shit?"

Bryce shrugged. "Once you're used to it, you feel naked without it."

Taylor-May teased, nudged his shoulder. "That's a strange kind of naked, Karma."

Bryce chuckled. "Yeah, I guess it's more mentally naked. I can't sleep if I have to look over my shoulder, so this helps. Plus, I'm always on the move."

He switched topics. "Did you test the boat engine after you put it in the water?"

Taylor-May was still focused on the 3D imaging, eyes flicking between the screen and the rest of the setup. "Yep."

Bryce nudged her back. "Good. I need you to write down everything you know about this operation; names, connections, other sub operations, locations. Anything you know, please put it on this laptop. Anything you remember. The more intel I have, the better."

She looked up at him, surprised by the casual physicality, but didn't pull away. "Okay."

Janice watched them, shaking her head as she pushed up from the table. "You hungry?"

Bryce turned his attention to her. "Yeah, I am."

Janice disappeared into the kitchen. "Sounds good. Me too."

For a moment, Bryce and Taylor-May just looked at each other.

Then the police radio crackled, cutting through the moment with an unexpected voice. A voice Bryce recognized.

"Unit-3 Alpha. We have visuals on the tracker. It's not a black Jeep, it's a red G-Wagon Mercedes. We had it pulled over on Interstate 40, mile marker 62, and found contraband."

Bryce smirked. Perfect.

They took the bait.

But they were still coming.

The radio crackled again.

"Requesting further orders. Copy Alpha Three, stand by."

Bryce reached over, turning down the volume as he pulled out his map. A smirk played at his lips.

"Well, he got further than I thought." He folded the map, glancing at Taylor-May's confused expression.

"They put a tracker on my Jeep, so I gave it to a more deserving individual." He checked his watch. "He was an asshole. It's only fair he shares in the fun."

Taylor-May scoffed. "You gave it to him?"

Bryce shrugged. "Love how opportunities like that work out."

Janice's voice called from the other room. "Come eat."

Setting his SAT phone down, Bryce and Taylor-May walked into the kitchen. She stayed close to him as they ate their chili.

Janice looked up from her bowl. "I'll make you a real home-cooked meal when we get out of this."

Taylor-May smiled. "She makes the best chicken dinner, fresh biscuits, garlic mashed potatoes."

Bryce glanced down at his bowl. "Well, this is the closest I've had to a home-cooked meal in a long time, so thank you. It's nice."

For a while, they ate in silence, enjoying the rare moment of normalcy.

The SAT phone buzzed, popping the little bubble of peace they'd carved out.

"Excuse me." He stood and answered. "Hey, Anthony. Any luck?" Bryce put on his ear bud and nodded as he listened. "That's great. Send it to me, and I'll wire you some money. Perfect. One more favor, track the address I gave you and see if we can get some eyes on it. I'm working with Troy now, so you won't get in trouble. I know they can't operate on American soil, but there are ways around that. Please. Yeah? Good. Let me know. Bye."

He sat back down, finishing the last of his chili.

"You want some more?" Janice asked.

Bryce looked up. "Yes, please."

Taylor-May grabbed his cup and brought it to her mom, who scraped the rest of the chili into it before handing it back.

She returned, settling beside him, eyes drifting to the 3D monitor.

Bryce smirked. "Am I boring the pants off you?"

Taylor-May turned, smiling. "Not yet. But if it helps, I'll take them off."

Bryce raised an eyebrow. "Noted."

She inched a little closer, but before she could say anything else.

Puulurp.

A loud fart echoed from the other room.

"Excuse me!"

Bryce and Taylor-May froze, both trying and failing to hold back laughter.

"I can hear you laughing!" Janice shouted.

Bryce coughed, clearing his throat. "Sorry."

Beep.

The humor vanished instantly.

Bryce turned to the monitor, typing quickly on the keyboard. The screen went dark for a second, then lit up again with new data.

Beep.

The laptop screen flickered. Four coded links appeared. Bryce clicked on one.

A satellite feed loaded showing night vision, high-resolution. A house filled the screen, and multiple cars parked around it.

"You know this place?" Bryce asked.

Taylor-May frowned. "Yeah. That's Sam's place. The deputy's house." Her expression darkened. "Shit, it looks like it's all of them together."

Bryce's eyes narrowed, scanning the image. His focus locked onto an oversized delivery van.

"You recognize that?"

Taylor-May leaned in. "No."

On the screen, the van's doors swung open. Three men in black tactical gear stepped out, hauling heavy Pelican cases toward the house.

Bryce exhaled sharply. "Not very subtle, are they?"

Taylor-May crossed her arms. "You don't have to be when you run the town."

Bryce clicked the record button before opening another feed. A different house appeared on the screen.

"What about this one?"

Taylor-May shifted uncomfortably. She hesitated.

She whispered, "That's where I meet my contact with the FBI."

A sheriff's cruiser pulled into the frame. A black sedan was already parked out front. The sheriff climbed out, Jack close behind. Together, they walked into the house.

Bryce hit record again.

"You know them?"

Taylor-May's jaw tightened. "That's Sheriff Fred and Agent Jack. My FBI contact."

She stepped closer to the screen. "I'd recognize Jack's smug walk anywhere."

Bryce didn't look up. "No effort to hide it. They're comfortable."

He tapped a few more keys. New data filled the screen.

Bryce smiled, typing a few more commands before hitting enter. Then, grabbing the SAT phone, he walked into the other room.

The screens went blank.

Taylor-May looked over at Bryce. "We lost it!"

Bryce turned and smiled.

"It'll come back in a second. Ant rigged it to cycle through commercial satellites. Like jumping cell towers, but in orbit. Keeps it off radar. Twenty, maybe thirty seconds at a time. Not exactly legal... but tough to track. We're skating the gray area."

He looked at the sat phone. "I need to make this call. Keep watching. The feed will come back. Log everything you see. Every detail counts."

Bryce closed the door behind him.

Sitting on the edge of the bed, he worked to steady his breath. His fingers hovered over the SAT phone before scrolling through his contacts.

He hit dial.

It rang once.

A deep voice answered. "This is Troy."

Bryce nodded to himself. "Sergeant."

After a moment of awkward silence.

"Karma."

Bryce didn't waste time. "I have everything you need, including Agent Jack's little meeting with the sheriff. It's in your inbox now."

Troy's keyboard clattered faintly through the line. "Where did you get this?"

Bryce stood, pacing. "This is all me. No one else. But you need to promise me something. You get them witness protection."

More typing. Troy sighed. "They'll have to turn themselves in."

"Perfect. They can do that. Get a chopper here now. They'll cooperate however you need. But listen, they're mobilizing. Within twenty-four hours, this whole town is going to be on fire."

Troy's voice hardened. "This is an internal problem. I'm working on it."

Bryce shook his head. "No. It's an external problem because I have a warrant—illegal and legal. They're blaming me for dead cops they killed, and I've already had to drop civilians. I can't go back to jail, Troy. I'll handle this. But I need you to wipe my slate clean."

Troy exhaled. "And how exactly do you plan to handle this?"

Bryce stopped pacing, jaw tight. "You can't declare war on the cartel. I can."

Silence.

"I know where Javier is. I can get there. If you clear me, I'll take him out. They won't believe I'm dead, but if I kill him in a big enough explosion, I walk away clean. Kill the money, kill the disease."

Troy finally spoke. "That's a big if."

"I don't miss."

More typing. "If I do this, I'll need time."

Bryce checked his watch. "We don't have time."

Troy's tone sharpened. "You're used to waiting, Karma."

Bryce clenched his jaw. "Thanks."

Click.

Troy hung up.

Bryce set the SAT phone down. His hand trembled slightly. He flexed his fingers.

"Breathe. Fuck."

Checking his watch, Bryce stepped back into the living room.

Taylor-May and Janice sat at the table, eyes locked on the satellite feed.

Taylor-May looked up and smiled. "It came back on."

"Good," Bryce said, scanning the room. "We've got twenty-four hours."

He paused.

"There's a war coming. We need to be ready."

Bryce grabbed a map, spreading it out on the table. They joined him, standing across, waiting for instructions.

He pointed to a ridge outside the valley. "I need you to drive the Jeep here and park it under the tarp. Keep the keys in it, but stay low."

Then he tapped four separate rock outcroppings. "These are your vantage points. Twenty feet apart. Stay behind cover. Never fire from the same spot twice."

He grabbed two TRG-42 rifles from Jed's stash. "Use these. They're already set up for night vision."

Taylor-May took hers, frowning as she examined the scope. "You want us to shoot together?"

Bryce nodded. "Fire at the same time. They'll have a harder time figuring out where the shots are coming from."

Janice chambered a round, nodding in understanding.

Taylor-May tapped the scope. "What if they come during the day?"

Bryce met her eyes. "Then we fight. But they won't. They'll wait for sunset, light enough to see us, dark enough to hide. They'll start with suppressive fire from a distance, then move in a pincer maneuver, thinking the cliff behind us is a disadvantage."

He locked eyes with them both. "I need you ready before they get here."

He lifted his Kevlar vest, showing the faintly glowing Xs taped to the front and back. "This is infrared tape. You can't see it with the naked eye, but through your scopes? It's clear as day. They'll have night vision, too, so shoot anything that doesn't have an X."

Taylor-May swallowed, gripping the rifle tighter.

Janice looked over the map one last time, then nodded. "We'll be ready."

Bryce exhaled. "Good."

Then, quietly, he added, "This ends tomorrow."

"If the Jeep gets destroyed, get to the boat and go. If the boat's compromised, take the truck. Drive out of state. Call Troy."

Janice studied the Kevlar vest Bryce handed her, nodding as he placed a burner phone in each of their hands.

"My number is the only one in there. Call only when you're safe."

Taylor-May gripped hers tightly, her jaw set.

Bryce exhaled, scanning them both. "Wear your Kevlar. Paint your faces black. No exposed skin, nothing for them to aim at." He rubbed the tension from his neck. "Now start packing. Get as much sleep as you can. We don't know when we'll get another chance."

He turned to scan the supplies laid out on the table, running through the checklist in his head.

"Before you sleep, I need to make suppressors for our rifles," Bryce said, counting off on his fingers. "I need as many washers as you can find, a metal pole at least three feet long, and a vise. I've got the drill and welder."
Janice nodded, already heading for the back room. "I'll get it."

Bryce sat down, pulling out more gear. From the back came the sounds of boxes being shoved, tools clattering to the floor, and Janice's muffled cursing.

He handed a Kevlar vest to Taylor-May. "Here, help me get everything organized. I need to make sure you both have what you need in place now."

"Damn it!" Janice muttered, followed by a thud.

Bryce and Taylor-May exchanged a look as another curse echoed from the back.

They worked fast. Taylor-May laid out the vests and weapons, double-checking ammo, water, and protein bars. Bryce moved methodically, ensuring every rifle and sidearm in the cabin was loaded and positioned near each exit.

He knelt to inspect the hidden escape hatch beneath the rug, checking for light leaks. Satisfied, he pulled a large duffel onto the floor beside the table and began stuffing it with backup supplies.

Janice reappeared, carrying an old wooden box filled with assorted washers. She dropped it onto the table.

"That's perfect," Bryce said, glancing inside.

Janice wiped the sweat from her forehead. "Found a vise in the back, but I can't lift it."

Bryce followed her to the storage room. She pointed to an old cupboard. "It's behind that."

Bryce moved the coats aside, revealing a heavy, dark-brown vise bolted to a board. He pulled it free, and a hidden slot unfolded a homemade workbench built right into the wall.

Janice pointed at a metal pole nearby. "There. You should've asked for a tank while you were at it."

Bryce chuckled. "You're right. I need to work on my asking skills. Not used to getting what I ask for."

Janice hesitated, her expression flickering part amusement, part something heavier.

Then she forced a laugh. "Yeah. Me neither."

Back in the main room, Taylor-May sat by the fish finder, watching the screen intently.

"You're quite the practical artist," she said, glancing at Bryce.

He laughed. "That's one way to put it."

He sat down, sorting the washers into stacks by size.

Taylor-May leaned in, grinning. "Are we playing poker?"

Bryce smirked. "Not quite. But if you want to join me, be my guest."

Janice pulled up a chair. "Can I help?"

Bryce nodded. "Yeah, we need to match them up."

The three of them sat at the table, stacking the washers in neat rows.

Janice frowned. "Why are we doing this?"

Taylor-May glanced at the metal pole. "He's making a silencer."

Bryce smiled. "Suppressor. Silencers are for movies."

Janice arched a brow. "And what do the washers do?"

Bryce held one up. "They disperse the gas from the muzzle, disrupt the hot flow, control the expansion, cut the noise and flash." He set the washer down. "It won't be silent, but it'll keep us from being spotted when we fire."

Janice and Taylor-May exchanged a glance, understanding settling in.

Taylor-May cracked her knuckles. "What else can we do?"

Bryce checked his watch. "We need to rotate watch. Can either of you sleep?"

Janice and Taylor-May both shook their heads.

Bryce exhaled. "I need you both at the top of your game. I'll walk you through some breathing exercises."

Janice snorted. "I did Kegel exercises back in the day."

Taylor-May burst into laughter.

Bryce grinned. "Well, that's a start."

He stood, gesturing toward their makeshift beds. "Both of you lie down. I'll walk you through it."

Taylor-May's smile curved slow and deliberate, her eyes flicking toward Bryce as she kicked off her shoes and unzipped her pants.

Bryce gave her a deadpan look. "As much as I'd enjoy this weird striptease with your mom in the room, you both need to be ready to move the second you wake up. So keep your clothes and shoes on."

Taylor-May sighed dramatically, zipping her pants back up as Janice shot her a look that could only be described as motherly exasperation.

They each lay down on their blankets, using their bags as pillows. Bryce handed them both earplugs.

"I'll be making some noise welding the suppressors. Put one earplug in so you can still hear me. If I wake you up, you can put the other in."

Bryce sat cross-legged on the floor, voice low and steady. "We're starting with controlled breathing. It's the four-seven-eight method. Inhale for four seconds, hold for seven, exhale for eight. It'll slow your heart rate, relax your body. Now, follow my lead."

He inhaled. They followed.

After a few repetitions, he continued. "Now, while keeping that breathing pattern, start tensing and relaxing each muscle group, one at a time. Start with your toes, then your calves, then your thighs, work your way up. With each exhale, picture the tension leaving your body."

The tension in their bodies slowly melted away, their breathing deep and steady.

"Now, visualize a calm, peaceful place," Bryce continued. "Could be a beach, a forest, a lake, somewhere safe. Focus on the details. The colors, the sounds, the temperature. Hold on to that feeling."

Their breathing slowed, deep and even. Minutes later, both were asleep.

Bryce sat still, listening for a moment before standing. He checked the monitor—still clear.

Good. Time to work.

He cracked open a bottle of water, drinking deep as he ran through every possible attack scenario in his mind, playing it out like a mental chessboard.

From across the room...*snrrrk.*

Janice had started snoring.

Bryce nearly choked on his water, stifling a laugh.

Shaking his head, he got to work.

He carried the washers into the back room, setting them on the bed to use as a workbench. Digging through the cabinet where he'd found the vise earlier, he pulled out an old pair of leather gloves and a thick apron, setting them aside.

Then he grabbed his bag from the kitchen and retrieved the portable arc welder. He frowned, realizing he needed better ventilation and more power.

Stepping back into the main room, he checked the monitor. No movement.

He slipped through the crawlspace behind the kitchen, each step careful and controlled. At the Jeep, he turned the engine on, grimacing at the low rumble. He watched the cabin.

No movement.

The earplugs were doing their job.

Bryce backed the Jeep closer to his bedroom window, then shut it off. From the back compartment, he pulled out a gas mask and plugged an extension cord into the inverter outlet. He fed the cord through the window, then climbed back inside through the crawlspace, pausing again to check the monitor.

Still clear.

Back in the room, Bryce stuffed a towel under the door to keep the fumes contained. He flicked on the red light first, then switched to standard overheads, letting his eyes adjust before plugging in the welder.

Time to move fast.

He drew his knife and sliced into the window frame, pulling out a strip of pink fiberglass insulation. Once he had enough, he tossed it beside his Jeep's repair kit. He'd need it later.

Bryce measured out the pipe and cut it into nine-inch sections. He laid down a fireproof tarp and donned his gas mask, welding goggles, and gloves.

The arc welder screamed to life.

Sparks showered the tarp as he worked with practiced precision, cutting and shaping the steel. He paused only to scan the room for stray embers, nothing burning where it shouldn't.

He laid out a set of washers, aligning them to form a makeshift baffle system. Clamping the first pipe into the vise at a downward angle, he welded the washers into place one at a time, moving from the muzzle-end back.

Test fit.

Too tight.

He swapped drill bits and re-bored the washers, widening each just enough to slide smoothly over the rifle's muzzle.

Second test. Perfect.

With the process dialed in, the next suppressors came together faster. Cut, weld, fit, adjust. Bryce moved with methodical speed. Controlled, deliberate, lethal.

He'd used dozens of suppressors in the field, but building one from scratch? This was new. Improvised. Field-tested theory made real. Holding the weight in his hands now, feeling the metal cool against his gloves, there was a quiet satisfaction in the craftsmanship.

He clamped the last two pipes in the vise, finishing the final bore cuts. One by one, he fitted each suppressor to its rifle.

A perfect seal.

Bryce exhaled, rolled his shoulders, and nodded to himself.

Suppressors. Done.

He locked the first rifle back in the vise and prepped the final step. Using the fiberglass insulation as a heat barrier, he slid the suppressor snug over the muzzle. Sweat trickled down his temple, but he didn't dare remove the gas mask, not with fumes still clinging to the air.

From the Jeep's repair kit, he pulled a red mini-tube of high-temp RTV silicone. He used it once on a cracked exhaust manifold. It would hold.

Not perfect. But it wouldn't melt under the heat.

He applied a bead around the collar, then gave it one final tack weld to lock it all in place.

First one. Complete.

He repeated the process twice more, working methodically. His hands moved on instinct.

By the time he finished, the sky was beginning to lighten. Bryce glanced at his watch. Sunrise was close. He unplugged the welder, coiled the cord, and fed it back through the window before shutting off the Jeep.

He peeled back the tarp, letting fresh air in, then yanked the towel from under the door. Even so, the acrid tang of burnt metal still clung to the air.

He grabbed the girls' rifles and his H&K, slipping out through the hidden exit in the floor. The cold earth beneath the cabin sent a shiver up his spine, the crisp morning air cutting through the exhaustion weighing on his muscles.

The Jeep hummed in the distance, its engine a low murmur beneath rustling pine and creeping dawn.

Bryce moved with precision, checking his surroundings before kneeling beside the Jeep. He unplugged the extension cord from the inverter, coiling it neatly and tucking it into the back compartment. With a quick turn of the key, the engine cut off, plunging the world into near silence.

He took a slow breath, adjusting to the stillness.

From inside his pack, he retrieved a bottle of water, taking a deep drink. The welding fumes still burned in his sinuses, but he pushed through it. His body ached. Exhaustion clawed at the edges of his mind. But the work wasn't done.

He examined the suppressor attached to his H&K, running a hand along the cool metal. It wasn't perfect, but it would do.

Raising the rifle, he aimed at a distant dirt mound he had marked earlier.

Pop.

A muffled shot.

No muzzle flash.

Bryce smirked. That'll work.

He tested the two rifles he'd modified for Taylor-May and Janice next. Each one fired smoothly, the suppressors doing their job. That was one more advantage in their favor.

Before heading inside, Bryce crouched near the treeline, scanning with his night vision goggles. The world glowed in eerie green. The mist rising from the lake curled like shifting ghosts. No movement beyond the lazy sway of the trees.

Good.

Back in the cabin, he stepped over the hidden floor exit, replacing the rug as he shut it behind him. Red lantern glow painted flickering shadows across the cabin walls. Bryce paused, glancing toward Janice and Taylor-May, their breathing slow and steady.

Janice snored softly.

Taylor-May stirred just enough to glare at her mother before rolling over.

Bryce smirked. He'd almost forgotten what this felt like.

Setting the rifles near the designated exits, he checked and reloaded each magazine, the steady click-clack of rounds sliding into place, grounding him in the reality of what lay ahead.

Then he moved to the monitors, fingers hovering over the keyboard as he cycled through the feeds.

Nothing.

The cartel and the sheriff's men were still waiting. Calculating.

But not for long.

He exhaled, rolling his shoulders, trying to shake off the tension. Reaching into his bag, he tore off two more strips of infrared tape, pressing them onto the back of his Kevlar vest. One more layer of safety.

Taylor-May stirred again, stretching before pushing herself up onto her elbows. She blinked the sleep from her eyes, then rose and walked toward him.

She placed her hands on his shoulders, kneading gently. "Hey," she whispered, her breath warm against his ear. "You need sleep too. I've got the monitors. I'll wake you if anything moves."

Bryce leaned into her touch for a moment, letting the exhaustion settle in. "Sleep sounds good. But this is nice."

Taylor-May grinned. "Get some sleep, Karma. I'll massage your whole body when this is over."

He smirked. "Deal."

She helped him to his feet, guiding him toward the back room. Every muscle ached. His body had never felt heavier. He slipped behind the curtain that served as a makeshift door, blocking out the early morning light.

His gun rested within arm's reach as he laid back, eyes drifting shut.

His mind kept working, mapping out every angle of attack, every escape route, every worst-case scenario.

They had maybe twelve hours.

Then the real war would begin.

Chapter Thirty-Nine

We're In Charge Now

The living room reeked of testosterone and sweat, more than any house was built to contain. Thirty-five men occupied every available surface. Folding chairs, couches, counters, even the floor. Each wore camo, their hunting rifles and handguns within easy reach. A few carried semi-automatic weapons slung over their shoulders, but it was clear they'd never trained with them properly.

They thought they were an army.

They were not.

Ahmed, Hassan, and Nadir stood at the front of the room, a stark contrast to the ragtag militia before them. Dressed in black tactical gear, military-grade Kevlar, night vision goggles, and Russian PKM machine guns strapped to their bodies, they radiated controlled lethality.

Ahmed surveyed the group, his gaze sharp and unforgiving.

"Who speaks for you?"

Silence.

Then the deputy stepped forward, hesitant. He scratched at his stubble. "Uh… I guess I do, since the sheriff isn't here."

Ahmed sized him up, expression unreadable. "I was told you had forty-five men."

The deputy's eyes flicked to the floor. "Oh yeah, well… Bryce killed six, no. Wait; Jax, Jacob, Rich, Tim, Johnny, Jake, and Tony, those guys, the dudes from the county over. Yeah, ten or more in total." He coughed. "Tank and Gary hit the road. They don't want any part of this." His lips pressed together. "Honestly, it's for the best. They were city folk, would've just gotten in the way."

Ahmed gave a slight nod. The numbers made sense. The excuses? Pathetic.

The room went still. Men shifted under Ahmed's stare. The sheriff had given them orders, but Ahmed owned them now.

His presence confirmed it.

A silent signal, a flick of his fingers, and Hassan stepped forward, flipping open a large Pelican case. Inside, military-grade weapons gleamed beneath the dim light.

"In fourteen hours, we move," Ahmed announced.

He placed a marked map on the table, stabbing his finger at a precise location.

"Here. The Williams family cabin. Some of you may have known them. After tomorrow, they will all be dead."

The words landed like a hammer. A shift rippled through the room, unease. Some flinched. Some glanced at each other. But no one spoke.

Until someone did.

Bubba hesitated, then raised a hand.

Ahmed's eyes cut to him, slow and deliberate, like a predator spotting movement. His voice was an edge of steel.

"I will take questions after I am done."

Bubba jerked his hand down.

The air thickened.

"We will break into three groups," Ahmed continued. "The sun sets at 5:45 p.m. We will be in position by 5:20 and attack at dusk. They will be blind, unable to shoot back with any accuracy. We will overwhelm them in full force."

A voice cut in from the back, ignoring the warning. "Why can't we attack at night?"

Ahmed's jaw flexed. A twitch, just the smallest sign of restrained violence.

Nadir stepped forward instead, his voice calm. Clinical.

"Because you are not trained for night combat."

He let the insult settle before continuing.

"You do not have enough experience with night vision. And unless we trained you for months, you would only shoot each other. Night vision flattens depth, no shadows, no perception. We are trained. You are not.

By attacking in unison, what is called a pincer or flanking move, we create a sustained barrage, making it impossible for them to defend themselves.

The plan is sound. If anyone speaks out of turn again, they will die.

We do not have time for questions. We do not have time to teach you. Forget we were ever here, you live.

Speak of us, and I'll kill you, your family, and anyone you talked to."

A slow, suffocating silence pressed down on the room.

No one moved.

No one even breathed.

Ahmed let it linger. He wanted them to feel it.

Finally, he tapped the map again. "You will each be given comms, set to different channels. Gus or Omar will be in direct communication with your group's channel.

When the sheriff speaks, it will be my voice through him, amplified over a bullhorn. If this takes too long or gets too loud, other law enforcement will arrive.

When they do, we will be gone. But the target will be eliminated."

His voice dropped lower. Colder.

"We will know if you speak of us. If you do, I will personally kill your family in front of you first. Do you understand?"

A wave of nods. No hesitation now.

Good.

Fear had settled in.

Now, they would obey.

Ahmed nodded once. "Get in line."

One by one, they stepped forward. A box of ammunition. A rifle. A Kevlar vest.

One man hesitated, staring at the vest in his hands. His brow furrowed.

"Why does this smell like bleach?"

The room froze.

Ahmed's head turned slowly toward the man.

A pause.

Then his voice, razor-sharp.

"Because it's fucking clean. Keep moving. Check your weapon. Put the vest on. Or I take you out myself.
Do you understand?"

The man nodded, hurrying away. The vest was on before he even took his next breath.

Ahmed watched them file through, one after the other, each one falling further under his command.

Fear had made them useful.

And fear would keep them that way.

Chapter Forty

Zero Bright 40

"Shit. Bryce!" Taylor-May screamed from the other room.

Bryce jolted awake, instincts firing before thought. His hand closed around the gun as he moved without hesitation, straight into what was no longer their war room.

Janice stood beside Taylor-May, arms crossed, her face pale but set like stone.

Bryce blinked away the remnants of sleep and checked his watch.

Seven hours.

A record.

Leaning over the table, he took in the screen. Armed men mobilizing. The sight ripped the fatigue straight from his bones.

Taylor-May was at the laptop, her voice sharp with urgency.

She watched the grainy black-and-white feed from an aging satellite.

"They're loading up. At least thirty of them, maybe more. They just keep coming out of that fucking house."

She leaned in. "More trucks pulling up. Crates. Weapons. It's like..."

The satellite feed cut out. The screen went black.

"Shit," she whispered. "We lost it. Shit." She stood and started pacing. "That's a lot of fucking people. That's like two towns' worth of bad fucking people."

Bryce stepped in, noting the tension in her face. He slid the recording drive into the secondary laptop.

"Let's rewind," he said, his voice eerily calm, scrubbing through the buffered footage.

Taylor-May frowned. "Can't we get better quality?"

Bryce's fingers flew across the keyboard. "It's a crapshoot. Depends on what satellite's overhead. This one's probably an old commercial bird, wasn't even supposed to have a camera. The junk we've left in orbit's almost as bad as what we've dumped in the ocean. It's a fucking mess."

The screen flickered back to life.

Bryce leaned in, speaking more to himself than anyone else. "Black Kevlar over mixed tactical gear. Some in hunting camo. All of them carrying high-caliber rifles."

He zoomed in on the bed of one of the trucks. "Looks like they've mounted a belt-fed .50 cal. If that thing makes it up here, all our plans change." He scanned the room. "That'll cut this cabin in half in seconds."

On-screen, the men moved with tight formation, stacking crates, locking mags, loading weapons into trucks.

"Thirty-plus," Bryce said. "Maybe more. Three giving orders." He sped the feed forward, pointing at three figures outside the main group.

He froze the frame. "Not street muscle. Elbows tight. Muzzle control. Former military or specialized cops with combat training."

He took a beat, mentally cataloging the threat.

Then he toggled back to the live feed.

The lot was empty.

Trucks gone.

House still.

"They're on the move," Bryce said flatly.

He turned to Taylor-May. "You need to move. Now. Take my Jeep to the hide across the valley." His tone was sharp, cutting through the room like a blade.

He pointed to the map, his voice flat, stripped of emotion, just cold, tactical precision.

"You've got two alternate positions. Shift after your first shots. Fire in sync, it makes it harder for them to triangulate. Only shoot when you've got a clean line of sight."

Taylor-May and Janice traded a glance, then nodded.

"Move now."

Bryce handed them Kevlar vests, oversized, but they'd do. They both put them on. He adjusted the Velcro straps, cinching them tight.

Janice hesitated, staring at the screen. "We don't know for sure they're coming."

Bryce shrugged. "Then this is good practice."

But he knew.

Janice exhaled sharply. "Shit." She grabbed her rifle, inspecting the suppressor. "Looks good. You test it?"

Bryce nodded. "Yeah. But when you get up there, fire a quick shot to zero it in."

Janice turned, walking outside to start the Jeep.

Taylor-May lingered, arms crossed, biting her lip.

"You don't have to do this. You could come with us."

The Jeep's V8 growled to life outside.

Bryce stepped closer, resting his hands on her shoulders.

His voice was calm, but his eyes were steel.

"I do. We're not running. We're drawing them into our kill zone. This ends here. If we give them space and time, we lose control. And we won't win that fight. They're too big, too well-funded. I've seen the kind of teams they send. Doesn't matter if you've got a full Secret Service detail protection is reactive. Attacking is easy. Defending takes constant vigilance. One mistake, you're dead. You don't want to live your life looking over your shoulder, wondering if today's the day they catch up. But if we make this loud, if we burn them down in one place. We shine a light on the whole thing. Make it look like we all died here, and the pressure comes off. You get your lives back."

Taylor-May pulled away. "What the fuck, Bryce? Do you have a death wish?"

Janice stomped back in. "Damnit, Taylor-May, let's go. We're in this shit together. Without him, we'd be dead. So kiss him if you want, then move your ass."

Taylor-May scoffed, glaring at her mother. "I don't want to kiss him."

Janice exhaled hard. "This shit's really happening. Fuck these fucks. Textbook Second Amendment shit. In case of government collapse or cartel death squads, break glass. Nobody else is fucking coming. Fuck this whole goddamn mess."

Taylor-May walked out in a huff.

Janice rolled her eyes and turned to Bryce. "Sorry about all this damn shit. Thank you, Bryce. We'll protect you from that hill."

Bryce gave her a small nod. "I know you will. Now go."

Janice stood in the doorway, lost for words. Tears welled up in her eyes as she looked at Bryce.

Bryce's expression shifted as something deeper surfaced.

"This is what I was trained to do." His voice was quiet, but unshakable. "But now I get to do it for people I care about, against an enemy that doesn't care about us or this country. I got this. We'll get through this. Now leave."

Janice kicked over an empty Jack Daniels bottle next to the door on her way out, muttering curses under her breath.

Taylor-May walked back into the doorway with her hands on her hip, watching Bryce gather the phones and hard drives before putting them in the duffel bag.

She swallowed hard. "I don't know what the fuck to say at a time like this."

Bryce smirked, still focused on his work. "Then don't. Just get to that hill and don't shoot me."

Taylor-May exhaled, running a hand through her hair. "Yeah. Okay." She hesitated, like she wanted to say something more, but turned and walked outside.

Bryce followed, squinting into the setting sun, slicing through the open door like a blade.

He checked his watch. Forty minutes to sundown.

Time was bleeding fast.

He hoisted the duffel into the back of the idling Jeep and slammed it shut; the sound cracking through the trees.

Two sharp knocks on the tailgate.

The V8 rumbled, ready.

Tires spit gravel as the Jeep launched forward.

Taylor-May and Janice disappeared down the winding frontage road, swallowed by trees and shadow.

They were gone. Safe for now.

Bryce slipped back into the cabin, eyes locking onto the laptop.

A new satellite feed flickered to life. Unstable color, but usable.

He typed in the local grid coordinates and widened the view manually, mile by mile. The dense forest blurred into ridgelines and narrow roads, barely visible cuts through the dark terrain.

There it was, his Jeep. Small, fast, pushing west down a cracked stretch of forgotten asphalt.

He zoomed out again. Tilted the angle. Scanned east.

A flicker.

Convoy incoming.

Vehicles crept through the trees in staggered formation trucks and SUVs crawling along the old access road into town.

The white Sprinter van led the way.

Behind it, an off-road pickup rolled forward, a belt-fed .50 cal mounted in the bed.

Bryce hit record.

A flatbed trailed the group, carrying three dirt bikes. Last in line, the sheriff's cruiser followed with its lights on, painting the whole operation like a legitimate escort.

Bryce's jaw tightened.

No more time.

"Fuck. That was close."

His mantra from the teams echoed back:

Slow is smooth. Smooth is fast.

Gearing up wasn't just muscle memory, it was focus. Calm in the storm.

He only had now, and he'd make it count.

Kevlar first. He put it on tight, centered, plates locked.

Knife sheathed under his left arm. Elbow pads strapped snug.

The ghillie suit pulled over, hood down for now, netting draped loose.

Weapons laid out. Night vision goggles secured.

Every move rehearsed a hundred times in his head.

He didn't move fast. He moved right. Speed came from control, as it always had.

Each weapon went to its place.

The Glock rode on his hip.

He then strapped down his two most valuable tools.

He'd already planted staged weapons at each corner of the cabin, different calibers, different models.

Let them think more than one person was inside.

Next, he made sure the HK was slung across the duffel, right beside the LaRue—7.62 NATO, gas-operated, precision-tuned.

It was built to punch through cover, drop targets past 800 meters, and still run smooth under pressure.

The Vortex Razor optic sat tight on the rail, with a clip-on thermal locked in front.

No wobble. No over-travel.

Just raw accuracy and stopping power.

It wasn't just a rifle.

It was dominance at range.

He toggled through the modes: white hot, night vision, back to daylight. The image held steady. Battery full. No drift.

He set it all by the hatch, just close enough to grab on the way out.

The duffel beside it zipped and loaded. Laptop, SAT phone, spare mags. His range card folded flat inside the lid of his chest pack.

He crossed to the far corner and dragged the propane tank into position. Fishing weights and hooks clinked softly against the metal.

Next to it, he angled the motion-sensor floodlight toward the door, its faint indicator light steady.

Everything where it needed to be.

No second trips. No wasted motion.

He exhaled slowly.

They wanted war.

They were about to get it.

Another floodlight was wired differently, a long cable snaking from its base toward the entrance. Bryce crouched, adjusting the sensor, angling it toward the door.

One step closer.

He grabbed an old pair of jeans and a jacket, stuffing them until they took shape, a body silhouette slumped near the propane tank.

He took another jacket, Taylor-May's pink camo, and propped it in the far corner, shaped over a bundled sleeping bag. Janice's red pullover went on another, hood stuffed, sleeves arranged just enough to suggest human form.

Three corners, three shapes.

Let them think everyone was still inside.

He tied a broomstick to the window frame with a strip of paracord, angling it just right. From a distance, it would read like a rifle barrel, barely visible, just enough to pull eyes.

He'd fire from a different angle entirely.

Keep them guessing.

Push them toward the kill zones.

These decoys weren't part of the blast, they were part of the lie.

Better to let the fire write its own story. No survivors. No questions.

The illusion was complete.

Bryce stepped back, surveying the scene.

His hand shook, a tremor, small at first, then growing.

Bryce clenched his fists. Exhaled sharply. Forced control back into his limbs.

"Come on, Karma. Focus for two minutes."

His voice was low. Steady. Not a plea. A command.

One last step.

He ran his hand over the sensor. The light snapped on, casting harsh shadows across the cabin walls.

Bryce moved the wire next to the propane tank, his breathing tight, controlled. But he didn't connect it. Not yet.

Final check.

He unscrewed the bulb from the floodlight. He'd light the room in a different way.

One more scan of the room. Everything was in place.

He slipped on his shooting goggles. No need to catch debris in the eyes during the chaos.

Nothing could stop this mission.

Then he bolted for the door.

Chapter Forty-One

The Other Side

The convoy tore down the old frontage road, engines growling as the sun bled into the horizon. Thirty minutes until sundown.

Hassan sat behind the wheel of the lead van, eyes locked on the fading light ahead. Every second that passed worked in their favor. By the time they reached the dirt road leading to the cabin, Bryce would be adjusting to the shadows. Struggling to track movement through the shifting light.

That was their advantage.

Behind Hassan, three trucks followed in tight formation. The men inside were packed in, weapons locked and ready. No one spoke. The air pulsed with tension, fear, and adrenaline.

At the very back, the sheriff's cruiser trailed behind, maintaining the illusion of pursuit.

But the sheriff wasn't hunting them.

He was clearing the way.

As the convoy neared the unmarked dirt road, Ahmed's calm voice crackled over the comms. "Slow down. Pull off. Everyone out."

The lead van veered right, crunching onto the dirt shoulder. The rest of the convoy followed suit, kicking up a cloud of dust as engines cut out.

Doors burst open.

Twenty men spilled onto the roadside, moving with practiced efficiency. Boots hit dirt. Rifles came up. Kevlar straps tightened.

Ahmed stepped out last, his eyes sweeping the line with icy precision.

"From here, we move on foot." His voice carried no room for questions. "Trucks will follow at a crawl. No lights."

Hassan nodded. They needed absolute silence to get into position before launching the assault.

At the rear of the convoy, three dirt bikes were unloaded from a truck bed.

They weren't for the assault.

They were for Ahmed, Hassan, and Nadir.

The bikes were staged off the main road, hidden behind a dense patch of trees, their engines cold, primed for a quick getaway. If anything went wrong, if law enforcement arrived too soon. Ahmed and his two closest men would disappear before anyone knew what had happened.

He wasn't just leading the attack.

He was making sure he had a way out.

Ahmed turned to the driver of the truck with the mounted .50-caliber.

"Be ready. Once we're in position, you lead the assault."

The driver gave a sharp nod. "Understood."

Ahmed stepped back, watching the operation fall into place with brutal efficiency. The convoy had spread out, men disappearing into the trees, rifles raised, moving like trained operators, even if most were just mercenaries forced into this war.

The plan was set.

Ahmed exhaled and turned his gaze to the fading sun.

Thirty minutes left. Then, Bryce Rath would die.

Chapter Forty-Two

It's Downhill From Here

Bryce sprinted for the truck, heartbeat hammering in sync with the plan.

He'd loaded everything into the cab two days ago.

He yanked the door open. A large, reinforced trash can was strapped to the truck's bench seat. Exactly the way he wanted it.

On top sat an array of items: three blocks of wood in varying sizes, a bungee cord, and three cut lengths of rope, each pre-measured for a specific task.

He grabbed the log he'd cut to anchor the front tire and placed it ten feet ahead, right on the access line he needed.

The perfect starting gate.

He had no intention of climbing in.

He shifted the truck into neutral.

With a calculated grip, he rolled it forward until the front tires perched just above the hill's crest, resting on the log—positioned like a missile aimed at the switchback's massive tree.

Then he set it in park.

Reaching across, he turned the key. The engine roared to life beneath his hand.

Every second counted.

He jammed a wooden block under the gas pedal, anchoring it so the engine wouldn't pull forward until he was ready.

Next, he tied off the steering wheel with a short rope.

No last-second swerves. No margin for error.

He reached across the bench seat and grabbed the three-foot log and the two pre-cut ropes, one long, one short.

Then he shifted the truck into drive. It lurched, then idled in place. The front block held firm.

He carefully placed the log over the gas pedal.

The truck didn't move. The block beneath held true.

Still, it was one of the few parts that concerned him.

But then again, so did everything else.

He coiled the bungee cord over the top log, building tension, ensuring that when the block beneath was yanked free, the truck would launch at full throttle.

Again, Bryce waited, ready to pull the block if anything shifted.

Nothing happened. Everything held.

That was good. Same as when he tested it two days ago.

He grabbed the long rope from the back of the truck and tied it to the trigger block beneath the gas pedal and the wedge braced in front of the tire, threading it through the hole he'd drilled in the door, after realizing the plan wouldn't work without it.

Janice hadn't appreciated that at first. But she got over it.

He tested the rope's tension. Both ends held firm. They were ready to move. He nodded to himself, then sprinted back to the cabin, threading the line through the door.

Every move was methodical. Planned, revised, and committed to memory long before tonight.

Then he ran back to the truck.

Carefully, he hefted the propane tank from the bed. It was wrapped in a lattice of fishing weights and steel hooks, designed to turn shrapnel into a storm of death. Just like the others.

With the door closed, he passed it through the window.

Gently, he set it inside the reinforced trash can and double-checked the seatbelts. The can was packed tight with smaller gas cans, both to secure the payload and amplify the blast.

From his pocket, he pulled a burner phone.

He peeled away the strip of tape marked **G7** and pressed send. His phone buzzed almost instantly. Connection confirmed.

He unwound the wire and attached it to the tank, then sealed the burner inside a custom foam casing built from spare Jeep parts. It clamped tight against the side of the can.

It wasn't just stable. It was locked in.

He'd spent more time securing that phone than anything else he'd built.

Once the casing was closed, it was done. Sealed. Ready.

Bryce exhaled, steadying his pulse.

He climbed out, pausing only to wipe sweat from his brow.

His watch read thirty-three minutes until sundown. That meant ten at best. He'd give himself five. Timing was everything.

Back at the cabin, he pulled the rope tight. When it was time, the truck would move.

His adrenaline burned cold. Laser focus.

He opened the laptop. The screen flickered, then stabilized, revealing a live satellite feed.

Clearer than before.

A newer bird had linked up.

Relief passed through him.

He zoomed in.

The convoy had pulled off near the dirt road entrance. Trucks idled. Men spilled out.

Sloppy. Overconfident. Gang muscle pretending to be soldiers.

Then he saw them.

Figures in black. The same ones he'd clocked earlier. Their movements were tight. Controlled. No wasted motion.

Professionals.

His gut tightened.

That walk—he knew it.

These were men who lived with rifles in their hands. Warzone rhythm. Combat posture. Muscle memory you don't fake.

Something serious had just entered the field.

The feed cut out.

"Shit."

Bryce listened, still and focused, waiting for the next signal to open.

The sun dipped lower, casting long, broken shadows across the trees.

The feed returned.

The team was already moving.

His attention snapped to the largest threat creeping up the dirt road.

The gun truck. A belt-fed mounted .50 cal.

They were doing exactly what he would've done.

He took a slow breath, steadying his hands.

"Shit."

He watched the truck vanish beneath the treeline, engine low and guttural, four-wheel drive grinding against the incline.

He heard it now. They were getting closer.

A slow-moving hammer of destruction clawing its way up the ridge.

They still thought he was blind. Thought they had the element of surprise.

He knew they were trying to surround him.

Their first mistake.

Bryce stared at the rope in his hands.

No more time. Everything had to work now. No room for second chances.

Wait for it.

He watched the truck break through the trees. Moving heavy. Fast. Barreling toward the narrow choke point.

They weren't hiding anymore. They were charging in.

Now.

Bryce yanked the rope.

The rigged battering ram snarled to life. The engine howled.

It launched down the hill, tires spitting gravel, bearing down on the convoy like a guided missile.

Gunfire erupted.

Bullets tore into the truck's frame.

Shouts. Panic.

Bryce didn't move.

His breathing slowed.

Pulse steady. A measured beat in the chaos.

The .50-caliber roared.

It shredded the truck from multiple angles, its bark thunderous and final.

Bryce didn't flinch.

He just watched the feed.

If he didn't take out that truck, there was no winning this fight. Not here. Not anywhere.

The crunch of metal slamming into a massive tree at the turn gave him strength. That was the target.

The .50 cal kept firing. Chewing into the frame until it killed the engine.

Silence.

No explosion. Good.

Let them come.

Bryce's muscles tensed. Running contingencies.

Wire disconnected? Fuel didn't rupture?

Shouting.

They thought they won.

They rushed the wreck.

Too fast. Too confident.

Bryce reached for his phone. Hands steady.

The feed dropped. Static danced across the screen.

He closed the laptop. He didn't need to see it.

He already knew.

Gunfire cracked in the distance.

Voices tangled in panic.

The moment narrowed. Every detail was crystal clear.

His focus locked in.

This was the edge.

Bryce exhaled, slow.

"I'm sorry."

He hit send.

Chapter Forty-Three

Death To Them All

The hillside erupted in silent chaos as the men scrambled upward, eyes wide with fear and adrenaline. Some had dreamed of a moment like this their entire lives.

With all the firepower and cartel mercenaries behind them, they expected a quick ambush. They felt unstoppable.

One man and two women against all of them, no contest.

Those with military training moved differently, darting tree to tree, using shadows, never exposed for long. Their steps were quick and deliberate, a lethal dance between cover.

They weren't excited. Not even close.

They knew exactly what a MARSOC Raider was trained to do. And they knew what Bryce had already done to them and survived.

Some still woke up at night, haunted by the first hunt, dogs chasing him, never getting close. The screams of the men caught in his traps he made to not hurt dogs or kill, just to slow them down.

They'd never felt so trapped. They were supposed to be the hunters.

Some just needed it to end, so they could reclaim whatever piece of themselves was lost that day.

Their orders were clear: move silently up the hill and wait for the truck.

But the gangsters?

They floundered.

Unused to being prey, they stumbled through the brush, clumsy, loud, easy targets.

Ahmed moved like a phantom, his body melding into the terrain, rifle steady, eyes sweeping every inch of the ground ahead. They all annoyed him. He didn't care if they all died as long as they killed Bryce Rath.

As he walked up the steep embankment, something felt wrong.

He spotted the 4x4 truck with the mounted .50 cal crawling up the slope, tires clawing at loose gravel.

His instincts screamed.

"Get that fifty up the hill now! Full throttle! Move!"

The heavy 4x4 pushed its engine to the limit. It fish tailed trying to get traction as it fought to climb, kicking up rocks and dirt in its wake.

Ahmed was about to order the rest of his men to follow when another engine tore through the tension. From on top of the ridge, approaching fast.

Ahmed dropped to a knee, rifle up, body coiled tight.

"Groups A and B, keep advancing," he commanded, voice sharp. "Group C, focus fire on the hill. Get that .50 cal in position now. Do not let that truck cut you off. Move!"

Johns and Janice's old pickup barreled from the hilltop, bouncing and skipping down the hill faster than it ever had in all the years they had it. It advanced toward the 4x4 with no hesitation. No fear.

Gunfire erupted, short bursts from the trained, chaotic panic-fire from the rest.

But the truck didn't swerve. Didn't stop.

It was coming straight for them.

"Light it up! Hit it with the fifty! Do not let it through!" Ahmed snapped, shifting tactics on instinct.

A deep, thunderous burst of .50 cal fire shattered the forest, drowning out the sporadic cracks of rifles and pistols as the truck stopped before the switch back in front of the tree.

The old truck's frame didn't stand a chance.

Metal twisted.

Glass vaporized.

Rounds punched through its core like paper.

The vehicle lurched, veered, then slammed into the tree with a brutal crunch right in front of the 4x4 with the .50 cal.

Its engine sputtered, clawed for life, but the fifty tore through it again, silencing it for good.

Silence.

Then—

Cheers erupted. Whoops followed.

The sound of men who thought they'd already won the war.

More men opened fire, each one hoping to be the one who killed Bryce Rath. The man who had killed their friends and threatened the only work available.

"Cease fire!" Ahmed barked, his voice slicing through the foolish celebration.

Too late.

One man rushed forward, emboldened by what he thought was victory.

He flung open the driver's side door.

He froze.

A large trash can.

Ropes.

A log.

A trap.

Ahmed's roar exploded over the comms.

"GET AWAY FROM THE TRUCK!"

Too late.

Hell unleashed.

The world detonated.

Vaporized.

A fireball engulfed the hill.

The shockwave slammed into the valley, a concussive blast that ripped trees from their roots. The night sky ignited, flames clawing toward the heavens.

The first five men simply ceased to exist.

Gone in the blink of an eye.

The 4x4 went up with the truck, both torn apart in an instant.

The fire found the gas tank, then everything else.

Fuel fed flame.

Flame fed hell.

The explosion unleashed a storm of fishing weights, molten steel turned into high-speed projectiles, fanning out like a Revolutionary War musket line in a 180-degree arc, deadly precision that spared the house entirely.

A man in mid-scream was split in half, his upper body collapsing before his legs followed.

Another staggered backward, both arms missing at the elbows, eyes wide in blank horror.

One pitched forward, skull punched clean through. His brain liquefied before his body even registered the hit.

Others dropped where they stood, screaming, hands clawing at their bodies as razor-edged metal tore through flesh, organs, and bone.

Blood soaked the dirt.

The air stank of burning flesh.

The ground wasn't a battlefield anymore.

It was a graveyard.

Ahmed hit the ground just in time.

A fishing weight whistled past his head.

THUNK.

It slammed into a tree trunk behind him.

He turned his head slightly, breath catching.

Half an inch to the left and it would have punched clean through his skull.

Smoke curled upward, thick and choking, mingling with blood and burnt gunpowder.

Around him, his men lay scattered.

Some dead.

Some dying.

Others moaned, twisted and broken.

Another weight zipped past.

Ahmed dropped flat again, crawling with slow, surgical precision toward the thickest tree he could find.

His pulse thundered.

Each breath was deliberate.

He forced his body into stillness.

Bryce was out there.

Waiting.

Watching.

Ahmed clenched his jaw.

This wasn't an accident.

This wasn't luck.

This was warfare.

And his enemy was a professional.

Retreat would have been smart.

But Ahmed didn't retreat.

Not yet.

Not until Bryce Rath's corpse lay at his feet.

He barked into comms, his voice sharp with fury:

"All teams, advance on the house. Now!"

Chapter Forty-Four

No Turning Back

Dust floated in the still air, caught in golden slivers of light spilling through cracks in the blackout curtains.

Each particle glowed, suspended in silence.

The blast had rattled the cabin, shaking loose decades of settled dirt.

He knew it was a direct hit.

Screams echoed up the hill.

The .50 cal had gone silent.

But there was no joy in killing.

There never was.

This wasn't vengeance.

It wasn't even justice.

It was nature's law—eat or be eaten.

There was no emotion now.

Only survival.

And he intended to survive.

He knew they would keep advancing.

He was ready for that.

What they weren't ready for was everything that came next.

Bryce's breath quickened, his heartbeat thudding in sync with the monitor vibrating on his hip.

He pulled the tablet from his chest pocket and tapped the screen, switching to 3D view.

He had set the sensors as far out as they would reach, but the perimeter was still smaller than he wanted.

Still, knowledge was power.

It was the high ground.

And he needed every second to pull this off.

Three men were already inside the outer perimeter.

His hip vibrated.

Six more were moving in from the northwest.

Another buzz.

They were coming.

Creeping.

Hunting.

He switched off the pager. That was all he needed from it.

Now it was just a distraction.

The fish finder beeped—urgent, sharp.

Bryce moved on instinct.

He grabbed the nearest rifle, gripping it tight as he dropped below the window.

He didn't need to look.

He trusted his angles.

His calculations.

Crack. Crack. Crack.

His rifle snapped off three shots toward their last known position. Without hesitation, he rolled into cover, flipping the old family redwood table—a solid slab of logging-era timber, scarred but unshakable.

Wood groaned under its own weight, dust exploding from the impact.

Rounds tore into the cabin's exterior.

Lead slammed into thick walls, shaking the structure like a war drum.

Splinters flew. Logs cracked. Dust billowed.

But the cabin held through the first barrage.

He moved fast.

A quick glance at the monitor—

The enemy had scattered, taking cover.

Good.

Bryce grabbed his burner phone. Scrolled to H4.

Send.

BOOM.

The smaller propane tank detonated.

A fiery shockwave ripped through the forest.

The rock outcropping—one of the defensive positions he'd predicted they'd use—vanished in an instant.

The men hiding there were flung like rag dolls, swallowed by fire and shredded by fish hooks and lead weights.

The forest shuddered.

Leaves and ash rained down from the trees.

Inside, dust danced in the golden shafts of light.

***

Then silence.

Except... something was wrong.

Bryce's nostrils flared.

The blast had left the air thick with smoke and heat, but this was different.

There was a sharp, chemical sting clinging to the back of his throat.

Not scorched earth.

Not metal, ash, or fire.

Not even charred flesh.

It smelled like bleach.

His gut clenched.

He'd deal with that later.

The fish finder shrieked again.

Bryce crawled low, rifle in hand, toward the dining-room window.

He swapped it for another rifle—one he had staged beside the propped-up decoy: Janice's sweater, stuffed and posed in the window frame.

His fingers found the trigger.

Muscle memory took over.

One shot.

Then two more.

Different rifle.

Different caliber.

Different cadence.

Let them think Janice was in the cabin.

Let them think Taylor-May was too.

Let them believe all three of them were trapped.

It would keep the enemy focused right where he wanted—on the cabin.

And that was all he needed to disappear, taking every last one of them down in the process.

This would make the national news.

And with it, another crack in the system he planned to tear apart.

Screams echoed through the trees.

He'd hit one.

Time for the rest.

C2—Send.

BOOM.

Another explosion tore through the treeline.

A brutal chain reaction.

Fire and steel ripped through everything in its path.

Shockwaves slammed into the cabin.

The table rattled. Walls shuddered.

Bryce checked the monitor.

Silence.

The screen flickered, dust settling in a grim, smoky haze.

Only fragments of men remained in that quadrant.

He checked his watch.

Twenty minutes to sunset.

The fish finder chirped again—different quadrant.

Bryce fired without hesitation.

A scream followed. Sharp. Agonized.

He rolled back behind cover as bullets shredded the walls.

They were getting closer.

Wood buckled. Logs cracked.

Rounds tore through like axes.

Gunfire hammered the cabin.

Loud. Relentless. Deafening.

Bryce moved.

B4—Send.

BOOM.

A double detonation.

A hailstorm of steel.

The blast rattled his bones.

Red-hot fishing weights slammed into the trees, echoing like war drums.

More screams.

Then ringing silence.

He checked his watch.

Ten minutes.

Felt like an hour.

He crawled to the large propane tank, wired in a motion sensor, and connected the battery.

The cabin was coming apart.

Perfect.

Let them think he was pinned.

Let them believe they were closing in.

***

Gunfire roared again.

They were getting closer.

Inching toward the final assault.

Bryce reached the hole cut in the floor.

He checked the duffel, chose the HK for close contact, and pulled it free.

Quick, practiced movements—

Laptop inside. Zipped shut.

Sniper rifle strap. Tight. Ready.

He grabbed the phone, scrolled to the next number.

Lifted the duffel with one hand.

Dialed.

BOOM.

The earth shook.

A blast ripped through the trees, yanking them from their roots.

He dropped the duffel flat.

The shockwave would mask everything.

No one would see it fall.

Sunlight flashed across the shrapnel mid-flight, glinting like molten razors as it tore through trees, flesh, and bone.

The enemy staggered in the aftermath.

Blinded. Broken. Bleeding.

Some fell.

Some crawled.

None unscathed.

Bryce moved.

He dialed again and shoved the phone into his chest pocket.

The next explosion ripped through the forest.

The cabin shuddered to its foundation.

The forest roared.

Fire and smoke devoured the golden light.

Shadows stretched across the cabin floor.

The light was dying.

And Bryce was ready.

Now it was time to leave.

Chapter Forty-Five

Keep moving

Ahmed lost count of the explosions. Each team he directed to attack was taken out.

Each blast tore through the forest like a beast awakened, ripping trees apart and flinging debris skyward. Craters bloomed in the earth. Fire licked the canopy. Flames clawed at the twilight, smoke rising in twisting tendrils.

The air shimmered with heat and violence, the forest now a hellscape of fire and falling embers.

Golden ash drifted like malignant snow.

Amid the carnage, Ahmed stood still.

Eyes narrowed. Unshaken.

A fishing weight zipped past him, slicing the air like a bullet. He didn't flinch. Another detonation rocked the perimeter. A wave of dust rolling through the clearing, catching the last rays of daylight, a swirling vortex of shimmering destruction. A violent beauty, masking the deadly dance unfolding beneath it.

Ahmed's lips curled. A grudging admiration.

Bryce's tactics were brutal. Calculated. Effective.

Without breaking his gaze from the smoldering battlefield, Ahmed activated his earpiece.

His voice, steady as iron, cut through the static.

"Group A, get in position to breach. Hold until my command. Group B, cover every exit. No one leaves. If they slip, it's your failure."

Behind him, the sheriff crawled up, breathless, disheveled, his face twisted in panic.

His body leaked fear from every pore.

"What the hell, man? You said you'd help! All you've done is get all my men killed! I could've done that myself!"

Ahmed barely glanced at him.

His hand lashed out, a vicious slap.

The sheriff staggered back, skull ringing.

The force sent a shockwave through his spine.

The kind he hadn't felt since high school, the hit that sent his teammate to the NFL and left him in obscurity.

Now, that same feeling washed over him.

Outclassed. Helpless.

Ahmed, unbothered, raised his binoculars again, scanning the battlefield.

He gave a nod. Nadir vanished into the smoke, sniper rifle in hand. Hassan followed, a shadow slipping through the dying light.

"Where's the Kevlar vest we gave you?" Ahmed asked coldly.

The sheriff stammered, his hand instinctively touching his chest. "D-didn't fit."

Ahmed's jaw twitched. He remembered the XXXL vest they'd brought.

The fat tracker must've taken it.

A mental note: Never underestimate American obesity again.

"Listen to me, Sheriff." Ahmed's voice dropped, lethal as a blade. "When the fire trucks and backup arrive, you're going to act like you're in charge. Tell them it's an active shooter situation. Let American law enforcement protocols take over. Use the 'Run, Hide, Fight' narrative. They'll assume it's still active. It'll stall their response."

The sheriff swallowed hard. Ahmed's eyes locked onto him. Cold. Pitiless.

"You keep this active until I say otherwise," Ahmed said, his voice dripping with menace. "Everyone who died here was a deputy. That's what you'll say. Do you understand?"

The sheriff nodded weakly, spirit crushed. He turned to walk away.

Ahmed's gaze darkened. He stepped closer, locking eyes with him.

"I wasn't finished."

The sheriff froze, too scared to test Ahmed's patience again.

"Hassan can put a round through your skull from fifteen hundred yards. In pitch black. Through cover. Your badge won't save you."

His voice was ice.

"If you so much as hesitate, your wife and daughter will be sold, broken, and gutted like animals. And we will take our time."

The sheriff's face went pale. Blood dripped from his nose. He hadn't even realized it.

Ahmed's lips curled into a predator's grin. The stench of fear was intoxicating.

He pressed a finger to his earpiece.

"Groups E and D, move into sniping positions. Step carefully. Bryce has made it clear—one wrong move and you're dead. Now move."

He raised his binoculars and scanned the tree line.

The cabin sat still.

A shadow shifted inside.

He saw it—just a flick of the curtain, caught by the wind.

That was enough.

A slow smile crept across his face. He had him.

Ahmed's finger hovered above the mic.

Another explosion ripped through the forest, forcing him to duck as weights tore through the trees.

He waited, already familiar with the delay between detonation and the barrage of shrapnel.

The last of the weights hit with a final snap.

His breath remained steady.

Heart calm.

He lived for this edge.

"All teams, hold your fire. Group A, go."

He whispered it like a death sentence.

The crackle of movement filled his earpiece as the remaining members of Group A advanced.

Ahmed watched. Waited.

Bryce was smart. Dangerous.

But Ahmed had the numbers.

The firepower.

The will to finish this.

Flames roared higher, turning the forest into an inferno.

Ash rained like a curse.

Ahmed paid it no mind.

This was his world.

Chaos. Destruction. He thrived in it.

The breach team closed in.

The final assault was imminent

Ahmed's fingers tightened on his sniper rifle.

His aim locked on the last place he saw movement.

One more move.

One more chance to end this.

The wind shifted, carrying the stench of burning wood and gunpowder.

The trees groaned under the heat.

But Ahmed's focus didn't break.

His moment was coming.

And when it did, he would be ready.

Chapter Forty-Six

Hellfire

Bryce dropped through the floor exit in a blur as the blast masked his escape. He slammed into the ground, landing hard and rolling over the duffel to protect the weapons.

Pain jolted through his frame, but he didn't stop. He dragged the bag into the thick weeds and pulled free his HK.

He swept the area in tight sectors, moving in small, deliberate arcs—just enough to cover his key approach angles without giving away his position.

Slow is smooth. Smooth is fast.

Now he would move with the wind, making every shift invisible.

Every motion was silent, undetected until darkness settled around them.

The earth was dry, disturbed, still warm from the day's sun.

The air reeked of bleach, gunpowder, and scorched wood laced with damp soil.

It coated his mouth with the taste of war.

He wanted to spit, but his training wouldn't let him.

He kept moving.

Above him, the world exploded.

Gunfire chewed through the cabin.

Rounds tore into the wood, splinters bursting like shrapnel in the golden light.

The setting sun cut through the chaos at a brutal angle, blinding Bryce with its intensity.

He couldn't see. Not yet.

But he didn't need to.

Timing was still on his side.

He stayed low, pressing into the earth, slowing his breath.

Dust and debris rained down, sifting through the collapsing floorboards, caught in the slanted beams of dying daylight.

Fire was falling from the sky.

Then, silence. The gunfire ceased all at once.

Shouts. Orders.

The sharp bark of commands over radios.

Boots crunching through dirt and debris left by the mayhem.

The unmistakable clatter of fresh magazines locking into place.

They were advancing.

Bryce exhaled through his nose. He needed the light to die.

His world narrowed to targets and shadows.

The golden hour stretched across the battlefield in long, defiant streaks. Beautiful. But deadly. If he moved too soon, he'd be dead before he could even fire.

Heat from the flames above licked at the air, smoke rolling down like a slow tide. It mixed with the dust, creating a thick haze that blurred the line between earth and sky.

They were moving.

He angled the screen under his arm to shield it from the sun, scanning the feed. Thank God he'd placed the monitors in the only zones the blasts wouldn't reach.

They were coming fast.

Three men crept past the outer perimeter. Four more advanced toward the left side of the cabin. One dropped prone, setting up a sniper position while two others shifted into overwatch.

The monitors wouldn't last much longer.

Bryce made a mental note of their positions, each one mapped to the range card he'd drawn by hand.

He watched as the men advanced toward the door in tight formation.

He was waiting for them.

The breach team.

Stacked at the entrance.

Trained. Precise.

He could tell by the rhythm of their footfalls and the way they moved across the screen.

One.

Two.

Three.

Boom.

A flashbang arced inside, detonating with a brilliant white pulse.

They moved fast.

A kick to the door. Muzzles leading.

The breach team surged in.

Gunfire shredded the floorboards, tearing through every dummy he had staged.

Then came silence.

And that's when Bryce heard it.

That sound.

A sharp inhale.

A pause.

The flicker of realization.

They knew something was wrong.

Then it happened.

A violent rush of oxygen pulled into the cabin.

WOOMP.

The motion sensor bomb detonated.

Everything turned to fire.

The explosion hit the entrance first, incinerating the breach team before they could scream. Ripping through everything, turning wood into missiles and bodies into vapor, flinging the remaining men within twenty yards like rag dolls into the fading light.

Bryce ducked lower.

The fireball shot skyward, gold against gold, a monstrous wave of heat swallowing the last streaks of daylight.

Shrapnel rained down.

Fishing weights, superheated, sharpened, and deadly, tore through the forest, ripping through bodies, embedding deep into tree trunks with sickening thunks.

A burning log cracked loose from the ruins of the cabin and tumbled down the hillside, rolling end over end, setting the underbrush ablaze.

Screams.

Short. Garbled.

Then nothing.

Bryce finally lifted his head, blinking through the dust and smoke.

The last light of the sun slashed through the carnage, illuminating what was left of the men who had tried to kill him.

Bryce ducked at the sharp hiss of weights zipping past, chipping away at the rocks shielding him.

They must have been ricochets.

A flaming log crashed against the boulders beside him, its embers casting an eerie glow over the blood-streaked ground.

His fingers clenched around his HK, knuckles white.

Chaos. Absolute chaos.

The remaining men stumbled back, disoriented. The forest was alive with cries of pain. Smoke rolled over the valley. Shadows danced in the flickering light.

He didn't want to kill.

But they gave him no choice.

Bryce forced himself to move.

He tossed the screen aside, his monitors now obliterated by the blast.

Reaching into the duffel, he pulled out a long black rope and switched out his HK for his sniper rifle, then zipped the bag shut, tying one end of the rope to its straps.

Using the thick smoke as cover, he secured the other end to a boulder and rolled the bag over the edge of the cliff, lowering it into the valley below.

Letting the rest of the rope fall, he turned back toward the burning battlefield.

The screams continued, growing louder as the night deepened.

The sky had turned pale blue, masked by smoke and carnage.

Then, just like that, the sun was gone. He was free to move.

They had lost that battle.

But the war still raged.

Darkness was his element. But that didn't mean he felt safe.

Bryce moved carefully behind the smoldering logs, inching toward the rock outcropping where he had seen the sniper setting up.

He raised the rifle and switched on the night vision.

The scope flickered green.

The world bloomed in shades of infrared.

There.

The sniper lay prone, his rifle locked in position. His scope glowed faintly.

Bryce exhaled. Slow. Steady.

Squeeze.

Tok.

Through the scope, the sniper twitched, then slumped. Lifeless.

No glory. Just subtraction.

The homemade suppressor had worked.

The sound was strange, unfamiliar.

But it worked.

That was all that mattered.

He shifted position, staying low.

Every breath felt borrowed.

Three more snipers.

Squeeze.

Tok. The first dropped.

Squeeze.

Tok. The second never saw it coming.

Squeeze.

Tok. The third flinched—too late.

One wrong move, and it was over.

Three kills.

Time to move.

Bullets tore through the logs around him as the remaining forces opened fire blindly into the smoke.

They weren't shooting at him.

They were shooting at shadows.

Sirens wailed from the valley below.

But help wasn't coming. Not for him.

At first, the sound barely registered.

Then the red-and-blue emergency lights painted the treetops.

Reality hit.

More were coming.

Usually, sirens meant help.

Not this time.

Bryce checked his watch.

Minutes had stretched into hours.

He had to disengage—

Before the second wave arrived.

A bullhorn cracked through the noise.

"Bryce Rath, we have you surrounded! We know you have kidnapped Janice and Taylor-May!"

Keeping low, he crawled toward the cliffside, staying in the shadows.

A twig snapped just feet away.

Bryce coiled, knife already in hand, ready for wet work.

A man emerged through the brush, breathing hard. Scared. Confused.

Then a voice called out.

"Hey, you see 'em?"

The man frantically searched the area.

Bryce shifted, peering over a fallen log, struggling to see through the flames.

More police chatter filled the radios.

"Turn off the damn sirens!"

The wailing stopped.

Now, only the crackle of fire and the distant echoes of pain remained.

"Come out with your hands up! We have you surrounded!"

Searchlights cut through the trees, moving like ghostly fingers through the rising smoke.

"Shit."

Bryce sheathed his knife.

The man nearby had no idea how close he was to death.

Another voice rang out in the chaos.

"What the hell are we surrounding, Sheriff? The cabin is destroyed! Most everyone is dead. We don't know if we got them or they got us!"

A bullet slammed into the rock next to Bryce.

Someone had eyes on him.

Too close.

One inch left, and he wouldn't be thinking. He'd be bleeding out.

Another shot tore through the air.

His body screamed.

His mind stayed locked in.

Searchlights locked on.

"I have eyes on him!"

"By the burning log!"

"Which burning log? They're all burning!"

Flashlights swung toward Bryce's position.

More gunfire erupted.

Frozen. No way out.

Then—BOOM.

A searchlight exploded, sending shrapnel into the men below.

Bryce blinked through sweat and blood.

There was no pause. No mercy.

Screams. Panic.

Another blast. Another light gone.

Gunfire turned in every direction, shooting at ghosts.

A man shouted from the forest. "Where did that come from?! That didn't come from the rocks!"

Two more lights shattered, shards flying into the crowd.

Men dropped, clutching their faces, screaming.

The sheriff's voice cracked over the radio.

"Where the hell is that coming from?! Who's firing?!"

A pause between static and screaming.

"Light it up. Get some goddamn eyes on the ridge!"

Someone deeper in the woods yelled back.

"YOU turn on a light tubby! I'm not trying to get shot."

The sheriff spun around. "Who said that?!"

Bryce didn't wait.

He scanned the treeline.

Found it.

A long, dark muzzle of a rifle, searching. Hidden in the forest. Aimed directly at him.

It moved.

Squeeze.

TOK.

Threat eliminated.

The sniper dropped.

Bryce didn't stop scanning.

He steadied his breathing, sweeping the forest with night vision through the scope.

The sheriff addressed the arriving officers, his voice thick with nerves. Thankful the search light was just shot out. He was surprised they were still alive, but at least he didn't have to lie.

Bryce took advantage of the commotion, sliding over the side of the cliff. He gripped the rope, belaying down in a controlled descent.

Until gunfire erupted.

CRACK!

Bullets chipped away at the rock, stone shards slicing past his face.

"Found him! He's going down the cliff!"

Ahmed's voice cut through the radio.

"Fifty thousand dollars for the man who kills him."

The hillside lit up.

This was war.

And he was built for it.

Muzzle flashes flickered like lightning in the darkness, gunfire raining down in an unrelenting barrage.

Bryce forced himself downward, sliding faster than he wanted, but there was no choice.

Then a misstep.

The jagged outcrop gave way beneath him. His foothold gone in an instant. Gravity took over.

His grip vanished as the rope burned through his gloves.

He fell hard, rolling down the hill like dead weight.

A rock met his temple.

Blackness.

Pain didn't knock, it just kicked the door in and stayed awhile.

Voices.

"I think he's down the hill. You got any lights?"

KATHWACK.

Two bullets grazed off Bubba's vest, slamming into the fallen tree behind him.

"OW! Goddamn it!"

Bubba spun, firing blindly into the woods.

The others followed, unloading round after round into the dark unknown.

The radio squealed. "Hey, stop shooting, assholes! You're gonna hit us!"

Bubba growled. "Who the hell is 'us'? And why are you shooting at me?!"

Two guys dropped beside him.

Bodies folding into the dirt.

The sheriff's voice crackled over the bullhorn.

"GET DOWN, IDIOTS!"

Bryce gasped awake.

Pain crashed through his skull like a sledgehammer.

The world tilted, his mind struggling to catch up.

He felt around in the dirt, searching for something, anything.

A rock. A branch.

Then he found cold metal.

His fingers closed around his sniper rifle.

His duffel bag was nearby. He pulled in the rope and stashed it in his duffel, and continued to grope blindly, finding his night vision goggles just as a sliver of moonlight cut through the trees.

A lucky break.

Or a death sentence.

He slipped on the goggles.

Green light flared.

The world snapped into flat clarity.

No time to think. Only act.

He wiped blood from his eye.

And froze.

Four men.

Above him.

Lying prone on the hillside.

Rifles trained on the valley floor.

Fear clawed its way up. He forced it down.

One of them whispered, "Get a damn searchlight down there. It'll be like shooting deer at night."

Bubba barked an order.

A bright light snapped on. It blinded him.

Bryce clenched his teeth and rolled.

Gunfire erupted, tearing through the spot he had just occupied.

Another searchlight exploded.

Bam.

A panicked scream followed.

The radio came alive.

"What the hell, Bubba?! Warn us when you're gonna turn a light on! You fucking blinded me!"

Bryce used the chaos.

He ran.

Pain flared across his skull with every step, his balance unsteady from the fall. But he pushed forward, stumbling toward the tree line, duffel bag over his shoulder, the sniper rifle tucked into his chest. He was prepared to fire at the first sign of movement.

Shots rang out.

Janice and Taylor-May continued to open fire from the mountain. Suppressing rounds slamming into the cliff's edge, keeping the enemy pinned.

Bryce dove behind a thick tree, heart hammering.

The men were still blindly spraying rounds into the woods, firing where they thought he'd be.

Bryce willed himself up, pushing off the ground.

CRACK.

A bullet splintered the tree beside his head.

He dove again.

"Fucker."

The duffel bag was a liability.

He ripped it off his shoulder and hurled it up the hill.

Bullets followed.

"There you are!"

Bryce flipped up his night vision goggles, knelt, and aimed.

His hands were steady despite the pounding in his skull.

Squeeze.

TOK.

A sniper slumped forward, his weapon sliding from his grasp.

More gunfire erupted from above.

The girls were laying down cover fire, forcing Bubba's men into the dirt.

Bryce focused.

Breathe.

His hand shook as he wiped blood from his right eye.

"Come on, Karma. You got this."

He pushed off the tree and sprinted for the next cover point.

A click snapped from up the ridge—an empty mag.

"Shit."

Bryce ran.

Regret had no place on this battlefield.

The sound of dirt bikes echoed in the distance.

He climbed. Hard. Fast.

"Hey! Don't shoot me! I'm coming up!"

The camo tarp covering the Jeep came into view at the crest of the hill.

Bryce ripped it off and tossed the duffel into the back.

The interior light flicked on.

He killed it instantly.

"Holy shit, Karma! About time!"

Taylor-May ran forward and crushed him in a hug.

He held on for a second. Not long.

It wasn't over.

He couldn't give in to emotion.
Not yet.

They had to move.

His voice was hoarse from the smoke. "Yeah. Let's go."

Bryce climbed into the driver's seat, started the engine, and checked his mirrors.

Janice dove into the back seat, rolled down the window, and aimed her gun out.

"You got most of them, but five are coming now. The police showed up, but they never entered the fight."

Taylor-May slid into the passenger seat, grinning wildly.
Her grin caught the moonlight, feral, unstoppable.

"You sure know how to show a lady a good time."

Bryce smirked in spite of himself. "Yeah? Well, buckle up. This is gonna get interesting."

He handed her his automatic weapon and pulled extra mags from his chest pocket.

Then he jumped out of the Jeep.

Taylor-May looked back, confused. "What the hell are you doing?"

Bryce ran to the back, yanked open the hatch, and shoved the Pelican cases into position—strapping them across the rear window.

"I'm adding armor."

Taylor-May watched in confusion as he secured the cases into makeshift plating.

"This should stop most of what they throw at us. It was the best investment to make them kevlar lined."

Bryce climbed back in, making sure all the interior lights were off.
Night vision goggles: ON.

"Here we go."

He clicked a button on his goggles, shifted into gear, and tore down the bumpy dirt road.

Every jolt drew a quiet curse from Taylor-May or Janice.

The only sound outside was the dirt bikes—
Screaming through the forest.
Getting louder.

They were coming.
Coming for them.

Bryce gripped the wheel tighter and pushed the Jeep faster, weaving through the treacherous switchbacks.

Every move mattered.

One mistake, and they were dead.

But Bryce Rath didn't make mistakes.

Not tonight.

Not ever.

Chapter Forty-Seven

Who's in charge?

S moke and fire clawed at the remnants of the cabin, a once-pristine sanctuary now reduced to a nightmarish battlefield. The air reeked of burning wood and charred flesh, a thick haze obscuring the full horror of the scene.

Jagged craters marred the earth, gaping wounds from IEDs that turned the ground into a macabre graveyard.

Shattered trees stood like skeletal sentinels, their tops still ablaze.
Body parts and debris littered the dirt, buried beneath layers of ash and destruction.

The sheriff stood at the edge of the devastation, the bullhorn trembling in his hand.
He leaned against a nearby boulder to steady himself as he lifted it to his dry lips, unsure of what to say.

A man's voice cut through, faint over the crackle of fire and the chaotic hum of activity.

"Who's in charge here?"

A police captain stepped forward, the silver bars on his tactical vest catching the glow of the searchlights.
His team, clad in heavy gear and armed with assault rifles, surveyed the wreckage with steely resolve.

The sheriff dropped into a crouch; the words hitting him like another explosion.
He lowered the bullhorn.

Then he rose again, trying to compose himself, and cleared his burning throat.

"I am," he rasped, forcing the words through cracked lips.
"We had a hostage situation... then an active shooter... then... this."

He gestured at the obliterated landscape, disbelief edging into his voice.

"My deputies... they're gone. IEDs chewed through them like paper."

The captain's jaw tightened as he took in the carnage.

Searchlights sliced through the smoke-choked valley, sweeping in fractured, ghostly arcs. Fires still burned in scattered pockets, casting a flickering light that revealed horrors in bursts and buried others in shifting shadow.

Limbs hung from treetops like grotesque ornaments. Torsos lay torn open and flung across the blackened earth, discarded like broken dolls.

Massive craters pocked the ground, each ringed with jagged burn scars and twisted debris. Pools of blood collected in the dirt, thick and glassy, reflecting the beams like oil-slick mirrors of death.

The stench was suffocating. Burned flesh. Melted plastic. Cordite. Beneath it all was something worse. Something human. Rotting, but masked with bleach.

It filled his throat, gripped his lungs, and coiled in his gut.

He knew the smell would follow him for the rest of his life.

High on the ridgeline, Bubba and the last of his militia swept their flashlights over the hills. Their movements were slow, uncertain. Faces pale. Eyes hollow.

None of them spoke.

They were still trying to understand what kind of man could do this.

They were out of their depth.

Confusion and fear spread among them.

The dirt bikes revved in the distance, their engines echoing through the trees.

A reminder.

Someone was still out there.

Watching.

Waiting.

The sheriff's earpiece crackled, and Ahmed's voice slithered through like a poltergeist.

"This is your only reminder, Sheriff. Speak a word and your family dies screaming."

Bile rose in the sheriff's throat.

He barely processed the next moment.

A high-pitched beep split through the air.

Sharp. Unnatural. Wrong.

Bubba frowned. "What the hell was that?"

BOOM.

Explosions ripped through the night.

The remaining militia were torn apart in an instant. A gruesome spray of red mist caught in the smoke and orange glow of the fires.

Greasy black smoke mixed with blood stinging the air.

The hillside bled like an open festering wound. Contrasted by the sharp, sterile tang of bleach.

New searchlights spun wildly in the aftermath, casting long shadows that flickered like wraiths.

Nearby officers and emergency responders instinctively dropped to the ground, covering their heads as shockwaves rattled the valley.

Gunfire had been expected.

But this?

This was something else.

The sheriff's grip on the bullhorn slackened.

It fell to the ground with a hollow thud.

Staggering back, his face ashen, he barely made it to the nearest tree before doubling over and heaving onto the forest floor.

Firefighters shouted in controlled chaos, working to clear the wreckage of the trucks blocking the narrow mountain road, now halted by the explosion.

They had to open a lane fast. If the fire spread to the tree line, no one would get out alive.

They needed to get the fire crews closer before the flames spread, before the inferno consumed the forest.

But the sheriff's mind was spiraling.

Fear. Guilt. Death. The weight of it all curled around his chest like a vise.

He wasn't a lawman anymore.

Just a man staring into hell, with his own sins staring back at him.

He wiped his mouth with the back of his hand.

Then froze.

A new scent. Something acrid, wrong, cut through the smoke.

Sharp. Chemical. Wrong.

He sniffed again, brow furrowing.

Bleach. Like from the vests.

His stomach twisted.

This wasn't just an attack.

This was a cleanup.

His voice trembled as he turned to the police captain.

"You," he pointed a shaking finger. "You take over. I... I can't stay here."

He pushed through the crowd of firefighters and officers, their eyes boring into him.

Some full of judgment.

Others were simply confused.

But none of that mattered.

Not now.

Reaching the base of the hill, the sheriff spotted an empty police cruiser, its engine humming softly in the night, lights still flashing.

He didn't hesitate.

Climbing into the driver's seat, he slammed the door shut.

Tires screeched.

The cruiser roared down the winding road. His mind was racing as fast as the engine.

His phone buzzed against the dashboard.

With a trembling hand, he grabbed it.

Jack's voice came through.

"Where are you?"

The sheriff gripped the wheel, knuckles bone-white.

"I'm on my way. They're all dead, Jack. Do you hear me? DEAD!"

He flung the phone across the seat. His heart hammered.

The cruiser twisted and turned through the mountains; the headlights slicing through the void like twin blades.

He was running now.

Running from the death and destruction he'd helped unleash.

Running from Ahmed's threats.

Running from the blood on his hands.

But no matter how fast he drove, he knew one thing.

He couldn't outrun what was coming.

Not justice. Not vengeance.

Just the cold certainty that Bryce Rath didn't miss.

And deep down, he knew that when he found him, there would be no escape.

Unless he found him first.

That was his only way out.

Take out Bryce Rath, or be taken out.

It was inevitable. Karma was coming for him.

Chapter Forty-Eight

Rough Extraction

Bryce gritted his teeth, guiding the Jeep down the narrow fire trail, skimming the edge of the canyon they had just escaped. The road was nothing but dirt and loose rock, barely wide enough for the Jeep. Thick brush clawed at the sides, and the deep ruts from past firefighting rigs made every turn a gamble.

Bouncing lights in the distance signaled their pursuers. Headlights wavered in the darkness, gaining speed, closing the gap.

Janice looked through her window, muttering, "Shit. Damn bike heads."

Bryce couldn't look back. He kept his eyes locked on the road through the green-lit world of his NVGs. The path ahead blurred into a swirling haze. Slowly, the marine layer crawled up the valley, thickening with each passing second. The fog would work for them or against them.

"Janice, count your ammo."

She rummaged through the back seat, using the soft glow of Taylor-May's phone to check her gear. "I've got about twenty left for the rifle."

"Conserve your shots. Don't fire unless they do," Bryce said. "They're on bikes. That gives us the advantage. Just keep your eyes open for any other vehicles."

Taylor-May gritted her teeth, knuckles white on the overhead handle.

"Fuck this shit!"

Bryce punched the gas.

The Jeep launched over a deep rut, the suspension groaning as the tires fought for traction on the loose dirt.

For a split second, weightlessness.

Then impact.

The chassis slammed down, rattling through their bones.

"Sorry," Bryce called, voice calm despite the chaos.

Taylor-May groaned, eyes squeezed shut. "Drive that shit. I wanna live!"

The fire trail ended abruptly, feeding onto the shoulder of Route Two. Pavement stretched ahead of them, barely visible in the rolling fog.

Bryce jerked the wheel, cutting onto the highway hard, tires skidding before gripping.

With one hand, he yanked out the SAT phone and dropped it into Taylor-May's lap.

"Turn this on under your shirt so it won't blind me. Call Troy."

She hesitated, then shoved it beneath her jacket. "There's something funny to say here, but I can't think of it."

The screen's glow flickered against her skin.

"Shit!" Bryce closed one eye, temporarily blinded, but thankful for the straightaway in the road.

"Janice, is there another jacket back there?"

Janice scurried around. "Yeah. Here, baby."

Taylor-May snatched it, draping it over the phone. "Thanks, Ma."

A faint beep.

"Okay, ready."

"Hold the green button until the light changes."

Click.

"You could've told me that before I turned the phone on."

Bryce smirked. "Where's the fun in that?"

Taylor-May rolled her eyes. "Ha."

The phone rang. Bryce secured it in the dash cradle.

Troy answered, voice sharp. "This is Troy."

Bryce didn't hesitate. "Sergeant, you're on speaker. We're on Route Two, trying to make it to the next county in one piece. Taylor-May and Janice are with me. We need a green zone Exfil Point. The whole damn town is after us."

Bryce could now use both eyes, having adjusted back to the night vision.

Troy exhaled. "Karma, you really don't know how to stay out of the shit. Hold on. Let me make a call."

Silence.

Taylor-May frowned. "No, hold music at the CIA? Weird."

"I think he just put the phone down," Bryce said.

"Oh."

Then—

A guttural roar split the night.

Not bikes.

A big-block engine.

Bryce's eyes flicked to the side mirror. The green glow of his NVGs caught the flicker of headlights gaining on them.

He adjusted the mirror so he wouldn't be blinded by the glare.

"Taylor-May, Janice, get low. Taylor, adjust your side mirror so only you can see it."

They scrambled.

Taylor-May twisted the mirror, eyes narrowing.

"Okay. Shit, Bryce. It's coming up fast. They're moving to your side!"

Bryce yanked the Jeep left, tapped the brakes, then slammed the accelerator.

The pursuing vehicle swerved, struggling for control.

BANG-BANG!

Two shots shattered the rear window.

"Anyone hit?"

Janice stayed low, rifle steady. "No. Didn't go through. Guess you packed the right shit."

Troy's voice returned, tense. "Karma, did they just shoot at you?"

Bryce swerved again, avoiding a pit maneuver. "Many times. Too many times. A lot of people died tonight."

Dead silence. Bryce heard Troy speaking off-mic.

"How bad is this gonna look?"

"I'll keep firing until we're safe. That's how bad it's gonna look."

Another pause. Troy came back on.

"I've got the sheriff from the next county on the line. He says you need to relinquish your weapons before crossing into his jurisdiction."

Bryce barked a humorless laugh. "Not gonna happen. Can't trust that. Do you have any FBI contacts that aren't working with Jack or Javier?"

Troy sighed. "Not that I know of. CIA and FBI don't exactly—hold on."

Static.

Then—

WHAM.

Metal crunched.

The Jeep fishtailed violently. Bryce fought the wheel, NVGs locked on the swirling green chaos ahead.

Taylor-May shouted, "We need a new plan!"

Bryce adjusted to the motion, scanning for the contrast between shadows and movement.

"Hold on."

Engines howled behind them, relentless, unshaken.

The fog thickened, rolling over the road, swallowing the edges of the world.

Troy's voice returned, urgent. "Okay, Bryce, there's a Coast Guard base near you..."

Then—

SMACK.

A sharp gunshot cracked through the night.

Glass shattered. The driver's side mirror flew off into the darkness.

Bryce barely flinched, more annoyed than surprised.

"Shit," he muttered, gripping the wheel tighter. The green glow of his NVGs painted the world in eerie monochrome, illuminating the road in shifting shades of infrared.

"Where's the base?"

Troy's voice came back tense, rapid, fingers clacking away in the background. "Fifty miles away... but in the opposite direction."

Bryce exhaled sharply. "Well, shit. Why didn't you say so?"

His foot slammed the brakes hard.

The Jeep screeched, nose dipping violently.

Behind them, the pursuing vehicle swerved, tires shrieking as the driver instinctively reacted, trying to avoid a collision.

That was all Bryce needed.

He slammed on the gas.

The Jeep launched forward, dirt and smoke spitting from the tires. The sudden acceleration forced Taylor-May and Janice back in their seats.

Bryce kept his vision locked on the terrain, navigating through the green haze of his goggles, reading the landscape like a map only he could see.

A headache was building, his brain straining to process at high speed through the flat, unnatural depth of night vision, but that was the least of his worries.

The forest bled past in rapid motion, fog swirling between the trees, twisting in the turbulence of their escape. The pursuing vehicle hesitated, caught in its own momentum, giving them the extra seconds they needed.

The Jeep fought a sharp turn. Bryce pushed the axle and suspension to their limits to gain as much distance as possible.

Then he saw it. An opening to the left. A wider shoulder. Just enough to disappear.

He yanked the wheel hard.

The Jeep skidded onto the dirt shoulder, barely visible off the sharp curve. The world tilted as the tires fought for grip.

"What the fuck are you doing?" Janice snapped, gripping the overhead handle.

Taylor-May didn't bother asking. She just braced and shut her eyes.

The Jeep slid into the bend, fishtailing before straightening out.

Dust and debris bled into the fog, thickening their camouflage.

Bryce jumped out, rifle in hand, and dropped into a firing position behind the front bumper. He checked the slope angle, gauging the ricochet risk before exposing his head. He lifted his goggles, closed one eye against the light, and released the safety.

The pursuing car roared around the bend, high beams searching, cutting through the mist.

Bryce stayed perfectly still.

The cruiser shot past them, a phantom of light in the dark. Its headlights bounced off the fog like a lighthouse on a dead sea.

The driver hit the brakes.

Too late.

Perfect.

Bryce steadied his aim.

Squeezed the trigger.

THUD-THUD-THUD.

The rear window spidered with three tight bullet holes.

Inside, the driver slumped forward, forehead smacking the wheel.

The taillights exploded. Glass rained onto the road as rounds tore through them.

Bryce moved fast.

He sprinted to the passenger side, angling his shot low, blinding them, owning the night.

Two rounds punched out the headlights, plunging the road into darkness.

He flipped down his NVGs. His closed eye adjusted instantly.

The green glow revealed the truth.

Inside, Agent Jack sat frozen, gun shaking, eyes wide. The sheriff bled out beside him, hand twitching toward a weapon.

Bryce waited until the gun angled away.

Then he yanked open the door.

Point-blank.

Jack sat paralyzed. Hands up. Mouth moving without sound.

Finally: "Wait—WAIT!"

Bryce didn't blink.

He shifted his aim.

Two quick shots.

The sheriff's head snapped back, blood spraying across the shattered dash as his gun fell to the floor.

Dead.

A flicker of relief passed through Bryce. No celebration, just one more threat gone.

Not enough.

But something.

He turned the muzzle back to Jack.

Paused.

This one might still be useful.

Bryce exhaled. "Shit."

He lowered the barrel by an inch.

"You have one chance to live. One. Do anything outside of what I say, and you die. Understand?"

Jack bobbed his head frantically. "Y-yeah. Yes!"

"Good."

"Open the door from the outside. Hands where I can see them. Exit the car. Slowly."

Jack did as told. Short breaths. Shaky hands.

"Move to the front. Lay down. Hands forward."

Jack dropped flat, fingers stretched ahead of him.

Bryce moved fast. Snatched the cuffs off the sheriff's belt. Secured Jack like a pro. Fast. Efficient.

Burning inside.

Bryce grabbed the sheriff's wallet and phone. Jack's ID. Closed one eye and flipped on the emergency lights. Bathed the scene in eerie red and blue. Slipped the cuff keys into his pocket.

Done.

He hauled Jack up, yanked his arms into an armlock, and dragged him toward the Jeep.

Inside, Janice turned, eyes narrowing as she watched Bryce cut pieces of the rope tieing Jack to the seat.

Bryce cinched the final knot, securing Jack to the headrest. Not going any-where.

Now to figure out what to do with him.

Bryce slid into the driver's seat. Back trail was clear.

For now.

"Alright, hold on."

The Jeep lurched forward, tires chewing up the road.

Bryce's eyes stayed locked ahead. NVGs glowing.

"What are the chances they think we'd go back through town?" he said calmly.

Taylor-May whipped her head around. "No. Bad idea."

Jack spoke up. "Yeah, they offered fifty thousand for your heads. Everyone on the hill is dead, but that message went out to every person within a hundred-mile radius.

Don't go through town. You'll get us all killed."

Bryce flipped open the map. A quick flash of red light. Then off.

"We don't have to go through it," he said, smiling. "We can go over it."

Taylor-May and Janice exchanged a look. Equal parts dread and exhaustion.

Janice groaned. "My tits are gonna fall off with all this off-road shit."

A laugh burst from the SAT phone.

"Janice," Troy crackled through, "if you make it out, we'll get you new ones."

Janice scoffed. "Mmm. Government tits? No thanks. They'd be lopsided and only look good from one angle."

The humor hit like medicine. Relief through sarcasm.

Bryce chuckled darkly and punched the gas.

The Jeep surged forward, bouncing over uneven terrain.

They had miles to go.

But now, they had a plan.

Chapter Forty-Nine

The Hunters

Three black dirt bikes rolled up to the sheriff's cruiser, their engines purring low with restrained violence humming beneath the surface.

The cruiser's lights still spun, casting fractured beams of red and blue across the trees.

Each rotation painted the ground in alternating shades of warning and death.

The wreckage was still warm.

Blood and smoke clung to the air, thick and unshakable.

Slumped forward in the driver's seat, the sheriff's head hung at an unnatural angle like a lifeless marionette.

Fresh blood streaked the shattered windshield, glistening in the pulsing red and blue glow.

The siren was silent now, but the radio crackled with an eerie hum. Static from a dispatch that would never be answered.

None of them spoke.

They dismounted in practiced silence, boots crunching against the dirt like the last sound a man hears before execution. Each moved with precision, sector-scanning baked deep into muscle memory. Their eyes swept the scene, absorbing every detail with cold efficiency.

A sharp nod from Hassan.

A flick of the fingers from Ahmed.

A short gesture from Nadir.

No English. Only Pashto, cold, clipped, absolute.

Ahmed reached into his vest and unfolded a map, its creases worn from days of relentless study. Beneath the flickering red-blue glow, his finger traced the terrain, stopping at the coastline.

The Coast Guard base.

The only place Bryce could run.

Every road, every trail, every escape route, the cartel owned them all.

If Bryce made it to that base, this was over.

Ahmed exhaled through his nose.

That could not happen.

He imagined what would follow if they failed. Not death, humiliation. Disgrace. Bryce would become a symbol. That could not be allowed. Not after everything he had sacrificed. He'd buried too many men on missions like this. If Bryce slipped through now, the whole valley would become their grave.

He gave the signal.

His men moved like a coiled viper, striking forward. They knew the mission. There was only one path left.

The motorcycles snarled to life, tires biting the earth as they vanished into the fog—shadows slipping into the night.

They reached a break in the road. Subtle. Faint tire marks. A shift in disturbed dirt that most would've missed.

But not Ahmed. He didn't miss things like that.

His instincts, honed in battle, locked onto the trail with deadly precision.

The mountain whispered a warning, but Ahmed didn't listen. He never had.

Failure wasn't an option. Not on this mountain. Not with Bryce still breathing.

He motioned forward.

They moved.

Silent. Efficient.

Predators, closing in on their kill.

The trail pitched upward, winding along the ridge.

Fresh gashes in the brush. Torn-up dirt.

The desperate mark of a man running out of time.

No words were needed.

They knew.

He was close.

Ahmed throttled forward, grip tightening.

"No one leaves this mountain alive."

Chapter Fifty

The Escape

Bryce kept his eyes locked on the road, the shifting green glow of his NVGs casting a flat, eerie haze across the landscape. The terrain blurred past in ghostly shades of infrared.

He gripped the SAT phone tighter.

"Sergeant, we'll hit the north side of the base in about three hours. I have FBI Agent Jack in custody. Can you get me some eyes to help us along the way?"

Troy's keyboard clacked in the background.

"I'll try to get a drone training op up, but don't hold your breath. Getting you clearance and protection from the base will be hard enough." A pause. "I'll see who I can contact regarding the sheriff and any other options. They can't intervene on public property."

Bryce pushed the Jeep harder, finally finding traction as they hit a firmer stretch of dirt path.

"We're two clicks from marker sixteen. Should be able to travel dark most of the way."

"Copy. Good luck. I'll call when I have anything for you. Flying out now to see what I can do on the way."

Bryce exhaled. "Thank you, Sergeant."

Troy's voice softened. "Godspeed, Karma."

Click.

The SAT phone cut out.

The Jeep found a narrow path used more by animals than vehicles.

Bryce downshifted, gripping the wheel as the Jeep drifted up the steep embankment.

It rolled over the dirt path, its shadow barely distinguishable under the sliver of moonlight.

Bryce stopped the Jeep at the end of the small dirt trail.

An open abyss remained.

He studied the map, making quick calculations as he read the topography.

Bryce glanced at Taylor-May.

"There's water and food in the back. Grab some."

Taylor-May hesitated, then nodded. "Yeah... Ma?"

Janice, moving mechanically, reached into the bag, pulling out bottles of water and snacks. She passed them around.

"Feels like I'm a soccer mom all over again."

Her voice tried to smile, but her hands trembled too much to lie.

Taylor-May gave a tight smile. "You never brought food to my soccer games."

Janice arched a brow. "It's because of that ungratefulness that I didn't."

Bryce took a long pull from the bottle, savoring the cold burn down his throat. "I trust the Sergeant, but keep your eyes peeled. No clue how many are still out there."

Janice cracked open her bottle, taking a slow sip. "Gotcha."

They ate in tense silence. The jerky was tough, but it kept them alert.

Janice tensed. Her breath hitched.

"Shit."

Bryce checked the rear-view mirror. "What?"

Janice folded her arms tightly.

"He's awake."

Bryce met Jack's glare in the mirror.

The agent's eyes burned with a quiet rage, barely restrained beneath the surface.

"You're alive because you're useful, Jack. Stop being useful and you're dead weight. Got it?"

Jack didn't flinch. He blinked once, glanced at Janice and Taylor-May, and looked away.

Everyone was barely visible in the moonlight that forced its way inside.

Jack turned to the window.

Met only by his own reflection.

A haunted version of himself staring back through the glass.

The marine layer crawled into the valley, dropping the temp and thickening the fog.

Visibility plummeted.

Bryce made a few more calculations, adjusting the contrast on his NVGs.

The Jeep whined as he shifted into four-wheel low, then he set the emergency brake, leaving the engine running.

He slipped off his night vision goggles and stepped out, kneeling low to let his eyes adjust with his rifle raised.

Sweeping the area in tight quadrants, he moved toward the mountain's edge.

Raising his binoculars, he mapped out their descent as best he could through the patchy fog.

It kept rolling in, thick and low.

He could feel the cold Pacific air pushing up the slope, tightening around him.

Far off, sirens wailed through the mountains.

A sound Bryce knew too well.

Then something worse.

The distant screams of motorcycles.

Growing louder.

Faster.

Tracking them.

How?

Bryce exhaled, pulse steady.

His mind raced.

They must be good if they're tracking us.

He focused on his breathing, clearing the noise in his mind.

His pulse slowed, not from calm, but from calculation.

Fear didn't help. Focus did.

And more importantly...

How are they getting off this mountain if they're as good as they seem?

Engines snarled through the fog, growing closer.

Bryce turned back toward the Jeep just as Jack screamed.

Inside, Janice was pummeling the agent, her knuckles already bloodied from the impact.

Bryce yanked the door open.

"If you kill him, getting into witness protection becomes a hell of a lot harder."

Janice's breath was ragged, fist still clenched.

Jack's nose was broken, blood streaming down his face. One eye was already swollen shut.

Bryce barely spared him another glance.

"I need you both to clear your weapons. Safeties on. Eject the rounds. It's about to get rough, and I don't need accidental discharges."

Muzzle discipline. Straps secured.

Bryce checked them without thinking. Muscle memory.

Taylor-May nodded, pulling the bolt on her rifle, clearing it.

Janice did the same, shaking out her fingers.

Bryce checked his own weapon before handing it back to Janice. "Stash it behind the seat. Strap it down with the blanket. No one's shooting. Hopefully, neither are they. Lock the doors. Roll up the windows. We need every ounce of structural integrity we can get."

Taylor-May secured hers, gripping the handlebar tight. "What the hell's happening?"

Janice's head snapped up.

Lights bounced through the fog.

Motorcycles.

Bryce exhaled. "Damn."

Jack's eyes went wide as he searched out the window. He muttered through swollen lips,

"Oh, no... they survived."

Bryce climbed into the Jeep and started it up. All the windows went up. He glanced back at Jack. "They who?"

Repositioning his night vision goggles, he searched for a clear path down the hill. Then he put the Jeep in gear, eased off the brake, and rolled into the drop.

They all held their breath as their stomachs lurched with the Jeep. It pitched forward, tires spitting loose rock into the dark void below.

There was no road here. Just gravity and the mountain's raw, jagged spine that dropped into the abyss.

Bryce fought the wheel like a man wrestling the inevitable.

The only light came from the green glow of his NVGs, painting the world in an eerie, shifting haze. Rock, trees, void, flashing in and out of existence.

The Jeep wasn't driving anymore.

It was falling.

Bouncing.

Smashing through low brush, skimming cliffs, dodging boulders the size of cars at the last possible second.

No headlights. No real control.

A freefall down a mountain that didn't want them there.

"They who, Jack? I need all the info you have on them."

Jack's head lolled, smacking the seat frame with each brutal hit, blood streaking down his chin and nose. He blinked, slow and unfocused.

Then he spoke.

"ISIS."

The Jeep caught air.

Janice cursed, gripping the handlebar as they slammed back down. The frame groaned. Tires skidded on shale.

Jack coughed, a hoarse, humorless laugh under the Jeep's rattle. He spat blood onto the floorboard.

"Could be ex–Afghan Special Forces. Guys we trained… then left behind. Or worse, Quds Force. Iranian black ops. Ghosts in civilian clothes. Either way, they're Tier One trained. And they're not fucking around."

Taylor-May didn't want to believe it. But she'd seen the coordination.

This wasn't gang work. It was something darker.

She stared forward, silent.

Bryce kept his mouth shut.

Focused on the wheel and survival, his mind raced through different options.

Jack inhaled through his teeth, breath shaky.

"I think they were already here. Just waiting. Didn't need much, just a signal. The cartel should not have that kind of pull."

A drop.

The Jeep pitched. Rear tires lifted. Sliding.

Bryce yanked the wheel, bouncing off a rock, forcing it into a half-controlled descent.

Jack's voice dropped like stones into deep, black water.

"They gave Kevlar vests to the militia."

A slow inhale.

"They took control the moment they arrived. I told Fred. What an idiot."

Taylor-May exhaled sharply, her grip tightening.

Jack licked the blood from his lips.

"But the vests…" His voice faltered.

"They weren't for protection."

The Jeep hit a log and skidded, tires chewing through it, fighting to regain traction.

"They were bombs."

The air went dead.

Heavier than any silence before.

Bryce reacted. "That's why it smelled like bleach?"

Jack nodded.

"They eviscerated them. All that's left is more marrow than bone. They made it impossible to tell who was who. Who pulled the trigger? Who gave the order? No one was ever meant to survive. This wasn't just a hit on you. It was designed, cold and calculated, built to erase everything. Even the questions. I'm the biggest threat. I know too much."

Jack looked out the window.

A tear rolled down his cheek.

The Jeep lurched.

Then became weightlessness.

The mountain punched back.

A bone-crushing slam.

Skid.

Jack's head slumped forward. Out cold.

Taylor-May gritted her teeth. "Are you *trying* to kill us?!"

Bryce didn't answer.

He was too busy trying not to kill them.

Chapter Fifty-One

Dark Void

At the top of the ridge, Ahmed raised a clenched fist to signal a halt. Then he motioned outward with an open hand, directing them to spread out across the slope.

The others broke formation, riding low and quiet, their engines barely audible as they vanished into the mist like shadows on command.

He dismounted with practiced ease, boots sinking into the softened ground. Kneeling beside a patch of disturbed earth, he scanned the terrain, then reached down, reading the dirt like a story only he could see.

Fingers hovered, then brushed the damp soil, fresh tire impressions, still sharp at the edges.

Pine needles crushed flat. A root split clean, not weathered.

The ground held residual warmth.

Heavy vehicle. Recent movement. Less than five minutes ahead.

The tracks led toward the cliff's edge.

From below, the low thunder of an engine rolled up through the fog.

A Jeep, laboring hard through raw earth and broken terrain.

Ahmed couldn't see through the dark, fog-choked void.

But he didn't need to.

He listened.

Suspension groaning.

Tires fighting for traction.

Gear shifts spaced by instinct, not panic.

Bryce.

Still in control. Axles grinding. Tires bucking rock. The panicked rev of a desperate engine.

They were fighting the mountain.

He closed his eyes. Listened. Calculated the angle, the speed, and the weight distribution in every bounce.

Not prey running free, prey boxed in.

Ahmed rose slowly, adjusting the sling on his rifle.

The hunt had already started.

And they were exactly where he wanted them.

He dropped into a shooter's crouch, wet brush whispering beneath him as wind sliced across the ridge.

The marine layer had rolled in, dropping the temperature and shrouding the ground in mist.

He adjusted the elevation. Windage. Recalibrated with brutal precision, compensation, not hesitation.

Through the FLIR-equipped thermal scope, he saw it. A glowing trail of heat signatures streaking down the mountain, one engine, four bodies radiating like embers in motion.

Bryce was driving blind.

No headlights. Just momentum. Instinct. Night vision goggles.

That wouldn't save him.

Ahmed exhaled, finger resting on the trigger.

High ground. Advantage. Element of surprise.

His crosshairs locked onto Bryce's body in the driver's seat. Night vision goggles strapped to his head.

He savored the moment, calm breath, steady finger.

One shot. One certainty.

He exhaled.

He squeezed.

CRACK.

The rifle kicked against his shoulder.

The Jeep dipped behind a boulder, shot wasted on empty steel.

Ahmed blinked, adjusting the scope.

Miss?

He never missed.

Something inside him itched. Off rhythm. Wrong.

That wasn't a miss.

It was interference.

He muttered a curse, shifting his position.

He should've hit.

He always did.

His grip tightened on the rifle.

Pride was a weakness. Still, it clawed at him.

"Position. Move," he ordered, voice low and cold. "We cut them off before they reach the tree line."

The motorcycles roared to life.

Engines snarling.

Tires churned dirt as they dropped lower. Each rider cutting to new firing angles.

Chasing shadows.

The hunt was on.

Chapter Fifty-Two

Too Close

S MACK!

A sniper round punched through the windshield, bursting the glass into a violent spiderweb of shards.

Bryce's night vision goggles exploded. The lenses shattered across his face in a flash of green and glass.

He felt the concussion of the shot a split second later.

Supersonic crack first. Muzzle report trailing just behind.

He logged the delay. Roughly three hundred yards. Maybe more.

Night shot. Clean angle. No hesitation.

They were using infrared. Probably a thermal overlay.

Whoever it was, they weren't guessing.

The bullet had missed his skull by inches.

But now his vision was gone.

Disoriented. Compromised.

Green static swirled where the world had been.

Everyone screamed.

The Jeep bounced off a rock, jarring sideways. Gravel spat up, hammering the undercarriage as Bryce jerked the wheel hard, ducking lower.

Not random.

Not a warning.

A killer's shot. Dead-center by design.

Bryce's voice cut through the chaos, low and sharp.

"Quiet."

Silence dropped like a hammer.

The Jeep skidded sideways, tires clawing for traction as Bryce threw it into a hard stop behind a jagged rock outcropping.

Motorcycle engines howled in the distance, the sound echoing off the cliffs around them.

They were moving, changing positions, going for the kill.

Bryce moved fast, thinking, calculating, adapting on instinct.

They weren't chasing him.

They were hunting him.

And he was done being the prey.

Escape wasn't an option. Not like this.

He turned to Taylor-May, speaking low, urgent.

"Take the Jeep. Drive down to the next row of trees. Draw them away."

Taylor-May's head snapped toward him, eyes wide.

"No. We stick together, you said..."

"Janice." Bryce cut her off, voice like steel. "My rifle and my umbrella in that side hatch. Now."

Janice twisted in the back seat, hands moving fast. She unstrapped Bryce's sniper rifle from the duffel, then reached for a long line running along the roof.

She pressed it, triggering a hidden compartment that slid open to reveal a large umbrella and several long rods she didn't recognize.

She grabbed the umbrella and handed both items to Bryce.

He quickly checked the mag, then wiped blood from his eye with the back of his hand.

The bullet had deepened the cut he got earlier when he fell.

Taylor-May shook her head. "Bryce, this is—"

"Not up for debate."

Bryce worked fast, dialing in his scope for heat signatures. The world had gone dark without his NVGs, but that didn't matter.

They were using thermals, so would he.

The mylar lining in the umbrella would fracture his heat signature just enough to vanish in the thermal haze for a few vital seconds.

Janice shoved the umbrella at him with a growl.

"Mary. Fucking. Poppins," she muttered. "What the hell is this?"

Bryce didn't answer. He snapped the umbrella open, angling it with surgical precision between himself and the ridgeline.

His voice was calm, certain.

"They're tracking us by body heat. We can't run. They'll see us. We'll never make it off this mountain."

The bikes went silent.

Their engines cut out.

One by one, their lights vanished into the fog.

A sliver of moonlight pierced the fog, catching Taylor-May's defiant glare.

Bryce pressed a hand over hers, recognizing the sudden silence.

"Count to twenty-five. Lights on. Floor it. Drive."

Her breath hitched. She hissed under her breath, "This is bullshit."

But she knew.

In her bones, she knew this was the only way.

Bryce's jaw locked like stone. His eyes scanned the horizon, then flicked back. His voice dropped to a haunting whisper.

"It's survival. When I tap the roof, the clock starts."

Taylor-May clenched her teeth and slid into the driver's seat, buckling in with white-knuckled hands.

A tear slipped down her cheek. She didn't wipe it.

Bryce continued in his deadly whisper, steady and low.

She saw him in his element, and it scared her.

"Listen to me. The only way we beat them is by staying alive."

Her breathing was shaky, but she gave him one tight nod.

Bryce exhaled. "I'll find you."

Another nod.

No more words.

He didn't know if Taylor-May would make it down the hill.

But she had to.

They all had to.

Bryce shut the door carefully, holding the handle and easing it closed to keep any sound from giving away their position. He tapped on the roof with his finger.

He had twenty-five seconds, which meant he had fifteen to find them and figure how to take them out. If he didn't, they were all dead.

Taylor-May's fingers tightened around the gearshift.

The countdown began.

Bryce turned before her eyes could break his resolve.

Chapter Fifty-Three

The Hunted

Bryce engaged every sense. Every instinct. The mountain had gone silent.

He turned from the Jeep and sprinted for cover, slipping behind a jagged rock formation.

Movement calculated. Timing tight. No wasted effort.

He knew the umbrella's waterproof coating and synthetic weave disrupted thermal imaging.

It blocked enough body heat to blur his signature. Not perfect, but enough.

He positioned the umbrella tight to the rock and angled it precisely.

This wasn't about hiding. It was about buying seconds.

The mountain was still. No sounds gave away their positions.

The countdown ran in his head. Fifteen seconds.

He crouched lower. Steady breath.

He brought up his rifle. Scope aligned.

Scanning in quick quadrants based on their last known positions.

Left. Right. Center.

One target. Then another.

The third was gone.

Not good.

Bryce adjusted his position and shifted his aim.

He made small corrections. Five seconds.

He slowed his breathing again. Waited for the flash.

The engine roared to life as the headlights broke through the mist.

Bright beams sliced behind him, tearing the fog into ribbons of shadow and glare.

The Jeep launched forward. Tires tore through the dirt.

Loose rock sprayed as Taylor-May gunned it down the slope.

The engine roared, fighting every inch for traction as it disappeared into the trees.

Bryce held his position. Watched.

If all three gave chase, he could move.

He could reposition and cut them down before they reached the bend.

But only one rider peeled off. Throttle wide. Chasing the bait.

The other two remained still. Not searching. Not panicking. Just watching.

They knew he was close.

They just didn't know where. Not yet.

The clock in his head kept ticking.

The hunt was already underway.

He steadied his breath.

No sound. No shift. Only readiness.

Then came movement.

BAM. BAM. BAM.

A biker strafed the Jeep with a full-auto burst, aiming for the rear tires. Disable, not kill.

Bryce didn't hesitate.

Tok.

His suppressed rifle round punched clean through the rider's chest.

The body tensed. Then the hillside detonated.

Not just sound.

Pressure.

A concussive wall of heat and shock punched the air like a freight train.

The rider vanished in a burst of flame and shrapnel.

His bike tore apart midair.

Dirt, rock, and fire exploded skyward, turning the fog into a blinding storm of debris and smoke.

The sound wasn't a bang. It was a roar. Deafening. Violent. Primal.

It cracked the mountain wide open and echoed down the valley in rolling waves, followed by the acrid smell of bleach.

Bryce hit the ground as shards of metal and scorched branches rained around him.

His ears rang. His vision tunneled.

The mountain wasn't quiet anymore.

BANG BANG BANG.

The remaining two opened fire, bullets ripping through trees, kicking up dirt and shattered rock.

But they missed. Their shots went wide.

They didn't know where he was. They were trying to flush him out.

And that was their mistake.

Bryce rolled, tilting the umbrella to keep his body heat masked as he moved.

They weren't just firing blindly anymore.

One laid down suppressive fire on the Jeep. Loud. Deliberate.

The other held position. Watching. Waiting.

They were trying to draw him out.

Force his hand.

Make him choose between staying hidden or saving them.

They were hunting.

But so was Bryce.

The wind shifted. He heard voices in Pashto. Low. Fast.

They were communicating. Trying to pin him down.

One circled left, moving fast and low, spraying rounds at the Jeep.

The other held position, covering his flank.

Smart. Disciplined.

But not smart enough.

Bryce exhaled slowly, moving with the rocks.

Heat masked. Footsteps silent on damp earth.

His eyes adjusted to the shifting black, his mind tracking every movement.

They weren't just soldiers. They were killers.

But he had patience. And patience won wars.

From the ridge above, a whisper.

A hushed, almost reverent murmur in Pashto.

Afghan. He knew the dialect.

These men were killers from birth.

They had fought for something once.

Then became ghosts, smuggled into America, waiting for a call that had finally come.

Tonight, they were here for him.

Bryce adjusted the umbrella, keeping his body heat masked as he moved.

He had to find them both.

Locate the second before making his first kill.

A soft crunch of stone. Movement.

Then a flutter.

Two doves burst from the rocks, disturbed by something unseen.

Bryce's pulse slowed as he locked in on the disturbance.

One was right there.

But where was the second?

This was patience.

One wrong move and he dies.

It had to be a headshot.

The first man was moving carefully, scanning the hillside, methodical.

Tok.

Clean shot.

The body crumpled.

No explosion. Good.

He needed at least one identity intact if he was going to track how they got here.

Then—

THWACK.

SNAP.

A bullet slammed into his vest.

The hit tore the umbrella and rifle from his grip, sending them skidding down the slope.

The blow knocked the air from his lungs.

His vision tilted sideways as his body pitched down the slope.

THUD-THUD-THUD.

He rolled, slamming into dirt and rock, tumbling deeper into the darkness.

BANG-BANG-BANG.

Gunfire shredded the hillside, rounds barely missing him as he rolled.

He landed hard on his shoulder, pain ripping through him.

He couldn't see his enemy.

And now? He was alone in the dark.

The rifle was gone.

The umbrella was gone.

Only his Glock and knife remained.

His breath came ragged, pain lancing through his chest.

His ribs screamed. His body ached.

And now he was the hunted once again.

He pressed himself into the dirt, listening.

Somewhere above, his enemy was repositioning.

He had the high ground.

Superior firepower.

The patience of a trained killer.

And now, where the hell was he?

The forest fell silent.

Bryce waited.

One move. One shot. One survivor.

BRRRAAAP.

A wall of automatic fire shredded the trees. Bryce dove flat.

Rounds tore through bark and leaves, splinters raining like deadly needles as he rolled to escape the barrage.

Lungs burned.

Ribs screamed.

Everything ached, but he forced himself forward.

Survive. Move. Keep moving.

That was all that mattered.

Bryce lunged for the nearest tree, pressing himself flat against the rough bark.

BRRRAAAP.

More rounds ripped past.

His attacker wasn't firing blindly. This was controlled suppression fire.

He's pinning me. Wants me stuck.

Bryce returned fire from behind the tree with his Glock.

He exhaled, controlling his breathing even as his body fought against him.

His lungs refused to work right. Not enough air. Not enough time.

Mag empty. Reload.

His fingers worked on instinct. Eject. Reload. Snap shut.

Two left. No margin for error.

Bryce pivoted, snapping off a burst of return fire.

BANG-BANG-BANG.

He didn't expect to hit. He just needed a flinch.

Ahmed vanished behind the treeline, evading the shots with precision.

Bryce took the opening, moving fast, staying low, repositioning behind a new tree.

The forest fell quiet.

Then, CLINK.

A metallic bounce in the dark.

Bryce's heart stopped.

He knew that sound instantly.

Grenade.

No time.

He dove sideways, arms over his head.

BOOOOM.

A shockwave of heat and shrapnel ripped through the forest.

Tree trunks splintered.

He slammed into another tree, his head cracking against the base.

Pain exploded behind his eyes.

Bark and debris tore into his arms.

His ears rang like artillery fire.

The world went dark again.

The forest spun.

Shit. Can't see. Can't hear. Can't move.

Bad. But expected.

This was the plan.

He disoriented me. He's coming to finish it.

Bryce fought through the haze, forcing himself onto his knees, blinking rapidly.

He searched the ground for his lost weapon.

Then a twig snapped.

Close. Too close.

He knew where I was the whole damn time.

A dark silhouette loomed above him, outlined against the night sky.

Ahmed. The last of the killers.

He stood on a jagged rock, looking down at Bryce.

The perfect execution point.

Bryce had no time. No rifle.

He continued to scratch at the ground, looking for his Glock.

But he wasn't fast enough.

Ahmed raised his rifle.

Bryce looked up. Straight into his own death.

Then—

THWACK.

A single suppressed shot cracked from the trees.

Direct hit.

Ahmed's head snapped backward, his body collapsing and falling in front of Bryce.

From the darkness far down the cliff, a voice called out.

"Shit yeah! I got that fucker!"

"Bryce, you good?! Don't shoot. I'm coming up!"

A flashlight bounced up the hillside, weaving through the trees.

Taylor-May.

Bryce let his head fall back against the dirt, sucking in a broken breath.

She saved me. Again.

Taylor-May knelt beside him, water bottle in hand, scanning his injuries.

"You good, honey?"

Bryce blinked at her, a weak smirk forming.

"Never better."

He coughed.

Blood.

"Okay... I've been better."

Taylor-May frowned, shoving the water at him.

"Drink. Now."

Bryce took a slow sip, ignoring the burn in his throat.

Every muscle screamed. Breathing was almost impossible.

Blood dripped down his face, warm against the cold night air.

It wasn't just from one wound. It was everywhere.

Still, he forced himself up.

Every muscle protested. He made his body move anyway.

The mission wasn't over. There was still a bounty on their heads.

He wiped the blood from his eye with the back of his hand, then looked at Taylor-May.

"We need pictures of their faces."

A slow breath.

Her flashlight revealed his Glock.

He bent slowly, pain screaming from every inch he moved.

"And we need to get off this hill."

Taylor-May groaned, but nodded.

"Do I need to carry your ass, Mr. Bossy?"

Bryce laughed, then instantly regretted it.

Chapter Fifty-Four

Guard Tower

The watchtower stood like a solitary sentinel, shrouded in thick fog, clinging to the coastal cliffs.

Below, the ocean's fury crashed against jagged rocks, its roar broken only by a distant foghorn, a hollow cry warning ships to stay away from the perilous shore.

A distant engine echoed through the fog, followed by the faint crack of breaking branches and twisting metal.

Subtle. Fragmented.

Just loud enough to draw a glance up the mountain.

The tower's dim floodlights barely pierced the mist, casting long, warped shadows across the rugged terrain. On the small, metal-paneled outpost, two men stood guard, the night stretching endlessly ahead.

Watchman One leaned against the cold steel railing, arms crossed, watching the shifting fog below. His partner, Watchman Two, sat on a weathered stool, boots propped on the console, picking at a protein bar with the disinterest that came from too many nights like this one.

The crashing and engine noise echoed through the trees, but without headlights in sight, they dismissed it. Too far off to matter.

"Man, I swear," Watchman Two muttered, glancing up at the sound before shaking his head. "Sometimes I just go along with things because it's easier than saying no."

Watchman One turned slightly, raising a brow. "What now?"

Watchman Two sighed, rubbing his face. "Alright, don't laugh, but my girl wanted us to do one of those spa days. You know, couples thing. And I figured, hell, I'm always stiff after the shift. Maybe a little pampering isn't a bad idea."

Watchman One smirked. "Let me guess, it didn't go as planned?"

"It started fine," Watchman Two said, waving the protein bar. "Hot towels, some oil thing, whatever. Then she suggests a milk bath. Says it's 'romantic.' Next thing I know, I'm buck-ass naked in a tub full of milk, thinking: 'Is this normal? Is this whole thing curdling or will it curdle if I piss? What happens if I fart? How long has this milk been here? Shit, milk is expensive. What kind of milk is this? Cow's? Almond? Whale?'"

Watchman One let out a laugh. "I'm almost scared to ask, but I'm not. How did it end?"

The whine of distant motorcycles cut across the tower.

Looking up, three bobbing headlights appeared at the top of the mountain.

Not enough to raise alarms.

Just enough to draw another glance.

Definitely not enough to ruin a good story.

Watchman Two groaned. "Well, first off, it smelled weird. Like, real weird. And second, I get out, and I'm just... sticky. Not relaxed. Not refreshed. Just sticky, damp, and questioning every choice I've ever made."

Watchman One chuckled, shaking his head. "That's what you get for saying yes to everything."

Watchman Two pointed at him. "It made sense... until it didn't."

Their laughter hung in the cool night air, settling into the stillness of the outpost.

CRACK.

A single shot echoed over the mountain, sharp, sudden.

It sliced through their laughter, silencing everything.

They both stood up now, looking up into the mountain, looking to see what was happening.

Then a distant engine growled, crashing over loose rock and splintered branches.

Dirt bikes whined in the fog, their small headlights bobbing like fireflies above the ridge.

Watchman Two leaned forward. "Who the hell tries to drive down a mountain in this fog?"

Watchman One looked over. "Who the hell tries to drive down a mountain, ever?"

One of the dirt bikes zigzagged down the slope.

It stopped. Its headlamp blinked off.

Then silence.

They exchanged a glance.

Nothing. For a minute, they stared up the mountain, waiting for something. Anything to explain the gunshot.

Then headlights burst through the fog as the Jeep's engine roared to life, scrambling downhill.

Another burst of gunfire echoed across the ridge.

Followed by a deep explosion thundered across the cliffs where the dirt bike had stopped, lighting the fog like a strobe inside a thundercloud.

The world shifted.

The shockwave shook the watchtower, rattling its loose metal panes.

Both men froze.

They turned toward the ridge, where fog hung thick, obscuring everything in a shifting white veil.

BAP-BAP-BAP-BAP!

Automatic fire cracked through the mountain air while the vehicle kept tumbling down the mountain.

Watchman Two adjusted the binoculars on the console. Only fog and the dancing lights down the hill.

Watchman One grabbed his radio. "Base, this is Guard Tower One. We've got active small arms fire and dirt bikes pursuing a vehicle down the east face. Large detonation confirmed north of our position. Do you copy?"

Watchman One looked over. "Guess the sirens and explosions finally made their way out here. At sunset, it sounded like I was back in Iraq."

Watchman Two leaned out, squinting deeper into the fog.

Static cracked through the radio, followed by a response:

"Guard Tower One, copy. Detonation confirmed near the high ridge. Engagement in progress. Possible hostile contact. Hold position and observe. Do not engage unless fired upon."

Watchman Two straightened, suddenly alert. "Hostile activity? Out here? You sure?"

The radio crackled again.

"New intel just came in. Be advised, The driver's name is Bryce Rath. Three passengers. Black Jeep Wrangler. Friendly. Do not engage."

Watchman One and Two exchanged a look, then turned toward the fog-covered mountains.

Then came more automatic bursts from the mountain.

Sharp. Echoing. Distant, but getting closer.

Watchman One tightened his grip on his rifle. "That's automatic fire."

"Yeah," Watchman Two muttered. "And that's not just one person."

Gunfire continued in short, violent bursts.

A deadly game of cat and mouse was unfolding on the unseen mountain.

Then it happened.

BOOM.

The distinct echo of a grenade rolled across the ridge.

A second explosion cracked through the cliffs, sharper and closer than the first.

The floodlights shuddered under the shockwave, rattling the steel bones of the tower.

The mountainside lit up again, brief, blinding lightning swallowed instantly by the fog.

Watchman Two staggered. "Jesus. What the hell is going on up there?"

For the first time all year, he was glad the rifle was loaded.

A gust swept across the cliffs, twisting fog into violent spirals.

BAP-BAP-BAP-BAP!

Watchman Two swallowed hard.

A small suppressed *thwack*.

Silence.

Then, yelling.

"Shit yeah! I GOT that fucker!"

The cliffside held its breath with them.

They waited. Listening.

Nothing.

No sound.

Seconds stretched into minutes. The silence became louder than the chaos before it.

Then they saw headlights cut through the fog, glowing in muted LED halos.

A new sound.

Distant. But growing.

A grinding roar. Metal on rock. Branches snapping. Tires clawing at the earth like something wild trying to survive.

Watchman One stepped forward, squinting. "What the hell is that?"

A voice crackled over the radio.

"Do not engage. A black Jeep will be arriving at the North Tower."

A pause.

Watchman Two looked over at Watchman One, shrugging. "Dispatch, there's nothing on the road. Over."

A sharper reply: "It won't be from the road."

And that's when they heard it. Not an explosion. A heavy flowing crash, reminiscent of a dinosaur from ages past, tearing through the forest in the fog.

Then branches exploded outward. The Jeep burst from the treeline, airborne, crashing down off a ledge and slamming into the drainage ditch beside the gate.

Metal screamed on impact.

What little rubber remained slammed the pavement, the rims grinding so hard it looked like the wheels might shear off the axles.

It skidded, scraped, dragged and finally stopped in front of the guard tower fence line.

Smoke and steam curled from the mangled engine.

A haunted screech of steel vibrated with every pulse of the struggling motor.

The once-pristine Jeep was now a wreck, dented, scratched, its frame riddled with bullet holes.

The windshield and drivers-side window were gone, leaving only jagged glass clinging to the corners of the frame.

A long silence stretched through the radios.

Then Watchman One glanced at Watchman Two. He cleared his throat and keyed the radio.

"Dispatch, we have visuals."

Command responded:

"Consider anything else a threat. Medical support is deploying to your position. Keep access clear."

"Copy."

The Jeep crawled along the fence line until it reached an opening, dragging and pulling itself onto the road toward the front gate.

The gate groaned open.

The Jeep lurched forward, its suspension shot, the frame groaning under the weight of everything it had endured.

It scraped its way toward the base, still bouncing like it hadn't realized the road was paved.

Inside, Janice groaned, rubbing her ribs. Then, without hesitation, she leaned over and punched Jack in the groin.

Jack gasped, doubling over, blood dripping from his face.

They were all in terrible shape. Each of them bleeding, broken, and fighting through the agony as they focused on the freedom of the open gate.

Janice scowled. "I feel like we just went over Niagara Falls in a barrel. My bruises have bruises. Get me out of this thing."

Bryce, barely conscious, his face smeared with blood, leaned heavily against the steering wheel, his breaths shallow.

He'd held it together long enough.

Then he collapsed as the Jeep stopped just inside the gate.

Taylor-May scrambled out, fighting the door to open. It came right off its hinges and fell to the ground. Blood running down the side of her face. She waved frantically, limping toward the tower.

"We need help! He's been shot. There's blood everywhere!"

An emergency vehicle screeched to a stop nearby with its lights flashing. Two medics sprinted forward, reaching for Bryce just as his body sagged. They caught him before he hit the pavement, already assessing his injuries as the gate slammed shut behind them.

A low rattle crawled from the fog.

A new sound.

Engines.

Loud. Heavy.

Two trucks rumbled up the main road, their engines growling long before their headlights pierced the fog. Two dirt bikes accompanied them.

Up in the guard tower, Watchman One exhaled, watching the approaching vehicles with a frown.

"Well," he muttered, "we could show them how cool our light is."

Watchman Two grinned. "Yes, we can."

He flicked a switch.

Like a second sun exploding, the light cut through, blinding, brutal.

The tower's spotlight tore across the road, an artificial dawn screaming through the fog.

The dirt bikers panicked.

The instant the light hit, they swerved wildly, blinded by the sudden brilliance. One lost control completely, his bike kicking out from under him as he crashed, tumbling violently across the gravel. The others weren't far behind, their bodies slamming into the ground in a tangled heap of limbs and steel.

Watchman One leaned against the rail, smirking. "Bet that hurt."

Watchman Two tracked the beam further down the road. "Let's see who's in those trucks."

"With pleasure."

The blinding light swung, locking onto the approaching vehicles.

The trucks jerked to a stop.

Inside the cabs, four men sat frozen, their faces washed in stark white, pupils contracting against the painful glare. In the truck beds, more men ducked for cover, shielding their eyes with their forearms.

A tense moment.

No movement.

Then, tires screeched.

The trucks spun hard, skidding as they turned, kicking up a storm of dust and gravel before peeling out and disappearing into the night.

Watchman Two exhaled. "Rednecks, gangbangers, and bikers... looks like they finally figured out how to play nice."

Watchman One watched the taillights fade. "Yeah. Light worked just fine."

"Wish that's all we ever had to do."

"Only works on roaches, though."

A quiet chuckle.

Watchman Two leaned back, stretching. "Screw the spa. Give me a light bath over a milk bath any day."

Chapter Fifty-Five

Get To The Chopper

Bright white lights. Antiseptic in the air. Cold metal beneath his skin.

Bryce blinked hard, his vision swimming.

His mind swayed between lucidity and black. He wasn't ready to go under.

Not yet.

The painkillers felt wrong. Slower. Deeper. Like they were meant to keep him down.

He knew where they led, and he wouldn't follow. He welcomed the relief for now. But he'd never let them take control again.

The Coast Guard medic's voice came through clearly, sharp and focused.

"Ribs are bruised, maybe cracked. Get him on oxygen. Keep him stable. We need to get him to a proper hospital, fast. Check for internal bleeding. Monitor his vitals. I'll make the calls." He stepped out, brushing past Taylor-May in the doorway. Then paused, looking at her.

"You need to get that looked at."

She gave a slight nod, waving him off. The pain was starting to take hold, but she wouldn't let it, not yet. Not until she knew Bryce was going to be okay.

Bryce blinked through the haze.

Taylor-May stood in front of him, her face slowly coming into focus, caked blood crusted with fresh red, trailing down the right side of her forehead.

"Bryce?"

Her voice was softer than usual. The bravado was gone.

He smiled.

She was safe. Janice was safe.

For the first time in years, it felt good.

Silence settled between them. The quiet hum of medical monitors filled the room.

Somewhere outside, the faint echo of a radio transmission crackled through the base.

A nurse stepped into the room. "Ma'am, I need to prep him for flight."

Taylor-May didn't move. She just looked at Bryce.

"I should go with you."

Bryce forced a small smile. It didn't reach his eyes. "I'll be fine. Besides, you've gotta keep Janice in check."

Taylor-May let out a breath, shaking her head. "This feels wrong."

Bryce met her gaze. "It is."

The truth neither of them wanted to admit.

The nurse guided Taylor-May from the room to examine her injuries.

The doors closed behind her.

Just like that, she was gone.

***

Thirty minutes later, the whirl of helicopter blades cut through the night.

Bryce was strapped onto the stretcher, his body secured for transport. A medic checked his vitals, nodding to the flight team.

Taylor-May limped to the edge of the helipad, arms crossed tightly over her chest.

A gauze pad was taped to her forehead.

She stood alone as the rotors screamed above.

The helicopter lifted into the fog, carrying Bryce into the dark unknown.

Chapter Fifty-Six

Where do we go now?

The next morning, Janice and Taylor-May entered a sterile briefing room. The air was cold, clinical, detached.

Thin shadows stretched across the cluttered desk. The hum of the overhead lights filled the silence as they stepped inside. Janice moved with a stiff limp, one hand pressed against her ribcage. Taylor-May winced with every other step, her neck braced in white gauze and tape, a split near her hairline stitched and swollen.

Their movements were careful. Controlled.

They walked through the wreckage of the last seventy-two hours, since everything changed, still feeling every jagged moment of pain.

Troy motioned to the chairs across from him. "Please, sit. Sorry for the mess. I had to commandeer the office."

Taylor-May eased herself into the chair, slowly, teeth clenched. Her shoulders remained stiff as her lower back met the cushion. "How's Bryce?" Her voice was steady, but the tension in her frame was unmistakable, a mix of worry, frustration, and something deeper than she wasn't ready to name.

Troy expected the question. He nodded slightly, like he'd already rehearsed the answer.

"For your protection, the Bryce Rath you knew is no longer alive. Off the record, you saved his life in more ways than one." His tone was calm. Measured.

"Let's focus on both of you for now. We're placing you under federal witness protection. While we build this case, I need you as far from the crosshairs as possible."

Taylor-May opened her mouth, but Janice beat her to it, her voice tight, jaw clenched through the pain. One wrist was wrapped in an ace bandage, and her knuckles were purple from punching Jack and her time in the jeep. "What do you mean?"

Troy's expression darkened as he leaned forward.

"I can't give you all the details yet," he said quietly. "The less you know right now, the better. What you need to understand is that your enemies are dangerous, well-connected, and relentless. Until we neutralize the threat, you need to disappear.

"As far as the world is concerned, you both died in that cabin with Bryce in the blast. That's why he staged everything the way he did. It was the only way he could save you.

"I have to say, I'm constantly impressed by that man.

"I'm sorry, but your lives have changed forever. The good news is you'll be together. And you'll be safe."

The realization of it all hit Janice like a second crash down the mountain. She winced as she shifted in her chair. "Just like that, everything we had is gone."

Troy nodded, flipping through the stack of paperwork in front of him. "For the time being, yes." His voice was steady but firm. "Bryce collected enough evidence to blow this thing wide open, but we can't make it public yet. If anyone connected to Javier catches wind of what we're doing, you're both dead before we can finish the case."

He pulled out a file, sliding it toward them. "How do you feel about Florida?"

Janice let out a dry laugh, then winced and clutched her side. "Florida? Jesus. Snakes, hurricanes, and assholes. What a combo."

Taylor-May didn't laugh. A butterfly bandage split her right eyebrow. She sat rigidly, staring at the documents without really seeing them.

The only piece left was out of reach and fading.

Janice must've sensed it. She reached over, her fingers trembling, and gave her daughter's hand a firm squeeze with her puffy, bruised knuckles. "It's gonna be okay, baby," she whispered. "We'll figure this out."

Troy gave them a moment before pushing the paperwork closer. "I need you both to read through these," he said. "It's for the witness protection program, new identities, new locations. Sign it, and we'll get you set up."

As Janice flipped through the pages, wincing every time she turned too fast. Troy cleared his throat softly. His tone shifted, softer than before, directed at Taylor-May.

"Bryce wanted to talk to you, but we had to move him immediately. There wasn't time. But..." He reached into his desk drawer, pulling out Bryce's faded, well-worn baseball cap. He held it out, and Taylor-May just stared at it.

Her bandaged fingers trembled as she took it, brushing over the frayed edges. It still smelled like him.

Inside the brim, tucked carefully into the fabric, was a folded note. She pulled it free, her breath catching as she unfolded the paper.

Please hold on to my hat. I'm coming back for it.

Thank you, Taylor-May.□

Bryce

Her throat tightened. The words blurred as tears filled her eyes. She wiped them away with the heel of her hand, trying not to wince.

Taylor-May looked up, her voice quiet but anchored by something new: purpose.

"Okay," she said, gripping the hat. "Where do we sign?"

Troy gave a faint smile, the tension easing as he slid the documents toward them again. "Right here," he said, pointing to the dotted lines.

As they signed their new identities into existence, a muted determination settled over the room. There was still fear. Still uncertainty. But there was also a flicker of hope.

Once the paperwork was completed, Troy stood and crossed the room, grabbing two bottles of water from a small fridge.

As he handed them over, Bryce's words echoed in his head: *Keep them safe. No matter what.*

Taylor-May carefully folded Bryce's note and slipped it back inside the hat, pressing it close to her chest as she stood, favoring her right leg with every step.

Janice stood beside her, silent but steady, her presence grounding in a way Taylor-May hadn't realized she needed.

She turned to Troy, her voice resolute.

"I'll hold on to this hat. And when Bryce comes back, I'll be happy to give it to him."

Troy nodded. "I know you will."

He paused, watching as they gathered their things.

"I'll keep you updated. But until then, stay safe. We've got a long road ahead."

Taylor-May and Janice walked out together, the weight of new identities pressing on their shoulders like armor they hadn't grown into yet.

But in Taylor-May's heart, a quiet fire burned, one Bryce had lit with his note. A promise. A purpose.

He hadn't just given her hope.

He'd given her a reason to keep going.

She held her head high as they disappeared down the hall, her grip tight on the old, battered hat.

No matter how far Bryce was or how dangerous the road ahead, she knew one thing for certain:

They would find their way back to each other.

And when that day came, nothing would stand in their way.

EPILOGUE

S an Diego, California
Two Weeks Later

The steady beep of a heart monitor pierced the darkness.

Bryce's eyes fluttered open, the fluorescent light slicing through his fogged mind like a scalpel. His ribs felt like a cage of broken glass. Each breath ground like shards in his lungs.

The pain was familiar. Almost reassuring.

He was still here.

A shadow shifted at the edge of the room.

"Took you long enough," Troy muttered, dropping into a chair beside the bed.

Bryce smirked weakly. "Didn't feel like rushing back."

Troy leaned forward, elbows on his knees, eyes sharp as he scanned Bryce's battered frame.

"Officially, Taylor-May and Janice think you're dead. Unofficially, they'll be waiting, if you ever want to see them again."

Bryce exhaled, nodding. "Thank you."

Troy arched a brow. "Yeah. Thanks for the sleepless nights and forty pages of redacted bullshit."

Bryce's smirk deepened. "You're welcome."

A long silence stretched between them.

Troy studied him, the bruises, the bandages, the weight in his eyes that had nothing to do with injury.

"I've gone through most of the intel you gave me. We need to make your death official because Javier will come for you."

"Yeah," Bryce muttered. "I expected that."

"I've got Jack locked down," Troy continued, voice lower now. "But this whole thing, it's bigger than I thought. I still don't know who to trust. Or how high this goes."

Bryce shifted against the stiff hospital sheets, staring at the ceiling. "Did you find a way in?"

Troy let out a dry chuckle. "Of course I did."

He reached into his coat, pulled out a thick manila folder, and dropped it onto the small table beside Bryce's bed. The edge smacked against the tray, scattering grainy surveillance photos.

"You should walk away, Karma. Take the win. You're a free man. No charges. No cartel after you, for now. You could actually live."

Bryce exhaled. "You ever wonder why I survived?"

Troy frowned. "What?"

"All of it. The war. The raids. My team wiped out. My addiction. But I'm still here." He turned his head, eyes locking on Troy's. "And I don't think that's an accident."

Troy didn't speak for a long time. Then he sighed.

"Well, I never thought I'd say this, but I believe in Karma. Because there's a lot that needs to be done. And after this last week, I don't know anyone better. Or anyone I trust more."

The heart monitor ticked on in quiet agreement.

Troy looked around to make sure no one was watching.

He flipped open the folder, revealing a map marked with red circles and criss-crossing lines—a tangled web of power and blood. His finger tapped a spot near the coastline.

"Javier's compound. We've been tracking him for years. It's a fortress, mercs, ex-special forces, all paid to keep him breathing.

Every attempt to get close ends in body bags. Mostly because they always know we're coming."

Bryce studied the map. "That where you lost your guy?"

Troy nodded, sliding another photo across the table. "Drake Barber. Deep undercover. We lost contact three months ago. Could be dead. Could be working for Javier now."

Bryce's jaw tightened.

Troy flipped to the next page, revealing another surveillance shot. "This is Javier. He's a ghost. No digital footprint. No paper trail. Everything he does lives in the shadows. And he's expanding, fast. Taking ports. Smuggling weapons, drugs, people. They found mass graves. Bodies burned in underground ovens. Hundreds of shoes stacked like a Holocaust camp. And that's just what made local news."

"And now," Troy added, "he's got ties to ISIS and who knows what else."

Bryce ran a hand over his face. "Jesus."

"Washington won't do a damn thing," Troy said. "Not in the way that matters. They'll talk sanctions. Throw money at 'stabilizing the region.' Meanwhile, Javier's empire keeps growing."

Bryce leaned back. "So you want me to go in alone?"

"We can't back you. Not officially. Hell, not even unofficially. If you do this, you're on your own. No extraction. No backup."

"Wouldn't be the first time," Bryce said.

Troy slid a small envelope forward. "Four SIM cards. Burners. Pop one in, we talk, extract data. No trace."

Bryce flipped through the folder. "You got a way in?"

"Miguel Diez. He used to own a marina before Javier took it. If he's alive, he is working with Javier, or terrified of him. Probably both. But he's our best lead."

Troy exhaled. "You could disappear. Live on some beach. Never look over your shoulder again."

Bryce looked at him.

Troy didn't see a man broken. He saw a man reborn.

"I've slept better on mission than on vacation. While I can, I will."

Troy nodded with respect. "Alright. You'll get an account tied to a dummy pension. Pull cash from anywhere. You'll get a cut of every asset we seize. If you make it through this, you'll retire rich."

Bryce glanced up. "And you're my only boss?"

"No bosses," Troy said. "You're my silent partner. I handle the politics, logistics, and fallout. You do what you do best."

Bryce nodded.

"You showed me something," Troy added. "That I'd been wrong about everything that matters."

He pulled a passport and ID from his coat.

"Your new name is Andy. Forgettable. We'll age your ink, cover your biometrics, and plant your trail. You'll become a ghost no one's looking for. Get sunburned. Grow the beard. Look like hell. Then go blend into the sand and make your way down the coast."

He met Bryce's gaze.

"I used to think people like you were the problem."

Bryce raised an eyebrow.

"But the real monsters?" Troy said. "They built the system that hides them."

Silence.

"When you're cleared, we'll get you on a trawler heading for Mexico. From there, you vanish. Get eyes inside. Gather a plan. Then we hit them hard."

Bryce nodded, already calculating.

Troy knew what he was sending.

He wasn't sending a soldier.

He was releasing a weapon.

***

The Next Wave
San Diego, California.
Two Months Later

The Pacific stretched to infinity, each wave shimmering beneath the fading gold of the setting sun. A dolphin breached the surface, arcing clean through the water before vanishing again.

Bryce sat atop his surfboard, legs dangling in the cool sea. His beard had thickened. His hair had grown longer. The scars on his body ran deeper—but his mind was finally clear.

Salt hung in the air. No gunfire. No shouts. No war.

Only the rhythm of the ocean.

This was his second life. A path he chose, not one forced on him.

A wave gathered behind him.

He turned, paddling slow and steady.

The swell lifted him, held him aloft.

For a single heartbeat, he was weightless.

Then the board dropped in, cutting across the surface with grace and speed.

Water thundered beneath him, wild and indifferent.

He didn't resist.

The wave carried him, spun him, let him go.

He broke the surface, foam clinging to his shoulders, his breath slow and measured as he scanned the endless horizon.

He was alive.

He was healing.

The dolphins returned, gliding beside him like guardians of the deep.

A quiet reminder: freedom isn't given. It's earned.

He tilted his face toward the sun, lips barely moving as he spoke to the wind.

"Thank you for my life."

THE END

Acknowledgments

To my wife—my life editor, best friend, and the reason I write. I will love you forever.

Mom and Dad—you have always been and will always be my heroes and mentors. I love you.

To my friends and extended family—Thank you for your inspiration, for always striving to be your best, and for pushing me to chase what matters. Your belief in me helped make this real.

Karma Is Coming

Next Launch

Book Two of The Karma Files™

KARMA: NO HARBOR FOR THE DAMNED

THE KARMA FILES™

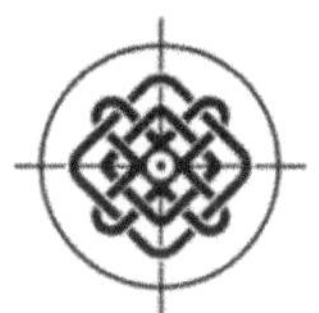

BOOK TWO: PROLOGUE

KARMA: No Harbor for the Damned

The Karma Files™

Mexico - Location Unknown

Javier Bravalez stood in a forgotten substructure. It was never meant for this, but "finders keepers" didn't translate well. The room reeked of sweat and fear.

Two men knelt before him, hands bound behind their backs, blindfolds covering their eyes. The space was sparse, just stone walls and a single overhead bulb casting long, eerie shadows.

In the center stood the Spanish Donkey. A simple, horrifying contraption designed to shatter resolve, flesh, and soul. Perfect for interrogation or pure torture, depending on its user. Its origins were unclear, but it could be traced back to the Spanish Inquisition. It resembled a crude wooden horse, its back a sharp, triangular beam tapered to a razor-thin edge. Jagged metal spikes jutted from it like rusted thorns. Crusted, bloodied shackles hung from its sides, waiting.

Nearby, bloodstained weights sat ready to be hooked beneath them.

The only sounds were the faint drip of water in the distance and the ragged breaths of the men before him.

Javier's second-in-command, Hector, shifted uneasily. A towering figure with a jagged scar running down his face, Hector had seen plenty of horrors, but even he hesitated now. Speaking in a local dialect:

"You don't have to be here for this, Javier," he said, his voice low. "The men can handle it. We'll find out where Jack went without you getting your hands dirty."

Javier turned to face him, a slow, cruel smile forming at the corners of his mouth. His dark eyes gleamed with something close to pleasure.

"No, no, my friend," he murmured, voice smooth, venomous. "This is the part of the job I truly enjoy. I need to know who betrayed me. And I need to make sure everyone understands what happens when they do. These two will be my message."

His boots echoed across the concrete as he stalked forward. He knelt beside the first man, inhaling deeply, savoring the trembling breath of his captive. Then, turning to Hector, he spoke in a voice laced with amusement:

"This is where power comes from. You either create the fear or the fear creates you."

Javier straightened, his expression darkening with delight as he motioned to his men. They moved swiftly, hoisting the first prisoner by his wrists and securing him to a metal pulley system bolted to the ceiling, a repurposed rail once used to haul butchered cattle.

Gears groaned, metal grinding under the strain. The trolley lurched forward with a high-pitched squeal. The man trembled violently as he was lifted into the air.

Javier tilted his head, watching with detached fascination as they slid him along the track directly above the Spanish Donkey.

The man writhed, muffled cries leaking from the gag in his mouth. His movements caused his bare legs to graze the rusted spikes below, drawing thin trickles of blood.

Javier glanced at the other captive. He shook uncontrollably, his blindfold damp with sweat.

"I want you both to listen carefully," Javier said, his tone casual, almost conversational. "I already know where Jack went. I knew the moment he ran. I also know Bryce Rath is dead, but I haven't seen a body. You two survived because you left. You deserted your post. That, I cannot allow."

He crouched down next to the larger man on the floor, his voice dropping to a whisper.

"This isn't about finding him. This is about ensuring everyone else knows what happens when you cross me."

He motioned, and a guard ripped the blindfold from the man's face. Tears spilled freely from Tank's eyes. He now saw Gary hanging over the Donkey. The razor-edged beam waiting beneath him.

"We can do this all night," Javier said softly. His smile widened. "He won't last that long. But we can."

He studied them, enjoying the way their eyes darted between each other and the sharp wooden blade.

Javier nodded, and one of the men reached over, removing Gary's gag.

Gary spat toward the floor, eyes locked on Tank. "Fuck this shit. I told you we should've kept going."

Then he turned to Javier, fury burning in his eyes. "Look, Mr. Bravalez, all I know is everyone got vaporized by the fucking men you sent. They killed everyone. What kind of message is that? Who the fuck sends a whole crew in Kevlar jackets to fucking die?

Fuck this shit, and fuck your fucking Donkey!"

He tried to kick the device, but its weight only hurt his foot and reminded him of what was coming.

Javier stepped forward, and Gary lost the last of his steam. He knew he'd just spoken his final words.

Javier looked from Gary down to Tank.

"It'll take him three hours to die if we add weight," Javier mused, motioning to the weights leaning against the Donkey, almost thoughtful. "Right now, with just gravity? Could take until tomorrow."

Gary and Tank began to cry. Their resolve cracked like thin glass.

Javier took his time pacing.

"Let me tell you something," he continued, turning toward them, his expression unreadable. "I already know the answer to my question. But this—"

He gestured to the Spanish Donkey and Gary thrashing weakly above it.

"This is about sending a message. A reminder of who I am."

With a slow, deliberate motion, Javier signaled.

The gears whined.

Gary dropped.

For a moment, only gravity.

Then—flesh met spikes.

A wet, muffled shriek cut through the air as Gary's weight pressed down, rusted metal digging into him. His screams did little to stifle the agony.

Javier chuckled. A low, satisfied sound.

"Ah," he mused, watching blood drip in down the donkey onto the floor, forming small crimson puddles on the concrete. "One of my favorite tricks."

He turned back to Tank, his face ghostly pale.

"You see," Javier continued, voice smooth, almost soothing. "The body's own weight does the work. The more he struggles, the faster it happens. The slower... well." He flashed a mocking smile. "You get the idea."

Javier leaned in close to Tank, his breath hot against the captive's ear.

"Do you know why I'm doing this? Why I'm enjoying it so much?"

He didn't wait for an answer.

"Because pain, my friend, is the only truth in this world. And fear—fear is the only currency that matters."

Behind them, Gary let out a final, desperate scream as the razor-sharp edge split him further. The sound cut off as his body gave out, stress and blood loss dragging him into unconsciousness.

A thick pool of crimson spread beneath him, the coppery stench mixing with the suffocating weight of terror that hung in the air.

Javier watched with savage satisfaction, his eyes gleaming in the dim light.

"Soon, he'll wake from the pain," he mused. "It'll happen over and over until there's nothing left of him but agony.

Well..." He smiled like a snake after poisoning its prey, gesturing at Gary. "He won't be telling us anything, anyway.

But you—" Javier turned to Tank, his cruel smile widening, "you still can."

Tank sobbed, his body shaking so violently that his wrists chafed against the restraints.

Javier straightened, turning back to Hector, who stood silently, his face unreadable. But Javier noticed the flicker in his eyes—discomfort, maybe even fear.

Good.

Javier's grin deepened. "Make sure everyone knows. This," he said, gesturing to the gruesome scene, to the Gary hanging limp and broken over the Spanish Donkey, "is what happens when you cross me."

Hector gave a tight nod, but it lacked the confidence Javier expected.

"It's important to remember who's in charge," Javier added softly.

Then he turned to Tank, whose tear-streaked face had gone pale, his lips trembling uncontrollably.

Javier crouched beside him, speaking in a mockingly gentle whisper.

"Your turn."

Tank whimpered, his words tumbling out in pleading, desperate sobs.

Javier chuckled, standing. "The good news? You won't be alone. The Donkey has room for two. You fled together, now you can die together."

As Javier turned for the door, he motioned to his men with an effortless flick of his fingers. The guards seized Tank, lifting him toward the pulley system.

Behind him, Tank's screams rose to a fevered pitch as he yelled out, "He's going to fucking kill you like he did all your fucking people! Fuck you!"

Tank was hoisted into the air. His weight strained the rig. It squeaked in protest, but the sound was lost under his pleading.

"I swear... please... I don't know anything else. Fuck you! He's coming for you!"

Javier kept walking.

The door clicked shut behind him, muffling the panicked cries and the clanging of metal as Tank was pulled over the Donkey.

The last thing he heard before stepping into the hallway was his own laughter, cold, merciless, and inescapable.

CHAPTER ONE: Where To Go Now

The safe house was dark, lit only by a sliver of moonlight bleeding through the curtained window. The air hung heavy with stale coffee and sweat, the stench of too many sleepless nights.

Troy sat at the edge of a battered table, phone pressed to his ear, tension radiating off him in waves. Jack paced the room, nerves frayed, eyes flicking to the door like it might explode inward at any second.

Troy's voice was low, almost a growl. "How the hell do you not have any DNA? Bleach? What do you mean, they wiped everything? You're telling me there's not a single trace left? No prints, no fibers, nothing?"

Jack stopped pacing and leaned against the wall, his face pale in the dim light.

Troy's grip tightened on the phone. "And the team? They didn't make it? You're telling me the two men who survived the shootout died in their hospital beds? How did that happen? I need answers, and I need to know who's after me. Now."

He glanced at Jack, who met his gaze with red-rimmed eyes, a cocktail of exhaustion and fear. Switching the phone to his other hand, Troy's voice hardened.

"Look, I don't care how hard it is. You've got a whole team. I need names. Connections. Anything."

Whatever came back wasn't what he wanted to hear.

He exhaled sharply, eyes closing just long enough to collect himself. When they opened, his expression was unreadable. Pure, controlled fury. He ended the call with a tap and pocketed the phone.

He turned toward Jack and whispered, "Talk to me. Tell me everything. I need to know how deep this goes, because I don't like what I'm hearing."

Jack hesitated, rubbing his stubble with a trembling hand. He took a breath, forcing himself to face the man who had saved his life but might still kill him if the truth was too ugly to live with.

"They got to me after I made some bad bets. I was desperate. It got worse when they threatened my family. Luckily, I had no kids. Then my wife left me. My parents were dead. Any family I had, I hadn't talked to them since I was a kid, so they didn't have much leverage back then.

"But they told me if I helped with a few problems, I could make some cash. They gave me inside info on bets, you know? It seemed simple at the time. This was back when I was working in Nevada."

Troy leaned back, eyes locked on him. The silence pressed in.

"Then they moved me to California. Called it a promotion. I was handed the Environmental Crimes Investigation role for Northern California. They knew I'd be in the mountains, remote areas where no one pays attention. Illegal logging, grow farms, wildlife trafficking, pollution... it was the perfect cover.

"Then they put me in charge. Me. Of all people. A one-man specialized unit overseeing environmental crime, working with the EPA, the Forest Service. But I was just their puppet. I still don't know who really pulled the strings. Once they got to the sheriff, everything changed."

He looked down, hands shaking, remembering the weight of a badge he no longer deserved to wear.

"The town was dying. All I had to do was keep the information locked down. I didn't report to anyone but them. My only job was to make sure nothing escaped our chain of control."

Troy's voice dropped, calm and cold. "And then what?"

"They wanted to send a message. Eliminate the competition. Make it look like the police were doing their job. We set up a rival gang. Framed them for drug trafficking. The message was clear: join us or disappear."

Troy's eyes darkened. He asked the question he didn't want the answer to. "Who gave you the bleach bombs?"

Jack shook his head, face pale.

"That's when it all went to hell. These guys... they weren't from Mexico or anywhere in South America. They were something else. Maybe ISIS. Maybe Afghan Special Forces. Smart. Trained. Too smart. They had no accents, masked everything. But they were too good to blend in completely. They never spoke Spanish. You know what I mean?

"Professionals. I've worked with dangerous men. Trained with some of the best. But these guys? They were different. Stone-cold killers.

"They turned a ragtag militia into a functioning unit overnight. They brought gear, weapons, and comms faster than I thought possible. Everything was ready. Like they'd been preparing for something for far too long."

The room was heavy with the weight of Jack's confession.

Then Troy's phone buzzed.

He snatched it up, pulse already spiking. "This is Agent Troy."

His face went hard as he listened, every muscle tensing.

"What? Shit."

He ended the call and shot to his feet, movements sharp and decisive. His eyes locked on Jack, dead serious. Urgency radiated off him like heat.

"We have to go. Now."

Jack didn't hesitate. He was no longer trying to escape. He knew Troy was the only person keeping him alive.

Whatever was coming was about to crash down on them like a tidal wave.

They bolted from the room, footsteps muffled against the old floorboards.

Troy grabbed his go-bag and yanked the refrigerator aside, revealing a hidden passage.

He pulled Jack through and shoved the fridge back into place just as the front door burst open.

Bullets tore through the walls. Sirens wailed in the distance.

The safe house swallowed them in shadows as they disappeared into the night, danger pressing in from all sides.

CHAPTER TWO : Time To Fish

San Diego Habor—Before Dawn

Bryce Rath walked along a weather-beaten pier in old sweats and a sun-bleached hoodie, a surfboard tucked under one arm. His beard was fuller now, streaked at the edges. His hair, longer, curled beneath the hood and clung to his neck in the damp sea air. He didn't look like a soldier. Didn't move like one, either.

That was the point.

He boarded the fishing trawler without a word. The few crew members milling around paid him no mind, just another drifter trading labor for a berth and a few bucks.

Bryce stowed his dry bag below deck, then returned to help rig the lines for the day's catch. The trawler groaned as it pushed off into the mouth of the harbor, steel hull slicing through a waking sea. The work was quiet. Simple. The kind of repetitive motion that kept his hands busy and his mind still. He didn't speak unless spoken to. No one pressed.

By midday, sweat slicked his back and rope-burn laced his palms. He tied off the final rig and let the ocean's rhythm work the knots tighter. Salt crusted his skin. Muscles ached in the right way.

It had been months since he'd slept in a real bed.

Longer since he'd slept like a man who still had a home.

He wasn't that man anymore.

Hadn't been since the mountains.

Since the cabin.

***

Offshore—South of Encinitas

He leaned against the port rail, watching a massive Chinese trawler drift past like a floating city, gray paint sun-faded and chipped. Steel winches crusted with rust. Nets dragging deeper than regulation should ever allow.

"They pull a million pounds a month," the captain muttered beside him. He lit a cigarette with a weathered Zippo, the flame barely catching in the wind. "Nothing's coming back. Not for decades, and that's if they stop."

Bryce said nothing. Just watched.

The captain pointed to a container ship further out colossal, black-streaked, its deck stacked with steel crates. It looked like it could split the ocean.

"Forty knots," the captain said. "They don't see you. And they don't stop. Even if they did, it wouldn't matter. Most of the damage happens lower. Ten feet under, steel boxes floating like mines. Hit one of those, and it's over."

Bryce nodded slowly.

Global collapse, one shipment at a time.

Not his fight.

Not yet.

But someday, maybe.

When this war was over.

***

Afternoon—Two Miles Off Encinitas

They dropped anchor past the breaks. Far enough from shore to look like a blip to anyone watching.

Bryce slipped below deck, stripped down, and changed into his wetsuit. He applied more sunscreen, sealed his dry clothes into a waterproof bag, and slung it across his back.

His hybrid board, a fish-tail custom he'd shaped in Baja, would carry him on the two-mile paddle to shore. A shortboard wouldn't survive the chop.

He gave the captain a parting nod.

The captain squinted at him. "You got someone waiting?"

Bryce shook his head. "Just the tide."

He slid into the water without another word.

***

Paddle In—Encinitas Coastline

He paddled low and long, keeping his profile down. Every few strokes, he glanced toward shore.

He scanned the beach automatically.

No lifeguards. No radios.

Three teens smoking near the bluffs.

A couple in the lot not watching waves. Watching people.

One drone overhead. Not police.

He didn't like that.

Still no red flags. Nothing that said ambush. Nothing that felt wrong.

The waves weren't much ankle-snappers on a long break, but they gave him cover.

He rode one in, casually sloppy, wobbling at the end. Performance art. Just a stoner with balance issues.

He stumbled from the surf and onto the beach, stripping the top of his wetsuit and letting it hang at his waist. His board slung under one arm, Bryce scanned his surroundings.

A young family caught his eye, kids laughing, mother passing out sandwiches, father digging a fire pit. Normal. Innocent.
The kind of life that couldn't exist where he came from.

He sat a few yards away.

Close enough to borrow safety.

Far enough not to intrude.

From his bag, he pulled a crushed protein bar and chewed slowly.

Planning his next move.

***

Beachfront Tension—Hour Later

The family didn't notice the threat right away.

Three locals, sunburned, hard-faced, twitchy, drifted up the sandy beach like sharks. Prison tans. Neck tattoos. One had brass knuckles. Another wore a fake service vest on a pitbull. The third chewed something white. Not gum. Not coke either.

Bryce clocked it all in two seconds.

They made a beeline for the family. Smiling with dead eyes. Asking for "protection money" in that fake-friendly tone that always came before violence.

Bryce stood. Stepped in slowly. Spanish slid off his tongue as he offered them his surfboard, his wetsuit, anything to get them to walk away.

They took both. Laughed. But it wasn't enough.

They wanted more. Wallets. Phones.

Bryce's jaw flexed.

He let the first punch land clean. Pulled with it just enough to spin down and look dazed. Blood trickled from his nose. Sand bit his palms.

The second guy grabbed his hoodie.

Bryce twisted his weight, let his heel slip under the first man's foot. One fell into the other, heads colliding with a wet crack.

He pivoted like he was staggering. Let the pitbull's leash wrap around the third guy's legs. The man hit the sand face-first.

From a distance, it looked like chaos.

Like luck.

Like a sun-fried surfer got the drop on three idiots by accident.

Perfect.

He let another punch connect, this time to the ribs. Just enough to bruise.

***

Cleanup and Cover—Thirty minutes later

The family was safe. Their money returned. No lasting trauma, just confusion and shaky gratitude. He told them to leave and not talk to the cops. The father insisted and Bryce told him to protect his family, not him. He doesn't owe him anything.

The father looked into his eyes and understood. He thanked him and took his family away.

The locals groaned on the ground. One staggered off. The pitbull barked at nothing.

Bryce collapsed into the sand. Let the blood dry.

***

Flash of Sirens—One Hour Later

Red and blue flashed behind the palms.
Bryce didn't run. Didn't flinch.
Let them find a sunburned surfer with a busted nose and no wallet.
Let them book him. ID him. Print him.
He needed to be in the system.
He needed to be seen before he vanished again.
This was just the first breadcrumb.
The web was already spinning.
Bryce needed Javier's men to see exactly what he wanted them to see.
A washed-up drifter.
No threat.
Not worth a second glance.

After Action Report

Thank you for reading Karma.

If this story moved you, I hope you'll share it with someone who'd appreciate the journey.

If you served, you are seen.

To the veterans, operators, and friends who helped shape this story:

Thank you.
Your insight, courage, and honesty made this possible.

About the Author
[Redacted] The author remains off the radar.

But if you're reading this...
you're already part of the mission.

Karma is on your side.
Follow the journey:
www.TheKarmaFilesTM.com